The
Champagne
Letters

The Champagne Letters

■ A NOVEL ■

KATE MacINTOSH

G

GALLERY BOOKS

NEW YORK   LONDON   TORONTO   SYDNEY   NEW DELHI

G

Gallery Books
An Imprint of Simon & Schuster, LLC
1230 Avenue of the Americas
New York, NY 10020

First Gallery Books hardcover edition December 2024

GALLERY BOOKS and colophon are registered trademarks of Simon & Schuster, LLC

Simon & Schuster: Celebrating 100 Years of Publishing in 2024

For information about special discounts for bulk purchases, please contact Simon & Schuster Special Sales at 1-866-506-1949 or business@simonandschuster.com.

The Simon & Schuster Speakers Bureau can bring authors to your live event. For more information or to book an event, contact the Simon & Schuster Speakers Bureau at 1-866-248-3049 or visit our website at www.simonspeakers.com.

Interior design by Kathryn A. Kenney-Peterson

Manufactured in the United States of America

10   9   8   7   6   5   4   3   2

Library of Congress Cataloging-in-Publication Data is available.

ISBN 978-1-6680-6188-6
ISBN 978-1-6680-6190-9 (ebook)

To the strong women in my life, most of all my mom

The
Champagne
Letters

Prologue

Barbe-Nicole Clicquot

■ CHAMPAGNE, FRANCE ■

Letter to her great-granddaughter Anne

JUNE 1866

If a woman does not tell her own story, then a man will surely do it for her. And even if he is a good man, he will be incapable of telling it true. Instead, he will twist and turn it so the woman in question fits his own imagination and preferences. He will recast events and experiences so he is the center of her story.

In my eighty-nine years of experience, including surviving that toad Napoleon and his wars, I have learned men always see themselves as the fulcrum that determines the balance of women and the world. If they had any idea how much is decided for them by the women in their lives, they would be shocked. They mistake loud, grand gestures for strength and disregard the quiet iron that underlies most soft things.

No, my darling Anne, if anyone is going to tell you my story,

1

it will be me, your great-grandmother, while I still can. I want to tell you all that happened because I ache to share it with someone, and the fear that my mistakes will be used against me is past. It is my hope that you can learn from me, by following in my steps where wise and avoiding any ill-chosen paths.

Though some will say I've always had a grandiose idea of my own importance, especially where the champagne business is concerned, that simply isn't true. Knowing one's worth isn't vanity, provided you also know your weaknesses and are honest enough to admit both. It isn't false modesty when I tell you that despite what I have accomplished, I know I will disappear from history's record. I am both a woman and a merchant, and those two things render me inconsequential in the minds of men who record important events. But their overlooking of my life makes it no less marvelous.

Let that be the first of the lessons I pass to you, my precious great-grandchild. Know your worth and tell your own stories.

Now, my story begins nearly sixty years ago when I discovered my husband, François, dead . . .

Natalie

■ CHICAGO ■

My home looked as if a bomb had gone off, obliterating my life. I shook my head. That was too negative. My life wasn't *obliterated*. Sure, I was leaving my dream home, where I'd painted every room, chosen each stick of furniture, and hand tiled the bathroom, but it was still just a move. People do it every day. There are entire companies dedicated to helping others haul their things from one place to another. So not obliterated, just . . . off track. I put down the cheese grater and took a deep breath.

After almost a year of therapy, I could hear my therapist's voice in my head all the time instead of just one hour a week in her office. "How could you reframe this in a more positive way?" she'd ask.

So *My life was ruined when the man I loved most in the world, for whom I would have crawled through broken glass, walked away from our twenty-plus-year marriage* became *Will isn't the man I thought he was, but his choices don't define me. My life isn't ruined; it's temporarily derailed.*

I'm fifty and no one will ever love me again and I will die alone, eaten by the pet cats that will be my sole companions became *I don't know what the future holds, but I'm a vibrant, smart woman who deserves happiness. And a cat if I feel like it.*

My husband's mistress, Gwen, is a lying, cheating, husband-stealing whore, who clearly doesn't understand the basic concept of women supporting one another and greatly deserves to have all her hair fall out became . . . Well, my counselor let me have that one. I suspect she figured anger was progress over despair. On the grief scale it was practically kissing cousins to acceptance.

I meandered through the house, searching for the tape gun to seal more boxes. I wanted to be someone who handled divorce with a sassy attitude, took up a new hobby like pottery, and discovered that I could give myself a far better orgasm than Will ever had, but the truth was, I felt abandoned. Not fully part of a new life, but unable to return to the one I'd had before.

My best friend, Molly, took me to a sex shop after Will moved out. I thought it might be good for my "healing journey," a way to get over the fact that nearly my entire sexual experience had been with Will, unless you counted my prom date, which I definitely did not.

At the shop, an older woman wearing an airbrushed sweatshirt bedazzled with "Number One Grandma" over two kittens sold me a vibrating silicone friend. So, on the upside, I had checked "better orgasms" off the postdivorce list. Now all I needed was a pottery wheel.

My new bracelet sat on the edge of the coffee table. I slipped it on before it disappeared into a box, never to be seen again. That had been another of Molly's help-Natalie-post-split projects. Worried that I wasn't bouncing back, she'd invited me to weirder and weirder activities, culminating in a Wiccan weekend retreat for women to find their "soul power."

The retreat had involved a lot of vegan food and chanting, and I'd ended up buying an overpriced crystal bracelet that was supposed to have magical powers. I couldn't remember all the details: rose quartz for self-compassion, moonstone for guidance, the rest I'd forgotten. I'd come back from the weekend filled with energy and hope that I was finally fully emotionally above water, but only a few days later I was back to waking up in the middle of the night and pacing in circles trying to figure out the exact moment everything had gone wrong. But maybe the rocks had a bit of magic. I'd been able to at least act like I was holding it together. Until now. Something about having to decide who would get our dented cheese grater had tossed me back into the deep end.

There was a knock on the door, but it opened just as I reached it.

"I brought champagne," Molly trilled, dangling a bottle aloft and swaying it back and forth as she barreled past me.

I stared out at the SOLD sign in the yard for a moment before shutting the door and trailing after her to the kitchen, my slippers shuffling along.

"I don't know where the champagne glasses are." I surveyed the wreck of my home. There were boxes everywhere, along with tumble-weeds of crumpled brown packing paper littering the floor.

"No problem. There'll be something we can use. Necessity the mother of invention and all that." Molly worked her way through the kitchen, opening and shutting the mostly empty cupboards. "Ah, here we go!" She pulled out two mason jars and spun the metal tops off with a flick of her finger, sending them skittering across the kitchen island.

"It's not really a champagne occasion," I mumbled.

"Every day is a champagne occasion if you want it to be. I splurged for the good stuff, Veuve Clicquot." Molly picked at the foil covering the neck of the bottle.

In a second the cork would smack into her face. It's all fun and celebration until someone loses an eye.

"Give me that." I grabbed a towel and twisted the cork, freeing it with a loud pop.

Molly clapped, took the bottle back, and poured a fizzy mason jar full for each of us. "To new horizons," she said.

"To new horizons." I clanked my jar against hers and took a sip.

Molly surveyed the space. "How's it coming?"

I shrugged. "It's coming." Moving was a Sisyphean task. For every box I packed, the remaining items in the cupboard multiplied overnight. Tupperware breeding with baking dishes giving birth to random kitchen gadgets. Everything had to be divided into his, mine, and things to be donated.

"You'll be ready for the movers?"

"I think so." I picked up a large serving platter and wrapped it in paper before tucking it into a box already partially filled with Bubble Wrap. I didn't know why I was keeping it. My new condo didn't even have a dining room—fancy dinner parties weren't in my future.

"What else can I do?"

"I don't think there's anything. It's all stuff I need to finish." Molly had earned her best-friend status over and over in the past few months. Most of our couple friends had drifted away as if divorce might be contagious. But not Molly. She'd helped with everything from picking up boxes to hauling loads to the Salvation Army.

"I took some time off to wrap up things here and get settled in the new place," I said.

"Good! You must have weeks of unused vacation." Molly wagged her finger in my face. "You need more balance."

I took a sip of champagne to avoid saying anything sharp. Molly had been harping on the topic for months. She didn't seem to understand I *liked* going to work. Insurance risk evaluation might not be the most exciting field, but there was a certainty to it that satisfied me. A sense of putting things in order, warding off disaster when possible, and returning things to normal when it wasn't. At my office, everything was still together. Each file in my cabinet had tidy, typed labels. Papers were stacked on the desk in priority order. Crisp check marks down the side of my daily to-do list made me feel capable and in control. I might not be able to control the mess of my own life, but I could take care of others' mayhem. I'd come in early, shutting out the noise of my personal life as soon as I swept in the door. I'd drop off the venti latte (extra foam) that I had picked up for our receptionist on my way and knit myself together by the time I sat at my desk.

Most people at work didn't even know I was getting divorced. At first, I didn't say anything because I was afraid that I would start crying, and then it seemed like a strange thing to bring up over the photocopier or while grabbing lunch in the break room. In the office I was the same Natalie Taylor I'd always been. Eventually, I had to tell HR because I'd needed to change my emergency contact and the beneficiary of my life insurance policy, but it had felt like a dirty secret. Disclosing something unpalatable that was best kept quiet like an intestinal illness.

I threw myself into work, taking on more and more files and volunteering for everything from heading the birthday celebration committee to updating our company policy-and-procedure manual. When my boss heard I was moving, he all but insisted I take time off after the extra work I'd done in the past year. He thought he was being thoughtful, and I didn't know how to tell him that routine was what held me together.

"It's going to be fine. It really is. I know you didn't want to sell, but it's going to be good. A fresh start."

If I had a dollar for every time someone used the term "fresh start," I would have been able to afford to stay in my house in our expensive Naperville neighborhood outside of Chicago. "I'll be okay," I said.

Molly lightly kicked my foot. "You're going to be more than *okay*."

I sighed. Okay still felt like a vast reach. Some days were fine, but others felt like I was moving through a thick fog as I took apart the only life I'd known as an adult.

Molly put down her glass with a thunk. She had that come-to-Jesus look in her eyes of a woman who had been binging the Brené Brown podcast for too long. "Look, it's time to pull yourself together. It's a divorce. Not death. You saw that article I sent you, right? The one on silver splitting?"

Even divorce had been rebranded. At least for people fifty and up. Apparently, we were all living our best lives as newly minted single people. The women they interviewed in the article were all starting businesses, learning Mandarin, taking up Pilates, and having sex with people young enough to have gone to school with their kids.

"Did I tell you Will brought Gwen to the meeting to sign the house papers?" I asked. "You should have seen Justine's face," I added with a smile. My lawyer reminded me of one of those sleek whippet dogs, thin and angular. Her clothing all looked vaguely European. Justine disliked Will more than I did, a professional courtesy that came with her high hourly rate. I hadn't needed my therapist to tell me I'd hired Justine to voice the things I couldn't say aloud. I might have complicated emotions where Will was concerned, but I had at least managed to employ someone who didn't.

"Hey," Molly said, breaking my train of thought. "Stop talking about Will and Gwen. Focus on the upsides of your new life." She must have seen the doubt in my eyes, so she pressed on.

"You won't have to compromise all the time. You can do anything. Move to Paris and take cooking classes. You love entertaining. Paint your new place any color you want. Decide to have popcorn for dinner." Her hands waved in the air, champagne sloshing in her glass. "Anything you want is possible!"

I stood in my nearly empty kitchen and tried to not cry. Why was it so hard to think about what I wanted? Was I that out of practice?

There was a knock at the door, and I flinched. "That's going to be Will," I said, warning her.

Molly's nose wrinkled up like she'd smelled something foul. "Why is he here?"

I took a fortifying gulp of champagne from my jar. "He came to get some things he'd left in the basement."

I stepped toward the hall, but Will was already opening the front door. "Hey, it's me," he called out uselessly. He stopped short when he saw Molly step out. "Oh, hi. Nice to see you."

"Wish I could say the same," Molly said.

I shot her a look.

"I'll go finish packing." She ducked back into the kitchen after giving him one more withering glance.

"She hates me," Will said when she was gone.

"No, she doesn't," I replied automatically. We both stood there awkwardly, knowing that was a lie. Molly and I became friends in college, but we'd quickly expanded to include our spouses. The four of us had gone on vacations together. We were godparents for their child. We held regular summer barbecues with Will and John manning the grill. They'd drink entirely too much craft beer and discuss sports with the intensity of doctors reviewing a terminal cancer diagnosis.

This was an occasion where previous ownership made a difference. I would get Molly and John in the split, just as Will had claim to the barrister bookcase in the living room that I had always loved but had originally belonged to his grandfather.

"Guess I'll get this out of your way." Will hefted his golf bag over his shoulder, clubs clinking together, and picked up a box of books that I'd dragged to the foyer. I watched him walk them out to his BMW and tuck them gently into the trunk like they were the child we never had.

Will looked around when he returned. "Is there anything else you need me to do?"

I shrugged. *Be the person I thought you were* didn't seem to be a reasonable thing to ask at this point.

"It looks weird so empty."

I stared into the shell of our dining room. I swallowed over and over.

Will's forehead furrowed. "You okay?"

I shrugged, trying for casual but knowing I wasn't pulling it off. I refused to cry. "Sorry, it's just so . . ." My brain searched for the right word to encompass the feeling.

"You know, this is hard on me too."

His words clanged in my brain, discordant.

"I'm also losing my home and previous life." His voice sounded shaky.

Something inside me tipped over. It might have been the sight of the empty room, or the last of my fucks picking up their bags and heading for the door. No amount of crystals, chanting, or reframing would make that comment okay.

A wave of pure rage boiled up from my stomach in a rush. "You're not losing anything," I said. "You're *throwing* it away."

He stared at me with sad eyes. "I can't be the husband you want." His voice was soft and low, but for some reason, that made me angrier.

"What, faithful?" I put my hands on his chest and shoved. He acted as if I'd wanted the impossible from him. That I'd expected too much, when the truth was, I hadn't asked nearly enough. How dare he want me to feel sorry for him? And what made it worse was that I did feel bad. I knew he was hurting, and the fact that I cared sat dark and seething in my chest.

"Maybe it would be best if I left." He held out his worn leather key ring. "You can give these to the Realtor."

I reached for it, then pulled back. "No. You take care of it."

"Look, I know you're upset—"

"I'm not upset!" I yelled, clearly lying. "Take care of your own damn keys. And you'll need to meet the cleaners, too, to let them in, make sure they get everything done before the closing. And there's still the ladder and mower in the garage. Those need to either be sold, or donated, or whatever. The new owners want a walk-through, and the yard service is coming one last time to trim the bushes out front." The list of to-dos spewed out of me. I was done. I wouldn't spend one more minute, not one second, on tasks to make this divorce easier.

Will sighed. "You told me you had time off to deal with all of this."

"Too bad. I changed my mind."

"Nat," he said, his voice full of strained patience.

"What? You changed *your* mind. You decided that you didn't want to be married anymore. Changed your view on the whole till-death-do-us-part thing, so yeah, I changed my mind about taking *my* vacation time to do this."

"You're upset, but you have the time off already. I'm in the middle of a project at work."

As if his time was more important than mine. But I'd taught him that, because I always treated it that way. We booked our vacations around his work schedule. We'd moved here for his job. When I was sick, I moved to the guest room so my cough wouldn't wake him. Even the meetings with our attorneys were at his lawyer's because it was close to his office. I'd put this man first my entire adult life and never noticed that it wasn't mutual.

"You have to do it. I won't even be here," I said, my voice flat.

Will's eyebrow shot to his hairline, a farther journey than it had been when we'd started dating. "Where are you going to be?"

"Paris," I said, surprising myself as much as him.

Natalie

■ PARIS ■

APRIL 17

I perched on the cab seat, gripping the torn leather with sweaty palms. I gasped aloud as the driver dodged in and out of traffic on the Boulevard Raspail, apparently hell-bent on ending my trip, and my life, when I was barely out of the Paris airport. I pressed my mouth together when I realized any sound resulted in the cabbie taking his eyes off the road to check on me in the rearview mirror.

This is an adventure. It's going to make for a great story.

This was my new mantra. Spiritual quests required one, and I'd decided that was what this trip was. It had more gravitas than saying I was on vacation. You can't deny someone on a quest. A quest has a purpose. Validity. A quest ends with Julia Roberts playing you in the movie adaptation. Vacation means you're played by Chevy Chase.

For the past year since Will's affair came to light, I'd kept my head down, simply surviving the upheaval in my life. I'd read every book

13

out there on divorce and starting over. I spun between motivational *Eat, Pray, Love*–type tales and, on the flip side, stories of women who chopped up their husbands and buried them in the garden. Honestly, the soil under the hydrangeas in our backyard was pretty soft. Will should thank me for going the motivational route. Now it was time for a reset. A chance to choose a new direction, a new life. Assuming I survived this cab ride.

Closing my eyes, I said a quick prayer as the car darted around a group of cyclists with a squeal of the brakes and a string of curses from the driver. I typed a quick text to Molly to let her know I'd landed and snapped a photo out the window as proof.

I had to admit I was more present in the moment than I had been for months. This must be what Dorothy felt like when she found herself somewhere over the rainbow: spun around, out of place, but also excited. I'd been waiting to feel different, to feel like I'd arrived on "the other side" of all of this. But I hadn't *done* anything different. Or at least not different enough. The end of my marriage was a cataclysmic shift in my life, a tornado, and it required me to take an equally dramatic step. A weekend retreat wasn't enough—hell, I hadn't even organized that; Molly had. Dropping everything and running away to Paris was about as dramatic as I'd ever been.

I wasn't the type of person to take off to Europe on my own. I didn't do risk; I managed it. I worked in insurance, for crying out loud. A solo international trip with only a couple days' notice was irresponsible. It was insanity. It was terrifying.

The cab darted in front of a pedestrian crossing the street, nearly taking him out. Then the cabbie slammed on the brakes, almost catapulting me through the windshield. The driver turned, resting his arm on the back of his seat.

"We are here."

I peered through the window. A small brass plaque by the door was the only signage for the boutique hotel. The exterior of the building was the same shortbread-cookie-colored limestone as most everything in the city, with large paned windows outlined in black. The door, a bright red, like lipstick on a pale face, was the only thing that stood out. As I fished through my fanny pack for cash to pay the fare, a well-dressed gentleman came down the stairs and opened my car door. He bowed dramatically as if he'd wandered off the grounds of a royal palace.

"Bonjour, bienvenue à la Delphine."

I smiled nervously. "Hi." *Why did I run away to France?* Why hadn't I run away to a country where they spoke English? Ireland maybe. Or Canada. Canada was supposed to be nice. Moose. Beavers. Handsome men in red Mountie uniforms.

"Welcome." The doorman held out his hand and guided me out of the car. For a moment I forgot I was rumpled and smelled sour after the long flight and sleeping in my clothes.

"Allow me to get your suitcase." He turned and spoke in rapid-fire French to the taxi driver, who popped the trunk.

"I can help," I said, standing uselessly next to the cab with my overstuffed tote bag.

"No, no, madame, it is my pleasure." He gestured to the open door of the building as he hefted my bag out of the car. "Please, make yourself at home. The clerk inside will assist you."

Stepping into the hotel, I took in the sumptuous lobby that made me feel as if I'd crossed the door into a Jane Austen novel. I could already imagine sitting in one of the navy velvet chairs by the fireplace, watching out the window. Through an archway, a library with tables, clusters of comfortable chairs, and a bar at the back looked cozy and inviting. A gentleman sat reading the paper with a cup of coffee, and a couple hunched over a guidebook with glasses of white wine. The shelves of leather-bound books reached toward the high ceilings. Screw the rest of Paris; I might never leave this hotel.

"Bonne journée," the man behind the carved front desk called out. I stroked the wood as I approached him. It felt like cool satin under my fingertips. I slid my passport and confirmation number over. Never in my life had I stayed someplace so fancy. I expected a loud buzzer to ring out, declaring that I very much did not belong, then a hole to open under me and shoot me back out onto the street. This was a hotel destined for curated videos on social media feeds shared by people who used the term "influencer" non-ironically.

Normally I would never stay in a place that cost this much, but when you book Paris last minute in the spring, your choices are limited. I'd almost backed out of the trip altogether, but I couldn't face telling Will I'd changed my mind. My stomach twisted. What if I'd made a huge mistake?

This is an adventure.

The desk clerk's fingers danced over the keys as he pulled up my reservation. "Here we are, madame. Just one key, I believe. You are alone in the room, correct?"

My heart slammed into my ribs before sinking toward my feet. I nearly burst out that I was alone all the time. All I could picture was years of being alone until I died and the cat I hadn't even bought yet feasted on my corpse.

This is part of the adventure. My breath hitched as I tried to speak. I swallowed over and over. I hadn't cried in months. I wasn't going to start now.

"Madame Taylor?" The desk clerk looked panicked.

"My husband's gone," I managed to choke out, my face spasming with the effort to hold the tears in.

The man's eyes widened in horror, and his mouth pressed into a thin line. "S'il vous plaît, pardonnez-moi." He pressed his hand over his heart.

Shit. He thought I meant Will was dead. My throat tightened another notch. It would be easier if he were. If he'd left because he had no choice. Not that he simply didn't want me anymore. That he'd chosen someone else. What was wrong with me? Why was I about to cry over someone who was so very much not worth it? I was supposed to be past this. I started to shake. Oh God. Now the people in the library bar alcove were watching the drama. Their faces wrinkled in concern and their expressions made me want to cry even more.

It's a quest! my brain repeated as I gripped the side of the desk. *An adventure.* You didn't see Dorothy sobbing when she saw the yellow brick road, and she had a dead witch under her house.

"Madame? May I show you to your room?" A young woman straight out of a 1940s classic film appeared at my side. Her icy-blond hair was pulled up in a chignon and her outfit looked like it had never even conceived of wrinkling. Taking my hand, she placed it on her forearm as if she were about to escort me down the aisle. She spoke in French to the clerk, and he stammered something and, after a quick sharp word from her, handed over a plastic key card.

"Come, Marcel will bring your bag up momentarily." She guided me toward the elevator, moving smoothly like a pageant queen. "My name is Sophie."

The doors slid silently shut, and I took a deep breath, shoving my emotions down where they belonged. "I'm sorry, I must be overtired."

Sophie patted my hand, which was still linked over her arm. "It is okay. I understand." We exited on the fifth floor, and she led me down the hall. The outside of the building was old, but the inside had clearly been gutted and rebuilt. There wasn't a creaking floorboard to be heard or wonky light fixture to be seen. Every detail screamed luxury. The hotel had its own smell, as if they pumped perfume through the air. Jasmine. Orange blossom, perhaps vanilla.

"It's been just over a year," I said. "Honestly, I have no reason to be upset. This is supposed to be my grand adventure. My life reboot."

The woman made a noncommittal noise. She pressed the key card to one of the doors. It swung open, and I froze in shock, the words explaining that Will wasn't dead drying up in my mouth. This wasn't a hotel room; it was a palatial suite.

"You have my sympathy, madame. Time doesn't make a loss better, only a bit easier." Sophie gently pushed me into the room, where my feet sank into the thick carpet.

The bed was immense, topped with a puffy duvet covered in linen, the palest of pinks. The color of the inside of a puppy's ear. The expansive room was L-shaped, a sitting area with a camelback sofa and a chair at one end and the bed at the other. Through an archway, I spotted a large free-standing bathtub and marble floor.

Sophie passed me and pulled the heavy curtains open, the sunshine flooding the room. "There is a view of the Musée d'Orsay, and the Seine." She pointed out the window.

"I think there's been a mistake—" I said. The space was easily double—no, triple—what had been promised online, and the basic room had been eye-wateringly expensive. This? This room would require me to sell a spare kidney for one night, let alone two weeks.

She waved off what I'd been about to say. "I had Marcel upgrade you to a suite for your stay at our expense to make up for his thoughtlessness."

My face flushed red-hot. "Oh, that's not needed. Really. It's not him, it's me." The understatement of the trip so far. I opened my mouth to explain, then paused, looking around; perhaps it was a mistake I should let stand. Explaining it seemed more complicated than letting them think Will had died tragically.

Maybe that was the way I needed to see it, as a death. Grieve the death of my marriage and who I thought I'd spent the last twenty-plus years with and then move the hell on. I felt the resolve that had spurred the trip leak back in. It would be easier to grieve in a room with this view.

There was a soft knock, and a bellhop brought in my giant suit-case and effortlessly popped it up onto the tufted bench at the foot of the bed. Behind him trailed another young man about Sophie's age, his pencil-thin mustache struggling to hang on to his upper lip, holding a silver tray.

"Champagne," Sophie said, taking the tray. "To welcome you to the hotel and wish you, how did you say it? A grand adventure."

I recognized the egg-yolk-yellow label. "Veuve Clicquot."

Sophie's face lit up. "Oui. You know your champagne, Madame Taylor."

"Not really," I admitted. "A friend got me a bottle recently." I would have to text Molly pictures of this room. She wouldn't believe it.

Sophie expertly opened the bottle with a muffled pop. "Well then, I shall have to tell you the history of the wine. Perhaps it will help you on this journey, act as a guide. 'Veuve' means widow, you see." She met my gaze and smiled kindly. "After the Revolution, the only way a woman could own a business in France was if her husband had passed. Barbe-Nicole took over after her husband's death. She faced many obstacles." She shook her head sadly, as if she'd known the couple and their tragedy personally.

Sophie poured the champagne into a glass and passed it to me. "The Widow is a hero of mine. There's much that can be learned from a woman such as her. Once you have had a chance to rest, then

I will tell you all about Madame Clicquot and the other widows of the time."

"There were more?" I sank into the cream silk–covered chair, feeling the tension in my back release. I wanted her to tell me stories while I drifted off to sleep.

"Oui. Most of the great champagne brands were built by women: Pommery, Bollinger, Laurent-Perrier." She counted off the names on her slender fingers, her ballet-pink manicure flawless.

I sipped the champagne; the bubbles snapped in my mouth. "You know a lot about this," I said.

Sophie smiled, her chin lifting in the air with pride. "It is my job; I am in charge of wines here at the Delphine. I was born and raised in Épernay, the heart of the Champagne region. And the widows of champagne are legendary."

"Guess there's no telling what a woman can accomplish," I said.

"Exactement!" Sophie gave a curt nod, and I felt absurdly proud of myself, as if I'd come up with the answer to a tricky question. "Never stand in the way of a determined woman," she said, thrusting the bottle in the air like a salute.

Barbe-Nicole

REGARDING THE EVENTS OF OCTOBER 1805

Dearest Anne,

While I wish your life to be free of challenge and pain, I know that they are unavoidable. To live is to feel both joy and sorrow. Perhaps in some ways it is better to have difficulties early in one's life so that you know you can survive them. You must learn to thrive even when it is hard, to seize opportunity when it comes, for unlike bad luck, it won't linger. Some say that those of us who lived through the Revolution and then the Terror walled off our feelings, that we became less than fully human. This is not true, our hearts beat the same as any other, but we did learn to contain emotions so that they did not overwhelm our reason. Perhaps this is why even in my greatest moment of loss I could sense both the opportunity and the challenges it presented.

To begin, let me tell you of your great-grandfather's death.

■ ■

My gaze took in everything at once. François lying deathly still on the bed, his eyes already beginning to cloud. The jumble of blankets at his feet, as if he'd been kicking in his final moments, and most damning of all, the small bottle balanced on the table.

The maid, Margot, stood shaking in the corner next to the fireplace, her hands still gripping a coal bucket. Her eyes were wide in her pale face. Time seemed to slow as if thickened. My heart paused between beats.

One of my greatest skills had always been to see how things were connected, looking forward and back. To glance at the slope of a hill in winter and envision the runoff of rain in the spring. To crush a pinot noir grape still warm from the sun between my teeth and know how it will taste after pressing and aging in a bottle. To tally up figures in the ledger and predict their value at year-end. And in this instance, I could see it all, what people would say. What they would do. How it would be viewed by everyone from the cheesemonger to our priest and the parents of our daughter's playmates.

And I knew what this would do to our already shaky business. I could not allow my husband's death to define my life.

I stepped forward and, before I even touched my beloved, scooped up the bottle of arsenic. It was small, fitting easily into the palm of my hand. *Where had François gotten this?* I pushed away the question. It didn't matter. Our scullery maids used arsenic to keep the kitchen free of mice, and the cellar master used it to rid the cellars of mold. The important question wasn't where François found it, but why it was in his possession. The near-silent gasp of the maid let me know she'd seen me take the bottle. I turned to face her and held her gaze. There must be no question. No doubt.

Truth is the story we convince others to embrace.

"My beloved husband has passed from his fever." I bent and carefully straightened his linen nightshirt, then pulled the covers over his bare legs. My voice was clear and steady. There would be time for tears later. Cope. Adapt. Leave the tears for others who have the freedom for them.

Margot stared back, and I could practically see her thoughts swirling round her head like bees. She was pretty, but in a simple way, the type that fades with youth. She was a small, slight girl. In my mind, I called her the Mouse. I could overlook her vanity, for when a girl has beauty but limited brains, she must cling to its importance. But what I couldn't abide was that Margot was also *lazy*. She was constantly daydreaming and took double the time to complete any task as compared with another. Like a mouse, she did little to build her own home and instead stole the crumbs of others. I couldn't fathom why anyone would do something if they didn't intend to do it well. *Why did she have to be the one to find him?*

"He—"

"He must have been sicker than we realized," I said firmly, cutting her off before she could put the idea into words. She didn't know for certain what had transpired. Nor did I. The vomiting, the muscle cramps he'd had the past few days, could have been the result of sickness. The presence of the bottle didn't have to mean the worst. Everyone knows fevers are as unpredictable as the sea. François had returned from Germany two weeks ago, complaining of the greasy pork and how the loud, braying laughter of the men he'd met with had given him headaches. He retreated to our room, but no one in our household had been concerned. His behavior was not unexpected.

François's fits of melancholy were frequent, his dark moods leading him to claim illness and stay in bed. His father told me it had ever been such. My husband was a man who felt things deeply, both happiness and pain. It was as much a part of him as the way his hair curled above his ears or the blue of his eyes. *But to do this?* To me. To our daughter. My teeth ached, and I realized I was clenching my jaw. I forced myself to take a breath. Anger at the dead was like being enraged by the weather. It changed nothing.

Margot's gaze dropped to my hand, which was still holding the bottle out of sight. I stood still, not fidgeting. Let her ask, if she dare be so bold.

"Go downstairs and tell Madame Martin to send for the priest," I demanded. I was her employer. She had no right to question me.

The girl nodded.

"We'll need to send a message to my husband's father as well." I wanted to weep thinking of it. The news would break my father-in-law. "Have Madame Martin send up some hot water. My husband will need to be laid out." My mind began to create a list of all that would need to be done in the coming hours and days.

Margot blinked, as vacant as a cow in the field. She could be commanded only one thing at a time.

"Just go downstairs and have Madame Martin come here," I requested.

The girl nodded. She took a few steps toward the door, staying close to the far wall as if she expected François to leap up and grab at her ankles.

Margot stopped at the door. "I'm so sorry, Madame Clicquot."

I pressed my mouth together, my throat suddenly tight.

"'Tis a horrible tragedy," she added.

I nodded, but when I lifted my eyes, Margot was looking at my hand as if she could see through the flesh to the bottle of poison, and then back at my face. She paused, not moving.

The girl would be trouble. Margot wasn't bright, but she was no fool either.

"You may go," I said. Why was it that Margot wasn't smart enough to collect chicken eggs without breakage, but she had the wits to realize what the bottle could mean, and how she might use it to her advantage?

She didn't move, but I couldn't tell if it was insolence or her usual lack of effort.

"Go!" I barked. Margot finally moved into the hall toward the back staircase.

I waited until I heard the whisper of her shoes descending the steps. Panic fluttered in my chest like a bird trapped by the netting in the fields. I wanted to shake François and yell at him. *Why?* Things were going well. Not perfectly, but well enough. Why did he always see the darkness of the clouds and never the benefit of the rain?

I wanted to collapse to the floor and give over to sobs, but there wasn't much time. If I threw the bottle from the window, there was the possibility it would be found. And if I left it here, there would be questions as to its purpose in our bedroom. The truth of what happened did not matter as much as what people believed it to be. We would never know if the presence of the bottle was mere chance or the cause of his death, but I could afford no inquiry into his illness. My gaze searched about the space. I had no doubt Margot would suddenly discover a thoroughness when cleaning this room. She'd shake out each one of my chemises, feel the hem of my gowns for secret pockets, and unroll every stocking.

With a quick glance at the door to ensure the girl hadn't moved swiftly for once in her life, I wrapped the bottle in a handkerchief and shoved it into my bosom. I said a quick silent prayer for my breasts, which had never been small but, after the birth of our daughter,

Clémentine, had become ample enough to make short work of hiding one small bottle. I'd dispose of it later. I wiped my hand on my skirts as if the glass had left an oily residue. With the bottle gone, I had time for my husband.

"Why, mon amour?" I sank into the chair at the bedside, suddenly tired. I should have sat with him this afternoon. Distracted him with conversation. Read to him. Taken his mind out of its dark place. But I'd been too busy. François's trip had been successful. He'd returned with more orders than ever before, but that wasn't enough. It was just the beginning. We had to ensure we could meet those orders, secure bottles and transportation. And all of it at the whim of the weather and harvest.

A letter from our employee Louis Bohne lay discarded under a pair of gloves on the table next to the bed. I touched it lightly; it was an artifact from another time. When it had arrived a day ago, I'd thought my largest problems were the issues he'd raised with our orders. Louis had long stopped writing to François when he needed questions answered or a direction for his employ. My husband was either traveling or poorly inclined to keep up with the minutia of our business to be helpful in the day-to-day details. Louis had faith I would know the exact count of bottles in our cellar, the poundage of grapes expected, the correct tally in the ledger, and the state of our wines.

Every dream I had for the business was lying cold and dead with François in our bed. I stroked the thick paper as if it could tie me back to the moments before the maid had called out. Louis was our most trusted employee. His mind was quick and sharp. He would need to know what had happened. Perhaps he would have thoughts on what should be done.

François's body was still. I brushed his hair to the side of his forehead. I had failed my husband as his wife, but I could not allow his dream of our business to die with him.

I dipped a flannel in the pitcher of water and dabbed away a bit of dried froth at his mouth. I regarded my husband's face. He had always been handsome. We were not well matched in that regard. Oh, I was fine-looking enough with my strawberry-blond hair and petite frame, but I had my father's nose and little grace. My sister once said I danced like a puppet, as if strings jerked my limbs one way, then the other. But François had never minded. He called me "ma choupinette," his cute little cabbage. And in our marital bed, he'd always shown that his affection was true. His calloused hands roamed over me like he was playing an instrument. Unlike other women, I never worried that my husband would stray on his travels.

François needed me. It wasn't that he was weak, but rather, he was like a new plant. Vulnerable to harsh winds or heavy rain, he required tending and care. Like a vine grafted to one that was stronger, he did better with me at his side. But when he shone . . .

Oh, when he shone, he was incomparable.

Exhaustion settled on my shoulders like thick, wet wool. I should have done more for him. There were never enough hours in the day or enough patience in my heart. The house staff needed supervision. Vines had to be watched, the cellars inspected. The ledgers with their columns of marching numbers were like an army ready to revolt at any moment if I didn't stay vigilant. My daughter clung to my skirts, wanting attention. François's moods added another weight, and I suspect he knew I found them wearying. Tears held fast in my eyes, hot and burning. I could have found more energy if I had known how close to the edge he had been. If I had allowed myself to see.

I had no doubt Father Joseph would chastise me for failing to call him out when François was ill. The old goat. Our local priest was one of those dour men who used God as a cudgel to feel powerful. In my experience, it takes a large amount of arrogance to believe you alone have a portal to God and his thoughts. I refused to accept that our Lord would choose the scowling, overperfumed Father Joseph as his mouthpiece. A burning bush, yes. That man, never.

I lowered my head onto François's still chest, taking his cold hand in my own. The ache in my heart expanded, threatening to swallow me whole.

"Mon amour. I miss you already," I mumbled into the fabric of his nightshirt. "Rest easy." I swallowed over and over and then forced myself to lift my head. The housekeeper, Madame Martin, would be here soon. The staff would look to me for direction, for assurance that all would be well. Our daughter would need comfort. At six, she was old enough to feel this loss keenly.

I would order the Mouse to her room in theory to rest, but in truth to bury her silence. With every minute that passed where neither of us raised the question as to the cause of François's death, the greater the chance that no one else would ever know. But our silence also became a secret bond that would tie me to the girl. If I allowed even the tiniest hint of what may have happened to go beyond the Mouse and me, the priest would deny my sweet husband blessings into the next world. I could not abide that. The church preached that to take one's life was a sin, but I did not believe a loving God would feel the same. And if this priest felt he knew God's thoughts, why should I not be as certain?

The edge of the bottle dug into my chest. No one would know. They would have no choice but to accept that a fever had swept him away, even if they wondered and gossiped. As long as the Mouse stayed silent.

"I will keep your secret," I whispered into my husband's ear. I gripped the side of the bed, as if trying to hold him to this world. Then I pushed away the thought that I was keeping the secret for myself and our champagne business, not for him.

Natalie

■ PARIS ■

I stumbled off the hop-on/hop-off bus, dizzy from spinning first one way and then the other on the top viewing deck as the bus careened past every Parisian monument. The Eiffel Tower, Notre-Dame, the opera house, and around the Arc de Triomphe. Molly had suggested I start with a bus tour to get an overview of the city, but I couldn't stand it anymore. I felt disconnected from reality. I hoped it was just jet lag, but I worried it was a sign that the trip had been a horrible idea. Going halfway around the world wasn't going to fix anything, and I'd been delusional to think it would.

"Excusez-moi," a man said as he barreled past me, rolling his eyes. Realizing I was blocking the sidewalk, I scurried out of the way, feeling clumsy and out of place.

Up ahead lay the bouquinistes that clustered along the banks of the Seine by the Quai Voltaire. The row of green wooden stalls had flung open their canopies to expose stacks of new and used books jumbled together under the spring sunshine. Sophie from the hotel had mentioned them as a possible activity, so I walked that way, trying to look like I belonged and not like a tourist. Although if I'd wanted to blend in, I should have taken a scarf-tying boot camp like all Frenchwomen appeared to have done.

If the books had an order, it made sense only to the proprietors. Illustrated flower guides were shoved next to copies of Proust and cookbooks from the early 1900s. The owners looked less interested in selling than they did in clustering together, smoking, and debating in mumbled French. No one bothered me as I browsed from one cart to another.

I'd always loved reading. At my local library I used to play a game where I would choose one book at random off the nonfiction shelving cart at every visit and give it a shot.

I closed my eyes and let my fingers slip over the faded covers as I inhaled the musty scent of used books. My hand paused and I plucked a slim book from the pile. After opening my eyes, I blinked in surprise when I saw the cover: *Guidance from the Grande Dame of Champagne: The Translated Letters of Barbe-Nicole Clicquot to Her Great-Granddaughter.*

My breath caught. It seemed like an omen. Didn't any good quest require a mentor, a wizened figure to provide wisdom and guidance? Why not a long dead Frenchwoman? It seemed nothing less than ordained that I kept coming across her. The bottle from Molly, the tales of champagne widows from Sophie, and now this. Perhaps she'd be able to give me the direction I so clearly needed. I clutched the book to my chest and bent my head to smell the faint scent of perfume and old paper, feeling the stir of hope in my chest.

"Excuse me, how much is this?"

The owner of the stall, his thin, wispy hair like dandelion fluff pinned down only by a tweed cap, had half-heartedly wandered over.

Opening the book, he pointed to a faint pencil mark on the inside cover, eight euro.

A ripple of excitement ran through my body. It was much cheaper than I'd feared. I'd been prepared to pay ten times that. He took my pause as reluctance.

"Okay, cinq euro." The stall owner held out his hand, nicotine-stained fingers splayed, and repeated, "Five."

"Sold!"

■ ■

I settled into the creaky wicker chair at the café across the street from the bouquinistes, then peeled off my cardigan. The sun warmed the top of my head, and the buzz of the motor scooters zipping along the street provided an oddly relaxing soundtrack. The waiter would be back at any moment, so I reached for the menu, but my hand fell on the book instead.

There was a soft crack from the brittle spine as I flipped through the yellowed pages. There were copies of letters in French, with the translation in English immediately following. My eyes fell on the sentence *Seize opportunity when it comes, for unlike bad luck, it won't linger.* I snorted. That was the truth.

In the middle of the book was an illustration plate showing a painting of the Widow Clicquot. She stared out from the page seated in a chair that was nearly a throne, an open book on her lap. The painting must have been done later in her life. She was older, thick, and stout. I guessed her age to be somewhere in her sixties or seventies. Her hair was styled in long sausage curls on either side of her face and topped with a lace cap. She wore black, which I suppose was to be expected, given her widow status. Like any good Frenchwoman, she'd tied a scarf around her neck. She looked like a woman who seized whatever she wanted without apology. A woman in control of her destiny, not just along for the ride. My finger rested on the page, and I held my breath as if I almost expected her to speak.

"Madame?"

The waiter stood next to me; his long apron was blindingly white in the spring sun. I dropped the book and grabbed the simple one-page menu. My eyes danced over the French words as though, if I stared long enough, I would gain the ability to translate what they said.

"A glass of white wine?" I said tentatively.

The waiter sniffed. "Yes, of course. I will bring you Château Florales, if that is all right?"

"Sure, that sounds fine."

"No, no, no."

Surprised at the voice, I spun to see a man sitting down at the table next to mine.

"May I?" He reached past me and took the menu from the waiter's hands. He smelled of clean cotton dried in the sun. He mumbled to himself in French as he gave the sheet a quick glance, his dark eyes taking in everything. "The lady would prefer the Sancerre." He raised an eyebrow. "And perhaps something to nibble?"

I nodded.

"And the plateau du fromage." He directed the waiter with a flick of his finger. Once the waiter was gone, the man smiled and lowered his voice. "The wine he suggested is overpriced and thin. They sell it mostly to tourists. Trust me, the Sancerre is much better."

I wasn't sure if I was annoyed or relieved. "Thank you."

He nodded slightly. "I recognized you from the Delphine." He gestured over his shoulder in the direction of the hotel. "As we are neighbors of a sort, guests of the same establishment, I had to assist." He tilted his face to the sun and pushed a dark curl of hair from his forehead. "On such a beautiful day, it would be a waste to drink bad wine." He looked back at me, his face a mask of concern. "Life has enough tragedy already."

As soon as he mentioned the hotel, my mind placed him immediately. He was the man reading the newspaper in the lobby bar when I'd checked in and had my minor breakdown.

"It's my first time in Paris," I explained. "I appreciate your help. I don't know very much about wine."

He smiled. "Then you are in luck, madame, for I happen to know enough on the subject for the both of us." His liquid smile spread across his face and wrinkled the corners of his eyes. His nose looked like it had been broken at some point and not put back together correctly. I guessed he was younger than I, early forties, but his expression held a mischievous look that would be at home on a child's face. He wasn't conventionally attractive, but something about his mismatched features, or maybe the fact that he was French, made him intriguing. He held out his hand. "I'm Gabriel."

I shook his hand. It was warm, slightly calloused. "Natalie."

"Bonjour, Natalie."

The way he said my name with his French accent seemed to add additional syllables.

The waiter returned with a bottle and a silver ice bucket. "Oh, no." I held up a hand to stop him as he whipped a corkscrew from a deep apron pocket. "I'm sorry. I only wanted a glass."

Gabriel spoke to the waiter in French and then turned back to me. "Ah, then your luck continues, as I've decided I want a bottle and would be willing to share with you."

Before I could argue that he didn't need to do that, the waiter poured a small splash into a glass, and Gabriel swirled it, sniffed the top, and then sipped before nodding his approval.

"Join me?" I asked. It seemed rude to not at least offer since he was sharing his wine. I was certain he would turn me down, but he pulled his chair over to my table.

The waiter quickly poured another glass and I reached for it, first lifting it in Gabriel's direction and then toward my mouth.

"Wait," Gabriel called out. "First, close your eyes." His hand skimmed over my face, not so much touching me as hovering millimeters from my skin. "Go on. Close them."

I did as I was told.

"Now drink. Let the wine rest upon your tongue for just a moment and then swallow."

The wine was ice-cold in my mouth, warming slightly as it slid down my throat. I opened my eyes.

"Now tell me what you taste." Gabriel looked giddy with excitement.

"I'm not good at this," I said, feeling anxious.

He threw his head back and laughed. "There is no good, or not good. It is drinking. Don't allow yourself to be intimidated by wine. It is meant to be enjoyed, to be savored. There is no right, no wrong. There is only how the wine works for you."

I stared into the glass and the pale-yellow liquid inside. "It tastes . . . like flowers?"

Gabriel closed his own eyes and took a taste from his glass. "Elderflower. Mineral. Like chalk? Yes?"

I took another mouthful. It did taste a bit like minerals. A zing of excitement ran down my spine, like I'd suddenly figured out the right answer on a test. "What did you say this was called?"

"Sancerre. Some call it the sophisticated sauvignon blanc. All Sancerres are sauvignon blanc, but not all sauvignon blancs are Sancerre." Gabriel held up a finger as if giving a lecture. "To be Sancerre, it must be from France's Loire Valley."

"So, being from France makes it better?" I asked, suddenly feeling the kind of sassy that usually took me two or three glasses of wine to reach.

"A few more days here and you will discover that, indeed, everything French is just a bit better." He lifted his glass in my direction. "But perhaps some things from America do not need to be improved."

I felt myself blush. "You seem to know a lot about wine."

He gave a humble shrug. "I have always loved wine, but it is also my life. I'm a wine distributor. I specialize in selling rare bottles to collectors."

"Wow. That sounds . . . exotic."

"To me, it is simply my business. No doubt what you do would seem exotic to me."

I suspected this sophisticated man wouldn't be that interested in my career in insurance risk evaluation. It's the rare person who's excited by actuarial tables.

"Perhaps," I said, playing coy. "Are you here on business?" He must sell a lot of bottles if he could afford the Delphine.

Gabriel nodded. "I stay at the Delphine every time I'm in town. It is the best place in the city; the staff become like family." He rolled his sleeves up over his elbows and I had to fight the urge to put my hand on his forearm. Had arms always been that sexy, or was this just him?

"But enough discussion of work. Are you enjoying your stay in Paris?" He leaned back in the wicker chair as the waiter delivered a platter of cheeses, fruit, and grainy crackers. "Ah, be sure to try the Camembert with a bit of honey." He pushed the plate closer.

I dipped my knife into the soft cheese and smeared it onto a thin cracker. Gabriel watched as I drizzled honey on top and then popped it into my mouth. The thick cream of the cheese, hinting of grass and earth, with the sharp sweetness was transcendent. I caught myself just before I let out a moan.

"In life, so many things are made better by being combined. From honey with cheese to sharing a meal with a friend." Gabriel smiled and then turned serious. "But it is important to know that one can also shine on their own."

I froze, uncertain.

He shrugged again. "I could not help but overhear of your loss at the hotel yesterday." He lightly touched the back of my hand. "It is difficult to lose someone we care for."

In the moment, sitting in the sun in Paris with a handsome Frenchman, drinking the best wine of my life, and eating cheese that likely had the same fat content as butter, I suddenly felt that it wasn't as difficult as it had seemed mere minutes before. "It's been over a year since my . . ." I paused. "Loss. Part of the reason I came is that it's time for me to move forward." I didn't mention that it had taken Will a lot less time. What had the letter from the Widow Clicquot said in the book—life contained both joy and sorrow? Perhaps I was ready to try the happy portion of the equation.

Gabriel nodded approvingly. "I admire the strength of women," he said. "You and Sophie are an inspiration to seize life despite grief."

"Sophie?"

"Yes, the wine manager at our hotel. She is a widow as well. I do not know all the details, but she came to work at the Delphine after her husband died."

A shadow fell over my heart. It was one thing for me to pretend that Will was dead, but it was another to lie to a woman who had experienced genuine tragedy. Now there was no way to confess the truth. How do you tell someone who had been through the death of their partner that you'd made it up?

"Enough of sadness." Gabriel lifted his glass. "To rediscovered joy."

We clinked over the table. "To rediscovered joy."

Gabriel refilled our glasses. His phone trilled, and he pulled it from his pocket. "Excusez-moi." He glanced at the screen and fired off a quick text before draining his full glass in one long swallow.

"Alas, I must leave you," he said. He motioned to the waiter and pulled banknotes, held tightly together in a silver money clip, from his pocket, then passed a few over.

I sat up straighter. "Of course." It was the middle of a Wednesday. This man didn't have time to sit around drinking the afternoon away with me. "Let me pay half—"

He shook his head as he stood, rolling his sleeves down before pulling his suit jacket from the back of his chair. "No. It is my pleasure. You will stay and finish the wine, yes?" Gabriel gestured around. "Sit and enjoy the sunshine." He pointed to the book under my hand. "Perhaps read a bit?"

"Yes, I think I will." It suddenly seemed a very French thing to do on a weekday, to get tipsy and read in the sunshine. This beat the bus tour by a mile.

He smiled. "Perfect. It will make my day to imagine this scene."

"Thank you for the wine," I said.

Gabriel bowed. "Natalie, I am sorry to leave in such a rush, but my work is unavoidable."

I waved him off. "No, of course. I understand."

He smiled again before taking a few steps and then pausing. "Perhaps I will see you later at the hotel?"

"Perhaps," I said, pulling the book closer to me. I watched him walk away, weaving through the crowds. This adventure was what I needed to reboot my life; I simply had to stop wallowing in my grief. After snapping a picture of the café table with the wine and food, I sent it off to Molly. I dragged a grape through the puddle of soft cheese and popped it into my mouth. An afternoon of reading and getting slowly day drunk seemed like a perfect plan. After making sure there was no honey sticking to my fingers, I flipped the book open. I'd start at the beginning; it appeared I had a lot to learn.

"Natalie?"

Gabriel stood in front of me, looking flushed and slightly flustered. I glanced around his abandoned chair. He must have left something behind.

"Will you have dinner with me this evening?"

"Dinner?" I asked, as if I'd never heard of the meal before.

"Oui."

Dinner with a man I just met, who had to be ten years younger than me, was absurd. Sure, this had been nice, but what would we talk about? He was likely only asking to be kind. I opened my mouth to tell him I had plans when I glanced down at the book.

Seize opportunity when it comes.

"I would love to have dinner with you."

Barbe-Nicole

REGARDING THE EVENTS OF DECEMBER 1805

My most precious Anne,

You asked if I always knew I wanted to run a business. I can assure you I did not. People assume those who do brave, new things are special, preordained in some way for greatness. The truth is that those who accomplish much are simply those who dare to try and are willing to endure failing in the pursuit. I had not imagined myself to be a business owner as a girl, no more than I would have imagined sprouting wings. My parents had not raised me to dream of a life beyond being a wife, a mother, and a social leader in our community. But when François spoke about his plans for a vineyard, they took root in my mind. It was as if I could suddenly see things that had always been just out of my vision in the past. And when he died, I was unwilling to unearth my dreams and leave them to rot.

My entire family seemed determined to stand in my way, but I was equally as determined to seize control of my life. I had come to learn my rights in the three months following your great-grandfather's death. A single woman in France may not be able to own a business, and a married one could not sign a contract without her husband's approval, but a widow?

Ah, a widow could control her own destiny.

Of course, this would be easier to do if I hadn't been living in my father's house. After François's death, my parents insisted I stay with them, and it had been so easy to let them take over. There seemed no reason to remain in a home where every corner held memories of my husband. My sister stepped up to direct my staff and shut up the rooms. My father, along with Father Joseph, ensured that the funeral service was done with all the pomp required. My mother fussed over Clémentine, distracting her with treats from the kitchen and attention. The time under their roof provided a retreat, to have the maids draw the thick curtains of my old childhood room and allow me to hide in the dark.

It had been just what I needed for those first few weeks. But when I was ready to open the curtains and let the outside world back in, I found it more difficult to escape. Hands that wanted to help could bind one better than any jailor. I had thought I was pausing time while I grieved, but instead, it seemed I'd wound it back until I was once again a small girl, and not a woman grown. I would have to make a stand. I would declare my intent to remain in business.

■ ■

My mother's hands fluttered in her lap as if knitting with invisible wool and needles. "My darling, are you certain?"

She had asked this question no less than ten times. My words appeared to have no form, as no one heeded them. Now my father had convened a meeting at my father-in-law's home, as if sheer numbers would change my mind. I was weary of the conversation, and we had only just arrived.

"Yes, Maman, I am certain."

My mother fussed with her sleeves and looked at my father to say something. I knew she wished I was more like my sister or my brother's wife. At times I would catch her watching me as if I were a puzzle she was trying to solve.

Papa patted my shoulder, his heavy ring rapping against my flesh like a hammer pounding a nail into place. "Darling, you should take some time. You've had a shock. Grief is difficult. The holidays are coming," he said. "Perhaps in the spring or summer we can revisit this idea of yours."

My jaw tightened. It wasn't that I didn't grieve François. There were moments in every day that his loss struck me with a crushing blow. A split second when I would think I saw him from the corner of my eye, or go to tell him something, before I would remember all over again that he was gone. But the world had not stopped like François's heart. Next spring or summer would be too long to have my very existence on hold.

"Plans need to be made now for the coming year. The winter months are key. It's when we seem at our most quiet that the most work is happening below the surface," I pointed out. I glanced outside, where a light layer of snow had fallen the day before, the vines in the distance like frothing waves marching toward the house.

We needed to start pruning as early as January and plan for the new fields. There was tasting and blending to be done. While the vines were dormant, we could not afford to be.

Father crossed his arms over his chest. "Who is putting these ideas into your head?"

No one put ideas into my head. I was plenty capable of filling my own mind. However, it was my employee Louis to whom I owed my rebirth. Upon hearing of François's passing, he'd sent an immediate letter, reminding me that under the law I need not involve anyone else in my business. He'd rushed to return to my side by horse, ship, and carriage, over miles and miles, and arrived just a couple of weeks ago. While others treated me as a widow, Louis treated me as a business-woman. He did not draw on my emotions, but instead on my intellect.

Once he was in Reims, we crafted plans; the mere sight of our notes piled upon my desk excited me. Louis never doubted me. He had sold our wine across the continent. He was certain the business could continue to thrive, but I had no time or space to retreat. I sent up a prayer of gratitude for him, though I knew my father would not do the same.

"No one has given me ideas, Papa. I find work healing." I kept my voice calm even as my hands were tight fists in my lap. The heat from the fireplace behind me seared my back.

"It's just that Clémentine needs you," my mother added, petting her skirts like they were a lapdog. "She is feeling her father's loss."

I felt the barb in her words. My daughter had always preferred my husband over me. Even as a tiny babe her eyes would follow him around the room, a smile at the ready. For me she'd always been fussy, unable to settle in my arms, as if she could sense I was uncomfortable. François would sweep her out of my hands and spin her about, and her tears would turn to gurgles of joy. It didn't change as she grew. François never tired of her thousands of questions. *Where does the sun go at night? How do grapes grow? Do dogs believe in God?* He would crouch down so their faces were close and listen patiently, discussing topics with her as if she were his equal, pulling her close so she could stroke the side his face as she spoke.

Clémentine loved touch. She was always reaching for someone's hand, winding her fingers in their hair, or crawling into a lap. At nearly seven she was more pet than person. She could be shy and awkward with those she didn't know, but with those whom she was familiar, she would open like a flower in the sun and her talking would be nonstop. When I was working, I had to stifle the desire to swat her away. I found her clinging to my skirts like an anchor holding me to the house.

It wasn't that I didn't love my daughter. At times, I would glimpse Clémentine and feel a wave of love so deep that it felt as fierce as rage. I would give my life for hers if needed. But despite how I longed to be the type of mother who would fuss over her hair and spend time discussing her dolls as if they were of the utmost importance, I could not seem to marshal any patience for the day-to-day needs of a child.

Fatherhood had been a joy for François. I once watched them from the office window as they lay in the grass looking up at the sky for hours. Later in bed, I asked what they had been doing. François stated they were finding animal shapes in the clouds and creating stories for them, as if he could imagine no better use of his time. I wasn't a natural mother, but the fault was in me, not Clémentine.

The desire to be doing something, to be *useful*, was like an inescapable itch under my flesh. I'd find myself pacing the sitting room, my daughter watching me carefully as if I were a bird that had flown in from a window and who might batter herself against the walls at any moment. It was only when Louis had returned, his belief that I could run the business on my own, that I'd felt my spark return.

"Clémentine is doing well," I assured my mother. "Working will allow me to ensure security for her future," I suggested.

"You and the child are well taken care of," my father said, his face stern, tightening along his jawline. "There's no need for you to scrounge for money. I won't have people thinking that this family cannot care for its own." He yanked his waistcoat down, smoothing the fabric over his expanding middle.

I bit my tongue. I should have known better than to raise the issue of finances. My father tended to avoid any risk of failure. He was keenly attuned to his reputation.

When I was a child, my father had curried favor with the nobility, but when the winds of revolution blew stronger, he changed allegiances in the blink of an eye. He donned the tricolor cockade and liberty cap, marking himself as a revolutionary. Now he'd returned to fine fabrics and trim as he embraced Napoleon, switching back as easily as the seasons melted from one to the other.

What impressed me was not only my father's ability to pivot, but that he'd convinced himself of this change of heart as much as those around him. The man who had been a vital part of planning the last king's coronation and wedding to the Austrian princess Marie-Antoinette had no problem denouncing them just a few years later as if they were strangers. Perhaps it was unfair to fault him; his performance had guided our family through those turbulent years when so many others had foundered. But I could not escape the feeling that while bending to the prevailing wind meant one didn't break, it also meant they stood for nothing.

"I think—" I began.

"Barbe-Nicole, the problem is that you are always thinking. You need to trust that I know what is best for you," my father said.

"I am a grown woman, Papa," I reminded him.

"It may serve her well to be knowledgeable of the business," my father-in-law, Philippe, said from the corner of the room. "People will respect that she's taking care of the workers. The salesman, Louis, has continued taking orders. They will need to be filled, or we risk the business failing altogether."

His words made my father pause.

I held my breath. I wished Louis could be in this meeting to explain the importance of action. He understood that the business was on the precipice. He suspected the truth of François's death; I could see it in his eyes when we spoke. Or perhaps that sly maid Margot had whispered in his ear. I knew she liked him, although her station was well below his own. If she thought her secrets gave her an advantage she could use in the game of love, I had no doubt she'd take it. The girl was like vine blight, sneaky and destructive.

"But Barbe-Nicole has no head for running a business," my mother said, bringing my attention back.

I wanted to stamp my slippered foot on the carpet. It was I, not François, who had led the formation of our vineyard, ensured staff did what was needed, learned the magic of blending, ordered supplies, and worked with Louis to plan for orders and new markets, but for once I managed to hold my own tongue.

My father-in-law knew the truth. He didn't need to be convinced, and my parents never would be. They thought it unseemly for a woman of my stature to be involved with anything as common as trade.

"I was thinking we could hire someone to provide guidance, an apprenticeship, so to speak," Philippe said.

My father stroked his chin. "Who would take on such a project?"

"I've given it some thought," Philippe said. "Alexandre Fourneaux is a possibility. I took the liberty of speaking with him. He would consider a partnership. He has his own fields and cellars, but he is looking to expand. Alexandre would be able to steer the business, and he has funds for investment. He's experienced at both distribution and wine making. He would be a good steward."

My mouth turned downward, in an expression my mother called

sour. I did not require a nanny. I didn't like the idea of anyone "expanding" into what was mine. My father-in-law caught my gaze and ever so slightly shook his head.

"But Barbe-Nicole's role?"

Philippe waved off my mother's concern and turned back to my father. "If she is to own the business, it is best she understands it, lest anyone take advantage. Alexandre can guide her, certainly better than either of us."

"Is he married?" my mother asked, leaning forward.

My head whipped around to face her. François was barely cold in the ground and yet she couldn't help herself from scheming to get me down the aisle once again, this time with a man as old as my father. She at least had the decency to look down at her lap, fussing with the trim on her skirt, ashamed to have raised the issue in front of my dead husband's family. Thankfully, Philippe didn't respond to her question.

My father scowled. "I don't know. It's a difficult time for a business. We may be better to sit quietly."

Philippe raised his glass in my father's direction. "Come now, my old friend. We are men of cloth and fiber. Wool was our business; this move to champagne is new and now is not the time for us to learn a new industry. You and I both know we have only bought fields for our children. We've weathered much change already. With Napoleon as emperor and his eye on the Rhine even more will be coming. We have earned the right to spend these years in relaxation for all we've worked for, enjoying our grandchild, fine wine, and time for our own pursuits. Let Alexandre take the helm on this."

My father leaned back in the silk seat with huff, and I held my breath. "I suppose it is unwise to simply shutter the doors of the business. If you're certain this man will provide the guidance needed," he said eventually.

My father-in-law stood. "He will indeed. Barbe-Nicole, come with me; we shall select a bottle from my cellar and celebrate this decision." He took my elbow and guided me toward the hall.

As soon as we were far from the drawing room, I stopped, planting myself firmly. "I do *not* require a partner. Under French law I can run the business on my own."

Philippe sighed. "Under French law, perhaps, but without family support?" He shook his head. "I doubt that very much, ma chérie. Be reasonable."

I crossed my arms over my bodice. I did not want to be reasonable. "I don't know this man, this Fourneaux."

"I do. I have known him for many years. You can be assured; I would not have made the recommendation if I wasn't certain he would be helpful. Are you so arrogant that you don't feel you have anything to learn?"

I squirmed under his gaze.

"He knows wine. If your goal is to be a success, then he is one who can help you get there."

"Louis will assist me," I insisted. I knew Louis. I trusted him. He'd been with François and me since the start. He knew what I wanted to achieve. And he worked for me, not as a partner. I was done allowing a man to lead the way when I was capable—no, more capable—than most.

"Louis is a salesman. You will require more than that if you are to make the business a success. Especially with the winds of war blowing yet again. It will take a steady hand to guide us in the months ahead.

"And while I will give you that Louis knows sales and could likely talk the birds from the trees, he knows little of blending and the art of making the wine."

Philippe smiled and spread his arms. "I will put forward some funds to make the partnership work. Alexandre will bring the knowledge you require in addition to his own investment. Those who are smart are the first to admit what they do not know. It is the foolish who insist they know it all."

I bit my lip while I considered his words, staring into the eyes of a portrait on the wall, a distant relation of Philippe's. The man stared back from atop a horse, saber lifted, ready for adventure. This was a man in charge of his own destiny. To be a man meant to chart your own course, but I was not this man, nor any other. I took a deep breath. "To the business, Veuve Clicquot Fourneaux."

Philippe nodded. I could see his throat constrict, his cravat twitching, as he acknowledged the loss of his son. "Come now, let us choose a bottle to celebrate this decision."

I followed him down the hall. I had a mentor against my wishes, but if I was forced to have a partner, then I would learn all I could from him. In life, one does not always get to choose the people near us, but we do choose the relationship we have with them. And when the time came . . . I would take the reins, and I had no intention of ever giving them back.

Natalie

■ PARIS ■

APRIL 18

The last time I had a first date was nearly thirty years ago. The enormity of that fact seemed incomprehensible and vaguely horrifying, but it did at least explain why the entire process was so daunting. I felt awkward, as if I'd slipped on a new body and wasn't familiar with the controls. I suddenly had no idea what to do with my hands, as if they'd appeared for the first time at the end of my arms and were bobbing about looking for a purpose.

"Just a bit further," Gabriel said, looking over. "It is okay?"

"Mm-hmm," I said, plastering a smile on my face. I'd worn the completely wrong shoes. If we didn't get to where we were going soon, my little toe would need to be amputated. But I was determined to be a good sport, which meant if a toe was severed, I was prepared to cast it aside like a climber abandoned on the way to summit Everest. If the Widow could risk family disapproval to stand up for wanting her own business, surely I could risk possible amputation for a date.

I regretted my impulsive response to Gabriel's invitation. I'd agreed in part because of sunshine, wine, and advice from that book. But I'd also said yes because of Will. I wanted him to think about me out with someone else. But the truth was, unless I FaceTimed him for this event (something I was 100 percent sure was bad first-date etiquette), he wouldn't even know.

And given that Will lived with another woman, even if he knew, he wouldn't care. I hated that he still crept into my thoughts. I didn't know if my inability to fully move on meant I still loved Will despite what he did, or I loved who he used to be, or I loved the fantasy of him that had never really existed.

My last first date had been with Will. I was twenty. We'd lived in the same apartment complex near campus. He'd casually mentioned, as we stood by the bank of dented metal mailboxes, that a group of people were going to O'Brian's for drinks if I wanted to join. Months later I would learn that he'd bribed his friends, offering to buy the first round, so that he could extend a low-stakes invite to me.

My heart pinched, and I shoved the memory aside. Along with the one of me and Will ending that first night making out pressed against the cigarette machine in the back hallway of O'Brian's, the metal knobs burrowing into my back like eager fingers, pushing us together.

Gabriel paused, looking up and down the quiet street, and then motioned toward a tiny alley between two buildings. "Ah, there it is, through here." He strode forward.

I hesitated. The space was tiny and narrow, barely wider than his shoulders. What if it wasn't a sympathy date? What if he was a serial killer?

Did serial killers bring picnic baskets? The giant wicker monstrosity was hooked over his arm. It seemed an unlikely place to keep a machete and duct tape, but with this city's limited parking, you couldn't exactly keep everything in the trunk of your car.

He smiled crookedly over his shoulder at me. "Come along. Trust me. I promised to show you hidden Paris. One must adventure if they are to see it."

The word "adventure" pulled me along. Even if he was Jacques the Ripper, the ugly truth was that my current life was so bland, even something horrid would at least be different.

The alley smelled of stale urine, making my eyes water. Gabriel kicked a bottle on the ground with a mumbled curse and it clanked against the cobblestones. At the end of the alley, there was a locked metal gate and fence.

Instead of pulling out a key, Gabriel grabbed the top spokes of the fence and pulled himself up and over. Dear God, what if he expected me to do the same? I hadn't climbed a fence since junior high.

To my relief, he opened the gate from the inside.

"After you." Gabriel bent low.

I paused. Was this breaking and entering? He motioned me forward, and I slipped past him and around a corner. The view stopped me short.

It was a garden, boxed in on all sides by the backs of buildings. The center was a lush green with a winding path of pale pea-shaped gravel. There was a cluster of flowering trees and a bed of daffodils waving hello in the fading evening light.

"What is this place?" I mustered.

"Lovely, yes?"

I turned in a slow circle. "It's beautiful." The word, so inadequate to describe the magic, stuck in my throat.

Gabriel pulled a thick wool blanket from the basket, flapped it open, and spread it on the grass between us before motioning for me to sit. "The city is full of these private gardens. They are only for the owners in these buildings."

"Do you know someone who lives here?"

Gabriel winked. "No."

"Then how—"

"A man never tells his secrets. And those who have all this"—his arm swooped over the empty park—"don't even appreciate it. So those of us who would appreciate it must take it."

I sat on the blanket, trying to get comfortable. "This reminds me of one of my favorite books as a kid," I told him. "*The Mixed-Up Files of Mrs. Basil E. Frankweiler.*"

He paused, considering. "I do not think I know this book."

"It's about these kids in New York City who run away and hide in the Met Museum to live. I must have read that book hundreds of times. The idea of being alone with all those beautiful things fascinated me. Like having a lovely secret all to yourself." I glanced around the garden. "This place feels like that, magical."

Gabriel nodded, then glanced at his watch. "And if I'm not mistaken, then soon—"

The faint sounds of classical music spilled into the garden.

My mouth fell open as if he'd conjured the notes himself. Gabriel laughed.

"There is a quartet that practices at this time every day in that building." He motioned to a bank of windows on the far side of the garden. "I've heard them many times before. I thought it would provide the perfect backdrop."

I glanced around, half expecting police or an angry resident to fly around a corner demanding we leave. "Are we going to get into trouble?"

Gabriel shook his head. "No. We are doing nothing other than enjoying the beauty. Come now, let's see what we have." Continuing his magic trick, he began pulling items out of the basket, like a gourmet rabbit from a hat. Grapes, cheese, a bottle of wine.

"A picnic," I said.

"Oui. I planned to take you to one of my favorite restaurants, LeDoyen. Everyone from Monet to Napoleon has eaten there, but the earliest reservation I could get, even with my connections, was at eight. It occurred to me that with your travel you must have jet lag, no?"

I nodded.

He cocked his head to the side. "To have a late dinner with rich food, I suspect you would be sleeping in your soup. I would have to carry you home to the hotel, I think."

His smile made warmth spread through my lower belly. He didn't mean anything by the comment, but there was something oddly intimate about him discussing the idea of carrying me to a hotel.

"I thought to myself, *Gabriel Dubois, you are thoughtless. The lady will be too tired to listen to you chatter until the wee hours.* I promise, while this is not a restaurant, you will not go hungry, and you will see a side of Paris many do not."

The sound of a violin danced around, bouncing off the building. When he looked to the side, I took a quick picture before he could notice. No way I wasn't documenting this for Molly.

"It's remarkable," I said, letting myself melt into the blanket, inhaling the scent of fresh-cut grass.

"No, it's Mozart," he quipped. Gabriel removed the cork from the wine with a practiced tug on the corkscrew. "Do you know this piece?"

The music was familiar, but I had no idea what it was. I shook my head.

"It is titled *A Little Night Music*. They say Mozart composed it for Marie-Antoinette. He was a bit in love with her."

Gabriel swirled the wine in a glass and closed his eyes to sip. "Ah, lovely." He poured a generous amount into another glass and passed it to me. "A Bordeaux, Saint-Émilion."

His French accent made the words seem lyrical and liquid. The wine tasted soft, like velvet. Plum, black cherry, and a bit of a kick, like licorice. It tasted expensive, like consuming a designer handbag or jewelry.

"I was going to bring us a bottle of DRC, but it is too fussy for a picnic—the Bordeaux is a better choice."

"DRC?"

"Domaine de la Romanée-Conti is an estate in Burgundy. It produces some of the best wine in the world. But this wine is better suited for a picnic. Bordeaux spans the two sides of the Dordogne river. Saint-Émilion comes from the right bank," Gabriel explained.

"Is that the better side?"

"It is if you ask the winemakers from the right bank," Gabriel laughed. "French winemakers love to debate who has the best terroir, the best grapes, the best barrels." He waved his hand to indicate that was only the beginning of things they could argue about. He tore a baguette into pieces, the crisp crust shattering into crumbs, which he brushed off his sweater. "I wanted to bring one of my favorites, a bottle of Haut-Palmer. It is a tiny boutique winery near where I grew up, but it can be hard to find outside the region."

"I don't think I was aware how little I knew about wine," I admitted.

"At least you do not pretend. So many of my customers, they huff and puff, but they know very little. They don't love wine; they simply collect it. They think wine is something to put in a vault and brag about owning. I would much prefer the person who does not know much about wine but is passionate to enjoy it."

Gabriel shrugged. "To me, the unknown, the exploring, is part of the pleasure. Wine is like a woman: complex, beautiful, ever changing, volatile."

Wine is like a woman? I tried to muster annoyance with the cliché, but it sounded right coming from him. He used a small pocketknife to slice a bright-green apple, then fanned out the pieces. The juice dripped down his hand and he quickly licked it off. He glanced up at me, held my gaze, and then smiled, leaving me flushed.

Gabriel picked through the basket at his feet and arranged more things on the plate. "I collected some of my favorites. A bite of Paris for you." He pointed. "This is pâté from Galeries Lafayette, two kinds, this one with a bit of truffle." He kissed his fingertips. "The apple is just from the corner market, but very nice, crisp. A bit of cold roast chicken, some dried apricots." He pinched a chunk of bread around some of the pâté before popping it in his mouth. He rolled his eyes upward in exaggerated pleasure and then continued. "Cheese, of course. Reblochon, it's creamy and mild like a Brie, but a bit nutty. I thought of getting a Roquefort but wasn't sure how you felt about a blue cheese, so I went with a Comté instead." He nudged me to try a piece, his fingers touching mine just a beat longer than required.

"This is impressive," I said. "Thank you. It's a perfect introduction to Paris." Beyond perfect—it was something I wouldn't have even thought possible a week ago. The idea occurred to me that perhaps there was more to life than I had allowed myself to imagine . . . It made me recall the Widow and her determination to be more than just a wife and mother.

The music in the background paused and then the players began to play the same number again, this time slower. I leaned back, letting my weight sink toward the earth, my fingers entwined in the grass. I couldn't remember the last time someone had made so much of an effort to please me. The realization made me angry. Angry that Will hadn't seen me as worth the effort—hell, he didn't even see me as worth the basic respect of the truth. But what made me the angriest was that I hadn't even noticed his lack of effort in our relationship. The affair was his mistake, but mine was in not expecting more from my partner.

The sky was just beginning to darken, and windows in the back of the various apartments began to light up, giving us vignettes to watch. An old woman sitting with a cat on her lap, reading. A man bustling about in a kitchen, preparing a meal.

"It is like TV, no?"

I sipped the wine, flushing at being caught looking. "It is. I feel like a voyeur."

Gabriel shrugged. "If they truly wanted privacy, they would shut the curtains. People want to share their lives. It makes them feel real, worth watching."

"So, it's their fault we're peeping?"

"It is not a shame for a person to use what others make available. I like to make up stories for them."

I felt my mouth twitch in a smile. "Stories, huh?"

"Oui, see the woman there?" Gabriel used the tip of his penknife to point to the window of the old woman. "A spy."

My eyebrows shot up. "A spy?"

"Oh yes, it is always the one you don't expect. She is resting after a perilous undercover mission."

"And the cat?"

"Obviously a double agent." He pointed to another window. "The young man there, he is wondering how to tell his family he wishes to become an actor."

"On the stage in New York," I added.

Gabriel nodded. "And he is in love, but he fears it is one-sided. But if he can garner fame and fortune, he is certain the woman will fall for him."

"And will she?" I ask.

Taking a slice of apple from the side of his knife into his mouth, Gabriel paused. "I don't know. Do you believe in happy endings?"

My throat felt suddenly thick, and I tore a bit of chicken free to distract myself. "I'm not sure," I managed.

"Well then, we shall leave his story in, how you call, the in-between, limbo? And I for one shall hope for the best for him." Gabriel smiled and handed me an apricot. It was cool and heavy in my palm. "Try this for something sweet."

We sat in silence, tasting the various items and letting the music wash over us. The entire situation seemed unreal. The garden with the scent of freshly cut hedges, the violin and cello in the backdrop, the warmth of the wine in my chest and the sharp taste of the cheese in my mouth.

"You still wear your wedding ring."

I glanced down, realizing I was twisting my ring around my finger. I'd taken it off when Will left, but during the move I'd been afraid I'd lose it in the pile of boxes, so I had started wearing it again.

I nodded. "Habit, I guess."

He took my hand in his, turning it to the left and right to catch the remaining light in the stone. "It's beautiful. Very well made."

"You know jewelry as well as wine?" I asked.

"With my clientele, I see a lot of fine pieces." Gabriel ducked his head modestly. "If I may be so bold, however, it doesn't seem a ring I would have chosen for you."

I blinked in shock. I'd never loved the ring. Will had had it made for our twentieth anniversary. He'd traded in the small diamond he'd given me when we'd gotten engaged right after college graduation. I'd missed my old ring. This one was too . . . fussy. The large stone was forever snagging on my sweaters. I'd said nothing, not wanting to be ungrateful. Will had been so proud. He practically preened when I opened it, puffing up like a peacock spreading out his feathers.

Look at me.

The realization hit, stealing the breath in my lungs. Will hadn't bought the ring for me; he'd bought it for himself.

The ring had been a way for Will to check a box that he'd arrived, a symbol that he was successful. It was never about me at all.

Gabriel ducked his head, examining my expression. "I have upset you. My deepest apologies. It was not a subject to be brought up."

I shook away the emotions. "No, it's fine. You're right, really. The ring isn't my taste." When I returned to Naperville, I'd put the ring in the safe-deposit box at the bank. There was no reason to wear it anymore.

"I have a suggestion. Sometimes when one is trying to move on, things from our past can be a, how do you say, an anchor." Gabriel motioned to my hand. "Perhaps if you want to remake your life, start with the parts that do not suit you any longer."

"Redesign my ring?"

Gabriel nodded. "Or sell it to purchase something entirely different. A pendant, or a pair of earrings." He slid a sliver of apple between his teeth and winked. "Perhaps a tiara."

I stared down at the stone. The ring *was* mine. I distinctly remembered it being in the divorce paperwork, but for some reason it had never occurred to me I could sell it. It didn't seem like something that was mine as much as it belonged to our marriage, and I was the caretaker. If I did sell it, the smart thing to do would be to put the money toward retirement. Or pay off what this trip was going to end up costing instead of relying on funds from the house. But suddenly I didn't want to do the safe thing. The Widow didn't slink off and be safe. I would buy something new. Something for me.

"I'm going to do it," I declared. I tossed back a huge mouthful of wine. I wanted to stand up and spin in a circle. Or ask Gabriel to dance with me to the music.

"I will come with you," Gabriel said. "A shopkeeper may take advantage of you if he knows you to be a tourist. I can take you to a place I know from my clients. Very high quality."

I paused. I hadn't planned to do anything here. Not yet. Gabriel seemed to read my expression and unease.

"Don't worry yourself. A decision can be made another time. To-night is for simple pleasures." He raised his glass and tapped it lightly against mine, and I allowed myself to take a deep breath. The first one in what felt like months.

Barbe-Nicole

■ REIMS ■

REGARDING THE EVENTS OF JUNE 1806

My petite puce Anne,

I recognize myself in your tale of berating your dressmaker. I applaud you for not allowing someone to convince you that an item is good enough. One has the right to expect the best. I have never been willing to settle. Not in expectations for myself, for those around me, or in the wine I produce. To settle is to deny yourself the possibility of what could be. This does not mean it is easy to chart new directions. There will be those around you who say a situation must simply be accepted. When this happens, gather your wits about you, identify the direction you wish to go, and do not allow yourself to be swayed by those who lack your vision. This is the way I handled both my business and my personal life. If you thought others found you too demanding about the cut of a skirt, let me tell you of my own unwillingness to bend when things were unacceptable.

■ ■

The cellar stunk of sour rot, and it took all I had not to hurl the glass against the limestone wall. As I stared at the bottle of champagne, my mouth curled in disgust. My fingers drummed on the rough wooden table as if my distaste would be enough to change the product in front of me through sheer will.

Ropey.

Thick gelatinous strands wound through the bottle, like weeds reaching up from a pond. The consistency of what I'd poured into the glass was like loose egg white. It was vile.

Undrinkable.

We must have bottled too early. Instead of bubbles, we'd made this . . . abomination. I could have screamed in frustration, but I already had a reputation for my moods. As it was, the staff ducked and scurried out of sight when they saw me coming.

I'd overheard one field worker refer to me as the Crow. The black skirts of my widow's dresses fanned out behind me like wings as I marched down the rows of vines. Another worker had quipped back to beware my sharp beak and loud voice. They'd chuckled, scratching themselves through their worn breeches. I'd longed to yank the sweaty cotton cravats around their necks so their heads knocked together for insolence, but I consoled myself with the fact that while the crow may not be the world's most popular bird, it was smarter than most.

The cellar master, Pierre, twisted his cap in his hands as he stood to the side, awaiting my verdict. He glanced back and forth between me and Louis. I was not so naive that I didn't know he'd invited my salesman to be here as a calming influence.

"We can move the rest of this lot to another part of the cellar, ma'am. If we can get them colder, rack them a few more times—"

"Yes, I know the options," I snapped. We could pour the wine from bottle to bottle, trying to leave behind the dregs in the hope that it would clear, but there was no guarantee, and with every pour from container to container, we'd lose more product, like coins slipping between our fingers. My foot tapped under the table as my mind spun.

"With summer coming—"

"I am aware of the impact of weather," I said, shutting him down again. The heat would make the situation worse. There had to be way to avoid this calamity when making champagne; these losses were unacceptable.

The man flinched, his head pulling in like a turtle. He looked to Louis for relief. My salesman never seemed to have harsh words. If I was the crow, Louis was the songbird.

"'Tis not your fault," Louis said with a shrug. "To make champagne is to risk failure."

I pinched my mouth shut. I had not seen failure as an option. The year had started off so well. I'd been arrogant, certain that my choices had been blessed. And I had assumed that I *deserved* that success. That the loss of François meant that the world owed me better fortune— but the world was quickly teaching me it owed me nothing.

While our first shipment had eluded the blockades, the second was stuck on the docks in Amsterdam and, along with it, the hopes for our business. My business partner, Alexandre, blamed me. In fairness, it had been my idea to send nearly all we had, the entire harvest's worth. I'd been so sure we'd been clever, but then the damned British had ordered the Dutch port closed to spite Napoleon. Now all our wine was simply sitting there, the rising heat doing it no favors while men played at war.

I stood quickly, the chair letting out a rumble of protest as it slid across the limestone floor. "Let me think what we will do. I'll speak with you tomorrow." I bustled past Pierre and Louis so that I could be outside. I wasn't foolish enough to think any new ideas would solve our current problem, but I wasn't yet ready to accept our reality. *Ropey wine. Mon Dieu.*

As I exited the cellar, I blinked, momentarily blinded in the sunshine. I tilted my face up to the sky, loosening the shawl I'd wrapped around my shoulders, and let the spring heat warm me.

Louis followed me. "Will you take the cellarman's advice?"

I stared out at the vineyard. The orderly rows soothed me, like lines of text across a printed page. As if I could read the soil and its fruit and divine what would happen next. "We'll take a loss," I pointed out.

Louis nodded. "As it is, it is unsellable. Some is better than none."

I sighed. He was not telling me anything I did not already know, but his calmness soothed me. Even though the decision was inescapable, Louis still framed it as a question. Deferring to me, allowing me to at least have that sense of control. "Are you leaving again so soon?" I asked.

"If I didn't leave, you would berate me for not selling the next harvest, and if I am not here, you declare me not helpful."

"Am I so difficult?"

The corners of his mouth threatened to rise. "I would not say difficult as much as a woman particular in her wants."

"So you avoid the question," I said, slightly annoyed. I did not like to see myself as unreasonable. "You aim to sweet-talk the situation."

"Is that not why you hired me?" Louis cocked his head. "A salesman who cannot be charming goes hungry. Now leave me to sell the wines to come and I shall leave you to manage the grapes."

I waved him off. "Go on then. Do what you do best, and I will have to manage everything else by myself."

Louis bowed low. "As if you would have it any other way. Don't worry, Madame Clicquot. You and the business will survive." He paused and then smiled. "You are too difficult to permit any other outcome."

I shook my head and watched him leave. He was right. The news with the wine was troubling, but I was confident I would find a solution eventually. One person's stubbornness is another's persistence. Life is not one season or one bottling. Placing my hands low at the base of my spine, I stretched, thrusting my shoulders out and back, like my own personal crow wings, the cording in my corset straining. The muscles protested even as air filled my lungs. I spent too many hours at my desk.

I relaxed and then shifted, tugging the bodice back down. The high waist did not suit my figure. My mother was constantly at me to embrace the latest styles, adding military-styled trim even if my widow status meant I was destined for black and gray fabrics. While I was glad fashion had rejected the large skirts of years past, I couldn't muster an interest in what I wore.

The sun was dipping for the day. I would return to the office and create one of my lists of tasks. One cannot head in a new direction unless one has clearly identified their goal. I could also finish my correspondence. With luck there would be word from Alexandre that the port had reopened, and he could get the wine off the Dutch docks, although I doubted it. Lately, the only news that came seemed to be bad.

Speaking of bad news.

The maid Margot, the Mouse, stood at the edge of the house. She ducked her head, glancing up at one of the stablemen through her lashes. Was there no one the girl wouldn't chase? I half expected to see her racing after the stable master's hound. The dog was about the only other unmarried male to escape her grasp.

I couldn't make out what she said from here, but I could feel the sticky-sweetness of her words. I was afraid of what she knew and what she might do with the information, so I was stuck with her and her honeyed words and minimal effort. How much time had she spent on that ridiculous hairstyle alone? Time that she owed me as a worker. Margot wrapped a hair ribbon around a finger and smiled shyly at the man.

My gaze narrowed. My hands clenched into fists. *How dare she.*

■ ■

The door to Clémentine's playroom flung open. My daughter, perched at her desk, dropped her doll at the sight of me and pulled the open book in front of her closer.

"Mama, I didn't expect you."

I rarely saw my daughter during the day. Or, if I was honest, often in the evening either. I tended to stay at my desk until late. Too late, apparently.

"Where are the hair ribbons I got you from Paris?" I asked.

Her eyes widened, and she glanced around the room as if she expected them to be sitting there in a tidy pile. "I'm not certain."

"You didn't give them to anyone, did you?"

Clémentine blinked rapidly, her gaze sliding away from mine. "No?" There was no chance Napoleon would use my girl for espionage. She could no more lie than she could open the window and leap over the moon.

"I saw Margot with them in the front yard," I stated, ending the charade.

Clémentine's lower lip sucked into her mouth, and she began to pick at the flesh around her thumb with her other hand. I reached out and covered her fingers with mine to make her stop.

"Margot is going to practice hairstyles with the ribbons on her own hair and then use them on mine," Clémentine admitted. "She can do the loveliest styles, Mama. She says that she can be my lady's maid when I'm a bit older."

I felt my lip twitch, and Clémentine winced as if I'd snarled. I pressed my mouth into a placid expression. "Darling, Margot is not a lady's maid. She's a housemaid." *And a filthy, scheming rat.* I knew my frustration with the business was leaking into this situation, but I could no more pull it back than one can place spilled wine back in a bottle.

Clémentine's eyebrows met in the center of her forehead. "But why can't a housemaid become a lady's maid?"

My little revolutionary. Why not indeed. I would almost admire her thought if I considered it even remotely original, rather than poured into her ear by that creature.

"You will not need a lady's maid for some time yet, ma chérie; you are only seven. When the time comes, we will hire you the very best. Not one who must practice with borrowed ribbons." I brushed the loose curls from Clémentine's face.

Her face clouded. "You don't like Margot, do you, Mama?"

I weighed my words carefully. I did not like to lie to my daughter. So many people lie to girls and women. As if we wouldn't be able to handle the truth, as if we didn't deserve it.

I sat on the daybed and motioned for her to take her chair.

"You know how I respect hard work," I ventured.

Clémentine nodded furiously. "Grand-père Philippe says you do the work of five men."

I felt the first honest smile of the day on my face. My father-in-law was good to me. He believed me to be capable.

Unlike my own father.

Or my business partner, for that matter. If the wine in Amsterdam was spoiled, Alexandre would be convinced it was a sign we should stop any effort to sell in foreign markets. At least until the war ended. But who knew when that would be? He was wrong to focus on domestic sales. If the champagne house was to succeed, we must sell abroad. I was certain of this. And we would need a way to avoid the losses that came with imperfect wine. My hands pleated my cotton skirt as I pondered.

"Maman?"

I jolted in my seat, my focus returning to Clémentine. "I believe that to work hard is to do God's will," I said.

"But didn't God say we should rest of the seventh day? You often work on Sundays."

God could take Sundays off with ease because he controlled the weather and the outcome of the war with its blasted blockades, and was assured balanced ledgers. I, on the other hand, was but a mere mortal so had to work twice as hard.

"Oui, you are right, my poppet. I should take more Sundays off. That is time we should spend in prayer and with family."

Clémentine's smile was huge, and she fidgeted in her seat with pride for having done God's will and secured herself more time with me.

"However," I said, bringing her back to the issue at hand. "I don't believe that Margot works very hard. On Sunday or any other day. She is light in her attitude toward her duty."

"But maybe it's because she doesn't enjoy it. If Margot were doing tasks she liked, I bet she would work ever so hard, Mama. She said she would love to travel with me to Paris to shop for fabric and meet with the best dressmakers. She's heard of milliners who can make hats that look like fairy magic with feathers and tulle. And that there are bakeries where we could eat sweets until our tummies ached." Clémentine's eyes were wide as she imagined this fantastic world that Margot had spun for her. A world in which Margot would no doubt benefit greatly.

"Never fear, my darling girl. You will have all the dresses you desire when the time comes, and perhaps even a fairy hat, but for now, your focus should be on your studies."

Her face clouded over. My sweet daughter was not one for books. How was I to compete with the sugary fiction the wench was dishing out?

"Margot said you wouldn't want her to be my maid, but that she had a way to convince you. That you wouldn't be able to say no," Clémentine said. There was a shadow of stubbornness in her eyes. My apple did not fall far from my own tree.

It was pure luck to spot those ribbons, like Medusa's snakes, in Margot's hair. The little minx had overplayed her hand. There was still time to nip this in the bud. I couldn't fire the Mouse without fear that she'd spread more rumors about town. But I could remove the danger. She would not win my daughter's affections, nor use her to get what she hadn't earned.

I petted Clémentine's arm, and the girl leaned into me like a cat. "All of that is a problem for another day, ma chérie. Why don't you show me your dolls? I have not seen Mademoiselle Marie in some time."

Clémentine clapped her hands together and reached for her doll. I pulled them both onto the daybed next to me and let her prattle on about the doll and her adventures, murmuring interested sounds to fill any silences. My attention was enough to distract her for now, but it wouldn't be for much longer. I had hoped that keeping Margot employed and ignoring her laziness would be enough, but I could see now that the girl would keep reaching, scrabbling for more. The Mouse was growing fat in my home.

Natalie

■ PARIS ■

APRIL 19

Sitting in the lobby of the Delphine, my book of the Widow's letters propped on the table in front of me, I started to plan. I'd always liked lists, but reading about Clicquot's list making had made me realize that mine were always about reducing risk and preparing for possible failure. The Widow, on the other hand, created plans to achieve things others believed impossible. She planned for success. I'd become someone so afraid of risking what I already had that I'd never reached for what I really wanted.

Heck, I didn't even *know* what I wanted anymore. It was time to shift gears. Instead of avoiding risks, I needed to start taking them.

I was multitasking my list creation by deconstructing a croissant layer by flaky, buttery layer while waiting for my coffee. The window in front of me held my reflection and I stopped short. I looked like an ad from a Lands' End catalog. I wasn't certain I owned any clothing that wouldn't be described as sensible and machine washable. I didn't have a style unless you counted "suburban white lady."

As I picked at the fabric of the jersey pants I'd brought because they were stretchy and would travel well, it occurred to me that there were entirely too many elastic waistbands in my life. Everything I owned was designed to be overlooked. To blend in, to be safe. I didn't know what I wanted for my life, but I was positive the woman I wanted to be wouldn't wear anything in my closet.

I cracked open the blank journal Molly had given me when she'd dropped me off at O'Hare so I could record my adventures. I hadn't always been one half of a whole. I once had interests and passions outside my marriage, and I could again; I just needed to find new directions. I patted the slim volume of the Widow's letters as if it were a friend keeping me company. My life was not one bottling or one season either, as the Widow said. It didn't end because my marriage had.

I wrote in large, thick letters across the top of the page *My New Life Plan*. I quickly listed down the page *Travel, Find a Mentor/Guide for Quest, Start Reading Again, Go on Date*. Then I checked each one of them off with a satisfying swoop of the pen. The only thing better than a to-do list was being able to cross things off. Then I added below those items *New Wardrobe* and then, after a pause, *Have Sex*. I immediately scribbled that out, rewrote *Have Great Sex*, and underlined it twice.

"Here is your coffee."

I slammed the notebook shut. Sophie held out a silver coffeepot and I smiled. My nose twitched as she placed it down in front of me. The smell of the dark brew was enough to shake off the last of the jet lag that clung to me.

"Sugar?"

I shook my head. "No thank you, but I have a question. Can you suggest where I might go shopping?" Molly had made a list for me of touristy things to do in the city, but checking off a river cruise seemed less decisive than taking steps toward my new life.

"It depends. What are you shopping for?"

"I need a new wardrobe," I replied.

"Like a new dress for a particular occasion?"

"Like an entirely different look." I pointed through the window to a woman striding past on the sidewalk. She wore loose wide-legged black pants and a fitted linen white top with the required scarf tied at her neck. Her sunglasses were oversized. She looked effortlessly chic, an "after" shot in a makeover spread for *Vogue*. Confident. "Something like that." Or really, exactly like that. It took all I had to not tackle the woman in the street and peel the shirt off her back.

Sophie nodded. "Ah, I see."

Glancing at her, I realized how stylish Sophie looked as well. It didn't escape my notice that her skirt had a zipper and button without an inch of elastic to be seen. "Anywhere you shop would be great."

She smiled and blushed. "Let me make you a list of shops with a map from the desk so you can find your way."

I thanked her, then blew on my coffee and texted Molly.

Paris wonderful! Had a date! With an actual man!! Going shopping later—new clothes for new me.

A split second later, my phone rang.

"You had a date?" Molly hissed into the phone. "You were only in town one full day. Last I heard you had just gotten off a bus tour. How did you meet someone? What if he's some kind of human trafficker?"

My brain spun to do the math. "It must be the middle of the night. What are you doing up?"

"Hot flash. I was just lying there sweating. I saw your text. Don't worry, you didn't wake me up and John could sleep through an earthquake. A date?"

I pictured Molly curled up in bed with her blanket kicked off, texting furiously. I glanced around to make sure Gabriel wasn't nearby. "I think it was a date. Pretty sure most human-trafficking rings don't target women in their fifties. He didn't kiss me, but he took me on a picnic in this private garden in the center of the city. And unless I've completely forgotten how these things work, there was definitely some flirting."

"Oh my God, that sounds so romantic."

I giggled, resisting the urge to bounce in my seat. "I cannot even describe how amazing it was. He's a wine merchant and so . . ." I searched for the right word. "French."

"Well, you didn't waste any time. First that amazing hotel, and now this?"

Molly had appropriately swooned when I'd sent her the photos of my suite. She agreed that while Will wasn't technically dead, my marriage certainly was, so it was worth the ruse to keep the room.

"This trip has been the best decision I ever made," I admitted. The back of my throat tightened, and I wondered if I was at risk of crying.

"Very *Eat, Pray, Love*," Molly agreed. "Tell me more about this wine merchant."

"Wait, I'll text you a picture of him I took last night."

Molly made an appreciative noise when she saw the photo. "Nice."

I leaned back in the chair. "I met him here at the hotel. He's staying on business. His name is Gabriel."

Molly sighed over the phone. "That *is* so French."

"Right? And he knows all this stuff about the city and music and history. We talked for hours." I lowered my voice as if about to divulge a dark secret. "I'm not sure his exact age, but I'd guess he's at least ten to twelve years younger than me." *Please, God, don't let it be more than that. If I could have babysat for him, it tips from sexy to creepy.*

Molly made a weird sound, like a cat trying to bring up a hairball. I pulled the phone away from my ear. "What the hell was that?"

"That's my cougar roar," she clarified.

I giggled. "Let's hope you and John stay together, because I'm pretty sure that's more scary than enticing." I suddenly felt knowledgeable. Like the girl at the slumber party who had done *things*. Molly was back in middle-aged-married-woman land. I, on the other hand, was taking steps into uncharted territory. I was creating visions and plans.

"I'm going to sleep with him," I said, mentally ready to put a tick next to that item on my list.

"What?" It sounded for a moment like she was choking on her own saliva, or she was trying to make that cougar sound again. "You went on one date!"

"You know the cliché: the best way to get over someone is to get under someone else." The words sounded over the top, even to me, like I was auditioning for *The Real Housewives of Paris*.

"Be careful, okay?"

Molly's sudden serious tone irritated me. She was one of those people the Widow would say was lacking in vision, someone who didn't risk sending wine to foreign markets. Or maybe it was envy. "Don't worry. Everything's fine. I think it's required to have meaningless vacation sex. The French government might insist on it before they allow single women to leave the country. If you haven't, they make you fool around with the customs guy at the airport. It's like the law."

"But is it going to be meaningless for you?"

"I'm not going to *marry* the guy," I said. As I said it, an image popped into my head. A sprawling stone-and-timber country house out in the middle of a lavender field. Me in a giant straw hat picking vegetables from a garden. Gabriel, his sleeves rolled up to show his tanned sexy forearms, opening a bottle of wine on the patio and waving for me to join him. That was a vision I could get behind.

"All I'm saying is, watch your heart."

"I can take care of myself. I'm not a teenager."

"But you were the last time you dated. Don't get me wrong—you're a beautiful, smart woman. It doesn't surprise me that he's attracted to you. By all means, have fun with Mr. Wine Merchant. And I'm going to want all the details so I can live vicariously through your experiences. I just don't want you to get hurt."

I didn't like how she called him Mr. Wine Merchant. And for someone who wanted details, she certainly seemed ready to rain on my parade. Sophie approached, holding a slip of paper. I motioned for her to sit.

"I need to go; my friend is here, and the shops open soon," I said to Molly. Sophie smiled as she sank into the chair across from me. "You should go back to sleep. I'll chat with you later."

"Promise you'll text and send pictures of the clothes you pick. Keep in mind dry cleaning gets expensive."

I rolled my eyes. "Of course. Sleep tight." I clicked off my phone.

Sophie tapped the piece of thick stationery on the table. "Here you are. The first two shops are some of the nicer department stores in the city, but the third one is a small boutique. I think you'll quite like that place, very classic French style. Not for tourists." Sophie passed over one of the maps that the hotel desk gave out to guests, with all the major monuments and tourist sites marked. "I've circled the location of the shops on here. It is easy to walk, but if you get tired, there is the Metro."

"Thank you."

"Your friend on the call, she upset you?" Sophie asked.

I glanced up and Sophie pointed to where I had pulverized a corner of the croissant into microscopic crumbs onto the table. "Oh, sorry." I brushed the debris into the palm of my hand and poured them onto the plate. "She's just worried about me."

Sophie nodded. She pinched her lips together and then leaned forward as if about to share a secret. "When my husband died, my family and friends were very supportive. I don't know if I would have survived without them."

I felt another pang of guilt over having lied to Sophie about Will being dead. And while we both had pain from our losses, I doubted she would see it as similar, but in this we were connected. My throat tightened. Molly had been the first person I called when I discovered Will's affair. She was there when I couldn't get out of bed. She'd held my hair back as I vomited up the tequila I'd used to blot out the texts I'd found. She'd arranged that stupid Wiccan retreat to magic the life back into me.

"But then when I started to find my feet again, it was hard for my family," Sophie continued. "It wasn't that they didn't want me to be happy, they did, but they wanted me to be the same, and I will never be that woman again. I have changed."

Hot tears filled my eyes, and I blinked them away before they could fall. "Me too." Sophie had put into words what I hadn't been able to articulate, what the list had been about. I needed to let go of who I had been, to stop trying to get back to normal and, instead, step forward and embrace the idea of being someone different. To accept that my former self was broken, but that I could put the pieces together in a new way.

Sophie patted my hand. "Neither of us wanted to change. I suspect we both would have preferred the life we had, but it was not our decision to make." She gave a lazy shrug. "So, we must adapt to this new life. What we have been through has forged us." She glanced over and saw the book on Madame Clicquot, a huge smile breaking onto her face. "Yes, you are learning of the Widow. We are like her. We will make a life for ourselves. We will live boldly." She held up her arm in a flex, her tiny bicep curling. "But to do so means that at times . . ." Her voice trailed off. "At times, it will make the people around us uncomfortable. They miss the person we had been and do not understand that it is not as simple as just going back."

"I know my friend means well," I said. "But at the same time, it's frustrating."

She nodded. "You may find that you need a break from those who knew you when, until you are done becoming who you will be."

This woman should work for Oprah. She tossed off these brilliant asides like a seasoned TED Talk professional. "If you don't mind me asking, how long ago did you lose your husband?" I asked.

"Just over three years ago. I stayed for a while in Reims, but I knew if I wanted a new life, I had to carve one out, so I moved here to Paris."

"And you're happy now?" I hated how desperate I sounded. It wasn't fair that I was asking this young woman to assure me it was all going to be okay, but I needed her to say that taking risks would pan out.

"Oui. I am happy. A different happy, but it is good." Sophie looked over, making sure the clerk at the front desk was busy. "I will tell you my dream. Something I have wanted to do since I was a girl. I am going to open my own shop. I will sell wine and offer tasting and education. My courses will especially be for women, so more of them enter this industry."

She lowered her voice. "Men always think they know best. When I was studying, men who had never even touched a grape that their mother didn't wash and put in their mouth lectured me, even though I grew up playing in the vines. No, my place will be special. The wine shop I wished existed when I was starting in this business."

"I love that idea," I said. I could already imagine the place, wine racks up to tall ceilings and a large handcrafted wooden table in the center. People sitting around, taking notes on the wines they tasted, listening to a lecture from someone like Gabriel.

Sophie winked. Her eyes were alive with sparks of excitement. "I have already bought the space in Reims. I used money from my husband's life insurance. It is old and run-down, but I can see the potential. I am saving now so I can open it in maybe a year or so. On my vacations I go there and make, how do you say, repairs, renovation? You will have to return to France someday and take one of my courses when I am in business."

"Count on it."

She cocked her head as she looked at me. "You can do it too. There is no magic to creating a new future. It simply means letting go of the things that tether us to the past."

I nodded, the tears threatening again like thunderclouds. I touched the wedding ring hanging from a chain around my neck. I'd taken it off last night when I got back to the hotel but couldn't risk leaving it in the room. The problem was, I didn't know what I wanted for my life anymore. Everything had always been about what Will and I would do together. I'd put my marriage first and made it so important that it overshadowed anything of my own. I knew I wanted my new life to be different. Better, but I'd gotten only as far as a small checklist in a notebook.

Sophie tapped the back of my hand. "May I be so bold to ask you something?"

"Of course."

Sophie bit her lip and shifted in her seat. "It is a bit rude for me in my position."

"No, please, go ahead."

"I am done with my work at noon today. May I go shopping with you? You say you like my style and I know these shops very well." Her hands fluttered to her throat as she flushed. "If you would like to go alone, of course I understand. I do not mean to presume we are friends, only that I feel this connection with you, comprenez-vous?"

"I would *love* that," I responded, feeling a rush of excitement. It was as if one of the cool kids asked me if I wanted to join them at lunch. The fact that she was almost young enough to be my daughter was immaterial. "I can use the help."

Sophie smiled wide. "Parfait. It is a plan." She stood. "Now I must return to my work. I will meet you here at twelve. You will be good until then?"

I nodded, happy to wait to shop until Sophie could join me. I'd use the morning to walk the city or go and see one of the museums. Then an idea hit me. "You wouldn't know where I could get a haircut, do you?" I tentatively touched the tips of my hair. I'd worn it long for years.

Sophie's eyes lit up. "Oui, I know the exact place. I will make a call. The owner owes me a favor; he will sneak you in if I ask kindly."

I leaned back, imagining everyone's face when I returned to Naperville. Didn't every movie about a person changing require a makeover montage? It was time and I was ready. I was more than ready.

Barbe-Nicole

■ REIMS ■

REGARDING THE EVENTS OF MAY 1808

My darling Anne,

It was with great delight I received your correspondence. Do not worry about being candid with me; I am not so easy to scandalize. The advantages of age are that one has both seen it all and has less interest in judging others, as we soon face our own eternal judgment. It delights me to no end that instead of limiting yourself you are choosing this season of your life to grow and explore.

The fact that you and your mother are at odds is the way of things. She is focused on the risk and you upon the opportunity. I found my relationship with my mother a challenge and I suspect your grandmother, my daughter, would have plenty to comment on regarding my skills as a parent. Perhaps we are destined to always see our own wants in our children instead of their own. My mother wanted me to have a domestic life, to thrive and focus on the home and family.

And in return with my daughter, I lamented that she had no head for business. It is human nature to be irritated with others over what we most dislike in ourselves, or fear we lack.

And as for the fight you had with your mother, let me tell you of one of mine, which, oddly enough, also was based in part on discussion of matrimony.

■   ■

The shadow of the cathedral offered relief from the sun. The spring was unseasonably warm, and it left me with unease as to what to expect in the coming months. I stood with my parents on the steps after mass waiting for them to finish chatting with our neighbors.

I glanced up at L'Ange au Sourire sculpture. The angel's stone smile did little to lighten my mood, but I hoped God would be as inclined to share his favor as the angel always appeared to do for all who entered the church. Father tossed his head back and laughed, all while slapping the back of Monsieur LaPointe, while mother clucked over the newest LaPointe babe. Seeing that it would be a while, I slipped back inside the cathedral. My thoughts were too heavy for casual conversation.

I paused at the back of the nave, drinking in the silence and peace of the nearly empty space. No matter how many times I came to the church, it still took my breath away. The cathedral was built to create believers. The soaring arches drew one's eyes to the heavens. Sun streamed through the stained-glass window at the end, creating a mosaic on the stone floor of dappled blues, greens, and reds, like a garden of light. The faded scent of incense hung like a memory in the air. No wonder French kings held their coronations here. In this space it was possible to believe God could be bothered to spend time with man. The church had been banned during the revolution; religious services replaced with altars to reason. It had been a mistake. People need to have a space where they feel closer to God, where they can let go of thought and rest on faith.

Glancing back toward the entrance, I saw my parents still engaged with others. They hung on the word of every neighbor but seemed to have no interest in what troubled me. They wanted me to be like my siblings. Quiet and obedient. They loved to attend mass, but they went more as a social event than a religious one. My mother relished the opportunity to show both her piety and her newest gown, while my father attended to further advance his politics. It was a wonder either of them found any time to commune with God, they were so busy with other conversations.

The thought was uncharitable, and I mentally sent up a small prayer of contrition as I moved to the small chapel for the Virgin Mary and knelt.

I turn to you for protection, holy Mother of God. I beg you to listen to my prayer and keep Louis safe from danger.

I did not often rely on prayer. I pictured God as a master vintner, the entire world his fields. He had much to do and little time for those constantly asking for favors. Even now, rather than disturb God Almighty, I sought the help of the Virgin. It seemed to me she would be more sympathetic to a woman's plea.

Louis's crumpled letter felt heavy in the pocket of my dress. It had been folded and reread a thousand times since it had arrived. I suspected the seal had been opened on the sly during the journey. The Russians thought Louis a spy, a ridiculous notion. Louis was no more a spy that I was one of the ghostly dames blanches who haunted travelers in the countryside.

My mind tumbled through options. I would speak to Jean-Rémy

Moët. He might be my competitor in business, but he was also a Frenchman. He and Napoleon were close. If anyone could get a man into Russia to check on Louis's safety or to grease the wheels of bureaucracy, it would be Moët. As much as I hated to ask him for anything, this was not a time for my pride to get in the way.

I turn to you for protection, holy Mother of God.

I entertained a fantasy of dressing like a man and taking off on my own to handle the situation. The freedom that would come from riding astride, traveling distance quickly and unencumbered. Oh, to sit at any public house with a drink and be left unmolested. To move and say whatever I wanted. I sighed. That was more of a miracle than the Lord was likely to grant.

No, I needed to keep my request small, that God would see fit to ensure the Russians saw Louis as no threat. To allow him to return to France, that our wines would sell, that the summer heat wouldn't destroy the harvest, that the business would stay on the right side of the ledger, that Alexandre would continue his investment, that the war would end so we could focus on business, that the Mouse would vex me less, that Clémentine would remain well and happy . . . My pleas piled up in front of me, filling the cavernous space of the cathedral. It felt as if, with each murmured request, I were purged of a weight.

I turn to you for protection, holy Mother of God.

"Madame Clicquot."

I turned to see Father Joseph. He stood with his hands clasped in front of his black cassock. In my widow's wear, we were nearly matched. "Father." I ducked my head in deference.

"I am sorry to disrupt you at prayer, but I'm glad to see you. I tried to speak to you earlier this week, but your servant indicated you were not to be disturbed while working."

Father Joseph's displeasure at having been turned away, or that I worked at all, was evident on his face, his bulging toad-like eyes fixed on me along with a scowl.

I disliked kneeling before him. The old goat didn't deserve my adoration. I pulled myself to my feet so we were eye to eye. Madame Martin had informed me the priest had come by, but I had ignored the message.

"Yes, I apologize, Father. I meant to call on you, but business has kept me quite busy." I ignored the ache in my knees and forced myself to stand tall.

"Business should never come before the Lord," he said, raising his chin in the air, his jowls wobbling like congealed fat atop a stew pan.

You are not the Lord. "Of course. How may I help you, Father?" If he wanted funds for the roof, he would need to ask another. As it was, my business hung by a thread.

"I have heard some distressing news." He pursed his mouth and looked down as if forming the words were painful. "It has been suggested that your husband did not die of a fever, but that he gave in to the sin of despair."

Sweat broke out under my arms. It had been nearly three years since François's demise. I had assumed any discussion of his death was long past.

"I do not know why someone would say such a horrid thing," I said, stalling for time. I knew exactly who would have raised the topic, but I didn't dare speak her name in case it confirmed her story that we were in league to keep a secret.

"I am not at liberty to share who spoke with me, but I assure you they shared this news out of their own spiritual distress." Father Joseph shook his head. "To lose faith and allow oneself to fall into despair is a grievous sin."

I nodded. "Life is indeed a gift from God," I replied.

"I know that François was prone to melancholy. You understand that if I was deliberately misled in order to have him buried in consecrated ground, that, too, would be a sin? You would have an obligation to share with me any concerns or worries that you had in this regard."

I nodded again. Despite what a man such as this would think of my decision, I was confident that a kind and loving God would never bar the door to heaven for someone like François. His sadness was a cancer, and it was not his fault for the having of it. And if I as his wife did not know the ultimate truth of what François may or may not have done, how in the world could this man have seen into my husband's heart? "I trust you won't allow vile rumors to upset you."

Father Joseph stared at me, perhaps hoping that his disapproval alone would be enough to wring a confession from me. Little did he know I was so familiar with disapproval it felt as comfortable as a feather bed.

"I will say a prayer for whomever said this horrible thing, that they are able to see clear and be lighter in spirit knowing that François is very much deserving of salvation," I replied, casting my eyes downward in faux piety.

Why is Margot stirring up trouble now? If she had any religious concerns, she would have run to the priest long ago. She was like a weed in the garden, sprouting up and in the way. Constantly asking for favors, pleading for additional free afternoons, finding ways to sneak off with bites from the table. The entire staff likely wondered why I didn't let her go, but the girl would simply smirk at me when caught as if daring me to call her out.

"Are you here to pray for your husband's soul?" Father Joseph's eyebrow arched like a bristling caterpillar lunging to reach a new leaf.

He looked smug, as if he had caught me at something. That praying for François proved the dirty allegation.

I drew up straight. "No, Father. I am praying for my employee Louis Bohne, that he may have safe passage home. He has been traveling to Russia for business."

Father puckered his lips as if tasting a sour grape. "Doing business in Russia is not wise. There is a war."

Did he think I was so vacuous that I was unaware of the war? Or, for that matter, foolish enough to take his advice on matters of commerce?

"The head of your business, Monsieur Fourneaux, has spoken to me of his worries," he continued.

I bristled. "Monsieur Fourneaux is my *partner*, not the head of the company. That is why both of our names are on it."

"It isn't natural for a woman to conduct business," Father Joseph declared. "The Lord meant for a woman to be the helpmeet of her spouse. The man is the head."

"Ah, but was it not a woman, Jeanne d'Arc, who saved this town, this very church in fact, from the British?" I smiled at him. "God chooses whom he works through, and with him, all is possible." Let him argue that, the old goat.

His mouth twitched. There was talk that Jeanne may be made a saint someday, but I doubted it. Not if the men of the church were anything like Father Joseph. The only women he liked were meek.

"Ah well, I imagine who is the official head of the business will not matter," Father Joseph said.

A frisson of unease passed down my spine.

"I understand you will soon marry again." He smirked and winked. "Never fear, I shall keep it a secret until the banns are read. But you can rest easy that when that time comes, you can let go of

the worries of the business, and your need for prayer can focus on
the wish for a new child. And perhaps, for the soul of your first husband."

I felt red blotchy hives breaking across my décolletage as anger
pumped through my heart like blood. "Marry?" My voice was loud
and carried through the nave as loudly as the pipe organ.

"Have I upset you, madame?"

"What upsets me is discussion of my future. Who has told you
such a thing?"

The priest held up his hands. "Perhaps I have spoken out of turn."

My nostrils flared. "Mayhap all you do is speak out of turn."

"Barbe-Nicole!"

My father's voice was harsh, and I instantly felt like a child again.
He crossed the transept, his heels making sharp sounds across the
stone floor. Once in the chapel he grabbed a hold of my elbow and
hissed in my ear. "Lower your voice."

My father pressed his lips into a smile and nodded at the few curious townsfolk who found reason to get off their knees to get a closer
view of the drama. "My apologies, Father Joseph," he said. The grip
on my elbow grew sharper.

"Yes, I apologize as well," I said, forcing the words out. "It must
be the unseasonal heat."

Father Joseph waved off my apology, rocking back and forth on
his heels, jowls wobbling. "'Tis no account. It is well known: women
cannot control their emotions. I pray you find peace and comfort in the
plans your family is making." The priest made the sign of the cross in
the air above my head and then stomped away.

"Plans?" I asked, pulling myself from my father's grip.

"We will not discuss this here." He took my elbow again and led
me from the church. His legs were long, and each of his steps was

nearly two of mine, leaving me running alongside as we strode to where the coach was waiting.

"Come, before the rest of the town comes out to watch you." Father shoved me inside before clambering in and slamming the door behind him.

Maman's face pinched when she saw the thunder in my father's eye.

"Whatever were you thinking? You were yelling at the priest like some kind of common fishwife!" he barked.

"Oh, Barbe-Nicole." Mother shook her head, the feathers in her hat bobbing like a strutting rooster.

"What is this about marriage?" I asked.

"The contract between you and Alexandre expires in two years. There is no reason for him to throw good money after bad, unless there is more in it for him." My father paused and looked to my mother.

"He has a son," she said, her face flushing with excitement.

My mouth dropped. "His son is but a boy."

Mother waved off my concerns. "True, Jerome is younger than you, but in two years he will be twenty-three." She fidgeted in her seat, uncomfortable to have her scheming made public.

"And I will be thirty-three."

Father snorted. "If he can overlook your age, I do not see why it should bother you. If Alexandre's son and someday, God willing, a grandson were to inherit the house, then it changes the tone of the investment. He will continue, otherwise he will not renew that contract."

Was I supposed to take orders not only from Alexandre but also from his child? "Am I to have a say in this decision, or shall you marry me off like a cow at the market?"

Father flopped back into the seat, the coach swaying on its springs. "Please do not act as if you are a player in a theater with grand dramatic gestures. Where this love of drama comes from is a mystery."

Mother's face pinched again; she was clearly distressed at my father's unhappiness. "Your siblings are nothing like this," she said, as if to point out that any fault of mine could not be laid at her feet. "Of course you will have a say in your life, but there must also be reason."

"If Alexandre does not renew the contract, then I shall run the business on my own," I replied.

"With what money? Have you not noticed that your ledgers are bleeding? With a hot summer ahead, you may as well plan to toss half your wine into the streets. It will never survive the bottling."

"I am working on a solution," I insisted. I had been spending hours in the cellar pondering how we could get the lees, the clot of yeast, from the bottles without losing so much wine. There was a way; I just needed to find it. I could almost see it, hiding in the corner of my thoughts like a timid cat that needed to be lured into the room.

"Bah. You expect me to believe that you will solve the problem of cloudy wine and exploding bottles? You?"

I sat up straight. "Why not me?"

"Mon Dieu." Father shook his head and looked at Maman as if she would have an answer. "It is like trying to coax a donkey in the field." He rubbed his forehead.

My mother leaned forward. "My darling girl, think of your future. Think of Clémentine's future. Your father is certain that if Alexandre does not renew the contract, the business will go under. There is no quick end to this war."

"Napoleon's foolishness is not a reason for me to marry a mere boy."

Father's eyes bugged at my blasphemy. "Napoleon is the savior of France."

"Well, Christ can rest easy, as he is not likely to be replaced by Bonaparte based on the emperor's current performance."

Mother gasped as if I had declared a taste for black magic.

"I trust you are not so much the fool that you have shared that opinion with anyone else?" Father's face paled. "You would risk our whole family by disparaging the emperor? A man we have been fortunate enough to entertain in our home?"

Guilt bloomed in my chest. "No, of course not."

"You haven't the funds to take the business on your own," Father said.

My mind mentally tallied the livres in the hidden chest in my office. He was right. While I had been saving and tucking away every loose coin, I did not have all the funds I would need. I would have to consider more desperate measures. "I do not wish to marry, Father. I will not do it."

The wheels of the carriage rattled over the cobblestones.

"We will not talk any more of it today," Father said. "The boy is still too young to declare himself. There is a bit of time."

But I could feel time running out. In my mother's eyes I could see images of me in yet another wedding dress. *I turn to you for protection, holy Mother of God.*

Natalie

■ PARIS ■

APRIL 19

I couldn't understand what the clerk was saying to Sophie, but I could tell from her expression it wasn't good. The three of us stood in the dressing room looking into the mirror at my tits.

"She says you should be wearing a 36D," Sophie said, translating the European sizing to something I could understand.

"I've worn a 38C for years," I explained for the third time. "An expert at Nordstrom fitted me."

The Frenchwoman's mouth pursed into a tight pucker. "No."

"How is she supposed to know what size I wear when she hasn't even measured me?" I pointed out.

The clerk, who looked like her other part-time job might be judgmental prison guard, grabbed one of my breasts in each of her hands, giving them a firm squeeze. She then cupped them from underneath, like she was weighing grapefruits. She dropped them and crossed her arms. "36D."

I blinked rapidly. Had that actually just happened?

The clerk yanked open the dressing-room curtain, exposing me to anyone walking past the shop. I hunched over, doing my best to cover myself. The clerk strode off, then pulled open drawers and selected items. Unlike underwear stores at home, there were no racks. Instead, a few items were displayed like art, but most were tucked into thin wooden drawers that lined the wall. It was a giant library card catalog, each one opened to show frills, lace, and silk.

"She's mean," I protested to Sophie in a low voice. I far preferred the salesclerks at the other stores. The giant mound of slick, glossy shopping bags piled near the changing-room door was proof of how much I liked them.

"True. But this woman is the best. She is known all over Paris. Trust me, have I led you astray thus far?" Sophie nodded toward my reflection.

I reached up and touched my hair for the one millionth time that afternoon. Sophie had shipped me off in a taxi that morning to a salon across town. To throw myself into the spirit of taking risks, I'd told the stylist, Jean, to do whatever he wanted. Jean had circled me slowly like I was a bomb about to detonate and he had to decide what wire to cut to avoid full destruction. There had been a flurry of foil, fumes from the color processing, rosemary-scented shampoo, the snick of scissor blades, and, when he finally spun me around so I could see the mirror, a moment when I didn't recognize myself.

Jean had cut off six inches, leaving my hair in a messy bob just below my chin that looked like I'd just rolled out of bed, but in a way that everyone knew took effort. My hair, which I have sworn was straight my entire life, had been coaxed into loose beachy waves. I'd left the salon with a bag full of shampoo, conditioner, and mousse that he ensured me would result in the same look when I did it alone.

That had been the first chunk of money I'd dropped that day, but it certainly hadn't been the last. Whenever I doubted a decision or questioned the cost of something, I'd touch the slim volume of the Widow's letters in my tote, like a lucky charm, and remind myself now was no time to settle. An hour into the shopping extravaganza, my credit card company had called my cell to check if I approved these charges or if someone else had gone mad with my card. Clearly my bankers were more inclined to see risk than opportunity.

I was now the proud owner of a capsule wardrobe that, in theory, would work for any occasion. Sézane had been my favorite store, and I'd left there with a stack of impossibly soft sweaters, a scarf, and a Breton striped top. But the other stores had also provided a linen sheath dress, black wide pants, an oversized white button-down, and jeans that I had only dreamed of. I wasn't sure what the French did to their denim, but my ass had never looked so good. At Officine Universelle Buly, a place that looked more like an apothecary than store, I'd selected a new perfume destined to be my new "signature scent," which was not even something I knew I needed, along with ordering a custom hairbrush and comb set.

Then there had been shoes. An espadrille sandal for summer, black loafers, and a pair of low-heeled slingbacks. After a period of discussion, the clerks decided that my plain white tennis shoes, while a bit too clunky for their preference, would be passable.

My palms had a red indent from carrying all the shopping bags. My feet hurt, and I was ready to go back to the hotel for a cold Diet Coke, but Sophie had insisted on this last stop.

"I still don't know what's wrong with my underwear," I said.

Sophie sniffed dismissively. "It is certainly very . . . functional."

I glanced down. I was wearing my good underwear. If this wasn't up to par, thank God she hadn't seen the pairs I'd left behind in Naperville.

"I like being comfortable," I insisted. The last thing I needed was some itchy lace thong that left me scratching my crotch, looking like someone who had a buffet of STDs in her pants.

Sophie looked at me, confused. "Of course. Why would you buy lingerie that is uncomfortable? Something can be both beautiful and comfortable, you know."

I opened my mouth to argue that that hadn't been my experience when the clerk bustled back in speaking in rapid-fire French to Sophie. She held a bouquet of bras in every color.

"Okay, she has a few for you to try, and once you find some you like, she will pull the matching panties."

"Do you always match your panties to your bra?" I asked.

"Mon Dieu." The clerk made a sign of the cross. It was as if I had asked if she always wore the matching left shoe when she went out in the right.

"I suppose I could get one set," I said as I reached for a pale-pink bra. At this point, I had spent more on clothing in one day than I had in the past five years. But Sophie was right—new me wouldn't want to wear old me's functional underwear. The bra the clerk offered looked delicate and beautiful. A ballerina of bras. "In case anyone sees them at some point," I added, feeling risqué.

Sophie snatched the bra out of my hand as if it were a cookie I'd nabbed out of a jar and barked out a firm "Non."

"No?"

She shook her head. "The bra is not for someone else. It is for *you*. You should wear lovely things under your clothing so you feel special, like a secret with your own heart." She stabbed me in the sternum with a finger. "It's not about anyone else seeing it. It is about loving your body. It is about walking around in daily life knowing that you are beautiful and so you dress beautifully."

The clerk gave the first smile I'd seen her make since we arrived. "Oui. Exactement." She then spun me around so she could clip the back of the pink bra and then twirled me back again so I faced the mirror. It fit as though she had sewn it to my exact measurements. The silk was nearly liquid, and the lace was most definitely not scratchy.

My first thoughts were how it was a shame that my stomach was so soft and how I would look better if I would just lose that ten— hell, twenty—extra pounds, and how I needed a tan for some color, and trying to determine when my arms had developed that disturbing bat-wing flop. Then I stopped and closed my eyes to silence the thoughts in my head and opened them again.

I was beautiful.

"I'll take this one," I said. "Let's try another."

■   ■

The sway of the Metro as it rounded through the dark tunnels was almost enough to lull me to sleep, if it weren't for the occasional metal squeal of the wheels on the rail. I was going back to the hotel for a shower, maybe a nap, and then I was going to put on one of my new outfits and throw pretty much everything I'd brought with me away. When I got back to Chicago, I could already envision the giant bags that would have to go to the thrift store.

The train carriage squealed around another corner, and we coasted into a station.

"Thief!"

I jolted wide awake. Sophie barreled through the people standing near the door and filing into our metro carriage.

"Wait, what?" I cried out, trying to figure out if I was dreaming, but she was gone. The people around stared back blankly. I scooped up the shopping bags at my feet and bolted after her. I just fit through before the automatic doors closed, the recorded announcement blotting out other sounds.

The platform was crowded, and Sophie dodged between shoppers, tourists, and families, someone up ahead firmly in her sights. She zagged off the platform, headed for the marked exit. I did my best to keep her in view, panting with the effort. My anxiety rose with my heartbeat.

"Au voleur!" Sophie cried as she neared the giant staircase that led out of the Metro. She took the steps two at a time, propelling herself upward. I couldn't see who she was chasing, but I grabbed the metal handrail and pulled myself after her.

The heavy shopping bags slapped against my legs, the handles digging into my wrists. Brightly colored posters for museum exhibits, travel destinations, and beer and clothing brands flashed past the corner of my eye as I focused on sucking in air and not twisting an ankle.

I was still a full flight of stairs behind her, my breath coming in ragged gasps as I rounded the landing. Sophie bent over, no longer running. "What happened?" I managed to squeak out when I reached her side.

She pointed up the stairs as she stood. "That man took your phone from your bag."

My brain flashed red. I yanked open my tote and fished through the items inside, desperately wanting her to be wrong. Panic seized my chest. What the hell was I going to do without my phone? It contained my entire life, numbers, contacts, calendar—everything.

"What man?" I searched the staircase in front of us, half hoping some guy would still be standing there, waiting for us to catch up. Anger at losing my phone had given me a second wind.

"It is okay. He ditched it." Sophie spit on the tile as if cursing. "Afraid of police is my guess. If he doesn't have the item on him, they can do little." She stared out into the park just beyond the next flight. "He is long gone by now. Sous-merde."

I had no idea what that meant, but I could tell it was an insult. She held out my phone, which she'd stopped to pick up. The screen was shattered. It looked like a semitruck had run it over. I gently took it from her hand, afraid to even try to turn it on. There was a large dent in a corner.

"Careful," she warned. "The glass may cut you."

The phone screen remained black no matter what I did. Sophie patted my shoulder. "Ne t'inquiète pas. It will be okay. I should have warned you to be extra vigilant on the Metro. Thieves are every-where in the city."

How had I been so careless? I'd been sitting there half-asleep. I might as well have worn a T-shirt that said "TAKE MY STUFF." It creeped me out that I hadn't even felt the thief's hand in my bag. At least he hadn't gotten my wallet or the Widow's book, and in the end, he hadn't kept my phone. I should be grateful, but I felt like crying.

"Come now, no sadness," Sophie said, jostling me. "Today has been a good day."

"Well, it's not a good day now," I snapped. "Look, it's not your fault, but what the hell am I supposed to do without my phone?"

Two police officers rapidly came down the steps toward us. "Ça va? C'est quoi le problème?"

"Someone mugged me," I said. I pointed down the staircase. "On the train." I spoke slowly and loudly, as if volume might transcend any language gap.

"Mugged? Theft?" one of the officers said, his eyebrows meeting in the center of his forehead.

"Yes, oui," I replied. I wished I could speak French so I could explain myself more clearly.

Sophie stepped in and spoke to them, pointing toward the platform and then my smashed phone. "Pas de problème, tout va bien."

They spoke back and forth so quickly I could only make out a word or two. Tourist. Shopping. Phone. One officer took my elbow and began to pull me toward him. Sophie shook her head and took my other elbow. I had an uncomfortable flash of what a turkey wishbone might feel like. She took a step, and I was stretched between the two. I pulled my arms back from both of them.

The officer spoke, and I looked to Sophie for help, but he then switched to English.

"Perhaps Madame would like to make a report?"

"Yes."

"No," Sophie said. Her mouth pursed as she looked at me, and she jerked her chin as if motioning we should go up the stairs and out of the station. I stared at her, confused, but she didn't explain.

The officer spoke again in French, and Sophie cut him off, the tone of her voice sharp.

"You would like to make a report, no? About your telephone." The officer tapped the screen, and a tiny piece of glass fell from it and bounced on the tile floor with a faint tinkling sound.

I glanced at Sophie, who shook her head.

"No?" I replied uncertainly.

The officer took Sophie's elbow, but she yanked out of his grip. "We do not wish to make a report."

"But the American wishes—"

"No, she does not," Sophie barked.

My gaze darted back and forth between them. *What the hell is going on?*

"Are you certain that this woman found your phone?" one of the officers asked.

I glanced down. Was he trying to imply it wasn't mine? It didn't turn on, but I recognized the case.

"He is wondering if *I* stole your phone," Sophie explained.

"Why would you take my phone?"

Sophie rolled her eyes. "Exactly."

"We do not see any thief," the short cop said.

"My friend and I are leaving now." Sophie motioned for me to go up the stairs.

The taller of the two officers stepped in front of me. "Perhaps you would like to go with us to the station without your friend," he said, putting an edge to the word "friend."

My stomach turned sour. I didn't know what was going on, but it didn't feel right. "No, thank you."

"Excusez-nous." Sophie pulled me up a step to join her.

As we walked up the final flight, I felt their eyes boring into our backs. It took everything I had to not bolt for the open doorway. Once outside, Sophie didn't say anything until we walked nearly a block, then she plopped down on a bench and motioned for me to join her. "Fils de pute," she mumbled.

"What the hell was that?" My heart was still beating in double time. "Were those guys even real cops?"

"Oui. But they are, how you say"—she stared off toward the river, clearly searching for the right word—"no good police."

"Crooked?"

"I think yes, that is the English. They will try and make money from this."

"They can't do that," I insisted. This was France, not some third-world country.

"There have been stories of corruption in the news. Some of the police take advantage of the tourists." She shrugged. "They didn't know we knew each other. They would tell you there was a cost to file the report or some other story." She waved her hand. "There is always a way for bad people to take money."

I stared back at the train station, half expecting to see the two of them loitering by the entrance. I felt foolish. It hadn't even occurred to me that the police might not be trustworthy. One would think I would have finally learned that no one should be trusted after my divorce, but I appeared to be a slow learner. "I can't believe it."

Sophie sighed. "I am sorry. It has put yet another shadow on your day."

I shook off my unease. "No. I'm not going to let it. I'm sorry I snapped earlier. It's just a phone." She had spent her entire afternoon helping me and I was acting like a brat.

Sophie patted my hand. "We will return to the hotel, and you can call your friends in America on the hotel phone. Let them know if they need to reach you, they can leave a message at the desk. Your friends otherwise will have concerns."

I pictured Molly being unable to reach me. "They will worry." That was an understatement. Molly was the type to go DEFCON 4 and send a rabid Liam Neeson to come and find me.

"It was the same for me after my husband died. They think a widow is a child again. I know it is meant from a place of love, but it can leave one feeling less capable."

I pressed my mouth into a kind smile. Now was the time— I should tell her the truth that we didn't have widowhood in common. Will wasn't dead so much as dead to me.

Sophie arched an eyebrow. "Perhaps it is good for your friends to be out of touch with you for a tiny bit."

My thoughts of confession evaporated as I thought about what she was saying. Molly had texted several times a day since I'd landed. Wanting to know that I'd arrived, that I'd gotten to the hotel, what I was up to. She was excited, but there was a sense that she also thought I might need help. Ever since the divorce, she had been there for me, directing the show. And I'd needed that support at first, but it was starting to chafe. Molly was acting like my mother. And what had the Widow talked about—that someone who is our mother always wants us to be more like them than ourselves?

Maybe what happened with the phone was a good thing.

"Tell your friends they can text me personally, for, how do you say, proof of life?"

I laughed. "Yes, that's the term."

"I will talk to Stefan at the hotel. He will know a place that can repair your phone. You will have it back in no time at all." Sophie stood and pulled me up, then linked arms. "Now, come with me. We will return to the hotel, and I shall pour you a glass of rosé that will make this entire day good again. Not a shadow to be seen."

"It must be some good rosé," I said.

"Of course, I would give you only the best."

Barbe-Nicole

■ PARIS ■

REGARDING THE EVENTS OF SEPTEMBER 1808

Ma coccinelle Anne,

Oh, my dear, I must rectify a misconception in my last missive. To do bold things does not mean that one is without fear. In fact, if there is no fear, it is not a brave act so much as behaving in a foolhardy manner.

Let me tell you of a time when I trembled in fear of what to do. After enrolling Clémentine in a Parisian convent boarding school, I traveled there often to see her. While it was a good education—the entire family agreed upon this—to live far from family was not what my dear girl wanted. But sending Clémentine away removed her from Margot's clutches. I had not the time to keep an eye on the Mouse and her influence on my child, and if I couldn't yet take the risk of removing Margot, then it meant I had to remove Clémentine.

School had been good for Clémentine. While my daughter was no scholar, she would still learn, and the nuns would impress upon her skills in music and embroidery. I would not allow myself to cry over my daughter leaving home. There were women all over this country watching sons and husbands march off to war. If they could pretend to be brave, then I certainly could.

But what I was about to do took a different type of courage.

■ ■

Hiding behind the column of the church, I flipped my shawl over, exposing the different, brighter lining fabric, and wrapped it around my shoulders. It wasn't much of a disguise, but with luck the coachman wouldn't recognize me. He was used to seeing me in only dark colors. At first, I hadn't been sure if he was following me, but I'd caught him twice in the market, trailing just a few steps behind. I was a woman who believed in chance, but this was too purposeful for me to ignore.

I didn't know if he was following me at the request of Margot, my partner Alexandre, or my father, or out of his own idle curiosity. But I was certain I didn't want any of those people to know my purpose in the city. Ducking back out from around the corner of the column, I quickly wove down the row of sellers that pressed in from every direction. The vendors' stalls were interspersed with beggars, a fortune teller, women of questionable reputation, and a small child doing tumbling tricks for money, and everywhere—noise.

"Cabbages! Onions!" the woman in front of me bellowed from her rickety wheelbarrow. Her teeth were as brown as the soil and her breath reeked as if she ate only her own wares. The market was a cacophony of smells and sounds, and I raised my perfumed kerchief to my nose to block the worst of the stench. I risked a glance backward. The coachman was still off to the side, his gaze focused on the front of the church as he pretended an interest in a pile of turnips. He had not spotted me.

They said the population of Paris had swelled to the numbers that existed before the Revolution and the Terror, but it seemed to me that it must be even larger. Citizens filled the narrow streets and squares, bustling past each other and elbowing for space. Carriages barreled down roads, the inhabitants within bounced about like acrobats. Their journey to wherever they were going was difficult, as many of the streets were torn up and redirected; Napoleon had gone mad for construction in his desire to remake the capital. It seemed every corner held a building site with piles of rubble and dirt. Monuments had sprung up like marble weeds. I felt like flotsam being jostled and pushed along the river of humanity.

The church bells rang out, and it was good to hear their sound after the years of silence. The tolling reminded me to stop gaping about like a tourist, so I stepped over a pile of still-warm manure and a sludgy trickle of water and waste that ran down the road, and slipped down a side street. I'd chosen the establishment with care. Its proximity to the market made it easy to hide my true intentions, but I had no illusions that I could take my time. The coachman would be wondering where I'd gone.

"Miss, have you any change?"

A child no more than Clémentine's age stood before me, but this girl was all long, thin legs and arms, out of proportion to her too-small body, like a spider. Her eyes were wide in her gaunt face.

I stiffened as I realized she wasn't alone. There were three, no, four more children with her. They made a circle around me. The hair on the back of my neck rose.

"For charity, ma'am. For me and my siblings." The girl smiled, and she was missing a tooth. I knew not if it was a lost milk tooth or if she'd had one knocked out of her skull already. She scratched her head, and I could see a scurry of lice in her part. "Our father died in the Battle of Austerlitz."

The others shifted in place. At least one was out of my sight, and I fought the urge to spin about to see if he was growing closer. Beneath my skirts, my knees knocked together. I doubted they were siblings. They looked too different and too close in age. And I also suspected the story of a war-hero father was fiction. But while the girl spun many stories, it was clear the desperation in her eyes was real. I pressed my reticule to my side.

"I am afraid I have very little," I said, grateful that my voice didn't quiver despite my fear. While I had little experience with ruffians, I suspected they weren't much different from wild dogs, quick to pounce if they sensed weakness. "But allow me to give you something for your father's noble sacrifice." I shook the reticule, letting the few coins inside fall into my palm. The girl cocked her head as she listened to the sound, tracking that there were no more coins left. I suspected her hearing, like a wolf's, was keen enough to note the faint rustle of the tiniest of rabbits in the brush. She could tell from the sound alone the exact amount I had. I held out two of the coins. Her filthy hand shot forward and took them, making them disappear into the folds of her skirt.

"I am a widow, so I share your sense of loss," I said. Let her believe that François was a soldier, like her supposed father. She'd lied to me; it was only fitting I return the favor, both of us wanting to gain some empathy from our falsehoods.

The girl looked me up and down. She took in the weave of the fabric of my dress, my shoes with their buckles, the careful lack of any adornment other than my simple silver wedding ring. I'd been careful when dressing. My mother had wanted me to dress up, to wear something with embroidery or trim for the occasion of seeing Clémentine, but I'd insisted on the simpler wear that I wore about the vineyard. Sensible. Non-showy. However, even with my austerity, I realized that it was still clear I was not a woman of average means. My dress was not darned several times over, taken in, or out, as it passed between owners. The cotton fabric was simple, but not worn or faded, and perhaps most telling of all, it wasn't stiff with dirt and grime. It still smelled of the dried lavender that had been layered between my gowns in their chest. This girl could likely tally up the value of everything in my position faster than a banker.

But after a pause, she bobbed her head. "Merci, ma'am. God bless."

Before I could respond, the girl and her followers melted back into the alley from whence they'd come, like spiders scurrying to the corner of a web to await another, hopefully fatter victim. With them gone, I could breathe deeply again, my belly like water.

Just a few steps down, I saw the hand-painted wooden shingle outside the business I sought and quickly made my way there before another spider found me.

A small bell above the door rang as I entered. I took in the tidy space. It was sparse but smelled of tung oil and beeswax. A counter ran the length of the room, and several trays mounted on the far wall showed off some of the wares. A young man stood, straightening his waistcoat. "May I assist you?"

"I'm looking for Madame Poette." I'd done my research carefully. Madame was reputed to be honest and fair, one who could spot a gem in a pile of refuse. She was picky and selective. Some warned of a sharp tongue, but if anything, I suspected that would make me like her more. I would not deal with this man.

"My mother is busy, but I would be happy to help. Are you seeking an item for yourself or another?"

"I'm seeking Madame Poette," I repeated.

"'Tis fine, I shall handle it." A woman slipped between the curtains that separated the front of the shop from the back, waving off her son before he could argue further. "I am Madame Poette."

She was slight, hardly bigger than Clémentine, but there was steel in her blue eyes that I could see from across the counter.

"I have some items for sale," I said.

Madame Poette shook her head. "I am not looking for anything. I have plenty to sell as it is. And in these times, there are many more who need to rid themselves of things than there are collectors. Jewelry practically falls from the clouds in Paris."

I had feared as much. "These pieces are different."

She arched a weary eyebrow. "How so?"

"They are better."

The corner of her mouth tweaked upward, and after a moment, she motioned me forward to the polished counter. "Well then, you best show me."

"Turn around," I directed the young man. He opened his mouth to argue but shut it after a glance from his mother. Only once he was facing the curtain did I reach into the slit in my skirt so I could grasp the second reticule tied to the laces of my chemise.

Madame Poette nodded her approval at my hiding place. "Madame is wise to be careful. These times are better than in years past, but there are still many risks about."

"It doesn't matter the time," I replied. "There are always those who will steal from others." I gently unwrapped and placed the pieces on the counter: a brooch with a central emerald and a pair of diamond earbobs. My heart pinched. The brooch had been my grandmother's, and the earbobs a wedding gift from François. I wanted to swoop them back up, but emotion and memories are not anchored to things, I reminded myself. I would still hold those regardless of what happened to these baubles. But the pain of losing them was keen, a severing of a part of me. If I had another choice, I would take it, but I needed the money. And belief in my future was more valuable than mementos of my past.

Madame Poette grunted and pulled on spectacles to inspect the items. She turned them over and then tapped them carefully against the counter, listening to the sound.

"I have the sales letter for the earbobs," I added. "They were made by Légaré." She glanced up at the mention of the former king's jeweler but didn't comment. I pulled out the paper with his official seal affixed to the bottom and placed it on the counter.

Like me, Poette was a widow and a business owner. She could likely sense my desperation. I needed the funds. Alexandre was losing his interest in our business. He wasn't ready to walk away yet, but I sensed he was tempted. I was like a wife who watches her husband's eye wander before his hands. One knows it is coming and yet is unable to stop it.

Alexandre was growing weary of the challenges with champagne, wine that grew ropey or exploded in the bottle. He and my parents still whispered behind my back about a possible marriage with his son, but he was unaware I was not interested. He was too much of a gentleman to blame me for the risks I'd taken to get our wine to foreign markets.

At least aloud.

In his heart I knew he felt the choice had ultimately been mine, and he placed his empty coin purse on my ledger. And even with failures, we couldn't afford to play it safe; we had to keep pushing forward. I'd tried speaking with him so that we could make new plans, but he found excuses to avoid my company, preferring to send messages through others. This was no way to run a partnership.

If he withdrew his interest when our contract ended, then the house Veuve Clicquot Fourneaux would not have funds to meet our creditors' demands. And yet I still refused to marry the boy as a solution.

While there was great financial risk for me if Alexandre withdrew from the business, the positive of his leaving would mean the house would no longer carry his name. As long as I had money, the business could remain open. It would then be Veuve Clicquot Ponsardin, my married and family names. *My* house. *My* wines. If I had to sell my jewels to make it reality, then I would do it.

"Do you want to know why I need the money?" I asked.

"I respect your privacy," Madame Poette replied. "I'm certain that to part with such things you have reasons."

Everyone had reasons, but it was important to me she know that I wasn't someone whose family couldn't provide, or that I had to pay off gambling debts. "I need funds to keep my business afloat." I still felt the warm glow of pride when I mentioned having a business.

She shrugged. "If the business is not steady, perhaps it should be allowed to founder. When a ship has a hole, it is unwise to put more cargo in the hold."

I stiffened for a moment and then let the irritation go. I didn't need her approval. What I was doing was right. I could see it as clearly as she could tell real from paste. "My ship is solid," I replied.

"Of course. I am certain," Madame said. She stared at me as if considering, then slid the earbobs back across to me. "You should keep these," she said.

I steeled myself to show no weakness, to not let a hint of their loss show on my face. I pushed down the worry that I owed my daughter to pass these heirlooms to her. No, it would be better to pass a thriving business than a bauble. "You don't need to worry about my sentimental attachments."

"I am not. These are very fine, top quality. If I buy them from you, I'll have to give you less than their value so I can make my own profit. I will break them up to make something new, less expensive. There are only a few buyers who will buy these as is, but that is how you would make the most. You would be best to sell them directly to an aristocrat who can appreciate and afford them."

Her son threw up his hands and stormed out of the room, the curtain swishing. No doubt he wished it had been a door to slam.

"My son doesn't approve of my advice," Madame Poette said. "He would be more cutthroat. He thinks I am too soft, but I make you this suggestion as one businesswoman to another. There are too few of us about to profit at each other's expense."

While I appreciated her thoughtfulness, the businessperson in me could see that her son was right. "How would I find a direct buyer?" I asked.

Madame Poette shook her head. "Don't mistake my kindness for commitment to do the work for you. If you do a bit of looking, you can find a way. If you want me to tell you how to find a buyer, then I will do it myself and keep the profit."

I was torn between wanting the certain money now and holding out for the hope of better. Watching harvests had taught me nothing was guaranteed. But I had also learned in the tasting cellar that allowing time to work its magic could yield results. I scooped the earbobs back into my bag. "I will still sell the brooch." Touching it one more time for luck, I pushed it back toward her. It had served my grandmother, then me, and now I set it free to another woman. I would not allow fear of its loss to hold me back from destiny.

Madame nodded, and I hated myself for feeling pride at her approval. "This I can use." She picked up the brooch again and then offered me a figure.

"Mmm," I said, making a noncommittal sound.

Madame Poette's eyebrows arched. "It is a fair price."

It was. Truth be told, it was even a bit more than I had hoped to receive in these times. François would spin in his grave to have me sell a family heirloom for so slight an amount, but then he had left me to make my own way, and this was the offer. I would still need much more to reach my goal of independence, but these funds would be a strong stride forward.

And yet the urge to negotiate, to haggle, was there.

My eyes lit upon something in one of the trays on the wall, a small cameo pendant. It wasn't a very valuable piece. It had a pale-pink background with a white flower raised on the top. The sunlight from the window made the pink feel almost like a warm blush on a babe's skin. It brought to mind the new peonies that grew along the side of the house. Clémentine would love it. She adored the giant blousy blooms when the gardener planted them. The pendant would remind her of home.

"I will take the offer for the brooch if you add in that cameo." I motioned to the item behind her. She tensed; she also wanted to win the haggle. I sensed she was far more skilled at this game than I.

Before she could turn me down, I spoke again. "In return, with the next harvest, I will send you a case of champagne. *My* champagne."

Madame Poette paused and then nodded her agreement. She called out to her son to bring the lockbox. After wrapping the pendant carefully in a slip of muslin, she handed it to me along with the money the young man had fetched from the back. She wrote the details of the deal in her flowery script before scattering sand on the page to dry the ink.

"You own a champagne vineyard?" the young man asked, disbelieving. "What is it called?"

I lifted my chin in the air. "Veuve Clicquot," I said, already leaving off Alexandre's name as easily as I had rid myself of his son.

"I never heard of it," he said.

"You will. The whole world will hear of it."

Natalie

APRIL 20

*A*nd yet I still refused to marry the boy . . .

Unlike the Widow, I'd been desperate to marry Will. I was only twenty-five, but it felt like time was running out. Our mutual friends from college had already all been down the aisle, and I was starting to take Will's reluctance personally. He insisted he loved me, he "just wasn't ready."

There were several elaborate proposal fantasies on rotation in my head. A giant heart made from rose petals on a beach; a fancy white tablecloth dinner where the ring was delivered by a smiling waiter atop a dessert; Will renting out an entire theater, secretly filling it with friends and family, and then, in the middle of a romantic movie, dropping to one knee and declaring his true intentions.

Instead, he asked me when we were driving to the pharmacy to pick up his allergy meds. It hadn't even really been a formal proposal. More of a casual question.

"Do you really think you'd like to get married?" He stared up at the red light, waiting for it to turn.

"Sure," I replied after a pause, wondering exactly why he was asking the question. My feelings on the issue had never been in doubt.

"Then we should do it."

I waited a beat to see if he would call out "Just joking," or pull over to show that he'd set up a picnic with champagne in a nearby park, but we simply drove into the parking lot of the Walgreens and he turned off the car.

"Do you mean it?" I asked, listening to the ticking sound of the cooling car engine.

He squeezed my hand. "Yeah, I do."

When I told the story over the years, I made it funny. Rolling my eyes at Will's complete lack of romance. I took pride in the fact that I hadn't been some type of fiancée-zilla, that for us it was about being *married*, not about a one-day gesture. But since his affair and walking away from our marriage with barely a glance over his shoulder, it occurred to me that perhaps that proposal had been a sign. Not that he was too practical to be romantic, but that he hadn't deemed me worthy of a grand gesture even at the start of our marriage.

The Widow sold her jewelry to invest in herself and her business. Perhaps what I needed was a similarly grand gesture to myself. A public statement that I was moving on and forward. A proposal for a new life. And this store would be the place to do it, with its ornate interior, vases of flowers, and glass cases full of beautiful items.

I turned the ring over in my hand, my finger still bearing the slight indent where it used to sit. I missed the certainty of my old life even if it had never been as reliable as I'd chosen to believe. The idea of letting go of the ring was oddly terrifying, but I kept repeating the Widow's words to myself: *To do bold things does not mean one is without fear.* I so badly wanted to be bold. There was something symbolic about purchasing an item I'd have forever on this trip, this quest, that felt right.

"Ah, what do you think of this?" Gabriel lightly draped a diamond bracelet across my wrist. The gold links were like a rope, each circling a tiny stone that sparkled in the light spilling in from the skylight.

At my request, Gabriel had taken me to several jewelry stores to get opinions on the price I could get for my ring and ideas for replacement options. I was grateful for his help. I fell in love with an emerald ring at a place that specialized in antique jewelry. I liked the idea of owning something that had history. It seemed only fair that the ring had its own baggage since I had mine, but Gabriel insisted I wait to decide until we came to this shop, saying it was his favorite.

The store was down a small side street not far from the Tuileries Garden. The plaque out front declared the building had been built in the early 1800s, and inside it was like stepping back in time, minus the security cameras in every corner of the ceiling. The walls were a dark paneled wood, and the space had the hushed atmosphere of a library.

The staff deferred to Gabriel as soon as we walked in and escorted us into a private suite away from the showroom. It was set up like someone's home with a sofa and two chairs, both done in silk, and an oil painting of what I was told was the original owner, a small beady-eyed man with a mustache the size of a ferret draped over his upper lip. The clerk brought in champagne and sugared almonds for us to enjoy while she delivered trays of jewelry for me to consider. Her dark curly hair was cropped short like a skullcap, and she walked like the entire world was her runway.

I'd felt more comfortable in the slightly dusty antique shop bursting with well-loved things, but this was . . . an experience. It was deliciously over the top, but the amount I was considering spending deserved a bit of theater. I imagined this was how movie stars and the superrich did all their shopping. Must be why you never see Beyoncé in line at Target.

I turned my wrist one way and then the other, evaluating the bracelet while Gabriel and the clerk watched. Nothing she brought had a price tag. "Do you know how much it is?" I whispered to Gabriel, although why I bothered to lower my voice was a mystery. This clerk didn't seem to speak any English at all.

"Don't worry, your ring is worth nearly twelve thousand euro. It is enough for the bracelet."

I swallowed. Gabriel mentioned the amount like it was no big deal, which I supposed to a guy who wore a Rolex, it might not be. In addition to thinking Will was dead, Gabriel also seemed to be laboring under the illusion that I was loaded. He'd seen me return from the shopping trip yesterday, and for all he knew I bought like that all the time. I could only imagine what Molly would say about spending that much money on a single piece of jewelry, but I shoved her judgment out of my head. I was done living my life timidly and settling. I glanced at the bracelet. "I'd prefer something I could wear every day."

Gabriel dropped it back on a velvet tray like it was a discarded fast-food carton and passed it back to the clerk, making a request in French. "She will bring something else," he told me.

The clerk spoke, and I instantly looked to Gabriel, who answered her, and she nodded before bustling off.

"I hope I'm not wasting your time," I said. "I'm sure you have things to do other than wait for me to make up my mind."

"It is my pleasure. I was happy that you asked for my help."

I sipped the champagne. I loved the way Gabriel pronounced "pleasure." It was nearly pornographic. He seemed to find everything I said and did interesting. His attraction to me made me find myself intriguing.

I shifted on the sofa. The silk fabric was slippery, and I was at con-stant risk of sliding off and ending up on the floor, not least because I was a few glasses of champagne in already.

"Sorry if I'm being picky," I said.

He waved off my concern. "Not at all. It's important that you select the perfect item."

"I did like that emerald," I said. There seemed something fitting about replacing a ring Will gave me with one I gave myself.

"Let's see if you find anything here. The prices at that other store were inflated." He held his hands up as if I'd argued. "Not outra-geously so, but I think we can do better."

My heart squeezed at the use of the word "we." "Thanks for com-ing. Will hated to shop." I bit my tongue. I had to stop comparing everything in my new life with my old, as if Will were the yardstick.

Gabriel smiled at me in a way that caused what my grandmother colorfully referred to as "hot pants feelings." He leaned closer. *Dear God, is he going to kiss me?* Why had I let him talk me into trying es-cargot at lunch? My breath surely smelled like a garlic press left in the summer sun.

We were inches apart when he sat back quickly, reaching for his pocket. I nearly tipped forward into his lap. "Gah. Please excuse me." He stood and paced along the far wall, talking into the phone, his tone serious. When our gazes connected, he rolled his eyes and mimed with his hand, like a puppet, someone talking. He tugged a bit of hair right behind his ear as he listened. It was adorable. While he talked, I rooted through my bag for the tin of Altoids and crunched up two of the mints just in case.

One thing I'd loved about being in a long-term marriage was how well I knew Will. I could guess what he would order from any menu, how he liked his socks folded (never in balls, he swore it stretched the elastic), and how he tended to hum in his sleep. I could manage his moods. I knew how he kissed. Every step in our lovemaking was familiar, like a well-choreographed dance.

It was comfortable to be so knowledgeable about another person and to feel known in return. But there was something thrilling about someone new. Not knowing what to expect left me on edge, but also excited. Each moment felt like a wrapped present under the tree that could contain anything.

Speaking of unwrapping . . . I couldn't help but notice how well Gabriel's pants fit as he turned to a bookshelf. He clicked off the phone and spun around. I flushed, as if he could tell what I'd been thinking.

"I apologize. It is my work."

"Is everything okay?" I shifted, sliding on the sofa again.

"Yes, I believe it will be fine. I am hosting a dinner tomorrow for several clients and they are . . . difficult." He shook his head in annoyance.

I took another sip of my champagne. "How can people buying nice wine be in anything but a good mood?"

He tipped his head back and laughed.

An image of running my tongue along the line of his jaw, his skin tasting of salt, flashed in my head and I swallowed hard.

"You're so wise. How can anyone be unhappy with good food and wine? But there are challenges in my work." He topped up my glass, the sweating ice-cold bottle dripping on the thick rug, before filling his own. "Many of the wines I sell are rare, and as a result, expensive."

I nodded. Gabriel didn't dress like he sold boxed wine.

"In this business, there is not much trust when working with new people. They worry they do not know what they will get. Wine is temperamental. The bottles can't be kept someplace that is too hot or too cold." He tipped his hand one way and then other, to show the delicate balance. "It must be stored correctly so that the cork doesn't dry and allow too much oxygen to enter. And of course, the problem is, you do not know by looking at the bottle if it has been cared for until it is opened. And by then"—he snapped his finger—"poof, it is too late. If one spends five or fifteen thousand on a bottle of vinegar, they are not happy."

"Fifteen *thousand* for one bottle?" I asked, trying to not sound appalled. If I went up to a hundred bucks for a bottle of wine, I felt like Gatsby.

Gabriel nodded. "Oh yes, the majority of bottles I sell are not so expensive, but I have sold bottles for up to twenty thousand." He shrugged. "And that is nothing in this business. There was a bottle that sold at auction a year ago that went for a quarter of a million euros."

"For wine that's gone as soon as you drink it," I said in awe. For that kind of money, I would want a house, not something that I would literally piss away a few hours later—or even less, given my bladder.

Leaning back against the sofa, Gabriel held up his glass of wine and peered into its depths like it was a crystal ball. "It is the ephemeral nature of wine that makes it magic."

"Says the man who sells it," I pointed out.

He chuckled. "True. But I believe that wine is a reminder that life itself doesn't last. To save things for later because you don't want to use them is to deny them the very purpose of their existence. Wine was made to be consumed. Life was meant to be lived, to drink deeply."

I thought of all the fancy wedding china I'd rarely used because I was afraid I would break it. The dishes had outlived the relationship. The expensive skin cream that had expired in my bathroom cupboard because it was "too nice" to put on each day. The cashmere sweater I'd never worn because I didn't want it to pill, and then the moths got to it. I'd put every exciting part of my life to the side to save it for later and never realized I would run out of time to enjoy it.

"To drinking deeply of life." I clinked glasses with Gabriel, mentally adding *Use Fancy China* to my new life list along with plans to order some Waterford crystal wineglasses when I got home.

"To drinking deeply of life," he repeated, and then we each drained our respective glasses in one go. The champagne bubbles floated up through my head.

"Are these clients going to buy one of those quarter-of-a-million-dollar bottles from you?"

He smirked. "Nothing quite so expensive. I have several cases of grand cru from Burgundy that they are supposed to purchase, but as I have not worked with them before, they require a reference."

"Is that hard to get?"

Gabriel shook his head. "No, not for me. A woman who has bought wine from me has agreed to attend the dinner to reassure them." He sighed. "These clients have bought single bottles from me before, which I thought would assure them of my reliability, but suddenly they are worried about buying in bulk without confirmation I can be trusted." He rolled his eyes. "I am beholden to this woman, as this is a deal I have been working on for some time. For it to fall through would be a tragedy."

"I'm sure it will go well." I tried to ignore the wave of jealousy that swept through my body at the idea of this woman swooping in to help him.

"She is in her eighties, so it is very kind of her to make the effort to travel for this. I hope it is not too much," Gabriel said, his mouth pinching in concern.

She was in her eighties? Well then, that put a different spin on things. My mood bounced back.

The clerk returned with another velvet tray and placed it on the low table in front of us. A pendant caught my eye. "That's pretty." It was a large pear-shaped ruby with two diamonds set alongside, all held together in a thick silver open teardrop.

Gabriel went back and forth with the clerk. "She says you have excellent taste; it is a near-flawless stone. The setting is white gold and the artist who created it called the piece Phénix, or how you say, Phoenix."

I picked it up, the chain cool to the touch in my hand. It was lighter than I'd expected. The setting wasn't supposed to resemble a teardrop; it was a flame. I liked the symbolism of rebirth. Was that a sign? I was becoming one of those people who felt the universe was sending me messages. Or was that the champagne talking?

Gabriel took the pendant from me. "Here, let me put it on so you can see it."

I turned my back to him and felt the warmth of his hands on my neck, which still felt oddly naked since the haircut. The stone dropped gently onto my chest. The pendant was the perfect length, not too short, but also not buried in my cleavage.

The clerk held up an ornate silver mirror. I touched the necklace lightly with my fingertip. It looked beautiful. Gabriel leaned in, his face close to mine so we could both see the reflection.

"Do you like it better than the ring?" I asked. I still wasn't certain.

"Oui, it has a fire to it, like you."

I flushed, likely redder than the stone. It was a huge expenditure. Old me would never have bought something like this. And certainly not without taking weeks to ponder the decision and second-guessing myself. Granted, old me wouldn't have been selling her wedding ring either.

Unlike the proposal from Will, this would be a great story. How this handsome man I'd met in Paris took me shopping, the store with its fireplace and sugared almonds, the velvet trays, how I found the perfect thing to symbolize a commitment to my new life.

My purse fell off the sofa, and the thin book about the Widow slid out. It was as if she'd burst into the room to remind me to take risks.

Gabriel's finger traced the chain along my chest. "It is beautiful. The clerk says it is nearly the same cost as your rings, so it is an easy exchange."

My heart raced at his touch, and I suspected he could feel it. I stared into the mirror's reflection.

"If you are unsure, then perhaps not." He reached for the clasp.

The Phoenix. It had to be a sign. I pressed the pendant to my chest, stopping Gabriel from taking it off. I took a deep breath, squaring my shoulders.

"I'll take it."

Barbe-Nicole

■ PARIS ■

REGARDING THE EVENTS OF MARCH 1809

My darling girl,

I was sorry to hear you were upset. I know it is little comfort now, but I promise there will be a time when you will look back and not even have a twinge that the young man in question did not ask you to dance. You say you never would have gone if you had known how the evening would go, but predicting the future is challenging. Connections are intertwined and difficult to see in the present. It is only looking back that things become clear. Who knows what other things your presence may have put into motion? It is human nature to want easy answers, but life, and people, are so much more complex. We think if we knew the future we could control our destiny, but the fates mock our attempts to cheat them of their due.

Did I ever tell you of the time I went to a fortune teller? I'd taken it as a sign when I heard from Mademoiselle Lenormand that she

would see me. Getting an appointment with her was difficult; she was
known as the best in all of France. For her to have time when I would
be in Paris for Clémentine's birthday was too good an opportunity to
forgo. But the decisions I made because of that meeting would have
consequences.

■   ■

Logic told me that fortune-telling was nothing more than a show,
but sitting in Lenormand's home on the Rue de Tournon, crowded
on one side by a stuffed owl and smoking candles on the other, left
me wondering. How thick is the veil between one world to another?
The Bible was clear that to sport with such dark magic was a sin, but
so many things were listed as sins it was hard to tell if the good Lord
would really be bothered.

My need for clarity on the future outweighed any current concern for my soul. Louis had returned safely from Russia having used
his own sweet words to move the wheels of government, along with a
few well-placed bribes, but with every day there were new challenges.
While I could discuss business with Louis, he had no more idea of
what the future held than I did. To know more, I would have to reach
out to someone new, someone with knowledge of what had not yet
happened.

The fireplace in the corner threw too much heat for a tiny space
and I began to sweat. My wet cloak hung by the fire, steam adding to
the thick atmosphere of the room.

"The empress speaks highly of you, mademoiselle," I said, placing
my gloves in my lap. If I was going to see a soothsayer, I would visit
only the best. If Lenormand was good enough for Napoleon and his
wife, she was good enough for me.

"I have known Rose for a long time. Please, call me Marie-Anne." She poured coffee into our cups. She used Joséphine's former name. The empress had changed it to suit Bonaparte when they married. Lenormand's use wasn't accidental. She was letting me know that while my father's connections may have introduced me to the empress, she knew the woman better than I. She would be polite, but she would not bow or scrape to me, or anyone, I suspected. The fortune teller settled herself in the chair.

"I appreciate you seeing me." Her calendar was full of appointments with most of the wealthy in Paris. For a nation that was supposed to be founded on logic, we were all very keen on magic. Granted, with loved ones now off fighting and dying in Spain at Uclés, we were all seeking a way to connect to something otherworldly. A way to glean what the future held.

"I am happy to be of service, Madame Clicquot."

"Please, call me Barbe-Nicole." I was about to say something else when I was distracted, realizing that she had a bat—an actual bat— corpse dried and mounted to the wall near the ceiling. I swallowed and fought the urge to make the sign of the cross.

"What brings you to me today?"

I fidgeted with my skirts, the tiny print on the cotton nearly invisible in the dim light. "I have made a decision about my future," I said. "And I wish to know what will happen next."

Marie-Anne watched me over the cup of coffee. Her large eyes were wide set over her thin nose and chin. Her face was unbalanced, but not displeasing. We were close in age, but she left me feeling naive. She motioned for me to continue.

"I have decided not to marry again. This choice has upset my family." That was an understatement. The past months had been full of my parents, both together and separately, making one last desperate pitch for the case for Alexandre's son, Jerome, as if they could debate me into doing their will.

"My love of my deceased husband prevents me from binding to another," I said, stating the reason I gave my family.

Marie-Anne cocked her head to the side and considered me as if she were buying a fish in the market and was unsure of its freshness. "I don't believe it is a love for your former husband that keeps you from making that decision. Rather, I believe you prefer independence."

I flushed.

She sipped her coffee. "Please, feel no shame, Barbe-Nicole. I have never married. I prefer to be the master of my own home, so I do not judge you for your choice." She placed her cup down on the saucer with a rattle. "Before you came, I consulted the cards. I do this with all who request to see me. I will show you what I drew."

Marie-Anne reached for a worn deck, the Game of Hope. She flipped the first card over onto the table: the ship. "This card can mean travel or journey, but also trade. I think you come for business, not for questions of love or marriage."

I licked my lips. She could have guessed as much. My involvement in trade was not a secret. "What else did the cards tell you about me?"

She pulled the next card, an anchor. "I drew this when I asked the deck to tell me about you."

The anchor was the symbol I had burned into our corks to brand our wine. *Would she know that?*

"The anchor symbolizes hope, but also resilience, stability. It is a good card to represent one's character. It made me agreeable to your request to meet."

More likely it was the money in my purse and the relationship my father held with Napoleon, but her reasoning did not matter. "You are correct. I wish to know the future of my business."

Marie Anne passed the cards to me. "Shuffle these as you think of what you wish to know."

I took the deck; the cards with their thick paper slid beneath my fingers. When François died, I had been so certain that taking the helm of the business had been the right decision, and yet it faltered. Our company books were near the very edge. I'd been sure that sending the wine to Amsterdam was correct, and yet it had gone bad sitting on the docks. Solving the problem of the lees in the bottle had seemed simple but continued to elude me. I had no doubts when I'd sent Louis to Russia, and yet he had been lucky to get home at all. I chose to spurn a marriage with Alexandre's son and, as a result, any further investment from him. I'd believed I could make the business work, but what if I was wrong?

Was it foolish to trust in myself above all? I gripped the cards. *What does my future hold?*

I passed the cards back to Marie-Anne. She mumbled some type of incantation under her breath. I jumped when the candles flickered, their smoke dark. Was this some form of trickery? She laid three cards down in front of me, face down.

Tapping the first card, she began. "This symbolizes the present." She flipped it over, revealing the image of a mountain painted in faded colors. "This indicates things at present are a challenge."

I nodded in agreement. These were times of war. There was no surprise in this, simply a reminder to stay strong. Mountains were meant to be climbed, after all.

Marie-Anne reached for the next card. "The second card is what stands in your way." As she flipped it over, my heart seized in my chest at the image. The painting on the card was of a small field mouse.

"This card—"

"I know the meaning of this card," I said, cutting her off. Margot.

My back teeth ground together. Just like a rat, she scurried around the corners of my life. The housekeeper had caught the girl with some lace from my sewing basket, and I'd been forced to say I'd given it to her. I loathed that woman and her constant grasping. The cards were trying to tell me that she was the real danger I faced.

"One shouldn't rush the meaning of the cards," the fortune teller warned me. "They can be taken many ways. The mouse can mean depletion or disease, but also dwindling; at times, there is something small, overlooked, that can cause us the problem. This can be internal or external."

I was at no risk of overlooking the Mouse. I was well aware of her danger. "And the third card?"

"The third is the future."

I held my breath as she flipped it over.

"The crossroads." She pursed her lips. "You will have many choices and decisions ahead of you."

I knew this. I hadn't needed a fortune teller for this wisdom. "But what will *come* of my choices?"

Marie-Anne drew another card and placed it atop the crossroads. "The sun." She leaned back with a smile. "Success. Happiness."

Warmth spread through my chest, and I realized I was clenching my gloves in my hands. I loosened my grip. "Success," I repeated. "That is good." I let myself relax.

Marie-Anne laughed. "Yes, success is good. So is happiness."

I placed the small bag of coins on the table. "Thank you."

Her thin fingers, as fast as a pickpocket's, made the purse disappear under the table. "I am glad you are happy with the reading, but be aware, while the card means you will have success, it is hard to know how long it will take to come to pass."

I nodded. I could wait, so long as I knew the business would eventually succeed. "I imagine the prosperity of your business relies in part on seeing good fortune for others," I said.

"It is more advantageous for me to be accurate than overly positive, but you're correct—people are not as pleased when the cards are unfriendly."

"You predicted Joséphine would become empress, did you not?"

Marie-Anne ducked her head in false modesty. "It was not as clear as that. I predicted she would soon face great hardship, but then that she would marry a man and rise to the top with him." She spread her hands. "And so it has come to pass."

"And the hardship she faced?"

"I gave her the reading just before they guillotined her first husband."

I shivered. I hadn't heard that part of the story. I didn't like to think of those dark days. The sound of the crowds gathered around the Place du Carrousel and the guillotine, the whisper of the blade, the smell of blood everywhere in the streets. I wiped my sweaty palms on my skirt. "The empress must be happier now with her fortune."

Marie-Anne's face grew grim. "There are clouds ahead."

"Why? What do you see?"

The candles flickered again, and the temperature in the room seemed to drop, the fire in the corner of the room casting no heat. For a moment, I thought I could see my breath like a ghost in the air.

"To share another's fortune is to peek into their soul. It is best kept private." She motioned to my cup. "Finish your drink and I will read the grounds for you."

I tilted the cup, drinking to the dregs.

"Now place the saucer atop and flip it," she directed me.

I spun the cup and slid both it and the saucer back across the table.

"It is when things are upside-down that they become clear."

Something about what she said snagged in my thoughts. She swirled the upside-down cup atop the saucer and my gaze tracked the slow circles. There was a thought hiding from me, ducking out of sight every time I tried to pin it down.

Marie-Anne flipped the cup right side up, then pulled one candle closer as she peered inside. "Mmmm, intriguing."

"What is it?"

She held the cup out. The grounds inside had formed a burst pattern with a tail. "What does it mean?" I demanded.

"I am not certain, Madame Clicquot. But it looks like a star to me. You should look to the heavens. Your fate will be found there."

■ ■

The horses tossed their heads as I stepped outside the door. The icy drizzle falling from the sky shocked my system after the heat inside. I moved quickly, both to get out of the weather and to avoid any curious passersby. While there was no reason to keep it a secret, I'd rather no one know I had been to see the fortune teller. It was one thing to sin, another to reveal your transgressions to others. The coachman leaped down as soon as he spotted me to usher me inside. I had barely settled in the seat when the carriage pulled away with a clatter.

Pulling the thick blanket over my lap, I tried to calm the chill that ran through my body. I was glad I wouldn't see Clémentine until tomorrow. I wanted to give her all my focus. It is not every day a girl turns ten, but today I would not be able to clear my thoughts of Mademoiselle Lenormand. No, it would be better to arrive at the school tomorrow, laden with presents for her and not considerations for myself.

My thoughts raced with all I had heard and seen. Lenormand's entire home had been a carnival for the senses. The acrid scent of cheap candles when it was clear she could afford better. The way the room was layered in fabrics, a heavy nap on all the chairs, two or three cloths to cover the table, thick carpets where my feet nearly sank up to the ankle.

I stamped my feet on the floor of the carriage, trying to get the blood flowing. When I arrived at my cousins' house, I would need to warm by the fire before dinner. I felt cold to my very core. I pulled the basket I'd brought from home closer. The cook had filled it with treats from the country for my family, and I'd added two bottles of our latest bottling. I was eager to serve it and hear their thoughts. It was the first blending I had done all on my own. My taste was evolving, perfecting. I picked through the basket and pulled out a pastry to nibble upon.

Overall, the woman's predictions for my future had been positive. The sight of the sun card had confirmed what I believed; while I had been certain that declining any proposal from Alexandre's son was wise, I felt reassured by her agreement. My business would weather the challenges ahead. I simply had to stay the course.

And deal with the Mouse. I pictured Margot's face, her eyes growing smaller, her nose more pointed, in my mind's eye. All she needed was some twitching whiskers. Her gossip could diminish my business's reputation. My reputation. What was the word the woman had used? Ah yes, "dwindling." I'd been afraid to fire her because I'd been certain she'd cause trouble, but it was possible she was as much trouble if she stayed. But if I threw her out, people would want to know why she was let go. I needed to catch her in something. Something that was undeniable and that would taint her reputation should she then try to tell my secrets.

How does one catch a mouse . . . ? I needed some type of bait.

My stomach cramped. I'd eaten little when we headed out this morning. The coffee on top of an empty stomach left me feeling unsettled. I reached into the basket for another bite of pastry. The reading of the coffee grounds had been interesting. The shape had looked so much like a star.

When my sister and I had been children, we used to lie in bed and look through the open windows in summer and wait for a falling star. The first to spot it would get to make a wish. We squandered those wishes on so many foolish things: a kitten, a new dress, that we would marry a noble. What would I wish for now?

In my mind, I pictured Marie-Anne turning the coffee cup over and spinning it around: *When things are upside-down, they become clear.* The thought was like an itch in my brain. And I repeated it over and over again as we traveled through the city.

Upside-down, they become clear.

Upside-down, they become clear.

I gazed out the window. Glancing back at my lap, I realized I was holding a bottle from the basket upside-down, the neck resting on my skirt as I spun it by the base.

The lees, the clot of fermented yeast, had drifted from the body of the bottle into the neck. I could see flecks of yeast swirling in the wine, like snow falling.

When things are upside-down, they become more clear.

I sat straight up and held the bottle inches from my eyes so that I could watch the yeast settle, leaving the rest of the bottle clear. But how to get it out?

Then it clicked into my head.

Mon Dieu, it might just work. It would be a thing of beauty.

Natalie

■ PARIS ■

APRIL 21

*W*hen *things are upside-down, they become clear.*

Or is it when things are backward? I stared at the back of the giant clockface in the wall. It had to be at least twenty feet high. The clock could be seen by anyone walking outside the Musée d'Orsay, but here inside, it was backward. The hands, the size of fully grown trees, slowly reversed their way through time.

Through the clockface, I could see the Seine and Paris just beyond. It seemed magical, like I'd walked through a portal and the real world was outside, just out of reach. For the past year, I had felt like the life I'd spent decades creating was dead and behind me and I had wasted those years. But what if the time I had in front of me was more valuable? Everything was upside-down but, as the Widow would say, also becoming clear.

"After all this art, one needs fortification," Gabriel said, leaning back in his chair and patting his stomach. "You will join me in dessert, yes?"

"I don't know," I hedged. I had practically licked the crumbs from my lunch plate. Gabriel had suggested the quiche lorraine, saying the balance of bacon and shallots with the nutty Gruyère was perfection with a crisp green salad. He wasn't wrong. The quiche tasted rich and decadent, like something I'd expect to be served in a Michelin-starred restaurant, not a museum café.

Gabriel swirled the wine in his glass. "Do you like the Chablis? This one is more citrus forward, but I think it would go beautifully with a slice of their tarte au citron meringuée. It would be a waste to finish this bottle without a touch of something sweet. A travesty." He made an exaggerated frown, making me laugh.

"Fine, but only if we share a piece."

After waving over the waiter, Gabriel ordered the tart. A group of American tourists sat next to us at a long table, each with a name badge stuck to their clothing. *Hello! My name is Not From Here!*

A cluster of women at the near end watched Gabriel like he was the dessert. I could see them measuring him in his crisply starched shirt with monogrammed cuffs, fitted jeans, and his blazer tossed over the chair, in comparison to their husbands. The men in the group all wore Levi's that sagged in the seat, tennis shoes, and an assortment of golf shirts with business names stitched above the breast. I sat up straighter, proud to be with Gabriel and knowing that in my own new clothes, I looked like I belonged there.

If I'd come here with Will, I'd be in that group of wives. Admiring the café decor with the hammered-copper details, raising an eyebrow at the price for a "simple grilled sandwich," and bemoaning that the chairs weren't more comfortable after walking all day.

When had Will and I stopped talking about important things? Gabriel and I had spent the morning discussing art and politics. We chatted about what paintings we liked and why. We played a game deciding which of the works of art displayed we would choose if money were no object. He selected a picture by the impressionist Caillebotte, of men refinishing a floor. He said it reminded him of when he worked in construction, and I tried not to lick my lips at the image of him shirtless, engaged in some kind of heavy labor. I'd picked Seurat's *The Circus*, with the woman posing atop a horse in the middle of a ring, all done in pastel dabs of paint.

Gabriel wanted to know my perspective on everything. What I read, what movies I liked, how I felt about living in a city versus the country, whether I liked dogs. And more than that, he *listened* to my answers, his attention focused on me as if I were sharing nuclear codes instead of why blue was my favorite color.

Will and I had been reduced to mundane topics like the weather—*better wear your boots tomorrow*—or the house—*the water heater is acting up again*. When I tried to talk about things that were important, half the time I would catch him looking at his phone, or staring at the Bears game on the TV, insisting he really was listening. I'd forgotten how intoxicating, *how erotic*, it felt to have someone's attention. I'd forgotten that I was interesting.

I fiddled with the ruby pendant hanging from my neck, liking that it drew Gabriel's eyes to my chest. It turned out flirting is like riding a bike. You don't forget; it just takes a bit of practice. With luck, I wouldn't run off the road. "Let me buy lunch," I offered. "You got the museum tickets."

He waved off my offer. "It is the least I can do after I was such a cad last evening. I hated to cancel our dinner plans so last minute, but with my reference backing out, it has thrown everything into disarray. Of course, I understand she cannot travel when ill, but still, it is difficult."

I made a sympathetic noise. I'd been disappointed when he canceled our dinner plans, but I'd snapped out of it, reminding myself that the trip was supposed to be my own grand adventure. After all, he'd already spent most of the day taking me shopping. It wasn't as if I should expect to spend all my time and meals with him. I found a bistro close to the hotel and had a wonderful meal on my own, but I was still thrilled when Gabriel insisted on planning this day to make up for it. I hadn't been to the Louvre yet, but Gabriel declared that the Musée d'Orsay was his favorite museum in the city.

"It's fine. I understand you had to cancel," I said. "I'm just sorry you're having problems with work."

Gabriel sighed, then motioned for me to have a bite of the tart that had been delivered to our table with a flourish. "I appreciate your graciousness, but I very much dislike when work interferes with life. One should work to live, but not live to work."

The buttery shortbread crust of the tart crumbled in my mouth, along with an explosion of tangy lemon and sweet cream. Like with everything in France, I had to fight the urge to declare it was the best thing I'd ever tasted.

"Have you found someone else who can attend your dinner tonight as your reference?" I asked.

He shook his head, his mouth pressing into a scowl. "No, unfortunately I have not. It is too last-minute."

"What about Sophie?" I suggested, capturing a few crumbs of the tart on my fork. "She's bought several bottles from you for the Delphine."

"No, they will say she is a mere hotel employee." Gabriel held up a finger. "To be clear, I feel Sophie deserves more respect. She is very knowledgeable about wine, but they want someone like themselves: wealthy, investors. They cannot fathom that a mere worker"— he rolled his eyes to show what he thought of their attitude—"could appreciate what they can appreciate."

"What will happen with the deal?"

Gabriel shrugged. "I fear it may be ruiné, how you say, ruined?" Disappointment was etched on his face. It was as if a cloud had come over our table. "Months and months of work, poof, gone."

"I'm so sorry. Won't they wait until you can get another reference?"

"No. They will decide on a purchase for their cellars now. If not with me, then they will go with another broker." He smiled. "A shame you cannot be my reference. I am thinking you might say nice things about me. You could pretend to be a very important wine buyer who has chosen me above all the others."

I smiled. "I would, but I haven't done any acting since my high school production of *My Fair Lady*."

He laughed. "Of course. I was not serious, but I admit, I like the idea of you on a stage." Gabriel glanced at his watch. "Ah, we must go. It is almost time." He stood and tucked several notes under the plate for the bill.

I quickly finished my glass of wine. "Time for what?"

"I have something for you. Something to make up for the canceling of our plans last evening after I had promised you a good meal."

"Really, it was no big deal," I protested, gathering up my things to join him.

Gabriel stopped and put his finger under my chin to tilt my face up so we were looking directly at each other. "To give one's word and then not follow through is unacceptable. I am truly sorry."

My heart stilled. Gabriel was more apologetic for missing dinner than Will had been for all his lies and betrayal.

Gabriel dropped his hand, but I could still feel where he'd touched me, like a brand. "Now, come, a surprise."

I followed him toward the entrance of the café, past the massive clockface. Gabriel paused.

"Wait, we should get a picture." He motioned for me to stand in front of the clock, the large black Roman numerals circling the face. "To mark your experience."

"I don't have my phone," I reminded him. I wouldn't get it back from the repair place until tomorrow.

"I will take," he said, pulling his iPhone from his pocket. "I can send to you when you have yours returned. Face the city."

I struck a pose.

"La belle femme."

I turned to see Gabriel smiling at me. "What?"

"I am saying you look beautiful. There, with the light and the city behind you." He lifted his phone. "I will take another. This one, you face me with a smile." He glanced down at the screen once he took the picture. "Ah. Come see."

I always hated having my picture taken. Advice from magazines filled my head: the need to angle my body, slide one leg forward to elongate my look, tilt my head up and out to avoid the dreaded double chin, and above all else, ensure that the camera never caught me from below. I cautiously peered at the phone Gabriel held, hoping that I didn't look too bad.

I didn't recognize the woman in Gabriel's photo. My smile was huge, my eyes sparkled, and I filled the space with a bold stance. The outfit Sophie had helped me choose looked good, but it was more than that. I looked comfortable and at home in my flesh.

I looked happy.

Gabriel's finger swiped across the screen, and I saw the photo he'd taken with my back to him. I had my hands on my hips, looking out at Paris. I appeared in charge and confident. The kind of pose I imagined the Widow struck when she looked out over her winery.

"A good memory, I think," Gabriel said. He motioned to the clock just about to strike two. "Come, it is time."

"Where are we going?"

"You will see," Gabriel trilled, sounding proud of himself.

Just down the hall in front of the entrance to the impressionist gallery, a guard stood blocking the way. I saw the sign: TEMPORARILY CLOSED. My heart sank. While the museum had impressionists' works sprinkled around, the best work was in this hall. I'd been looking forward to this gallery the most.

The tour group of Americans was just in front of us. "The gallery will be closed for fifteen minutes," their guide announced. "There's a specialist coming to look at one of the works who can't be disturbed." The crowd grumbled. "You can rest here on the benches, or you can take a quick bathroom break," the guide said, shooing people away from the door.

"The impressionists are your favorite, are they not?" Gabriel asked.

"Yes. I went through a period of being fascinated with the artists of that time," I said. "I suppose liking Monet isn't very unique."

"Never apologize for what you love," Gabriel said. He pulled me toward the gallery.

"We'll have to come back after you show me your surprise."

He spun and smirked. "But this is the surprise."

"What?"

The guard saw Gabriel and smiled, moving out of the way. He ushered us inside the empty gallery. The wooden floor creaked under my steps. One beautiful work after another lined the walls, like a paint box of colors. I turned to Gabriel. "I don't understand." My voice was quiet and hushed. I didn't want to disturb the silence in the space. It felt holy, reverential.

"It is like your favorite book you mentioned, *The Mixed-Up Files.* The children who live in the museum." He shrugged. "Alas, security cannot allow you to stay here all night, but I did get for you this small amount of time." He gestured to the walls. "For this moment, this is all just for you."

"But the specialist—"

Gabriel winked. "I have convinced the guard that *you* are the specialist."

My brain felt fuzzy and disconnected. "But how—"

"Are you going to spend the entire fifteen minutes talking with me?" Gabriel's mouth quirked up. "Because I am not certain I can get another fifteen minutes. You would be better to spend your time with Monsieur Monet and his friends than with myself."

I started giggling. I felt drunk, but it wasn't the wine. I dashed around the room, taking in each piece. I backed up to see them at a distance, or to catch a view from the side. To see them without the crowds of people that filled the museum jockeying for a view, their cameras extended, made the art seem even more special. It made *me* feel special.

Monet's *Poppy Field* caught my eye, the woman in it walking through the waist-high flowers with a parasol over her shoulder. I'd had a poster of it in my college dorm room, but this was the real thing.

"With the impressionists I like to stand very, very close," Gabriel said, stopping his face barely an inch from the canvas. "The colors here are chaotic; it makes no sense. Then as you slowly move"—he stepped back just a half step, and then another—"you can see the colors come together. No longer chaos, they work together; they become some-thing greater. I think life is like this: in the moment, you can't make sense of it, but later, at the distance, it will all become clear."

I leaned toward the painting. The paints were swirled and dotted on the canvas, thick waves in one part and then barely dabbed on in another. Monet's brush had made these marks over 150 years ago. My breath was shallow in my chest with the beauty of it.

Gabriel had done this for me. Arranged this perfect moment. My throat thickened. I wanted to thank him, but I couldn't get the words out. I swallowed. His expression softened. He turned so we faced, placing his hand against the side of my cheek.

Time slowed. The crowd noise outside the gallery faded. Gabriel brushed a curl from my forehead and then leaned down to kiss me. His lips were soft, but the kiss grew more intense. His hand moved to the back of my head, and he pulled me closer, our bodies pressing against each other. Reality spun around, upside down, and back around like a ride at the carnival. And yet, for the first time in over a year, things felt crystal clear. This was exactly where I was supposed to be.

Gabriel pulled back. "This was okay?"

I nodded. My entire body was liquid, muscle and bone melting from the heat. This feeling left okay behind in the dust; this was *glorious*. I had forgotten how a first kiss could be, how it could be felt in every atom of my being. How it made my toes curl inside my shoes.

He tugged on my hand. "Come, we only have a few more minutes. Let us see the art like the characters in your book. Pretend that we slept here, with the art looking down at us. Now it is morning, and we are just getting up. We have it all to ourselves until we must hide away again."

We moved around the gallery, holding hands. His palm pressed to mine. We would step close to a piece, mere fractions of an inch away, my breath on the paint, and then back up. No matter which way I turned, whatever way I looked, all I could see was beauty. The sound of the security guard clearing his throat drew our attention. He tapped his watch face.

"Ah, time, it goes quickly in these moments," Gabriel said. "I wish I could spend the entire day, but I will be at the wine dinner until late. And alas, we should go, as I need to set up the event."

I didn't want the day to end. I fought the urge to cling to his side. An idea dropped into my head. "Would you sell me a bottle of wine?" I asked.

"I will gladly give you a bottle."

"But if you *sold* me a bottle, then it wouldn't be a lie that I was a customer of yours. One bottle or a hundred still count in terms of making me a buyer." I smirked at him, proud of my cleverness. It would feel good to do something for him after everything he'd done for me. "Assuming I like the wine, then I could be the reference you need."

Gabriel chuckled and then grew serious when I didn't join him. "Wait, are you certain? I do not want to put you in an uncomfortable position."

I was hoping he'd put me in a very comfortable position at some point later in the night, but I didn't plan to mention that now. "It will help you, right? It's not that big of a deal. They're not going to ask me to talk about wine in any detail, are they?"

He shook his head. "No, no, nothing like that. There is no expectation that you be an expert, just someone who appreciates fine wine."

"Well then, we're in luck, as I'm appreciating wine more and more these days."

He grew stern. "I would not ask you to do this."

I rested my hand on my chest. "You didn't ask; I offered. I want to."

He chuckled and then squeezed my hand. "This is . . . it is a miracle for me. I cannot tell you how much I appreciate it. My gratitude." He pressed his other hand to his heart.

"You'll have to show me how grateful you are later." I arched an eyebrow.

Gabriel made a low, guttural sound. "Hmm, I will have to think of something. Until then, if I want a good reference, I should be careful to choose a good bottle to sell you."

I pulled back as if offended. "Good? I'll have you know I no longer settle for anything less than excellent."

Barbe-Nicole

REGARDING THE EVENTS OF MARCH 1810

My darling Anne,

I am in awe of your recent social success. To shine in a crowd is a skill I never mastered. The truth is that I am not overly fond of large social occasions. I far prefer to read your letters detailing the balls than to attend them myself. Oh, I greatly enjoy a good meal or discussion with a close friend or two, but a loud event with everyone pushing to be seen and heard is better skipped in favor of staying home. I far prefer my own company and that of books to making small talk with someone as vapid as a grape. But you wanted to know about when I met the second empress. You asked about the dresses and music played. And I will share, but what I remember more than any detail of costume or conversation is that I took a momentous step that evening. Often when you make a decision that can change everything, you don't even know you've made it until much later.

■ ■

My father was determined to show the new empress, Marie-Louise, the very best Reims had to offer. I moved through the ballroom nodding in greeting to my neighbors. Everyone wore their best finery for the event. The young ladies, just barely out in society, favored white muslin for the occasion, embroidered in white thread. A few of the matrons still wore their skirts too wide, unwilling, or unable, to let go of that fashion. If one looked closely, they could see the wear the past few years had brought to some families. Seams were frayed and stains covered with a well-placed shawl, or a dark line revealing where a hem had been changed.

As I walked, I overheard snippets of conversation evaluating the Austrian archduchess on everything she wore, the style of her hair, and the accent in her voice. Bonaparte was said to have referred to her as "marrying a womb." She was more than twenty years younger than our previous empress, Joséphine. The same crowd of people who bowed and scraped to Marie-Louise tonight had done the same to Joséphine until the divorce. These neighbors of mine had grown to be shrewd sailors of society, tacking to match whichever way the political wind was blowing.

How easily a woman is forgotten as she ages, as if her looks and womb were her only assets. A man's love can be fickle; above all, a woman needs to love and care for herself in this world. She must never set her value based on the regard of others, or she risks being disappointed.

"Champagne?" Monsieur Lyon bowed slightly, handing me a glass.

I hadn't seen him approach or I would have slipped away. He'd come calling after François died, sniffing around to see if I was lonely. I could not fathom being lonely enough to welcome his attentions.

Not to mention I knew his interest was more in my vineyards than in me.

His soft, pudgy body was always encased in clothing just a smidge too small, like a sausage. Although it was not his size that bothered so much as his overall countenance. His tendency to sweat put a sheen on his face and neck and gave him an odor like greasy bed linens left out to air. Alas, those were his good qualities, as compared with his social graces.

I took the glass from him. "Merci," I said, stepping slightly to the side to avoid the stench that followed him like a rain cloud.

He tossed back his own glass. "Is this your wine? It's quite good."

"You sound surprised, Monsieur Lyon," I said. "Have you not heard that the demand for my champagne is growing?"

"I have. I also heard that the partnership between you and Monsieur Fourneaux is not to be renewed come July." He leaned closer, the smell of his mouth making my stomach turn. This close, I could see the blackened stumps of his back teeth. "Personally, I think you were wise not to marry his son. The boy is barely old enough for breeches. A woman has need of a real man." He winked and then adjusted his bitte through his clothing. "A true partner can help with business and in life."

With the size of his belly overhanging his breeches, it was a wonder he could reach himself, let alone any poor creature lying below him. I suspected the greatest satisfaction he provided a woman came from his absence.

"Today is not a day for discussion of business," I said. I had no intention of telling this odious creature that I would not be taking any new partner, business or romantic. I sent a silent prayer of gratitude for Louis's luck in selling my rose-pearl necklace while abroad. In the office strongbox, I had the funds needed to hold the business together on my own for at least a year, maybe two if I was cautious. I was rapidly running out of jewelry to be sold.

If Napoleon could bring these damn wars to an end, we would all fare much better.

Lyon jostled the man in the group nearest to us to pull them into our conversation. "You should be careful of playing too hard to get, Madame Clicquot. Wine may improve with age, but women rarely do." He laughed loudly, sending out clouds of his vile breath and looking for approval from those around.

"Monsieur, it is well known that intelligent thoughts have always been in your pursuit. How lucky for us all that you are faster."

I could practically see the gears in his mind turning to sort out my meaning, and then his mouth snapped shut, his face growing red.

He poured the remainder of his wine onto the floor of my father's ballroom. "You'll excuse me if I don't drink the rest. It is not to my liking."

I shrugged. If he thought his opinion of me or my champagne mattered, he was mistaken.

"It is no wonder that Napoleon chose the champagne of Monsieur Moët for his wedding," Lyon snapped.

My hackles rose in irritation. I would show Bonaparte and this pig Lyon that to sell me short was a mistake.

"Ah, my daughter, come, I wish to introduce you to the empress." My father swooped in and gripped my elbow. He nodded at those assembled around us and led me across the room.

When we were a few steps away, my father leaned in. "What has possessed you? Why are you starting disagreements tonight of all nights?"

"I am not starting anything," I protested.

"Monsieur Lyon is an important man."

My eyes rolled. "You need not worry; he is very much aware of his own importance. He does not require me to remind him of it."

Father sighed. "Must you be so obstinate? Perhaps you and the new empress will get along. She is also difficult." He shot a glance at her. "She's barely said a word or eaten all night. She acts like she's in the Bastille instead of at a party. Is it too much to ask that she smile?"

Marie-Louise likely loathed the French; we had beheaded her great-aunt Antoinette after all. And stories were that when she crossed the border for the wedding, she'd been forced to strip naked so as to not bring even a speck of Austrian dirt into France with her. No, I doubted that one fine party was enough to put her in good spirits for this twist in her fate.

My father stopped near one of the large windows. It had been propped open to give the space some air, to clear the thick scent of perfume, pomade, and burning candles. "Wait here. I will determine when it is a good opportunity to introduce you to the empress." He looked me up and down, his mouth pressed into a thin line. "Can you please keep any conversation light?" he asked. "Avoid difficult topics."

"Such as the rumors that Napoleon still sees, and is in love with, his abandoned first wife?"

Father rubbed the bridge of his nose. "Must you try me? You realize that if we have the emperor's favor, it benefits all of us, including your business?"

I flushed. I was being unreasonable. My father was right. Regardless of any feelings I had for Napoleon, or his new wife, any affection or goodwill toward my family was important. And my father had worked hard to make this evening's festivities a success. I touched his sleeve. "I will be gracious. You have my word."

Father's face softened. "Thank you, ma fille." He placed his hand on top of mine, and I noted that his skin had grown thin, more like onionskin than flesh. A flash of tenderness warmed my heart.

"Je t'aime, Papa."

He kissed my forehead. "Wait here. I'll call you forward when it is time." He paused and turned back. "Remember to curtsy."

Ah, how quickly court behaviors had returned. Vive la République indeed.

I stood near the window, glad for the chilly breeze. I'd had too much to drink. I fidgeted; the wooden busk in the center of my corset irritated me.

My father's footman Henri came to fuss with the window latch. He glanced over his shoulder and then whispered, his voice just loud enough to carry to me. "I'll agree to your plan."

A jolt of excitement went down my back, clearing away the fog of the wine. I had despaired that my idea would ever come to fruition. I was determined to get rid of the Mouse, but I needed an ironclad reason to terminate Margot's employment. One that would make any protest on her part appear to be merely sour grapes.

While the maid was petty and vain, and she might snatch a biscuit or a scrap of lace, she wasn't the type to steal silver or jewels, and I was not the type to stoop to placing something among her things.

I had learned long ago that one's own flaws are often the first thing to hang us. Margot was a vain coquette. She threw herself constantly at anything in breeches, always scrambling for a man that would allow her to better her station.

And so, I would provide one. One that would be nothing but trouble.

It hadn't taken much effort to encourage Henri to woo the girl. He was happy to chase anything in skirts, and the Mouse did not run very quickly. Henri was a known rogue. His employment with my father was always at risk. If anyone could lead the girl to trouble, it would be him.

"What do you want me to do with the girl?" Henri asked.

"I want you to spend time with her."

He raised an eyebrow. "Time?"

"I wish to let the girl go, but I need a reason to end her employment. You seem to be quite fond of activities that risk such things. Just let me know if she is a party to any of them."

Henri stiffened his spine. "Rumors of my ill behavior are overblown."

I waved off his words. I did not want to be involved in the particulars. The man was constantly in trouble: cards, betting on the dogs, messing with girls from town. I did not care what bad influence he exerted on the girl as long as it was something. "Bring me proof. No lies, mind you; it must be something that she has done, not you."

If Margot followed Henri and her base impulses to get ahead at any opportunity, she would soon find herself a mouse without a hole.

"I could lose my position," he said. "Your father has forbidden me to consort with any of the maids."

"And I have promised that I will care for you if it comes to pass."

"Margot is a nice enough girl," Henri said.

Despite decorum, I turned to look directly at him. "Nice?"

He swallowed hard, his Adam's apple bouncing against his tight collar. "Yes, she is loud and a bit crude, but she's kindhearted."

My eyebrows reached for my hairline. "Are you falling for her, Henri? Have all her whispered sweet words and touch led you to see the benefits of settling down?"

He flushed. "No, but I feel bad for the girl."

I turned away. If he wanted to marry her, I wouldn't stop him, but I suspected what he wanted more was money. I'd promised him I would make it worth his while to lead the girl astray into one of his schemes. Money I could ill afford, but it was an investment.

My father would call me over soon. I couldn't be seen in discussion with a servant at a social event. "Save your pity for those that deserve it. Trust me, Margot is trouble. When it is clear that her character is weak, you'll get your money."

The mention of coin was enough to silence him. Any feelings he had didn't run very deep, certainly not as deep as his own gambling debts. He moved off, sliding along the side of the room to stay out of the way of the guests.

Guilt sat in my chest, heavy and dark. I nearly called him back. It was not in my nature to do something like this. I wasn't one to treat people like chess pieces.

Then I recalled how Margot had run to the priest with her so-called worries. How she manipulated Clémentine's affections to get what she wanted. How the cards showed her to be my biggest risk. Her half-hearted efforts and sly glances almost daring me to challenge her. And I had not told Henri to force her into anything. She would make her own choices.

No, it was best to cut her out now before she rooted any further into my life. Before her gossip and stories spread and ruined my business as it dwindled away to nothing. Until it made me nothing. The cards showed I was at a crossroads, and I must act. It was ruthless, but necessary.

Father was now standing near the new empress, and he waved me forward.

I plastered a welcoming smile on my face and stepped forward, ready to curtsy. It was time for a show.

Natalie

■ PARIS ■

APRIL 21

'd been putting on a show since we'd arrived at the restaurant. It wasn't that hard; all that was required was listening to Gabriel's potential clients as if I found them as fascinating as they clearly found themselves. I provided a lot of nodding, appreciative noises, and laughter at jokes so pathetic they made me cringe. Granted, when not talking to me, they spoke only in French, so I spent a good amount of time smiling vaguely into space. Much like the Widow, I was not fond of these kinds of social events.

I'd come to act as a reference for Gabriel, but so far no one had asked me a single question other than my name. They were too busy impressing each other with what they owned, what they planned to buy, and by inference how much larger their penis was than anyone else's. A lot of time could be saved if they all dropped their pants and one of the waiters brought out a ruler. Most of the people at the event were French, although there were a couple of Italians and a portly

Belgian fellow who appeared to be wearing the entire contents of the Gucci store and a diamond pinkie ring so large it was obscene.

At least I looked good. I'd worn the linen sheath dress, with the pendant as my only jewelry. The outfit wasn't fancy, but it fit well. Or maybe it wasn't the dress at all; maybe it was just the way I felt in it, as if I were somehow taller. It was also possible that what had me feeling great was the silk bra and panty set I had on underneath. I'd taken time with my hair and, after some debate, worn a bright-red lipstick. When I'd looked in the mirror at the hotel before leaving, I'd filled with pride.

It was impressive watching Gabriel work the room, and not simply because of how divine he looked in a suit. He poured wine before anyone's glass dropped below half-full, slid into conversations in French, Italian, and English, charmed them, and then moved on to another cluster of men to work his magic. Every so often, he'd look across the room until our eyes locked and he would smile. It acted like a cable that connected us across the space. I could sense where he was, even if he wasn't in sight. The waiter rang a bell to let us know dinner was ready, and everyone took their seats at the collection of tables that had been shaped into a large U.

"I am famished," the man to my left said as he swept his napkin into his lap.

I nodded in agreement with what I hoped was a charming smile. It was nearly eight and I was about ready to start chewing on the starched tablecloth. The small canapés had been nice, but my head swam from all the alcohol.

Gabriel cleared his throat once everyone had settled and raised his glass of champagne. "A toast, if I may."

The group around the table paused their conversations. Gabriel had reserved this private room at the back of a midsize restaurant near the Louvre. The faint sounds of conversation, along with the clink of glasses and plates, drifted in from the main dining room along with the smell of browned butter and garlic.

Gabriel spoke in French, and the men nodded. "I will now change to English so my esteemed guest may be able to understand." He tilted his glass in my direction, and I smiled back, feeling oddly gracious, like I was the queen. "As I was saying, thank you all for coming this evening, and I trust that you have enjoyed the wines we've tasted thus far."

"Magnifique," a small bald man cried out, and drank the rest of his champagne in one go. The waiter standing at the back quickly moved to refill his glass. Apparently, I wasn't the only one who needed to soak up the alcohol with some food soon. This guy was a glass away from thinking karaoke was a good idea.

"While I do not sell Veuve Clicquot, it is Madame Taylor's favorite, so it seemed appropriate to start the meal with it. However, the rest of the wines we have had thus far, and will enjoy with dinner, are available for purchase," Gabriel said.

"So now you want more of our money," said the tall man sitting near the door with a smile of blinding white teeth that appeared to nearly glow in the dim light.

"Only if you wish to part with it, Monsieur Denmore," Gabriel fired back, and everyone chuckled. I was glad I hadn't been stuck seated next to Denmore for dinner. Gabriel had whispered to me at the start of the evening that this was his biggest client, the one most likely to buy in bulk, but the man was oily and repulsive. He'd put his hand on my ass twice so far, both times acting as if he meant to merely touch my lower back.

Gabriel raised his glass. "To the finer things in life"—he glanced at me—"that are made all the more valuable when they are shared."

The group around the table all raised their glasses. "Les belles choses de la vie!" a few cried out.

At that the waiters finally began to bring out the food. My mouth watered. They placed a small plate in front of me, on it a slice of baguette with some type of spread topped with what looked like a tiny fish.

The man next to me jostled me. "It is anchovy." He popped the entire bite in his mouth, breadcrumbs escaping as he chewed, proving that money didn't buy manners. "Matches parfait with the champagne." He rolled his eyes in pleasure. "And this is just course one. Wait until you try their bouillabaisse with snapper, and I am eager to see what red wine Gabriel will pair with the steak."

"Me too."

"You have bought his wines before?" he asked, suddenly looking sober. "You were happy?"

I carefully swirled the white the waiter had just poured, the chilled wine creating condensation on the side of the glass. "Are you telling me you haven't enjoyed everything?" I gestured toward the table.

He shrugged. "Wine at a dinner when they sell to you is one thing, wine when you get it home . . ." He let his voice trail off. "It can be another."

"The wine I bought was spectacular," I said, knowing what I said was true. Gabriel had rushed me back to the hotel after we left the museum and insisted on opening a bottle immediately so I could taste it. It cost almost $200, which was the most I'd ever spent on wine in my life, but I suspected it might be one of the cheaper bottles he was selling these people.

The man leaned back, looking relieved. When I glanced up, I realized Gabriel was watching, looking nervous. I surreptitiously winked at him, and a smile crept across his face. I imagined that he might have the same expression if we were to wake up together. Now I just had to get through the rest of this event. My nose twitched as the next course came out on platters.

■ ■

Gabriel pressed me against the wall in the hallway, his hands gently but firmly pinning mine as he kissed me deeply. The stubble on his jaw lightly scratched my face. My head swam from the wine and food. The dinner had been a success. Gabriel had packed up the wine and patted it goodbye as the men hefted case after case into the back of their cars. He had practically skipped back to the hotel, twirling me on the street corner as if we were dancing. He was elated. He'd sold more than he'd hoped.

"Come in," I said, my voice low and gravelly. He'd offered to walk me to my room, but I was counting on things going a bit farther than the doorway.

"Are you certain? I can go back to my own room."

I fumbled for my key, never more certain of anything in my life. I was desperate to touch him, to feel him inside me. This wasn't about checking anything off my list anymore.

"Yes," I said. If the key reader didn't work soon, I was prepared to batter the door down. The lock finally clicked open, and I dragged him into the room like it was a kidnapping, his shirt pulling free from his pants.

He chuckled and yanked out his phone, then tossed it over his shoulder onto the chair. "All night long I had to pay attention to all those people, but now, now, my focus is only on you."

I kicked off my shoes and reached for him. He tugged the top of my dress down and kissed my breasts. I melted. My legs wouldn't hold me up much longer.

Gabriel backed me up, shuffling along the carpet, until I was at the window; then, bending, he lifted me so that I rested on the ledge with a leg on either side of him. His hands ran up my legs, hiking the dress higher, and I moaned. He tore off his blazer and then returned to kissing my neck, mumbling in French. I didn't know what he was saying, but the words only made me hotter.

I grabbed his belt buckle and tugged, wanting him in my hands. I wanted him to make love to me right here with the view of Paris behind me, the cold glass on my back a contrast to the heat between us.

"Wait a moment." Gabriel pulled back slightly. His hair was mussed, and my lipstick was smeared around his mouth.

I was practically panting. My heartbeat thudded in every atom of my flesh.

"Is this what you want?" he asked.

Given that I was perched on a window ledge with my legs wrapped around his waist, I thought it was fairly self-explanatory.

Unless he didn't want to.

Oh God. I flushed bright red, and my arm shot up to cover my breasts.

Gabriel reached for my arm and pulled it down gently. "No, don't, you are so beautiful." He stood there staring, then kissed me softly.

"Then why—"

He ran the pad of his thumb over my lips. "I know you have not been with anyone since you lost your husband. I want this to be special. Not rushed because it is late, not fuzzy because you have been drinking." His lips brushed my ear as he leaned in and kissed my neck. "I want you to be aware of everything I am doing." He whispered the words, a warm breeze against my skin.

I squirmed on the ledge. "It's fine; I'm not drunk. I want this." The not-drunk part was a bit of a lie, but the wanting it was a hundred percent honest.

"Ma chérie, I want it to be perfect," he said.

"Perfect is overrated. But I'm willing to let you give it your best shot."

He threw his head back and laughed. Pulling me to my feet, he then ran his hand down the back of my dress and the zipper parted. The dress slid off into a puddle on the floor, leaving me in nothing but my underwear. I made certain to stand tall. Thank God for French lingerie. This was not a moment to be caught in Hanes Her Way.

Gabriel lifted me by my hips and tossed me onto the bed, the thick linens cradling me like a cloud. For a second, just a second, I remembered how Will and I used to laugh when we made love, and then I shoved him out of my mind.

Gabriel crawled onto the bed on his hands and knees so that he was over me. "My God, you are amazing."

I smiled. "You haven't seen anything yet."

He lowered himself until his body pressed mine even deeper into the mattress. I lost myself in his mouth and hands.

That was when there was a knock at the door.

Gabriel's head popped up, and he looked at me, his eyebrows arched.

"Ignore it," I said. I should have put up the DO NOT DISTURB sign.

The knocking got louder.

"It seems someone requires your attention," he said, sounding frustrated.

"Trust me, the only attention I need right now is yours."

He smiled, but then the knocking came again, along with Sophie's voice. "Natalie?"

Jesus. I crawled out of bed and grabbed the hotel robe from the hook by the bathroom. Gabriel scrambled so that he was standing next to the bed. But with his shirt rumpled, and the need to arrange himself in his pants, it wasn't exactly a mystery what was going on. He looked like a guilty schoolboy.

I tipped the door open and peered out into the hallway. Sophie stood there in jeans and a T-shirt, her face wiped free of any makeup.

"Natalie, I am so sorry to bother you."

"Now isn't a great time," I said. It was after one in the morning. What was she even doing here?

Sophie caught a glimpse of Gabriel, and she flushed. "Mes excuses."

"We were just talking," Gabriel called out. "Reliving a good evening."

One of Sophie's eyebrows arched. "I see." She turned to me. "It is your friend Molly." She held up her phone.

"What?"

"Your friend, she has been calling and texting, trying to reach you. She says if she doesn't speak with you, she will call the police to ensure you are okay."

What the hell?

Sophie continued. "I apologize. I am not sure what happened; I must have accidentally had my phone on Do Not Disturb all day. All the messages from her came in at once tonight." She threw her hands up in exasperation. "I am worried that she is desperate. There are many, *many* messages. I didn't want to come to your room, but I felt better me than the police."

Gabriel chuckled. "Yes, better than the police."

Sophie shot Gabriel a stern look, broadcasting that she didn't find anything about the situation amusing. I was with her. I was going to kill Molly. I grabbed the phone, and without even bothering to read the string of messages, I fired back a text.

Mols. This is Nat. Am Fine. Talk to you tomorrow.

Before I even handed the phone back, three dots appeared—she was replying.

How do I know it's really you? Call me NOW.

For crying out loud. I forced a smile onto my face. "Can I borrow your phone for just a minute? I'll pay for any charges."

Sophie nodded. "But of course."

I smiled at Gabriel and then ducked into the bathroom. After shoving some thick white towels out of the way, I sat on the edge of the tub and hit call.

"There you are," Molly said.

"What the hell are you doing?" I hissed into the phone, the sound bouncing off the white tile.

"I was worried."

I sucked in a deep breath, trying to let the scent of the lavender soap calm me. "Molly, I'm a grown woman. I'm on vacation, not off at war."

"I left two messages for you at the front desk yesterday and heard nothing."

I rubbed my forehead. "I don't know what happened. The clerk doesn't speak the best English. It's possible he messed them up, or maybe they were misplaced in a shift change."

"And I've been texting this woman all day, telling her I needed to speak with you."

"Her name is Sophie, and she didn't get the texts until now."

Molly snorted. "That's convenient."

"No, actually it's not. She just had to come across town to give me these messages in the middle of the night because you're acting crazy. I've been out of touch for only one day." I would have to make it up to Sophie for this trouble. Something that went further than a nice Yelp review for the hotel.

"I'm not sure why you're this upset. I said that it was important."

I rolled my eyes. "In the messages that I didn't get. And I'm upset because has it occurred to you I might not be alone?"

Molly went silent for a second. "Wait. You're not really sleeping with that guy, are you?"

"I was trying to!"

"You need to be careful. Look, it's not the sex that worries me, it's that you're not someone who does anything casual. You need to go slow."

"And you need to stay the hell out of it," I fired back, my voice rising. "I get you're my best friend, and I appreciate everything you've done for me, especially this past year. But you're married. You're not on your own and you probably never will be, so you have no idea what it means. You play at it by spending a night at my place and calling it a girls' night. You talk about how great it is to be able to do whatever I want, but you don't know how lonely it is. You have no idea what it's like to realize that it's been almost two years since anyone has touched you." My voice cracked on the last word, and the yawning gulf of pain from the last year that I hadn't let myself feel threatened to escape.

"I just wanted to help," Molly said quietly after a beat.

I shook my head. She just didn't get it. "No, you've made me your project. Someone you can tell how to live their life. What you need is a hobby."

She sucked in a breath. "That is not fair."

"I've barely been out of touch and you were ready to call the police."

"I was trying to reach you because I had important news."

"What is so important that it couldn't wait until I got home? You got a new recipe for kale? Or maybe the grocery rearranged the aisles? Oh, I know, you read a new article on the top five things single women in their fifties need to do and you know I'm not doing any of them?" I stood so I could pace in the small space.

"When I send you articles on stuff it's because I think they might help."

"And that's just it, you think all I am is someone who needs help. And you telling me how to live, what I need to do, lets you sit back and feel better about your own life. Because whatever is going on with you, at least you're not as messed up as me. If you would give me some space, maybe I could figure out what I wanted."

There was a beat of silence while we both digested the words that had flown out of my mouth.

"I called because I thought you'd want to know that Will and Gwen got engaged. I didn't want you to hear about it on social media, but I guess it doesn't matter, because as you said, you're busy getting over him by getting under someone else. Well, don't worry, I won't bother you again. You can have all the space you want." Molly hung up.

I grabbed the side of the sink to steady myself, and the makeup that had been on the counter hit the floor with a clatter. I slid down so I was sitting on the lip of the tub again, waiting for the breath to return to my lungs.

After a minute, I stood. Gabriel was waiting. Sophie needed her phone back. There was only so long I could hide out in the bathroom. I looked into the mirror, my eyes had dark circles where my mascara had smudged. I splashed cool water on my face, then stepped out of the bathroom.

Gabriel stood by the door. He was fully dressed, with his shoes on. Any romantic tension had evaporated. He and Sophie stood in an uncomfortable silence. I no longer felt sexy or desirable, just rumpled, and sad.

"I wasn't sure . . ." His voice trailed off.

"Yeah. It might be better another time."

He nodded, then crossed the room and kissed me gently on the cheek. "I will see you tomorrow."

I nodded and did my best to smile as he left. Sophie was still standing by the chair looking like she wished she could block every second of this awkward moment from her mind.

I passed Sophie her phone. "I'm sorry. My friend won't be calling again."

Sophie twisted her hands. "Everything is all right?"

I didn't even know how to answer that. The night had been magical, but now I very much felt like I'd turned back into a pumpkin.

"Come." Sophie pulled the covers back and patted the bed. I sat while she puttered around the room, getting a bottle of water from the small fridge and putting it on the nightstand with a glass. She pulled the blinds and then the curtains, the metal rings clattering along the rod.

"Go on." She motioned.

I pulled the robe off and slid between the crisp sheets as she pulled the duvet up.

"I will put the Do Not Disturb sign on the door so you can sleep. I think you will find in the morning things will look different."

I nodded.

Sophie walked to the door and turned off the room light. "Dors bien."

The door shut softly behind her, and I stared up at the ceiling. My feelings were all mixed up. I was livid with Molly and scared that we'd said things that would change our friendship forever. Then the feelings would flip, and I'd be proud that I stood up for myself. I didn't want to be Project Friend anymore.

The thought of Will being engaged was razor-sharp. I didn't want to even hold it in my brain in case I was cut. I was frustrated that Gabriel had left, but also maybe relieved. He was right—the night shouldn't be rushed and with both of us intoxicated. And maybe, just maybe, Molly was right too.

Barbe-Nicole

■ REIMS ■

REGARDING THE EVENTS OF JULY 1810

My precious girl,

My heart wept when I read your last letter. I know well how those around us, and our relationships with them, can create complexities and, at times, pain. Those that are close to us often wield the sharpest daggers and they know where to strike. I frequently found my work to be easier than people. I still spend time in the cellars. There are those that say I am old and have earned the right to stay indoors, to not dirty my hands with the tasks of wine making, but it is the labor that has kept me young. One needs purpose in this life. To me the smell of dust and mold on old bottles combined with the sweet rot of spilled wine on the floor is the world's most intoxicating perfume. But while wine is easier than relationships, when I look back, which one does with more frequency when there appears to be less to look forward to, I think more of the people in my life than the work.

But those relationships were not always easy or without their own heartbreak.

■   ■

The wine still wasn't quite right, but it would be. Like many things in life, it couldn't be rushed or hurried. It had to be allowed to take its time. I watched Louis's face closely.

"It is quite . . . unusual," he said eventually, looking over what I'd done.

I surveyed my project, pleased. My cellar master, Pierre, had built the shelf to my exact specifications. He used an old table and cut holes in the top so that bottles of wine could slide in, angled down with the neck pointed at the floor and the punt pointed at the ceiling.

"Yes. But look at this." I slid a bottle out, keeping the neck low, and held it up to the candle. The clot of lees, the dead yeast, had settled almost entirely in the neck. "If we turn the bottles about a quarter circle clockwise on a daily basis, it moves things along while not disturbing the wine. Kept like this for a month or so, the wine is perfectly clear once the lees are topped off."

The cellar master stood to the side. He crossed his arms over his chest in pride. "Look at that—even the Widow is satisfied."

"Am I that hard to make happy?" I chided him, knowing that my reputation was true in this case.

Pierre cocked his head. "I am an older, wiser man, Madame Clicquot. I know better than to answer that."

I chuckled and turned to Louis. "If we continue with the project on a large scale, we'll have to train a cellar worker to do the turning and build more of these shelves. It does add time to the process, but the results are hard to deny." I bit my inside lip in excitement to hear his views.

"The extra time is worth it if the product is better," Louis mused, looking at the bottle. "And the disgorgement?"

"We are still trying different methods of removing the lees with the least amount of spillage, but there's progress," Pierre told him. "It is already much better than the previous process."

My chest expanded with pride. I had made this happen. I slid the bottle I'd checked back into place. "Come." I indicated that Louis should follow me and leave Pierre to his work. I slipped down the length of the cellar, lightly touching bottles as I went past, like checking on sleeping babes. We would need every advantage possible. The world remained as upside-down as my wine. Not content to simply honeymoon with his new empress, Napoleon had just annexed the Kingdom of Holland. The man had no hobby other than politics.

"What do you think?" I asked impatiently.

Louis stroked his beard. "It's impressive. It could revolutionize the process of champagne."

"It would if I planned to tell anyone else." I rocked back and forth onto my tiptoes.

Louis arched an eyebrow. "You intend to keep it a secret from the other producers?"

I nodded. "It gives us the advantage."

Louis glanced down the cellar hall to ensure we were alone. "Surely one of the workers will tell Moët. It's rumored he offers money for suggestions that improve his wine."

I sniffed with disdain. "Of course he has to pay others; he hasn't the skill to make his own improvements. I keep my workers well satisfied and happy. They'll stay loyal. We are a family."

"Not all workers, I hear."

My gaze snapped back to his face. "What have you heard?"

"Madame Martin and I were speaking. She told me about the maid." He cocked his head. "Surely you can spare the girl some kindness."

I felt my expression sour. I had wanted to discuss my achievement after his time away, not this unpleasantness. Louis had no idea why I disliked the Mouse so much. I hadn't shared with him François's secret. "Come now, I look for your expertise with wines. I can handle my own domestic affairs."

"She's young. Are not most foolish at that age? And it seems to me the gentleman in question is more to blame."

The heat of my anger flushed my chest. "First, I can assure you he is no gentleman. Secondly, the 'girl' is a grown woman and certainly capable of making her own decisions."

"But—"

"What is this concern with my maid? Please tell me she has not turned your head as well. Have you not taken leave the past two months because of a honeymoon? Why did you marry your fine wife if you intended to chase after this lazy sot?"

Louis sighed. "My point is that if you are working to have a happy workforce, there is no reason to take out personal dislike on one girl. It makes you look spiteful. It's poor business."

"I have not asked you for your point on this issue," I snarled, smarting at his calling me spiteful. "Dare I remind you that while I may wear the skirt, this is *my* business. You work for me." I stabbed my chest with my finger. "When I want advice, I will seek it, and it is presumptuous of you to assume I would want yours."

The expression on Louis's face grew stony. "Yes, Madame Clicquot, I do work for you. Thank you for the reminder. If you will excuse me, I have much to do after my absence."

I watched him leave without saying a word. I would not request forgiveness for his hurt feelings when he was the one who had over-stepped. Louis was mistaken if he thought our friendship extended to being partners. I pinched my mouth shut. I had to do everything myself. Including saving the business from that girl.

I left the cellar in a huff. Despite what Louis thought, this was not a rash decision. People often confused bold action with bravery when the truth was, it was often harder to bide one's time. But it was finally time for me to rid myself of one troublesome mouse.

Madame Martin met my eyes as I came into the house and nod-ded. She would fetch the girl. After brushing dust and cobwebs from my clothing, I sat behind my desk, moving the ink stand and then straightening the stack of papers so they lined up even with the edge. I felt oddly nervous now that the time was here.

"You wanted to see me?" The Mouse stood at the door, her nose twitching. Madame Martin stood behind her as if to block her escape.

I motioned them both forward and then carefully looked the girl up and down. Her attempt to camouflage her situation with a loose apron fooled no one. Henri had found undeniable proof of the loose morals of the Mouse.

"It has come to my attention that you are in an interesting con-dition," I said finally.

Her cheeks flushed red-hot, and she opened her mouth to protest.

I raised a hand to cut off what she'd been about to say. "Please do not deny it."

Madame Martin sniffed with disdain from the doorway. "In a matter of months, the truth will be arriving for itself." She stared pointedly at the girl's midsection.

Margot swallowed over and over, her eyes swelling with tears.

"And the father of this child? Will he marry you?" I asked, as if I didn't know that Henri had taken the money I promised him and run.

Henri had dreams of new card games in America. I'd felt thick with shame when he told me the girl was pregnant. I should have known that Henri would take the easiest plan to the money. And no doubt the girl had made getting in her skirts easy enough, but I still felt bad for my part in it. I had assumed another member of the staff would discover them in an indelicate position. I had foolishly not foreseen a child would result, and the oversight made me angry with myself, which in turn made me even more angry with her.

The Mouse stared down at the Turkish carpet. "He has left town. I don't know where he is." Margot clasped her hands in front of her stomach as if to try to shield the babe within. "I thought he loved me, but . . ." Her voice trailed off. She looked back at Madame Martin, but there was little empathy there.

A flicker of guilt, like lightning in a dark sky, crashed through my chest. *What have I done? There is a child now.* I pulled myself straight in the chair, attempting to shake it off. I hadn't forced the girl to do any-thing, merely baited the trap and allowed her to make her own choices. Men were ruthless at war, and this was a battle I had to win. I could not afford a soft heart. I had done only what I must to save my family.

And your business, a tiny voice in the back of my mind whispered. It was always the business.

"Your employment here is ended," I said. There was no point in drawing out the inevitable.

The girl let out a sob and dropped to her knees. "Please, madame, let me stay!"

"That is not possible." I had anticipated and prepared for her anger, that she might threaten me with exposure of the true nature of François's death. I had imagined that Margot might be haughty and proud, but this, this tiny, quivering, scared little mouse, I had not expected, and I wasn't certain how to respond.

"I know I can't stay in the house, but I could work in the fields," she pleaded.

The image of her growing larger and larger, ripening out in the late-summer sun, was a nightmare.

"This is a reputable house. We cannot have you here," Madame Martin said.

"What will become of me?" she wailed.

All the words I'd prepared about how she had created her own situation and that her shame was her burden dried up on my tongue, like chalky soil denied rain. She hadn't created the situation on her own. I had used my knowledge of her to direct her path, just as we trained the vines in the field to grow in rows. Molding them to our will.

"Return to your family," Madame Martin replied. "You'll be paid your final wages. You need to pack your things and go."

"Madame Clicquot, please, I have no family." Margot's eyes met mine. For a moment, I remembered standing across François's bed with her, as if we had traveled in time back to that moment.

I stood. "For your kindness over the years to my daughter, I will give you some additional funds to help you until the child is born and you can work again." It created an additional expense I hadn't planned upon, but this unexpected guilt made it an easy cost to justify. I would not cast her out without at least some assistance. No matter what Louis thought, I was not unreasonable.

Margot's tears started anew. "And a reference?"

Madame Martin's eyes grew wide in disbelief. "A reference? For you? After this?"

Without a reference, the girl would certainly be doomed.

"Please, madame," the girl said, her voice cracking. "I know you to be a woman who does what is right and kind."

Was she hinting at how I'd lied to the priest about François? I stared at her as if I could see past her eyes and into her skull to read her thoughts and plans. "I will write you something," I said after a pause. "Saying you left our employment for family concerns." It was vague and unlikely to be much help, but it was better than nothing.

Margot pulled herself to her feet, ungainly and nearly toppling over. Her mouth pressed into a thin line, and she wiped her face free of tears so that no one else would see her thus. She was a proud little mouseling. She nodded to both of us, her head held high despite the weight of her errors, and left the room.

"You're too kind, Madame Clicquot," my housekeeper said. She stared down the hall after the retreating girl. "And she didn't even thank you."

"We have all made mistakes," I said. Was this one of mine? I'd been so certain that I had to rid myself of her risk at any cost, but now I wavered. She would be gone, and any further gossip she shared with a priest or anyone else would be disregarded. To feel pity for her was to ignore the fact that she had been willing to do whatever it took, from manipulating my daughter, to running to the priest to tear down the memory of François.

No. It was the right thing. If Louis knew all the facts, he would agree. Margot had to be pulled out at the roots, like a vine gone to rot.

I sat back down in my chair. "I will write something up and pull some funds for the girl. Please pack her a small amount of food and ensure that she is out of the house today. I don't want her here any longer than required."

"Yes, madame."

"I trust you can decide how best to share this news with the staff?" One benefit of this distasteful situation was that Margot was not a favorite of those belowstairs. She was charming, but too skilled at avoiding work and tended to put on airs. There would be gossip, the footmen no doubt trading ribald comments. The young maids would be reminded of the importance of chastity and the dangers of becoming a fallen woman.

Madame Martin nodded. "Never you worry, madame. I'll take care of everything. Monsieur Philippe sent word that he will join you for dinner as requested," she said, turning away from the unpleasant conversation.

I smiled, pleased. My father-in-law and I would raise a glass this evening to celebrate the business. The partnership with Alexandre Forneaux was officially at its end. The house of Veuve Clicquot Ponsardin now stood on its own.

"Excellent. Please ask Cook to prepare a simple meal. My father-in-law's stomach revolts so easily." While I had a lust for all sorts of food, enjoying the various delicacies that Louis and the other salesmen brought back from their travels, Philippe preferred less adventure on the plate.

I fussed over my father-in-law. I felt a tenderness for him as if he were the child and I the parent. When I declared my intention to run the house on my own, he'd invested more of his own money in the venture. Not a single word of Alexandre's son's suitability as a husband. No, he knew I wanted it all to myself, in *my* name. Between the funds I'd gathered from selling my jewelry, the limited sales made with the trade restrictions, and his contribution, we were set to weather any coming storms in the near future, God willing. I just needed the war to end.

"I will have Cook make the soupe au pistou Monsieur Clicquot is so fond of, with some cold chicken, and ensure the dining room has been aired."

I nodded my approval. A light soup of summer vegetables would be perfect. Madame Martin bustled off. I pulled a sheet of paper close and after a moment of thought scribbled a quick reference for Margot. One could hardly claim that she was hardworking, or preach of her upstanding character, so I decided on calling her "consistent," which was at least the truth. I sprinkled sand on the page and then set it aside.

It was the last unpleasant task before this new venture could sail forth. Had the girl not held her knowledge of the bottle above me, I would have ended her employ long ago. Things had resolved themselves as they should.

I rested my hand on the ledger I had just purchased. There was still a need to close out various accounts from the partnership, but this next stage required, no, *deserved* a new ledger and a fresh start. At my request the maker had tooled an anchor into the leather cover, and my finger traced the shape. François and I had chosen the anchor as the symbol of our house, an auspicious choice for a vineyard shipping its wines abroad. It was well known that anchors meant hope.

And I was filled with hope. I had done it! It was truly my own business at last. And it would be glorious. I thought of the fortune teller I'd seen over a year ago. I had faced the mountains. I had cleared away the Mouse and secured François's good name, and now I was ready for that success, choosing excellence at every crossroad. My champagne was good, and it was getting better.

There would be no quality other than the very finest from this house. I closed my eyes and made a vow.

The name Clicquot will mean only the best.

Natalie

■ PARIS ■

APRIL 22

The ringing of the phone on the nightstand was like a glass shard driving into my skull. *Why did I have so much wine last night?* My hand scrambled out from under the nest of covers and grabbed the receiver to make the sound stop.

"Hello," I mumbled. My mouth was pasty and sour.

"Bonjour, Madame Taylor. This is Nicolas at the desk."

I squinted at the clock on the bedside. Just after ten. Through a chink in the curtains, I saw daylight. Dear God, how had I slept almost the entire morning away?

"Mm-hmm," I said. I desperately needed a shower. And then maybe some toast. I was grateful Gabriel left last evening. I hadn't seen a mirror yet, but I was betting I looked less sexy, bed head rumpled, and more like a raccoon roused from a dumpster.

"The police are here, madame. They wish to speak to you. Would you like me to send them up to your room?"

I blinked, my brain scrambling to keep up. "Wait, the police? What do they want?"

Nicolas lowered his voice. "They say it is personal, related to a crime, madame."

A crime? Then it clunked into place. My phone. I dropped back onto the pillow. I wanted to tell them to forget it. I was going to pick up the repaired phone today. In the end, the crime hadn't turned out to be a big deal.

But if they had found the person who took it, they likely needed me to make a report to file charges. I knew from my job that people rarely wanted to be bothered with the boring paperwork required to process things, but without it, they may have to let the guy go. If I could help, I should.

I glanced around the suite. My dress was still in a crumpled heap on the floor and my shoes were kicked off into the corner. "Tell them I'll be down in five minutes."

■　■

It took more like ten minutes, and I still looked rough. I splashed water on my face and tried to do something with my hair, but there was still so much hairspray in it that it was hopeless. I sent up a mental prayer that there wouldn't be too many people in the lobby.

The desk clerk motioned to two people sitting stiffly in the library alcove. I smiled as I approached. "I'm going to have some coffee," I said. "Would you like some?" I raised a finger to draw the attention of the woman working.

The female officer stood. Her hair was slicked back into a tight bun, and her dark skin looked almost blue in the lobby's light. "This is not a social visit, madame."

I felt my eyes widen. Okay. Apparently, someone else had also woken up on the wrong side of the bed.

"Can you bring me a large Americano?" I asked the waitress as I dropped into one of the seats. At this point, coffee wasn't social; it was a required medical intervention.

The male officer pulled a notebook from his jacket pocket. "You are Madame Taylor from America, is that correct?"

"Yes, and listen, I'm willing to help you out with this investigation, but I'm not going to be in Paris for very long, so I can't get that involved."

The female officer arched one eyebrow. "I beg your pardon?"

"It's not that I don't want to help, but I only have some much time here and"—I motioned out the window—"there's a whole lot of Paris to be seen. The good news is that no one got hurt."

Gabriel had mentioned Versailles. Maybe I could convince him to take the train out there to see it. Or if he had to work, there was the food tour of Montmartre that Sophie had recommended.

My stomach did a slow turn. Maybe a food tour wouldn't be a great choice for today. I vowed only one glass of wine with dinner tonight. That would be it. I wanted to be able to remember every part of the upcoming evening. A shiver went down my spine as I remembered Gabriel's whispered words about his plans.

"You knew there was an investigation?" the officer said, bringing me back to the lobby.

"Well, I didn't *know*, but I guessed that's why you're here."

"And what would you like to say about the situation?"

The waitress placed the coffee down, distracting me with the rich smell. Thank God.

I took a careful sip. It was too hot, but I couldn't wait for it to cool. I blew on the top and took another sip. The officer drummed her fingers on the table between us. Someone needed to work on her public communication skills.

"I don't really have much to say," I offered. "It's a part of life in a big city. Things happen." I shrug. "It's not that big of a deal."

The male officer sat up straighter. "I can assure you, madame, that we take the heritage and reputation of France very seriously. We want his name, his real name."

"You and me both," I replied. "Do you have him in custody?"

"No."

I pushed down a sense of annoyance. If they hadn't even found the guy, then what was the point of all of this? I needed a shower.

"We want to know your involvement in this," the woman said.

"My involvement?" Was she going to victim blame me? "I was just there. I mean, yes, I was a bit careless—"

"I would call it a bit more than careless. The victim tells us you arrived at the event with Monsieur Dubois. That you acted as his reference for the transaction. That you were seen leaving with him, and the desk here has confirmed that he went to your room last evening."

I blinked, my focus growing suddenly razor-sharp. *What the hell is going on?* "This isn't about my phone?"

The female officer rolled her eyes. "No, madame, this is not about some phone. This is about wine fraud to the tune of nearly ten thousand euros."

I felt lightheaded. There had to be some kind of mistake. "Have you talked to Gabriel? If there was some problem with the wine, I'm sure he'll make it right." I glanced around as if he might be sitting in the lobby now with a croissant and a copy of *Le Monde* newspaper. "He has a room here. I'm sure he can sort this out." I raised my hand to flag the desk clerk over.

"Mr. Dubois checked out of the hotel two days ago."

My arm sank back into my lap. Gabriel never said anything about checking out. I replayed last night. I was almost certain he'd talked about going back to his own room.

"Are you sure?" I asked, my voice sounding small.

"Quite," said the female officer. She was looking at me like I was something she'd stepped in and was figuring out how to scrape off. "Perhaps if you were to tell us Gabriel Dubois's real name, then we could determine where he has gone."

"That's not his real name?" I asked, shrinking further into the chair.

She nodded knowingly. "Ah, you are saying this is something you also didn't know?"

"I'm not *saying* I don't know; I really didn't know," I said. I picked up my cup to drink more coffee, but my hand shook so badly I had to put it back down before I spilled it. "Can you please tell me what's going on?"

The female officer leaned back in her chair—she couldn't be bothered with me—but the male officer flipped back a few pages in his notebook to remind himself of the details.

"Last evening, we received a call from Monsieur Denmore. He stated that he had purchased several cases of wine at an event. When he got home, his partner noticed an error on the labels. This led him to believe the wine was fraudulent. Concerned, he immediately tried to reach Monsieur Dubois, but the cell number he had for him had been disconnected. Monsieur Denmore then reached out to us. A report was taken last night, and we were in touch first thing this morning with two other people who were at that dinner and inspected their bottles.

"The fraud department is involved, and they've indicated that, yes, the labels are certainly fakes. The wine itself hasn't yet been tested, but we expect when we get the lab reports back, we will discover that the supposed 'grand cru' has been substituted with inferior wine. We are waiting to hear from the others who were at the event, but we believe it likely that most, if not all, of the wine that was sold is fake." The officer looked up to make sure I was still following along. "The victims noted that you had acted as a reference, stating you were a frequent client of Monsieur Dubois and vouched for his reputation. Are you saying this is not true?"

My stomach clenched, sour and hot. "I bought a bottle of wine from him. It was fine." It had been fine, hadn't it?

"The people at the event were certain you indicated that you had bought far more than a single bottle in the past. You stated he could be trusted to provide quality wines."

Do I need a lawyer? "I never said that," I replied. I might have said it; the evening was a blur.

"But perhaps you allowed them to think that?"

I licked my lips. My mouth was dry. "Listen, I'm not sure I understand what's happening."

"What's happening is that Monsieur Dubois is a con artist. A wine fraud. And we are trying to determine if you are in business with him."

My stomach twisted again, acid rising in my throat. The sounds in the lobby faded around me.

"Are you all right, madame?" The female officer stood.

The rush of spit in my mouth was electric and sour. Oh God, was I going to vomit right here in the lobby?

"Breathe through your nose," the female officer demanded. She motioned to the waitress in the corner.

"Un verre d'eau," the waitress said, bustling over and handing the officer a glass of water.

"Drink," the officer commanded.

I was sweating all over, clammy, and cold. When I reached for the glass, my hand shook so badly that the officer held it for me while I drank.

"Thank you. I'm okay now." I wiped the back of my mouth. "There's no chance that you're wrong, that there's been some kind of mistake?" My voice cracked on the word "mistake."

The officer shook her head. "No, madame. There has been no mistake."

I swallowed. "I swear I didn't know anything. Gabriel told me he was a successful wine merchant. He needed a reference for people at the dinner. I had bought the one bottle from him, so I didn't think . . ." My voice trailed off. I didn't think. I closed my eyes. What the hell had I gotten myself into?

"It is your statement that you were unaware of the fraudulent nature of Monsieur Dubois's wine? You knew nothing?"

I nodded.

"So, you are a victim too?"

"I guess," I stammered.

"What luck that you only bought one bottle. Unlike the others who took your recommendation, who spent so much more."

My mind raced in circles, and a part of me wondered if this was some kind of drunk fever dream and any second now I would wake up back in bed.

"I need to go now," I said.

"We still have more questions," the male officer said.

"I can't help you. I'm telling you I don't know anything." I stood, fighting the urge to bolt for the elevator.

"Madame, I must insist—"

The female officer rested her hand on his shoulder, cutting him off. "Take this." She passed me an official-looking business card. "If you think of anything we should know, or if Gabriel is in touch, I insist that you follow up with us."

"Finc." I stepped toward the elevator.

"And Madame Taylor?" She waited until I paused and turned around to face her. "Do not leave the city without letting us know." She and the other officer walked out.

I stopped at the desk, clearing my throat. "Do you know when Sophie is working today?"

"Sophie is no longer an employee of the Delphine. I am happy to assist you."

I gripped the desk. "I need to speak to her. It's important."

Nicolas fished about and pulled a Post-it note free from a pile. "She left a phone number." He scribbled it down and slid a slip of paper toward me. I snatched it as if I expected it to disappear.

"Thank you."

■ ■

Two hours later, I could have wept with relief when I spotted Sophie sitting outside at the corner brasserie. She was the closest thing I had to a friend in this country. She stood and hugged me.

"Are you okay?" she asked.

"What the heck is going on?" I sank into the wicker chair across from her. I'd showered and had at least three more cups of coffee, but I still felt like I'd been hit over the head with a baseball bat.

Sophie motioned, and the waiter was at our table in an instant to pour me a glass of wine. She waited until he walked away. "I was let go," she said.

"Fired?" I realized I'd almost yelled the word and lowered my voice. "Why would they fire you?"

"This 'Gabriel.'" She made finger quotes around his name. "He, how you say, con me. I bought several cases of his wines for the hotel, because he said he is giving me a wonderful deal, but it turns out they were fake. He had always been so nice and polite to me that I saw no reason to doubt him. He has stayed at the hotel several times in the past. I didn't think it would be an issue." She bit her lip and shook her head. "Sacrebleu. He rang up so many charges to the room and then poof." She snapped her fingers. "Gone in the wind."

I felt hollowed out inside. "All of it was a lie?"

Sophie nodded slowly. "It appears so. The police spoke to the hotel manager this morning. They didn't even allow me to come in and say goodbye to my friends." She lit a cigarette and blew the smoke out in an angry plume. "They want no excuses. Management is very angry and wanting to blame someone. They feel I have tarnished the image of the Delphine by buying his wines."

I took a gulp of wine. "They can't fire you. It wasn't your fault."

Sophie leaned back. She looked like a French postcard, with her hair up in a messy bun, a striped Breton shirt, a glass of wine in one hand and the cigarette in the other. "I can fight it, yes; French employment law supports the worker. But I think not."

"What are you going to do?"

She took another determined puff on her cigarette. "I am returning to Reims and will open my wine shop."

"I didn't think you were going to do that for a couple more years," I said.

She shrugged. "Is one ever ready? No, I think I delayed because I was scared. I will do the work myself. Then I don't need to save as much to make it happen." She flexed her arm. "I am strong. I can build cabinets and paint. It is time. Perhaps this Gabriel does me a favor." She leaned forward, her forehead wrinkled in concern. "Perhaps he did us both a favor."

I gave a brittle laugh. "I think the only favor is that you saved me from sleeping with him." Oh God, what would Molly say? I'd picked up my repaired phone on the way here but hadn't wanted to call her or anyone else from home. She wouldn't gloat, but that undercurrent would be there. *I told you so.*

Sophie topped up my wine, her face grim. "Yes, it was fortunate that I came. But in the end, for you, he give the dream of Paris, no? A bit of romance as a way to move on from the loss of your husband."

There it was again. A sinking sense of guilt. I might be angry that Gabriel was a liar, but I'd lied to Sophie too. But at least my lies didn't involve possible legal action. I stared out at the traffic, watching the mopeds whiz past, feeling the vibration of their engines in my chest.

"He manipulated me into helping him rip a bunch of people off. The police tell me I can't leave town."

She waved off my words with her cigarette. "Bah. The police will do nothing. I hear he was very careful to ensure that the amount of his crime was not too high. In this city, with all that is happening, the police will not take time to do much more. And the people that he stole from are not victims anyone will cry over. They are arrogant with money to spare."

I thought of the wandering hands of Denmore and the endless boasting last night.

"If rich people want to buy expensive wine for a cheap price, officials think they get what they deserve. And on you, they have no proof," Sophie pointed out.

"Gabriel lied to me." The words caught in my throat. The pain of it was still blunt, not real, like when you cut yourself in the kitchen.

There is a moment when it doesn't hurt, and you observe your own blood pooling on the counter with dispassion.

"Men lie. This is the way of the world. His lies are perhaps just bigger than others. No, in the end you had a bit of a grand adventure; what he did will become a part of the story that you tell of your time here. Your friends back home will be most envious of this scandal of yours. It is not as if you love him; it has been but a few days."

Sophie seemed so certain. I hadn't loved him, had I? I'd been smitten, starry-eyed for sure, but it was more lust than love. It was embarrassing how easily I had fallen for everything he said. The Widow said that the truth is a story we convince others to believe, but my issue seemed to be that I convinced myself of things that were never true. "I feel like an idiot," I said softly.

Sophie smiled at me. "We are all fools at times. But we learn."

I considered everything that had happened with Will. I'd believed his lies too, all the working late and odd credit card charges. Then I'd flown halfway around the world and done the same stupid thing with a different person. The Widow was right. When I thought back on this trip to Paris, it would be this mess with Gabriel I would remember most. It's always the people who stick in our memory. "I seem to learn slower than most."

"Perhaps this is also the lesson that Gabriel give you. To be more careful with your heart."

"Perhaps." I watched the tourists and locals stroll down the sidewalks.

"Do not be sad, Madame Taylor. Keep in mind the grande dame Madame Clicquot. She rose from every hardship and so shall we. I will open my wine shop; you will continue your vacation and return home a wiser woman with stories to tell."

Barbe-Nicole

■ REIMS ■

REGARDING THE EVENTS OF SEPTEMBER 1812

My dear Anne,

Goodness, I was exhausted merely reading about all that is expected of you this season! It is natural for you to feel overwhelmed at the prospect. Do not be harsh on yourself by saying that others have much more to contend with—there is no winning by comparison. We all must fight our own battles; knowing others' wars changes nothing. When things are bleak it is human nature to think it will always be thus, but this is not true. I will tell you of a time when I felt at a loss, when I felt the weight of that darkness, so you know you are not alone and that there is a pathway forward.

One must experience the dark to truly value the light. The stars are in the sky all day, but it is only at night that we can see and appreciate them. So, when things in your life seem bleak, look to the heavens. You cope with today and plan for tomorrow.

■　■

The cork sizzled when it met the red-hot branding iron. The acrid
scent drifted up into the air. The worker thrust the iron back into
the fire and dropped the cork into a bucket of water. I fished it out
a second later, not waiting for him. The cool water soaked into my
sleeve, the fabric becoming thick and sodden, but I barely noticed.
I stared at the image burned into the bottom of the cork: a comet
streaking across a sky.

"You are happy, madame?" The worker shifted nervously as he
awaited my verdict.

Pure joy filled every inch of my body. I felt swollen, pregnant
with possibility. I nodded, unable to put the feeling into words.

The 1811 vintage was the best champagne I had ever made. No,
the best *anyone* had made. It had all come together perfectly: the soil,
the grapes, the sun and rain, the care the workers took as they har-
vested, the time in the cellar as it fermented. The alchemy of all the
different elements merging to become something greater than any
one part.

Magic.

The comet that had streaked the sky most of this past year had
portended something. It had been seen around the world, with reports of it coming from as far away as America and Egypt.

Had I not seen a star in the coffee grounds all that time ago at
the fortune teller's? Was it pure hubris to believe it had been a sign of
this wine? That God himself had noticed what I'd made? He sent a
star to signal the birth of his own son. Why not of this great creation
of mine?

I flushed, embarrassed at my pride. But I couldn't help it. The
champagne was perfection. But I wasn't alone in attempting to determine the meaning of the comet. There was no shortage of fortune

tellers declaring the comet meant all manner of things, some grand and some not. There were some who whispered that the comet predicted the end of Napoleon's reign, but the Toad was still there, despite what had happened in Russia.

My happy thoughts scattered. Too many families in Reims had lost sons, brothers, or fathers. The journals reported half a million French troops dead. Insondable. The number was too high to even imagine. My cousin reported that when the remains of the army straggled into Paris after the retreat, the men looked more dead than alive. Their uniforms were torn, spattered with all manner of things, but it was their haunted, hollow eyes that he remembered. People stood totally silent, watching them as they marched in.

I tossed the cork back to the cellarman. "I am pleased. Have all the 1811 sealed with these."

The cellarman nodded and returned to work. I liked to imagine that in the years to come, people would open this champagne and see my mark. 1811. The year of the comet. The year the house of Veuve Clicquot established itself as the very best. All the work, all the scrabbling to keep things together, all of it would come into line.

I stepped deeper into the cellar. I liked to walk among the wine. While I might not pick the grapes in the field, my hands were on every step of the production, and it satisfied me to see the outcome of that work. As I walked, my brain shuffled through the hundreds of tasks that still needed to be addressed.

Clémentine needed new school clothes. The girl was growing like a weed. Reports from the sisters said she was well liked among her fellow pupils, but my daughter was no scholar. I didn't need the update from Mother Superior to know this. Her letters home were evidence enough. As my mother reminded me, my daughter excelled in the womanly arts. There was a hint of disapproval there, the indication that I did not. Perhaps that was what bothered me more than my daughter's lack of intelligence, that she was more the woman the world wanted than I was. I shook off the thought.

The 1811 wine needed to be bottled and the blending done for this year. I worried we wouldn't have enough workers. Too many men held weapons instead of pruners, though many had no interest in fighting. There were those who tried to avoid conscription; there was talk in town of men who knocked out their own front teeth. If they couldn't tear open the cartridges with their mouth, they couldn't load a gun. It was a coward's way to avoid the fight, but I could not blame those who would try anything to save themselves. A ruined smile was better than a distant grave.

My project to improve the quality of the wine was going well. I'd expanded the number of bottles we turned upside down. The clarity was good, and there was less wine lost and fewer instances of the bottles exploding. I hadn't enough old tables to turn all the bottles I'd wanted, so I had the cellar master, Pierre, make me what I called a rack. Two large boards tilted together like a pitched roof.

"We shall create our own pyramids, madame," he'd explained, his chest puffed out. All things Egyptian were still widely popular. I teased him I would call him Pharaoh, but I could tell he liked it.

That would be another task. To explore if there were funds to increase Pharaoh's wages. Then there was the house in Bouzy, which called out for renovations. There was carpet and furniture needed, but the trade embargoes made things difficult. I would rather rooms be empty than full of items settled for rather than wanted. I made a mental note to write that to Clémentine. She was of an age where you want so desperately for your life to be full, with friends, with things, with achievements; it is all too easy to settle for good enough. It takes strength of character to sit in the absence of what you want and have faith it will come.

Then there was Phillipe. My father-in-law didn't seem well. I couldn't put my finger on any one ailment, but he appeared diminished. He walked with a cane now, his back hunched over, making him shorter. His voice was quiet, and I had to lean in to hear him.

"Excusez-moi," Pharaoh said, breaking my thought process. "May I speak with you?"

"Of course."

He paused, and his gaze flicked to the other workers in the room.

"Do you mind walking with me outdoors?" I suggested. If he wanted privacy, I trusted him enough to give it. "I wish to inspect the vineyard."

"Oui, madame." Pharaoh looked relieved.

Outside, we walked in companionable silence down a row. Pharaoh paused at one point to pinch a handful of soil and place it in his mouth, before nodding his approval and moving on. The old ones could taste a future grape by the dirt the vines were grown in. It was a skill gained only through time.

Pharaoh made certain there was no one around before he finally spoke. "Madame, I don't wish to overstep my position—"

I waved off his hedging. "Come now, Pharaoh, we've known each other for a long time."

He rocked back on his heels, looking over the vines into the distance. "The recent wine, the 1811, it is very good."

"Yes." I hadn't needed him to tell me this.

"I am thinking wine like this could be the making of this house."

I raised an eyebrow. He was leading somewhere. "I agree, Monsieur Casbon. Do you have a concern?" Perhaps he was going to ask for a raise in his wages. While he deserved it, it bothered me he would ask. It meant that I had left it too long. I disliked thinking I had overlooked something that needed to be done. It made me worry about what else I may have missed. I used to count on Louis to remind me of things, but our relationship remained strained. We spoke of business, but little else, and I sensed he held himself back.

Pharaoh glanced around, ensuring we were alone. "I would like to suggest, madame, that with your permission, once the wine is bottled, we wall up most of it in one of the back cellars."

I stopped. "Wall it up? With brick?"

"Yes, madame. If done in a back corner, someone not familiar with the space, even those who are, may not notice that the room has become smaller. It would be imperceptible."

A breeze blew over the vines, making a whispering sound that made the hair on my neck stand up. "Why would you suggest such a thing?"

Pharaoh looked down at the ground and then back at me. "I believe the war is coming here, madame."

"The war?" I repeated dumbly.

He nodded. "The Russians."

I shook my head as if I could toss off what he was saying as easily as water from a dog's fur. "Surely you don't believe things to be that bad. Napoleon may have suffered great losses, but he is pushing the Russians and their allies back."

"And like water, they will push back as well, flooding into France. And we have so little left with which to bar their entry. We gambled we would destroy them, but we did not."

"I see," I said. The weight of his words settled in my chest. The Russians had burned their own city of Moscow as they retreated rather than allow French troops to seize it. If they would do that to their home, what would the Cossacks do to ours?

"While I am an old man now, madame, I can still remember a young man's wishes after a battle. To be that close to death and then survive makes one want to inhale all that life has to offer: food, women—and liquor."

"Champagne," I added.

Pharaoh nodded. "To drink the stars themselves would be a fine way to celebrate. But these will not be paying customers, I fear."

I chewed on the inside of my cheek, his image playing out in mind. Drunken soldiers tearing into crates and yanking out bottles, the spray of the wine in the air, the sound of shattering glass. And me standing by, unable to stop it. I wanted to run from him and the story he was telling, but the truth moves faster than our wishes.

"You think we can hide most of it?" I asked. The weight of the decision made me want to reach out to Louis, but I hesitated. It wasn't clear what I feared more, having to apologize to him for what I said when we fought, or a letter detailing my plans falling into the wrong hands.

"Yes. But we shouldn't conceal all of it."

"Why not?" My mind was already calculating the space below in the cellars.

"A man's loyalty is one thing, but in a time of war it is often more, shall we say, flexible? If Reims is taken by the Russians, most in town will resist. Either with weapons or by subterfuge, but there will be others that will fall into line. They'll seek favor with the Cossacks."

I watched over the field. The sun was dipping in the sky. "You think someone in my employ would show them where to find the wine?"

Pharaoh shrugged. "I think the Russians would make it very tempting to tell. Too many people know about this wine. They know how good it is rumored to be. If you claim to have no bottles, well, people who work here will know this is an untruth. And some will profit from their knowledge."

I nodded. He was right. To save some of the wine, I would have to risk others. The list of things that needed doing that had seemed so insurmountable, so complicated, when I compiled it minutes ago now appeared simple with the new tasks that rushed into my head. The curse of accomplishment is the fear that one could lose what one has gained. Sometimes it seemed better to not reach at all.

"Thank you for bringing this to me," I said. "Choose a few men, those you trust, and begin to wall up some of the wine. Two-thirds if we can, but not all at once. Do it over time, at night after most have left."

"I'll find work that will keep most out of the back cellars until we are done. If we rub the fresh mortar with grit, it will look older. And my grandson likes to catch spiders. I will have him do so and place them on the new walls so they can spin their webs. No one will note the difference when we are done."

I smiled at the image of even the spiders of Reims doing their part. "We should have some time to make it work." Dear God, it would have to work.

Pharaoh nodded, although he looked suddenly weary. "The Russians will be wiser than Bonaparte. They will watch the weather and time themselves. Months, maybe as long as a year before they will come. And with luck, I am only an old man seeing danger that does not exist. I may be wrong, madame."

I patted his arm. "I am very grateful for your age and wisdom. Come to my office tomorrow with a plan and a list of what you need. And there will also be an increase in your wages. You will earn it, I expect, and I wish to show my appreciation."

Pharaoh stood straighter. The years of working in the fields and in the sun had etched his skin with lines like tooled leather. "I am proud of the wine, Madame Clicquot. It will be my pleasure to save it."

I felt a womanly gush of tears in my eyes and blinked them away. I swallowed quickly before I fell into unseemly gratitude. "Very well. Let us begin."

Pharaoh bowed his head and moved down the row, back toward the cellars. The weight of his words gathered on my shoulders with every step he took. Why did it always have to be so difficult? Life was a series of challenges, one mountain after another, stretching out, exhausting to even ponder. I sank down and sat on the earth, hiding beneath the vines.

I had done so much already to establish this house. Tears ran down my cheeks. The loss of François, disregarding my parents' wishes that I remarry, scrambling to find funds to operate without a partner, ridding myself of the Mouse before she could bring me down. And living with the weight of that decision every day since. The hours of learning how to blend the wine, to get the ledgers to balance, to manage staff that fought or had to be nudged to do their work. No one, not even Louis, could appreciate all I had done. And now this? War on my own land? Was there ever to be a time when it would simply be easy?

Giving over to despair, I sobbed, my tears hitting the ground and disappearing into the dry soil. I howled into the sleeve of my dress to keep the sound from traveling, and my chest ached with pain. I was simply so tired. So very, very tired and alone.

Eventually, I became too tired to even cry. I sat there on the cold ground, the smell of dirt and leaves like a fog about me. I was hiding, like Clémentine used to do, ducking into a wardrobe to avoid having to work on her sums. The sun dipped lower, and the shadows reached farther. People would be wondering where I had gone. I wasn't a child. I couldn't hide forever.

Taking a deep breath, I used a corner of the shawl to wipe my face. Strength isn't a fixed state. It is a series of choices in between moments of weakness. I would not choose to lie down and give up, which meant even though I had no idea how I would weather the storm ahead, I had to stand up and at least try. I wasn't foolish enough to think it wouldn't be hard, but every person must determine the price of their own worth.

And I was a proud woman.

Rising to my feet, I inhaled another deep breath, letting it settle my heart. Brushing off my dress, I did my best to pull myself together before going back to the house. When you don't know how you will handle a situation, when it feels as if it will all be too much, then simply focus on doing the next right thing and go from that point.

Natalie

■ PARIS ■

APRIL 22

held my breath in the jewelry store, fidgeting at the counter, even though I was certain of the answer. The truth does indeed move faster than our wishes. My job in insurance had taught me to go over every detail, double-check every line, look for anything that didn't fit when reviewing a troublesome case. When I looked back on my time with Gabriel, his help with selling my ring stood out in flashing red.

"It is glass," the clerk said, turning my pendant over. "An excellent piece of costume jewelry. One of our best." He tried to hand it back to me.

I swallowed hard. "What's it worth?"

His face scrunched in confusion. "Do you wish to return the piece? I can inquire if that is possible." He glanced over his shoulder for a manager.

I pinched the bridge of my nose. "Just tell me what it's worth."

"We sell it for two hundred euros."

I expected the reality to hit me like another gut punch, but I felt oddly calm. After I'd left Sophie, I'd walked the city for almost an hour, trying to sort out my feelings. I knew she said I should see what happened as part of my grand adventure, but there was a sense of shame. And disbelief that I'd lied to myself about the people around me again. Then it occurred to me that if Gabriel was a con artist about wine, the odds that he was a jewelry expert who just wanted to help me out were low.

"And the ring I brought in, can you remind me again the amount you paid me?"

The clerk looked at me as if trying to figure out how I had forgotten something that happened just a couple of days ago. "Our records show we paid you eleven and a half thousand euros. Minus the cost of this piece."

A hysterical giggle escaped my throat. "Right, of course, minus this." At least I hadn't let Gabriel take me for all of it. The irony wasn't lost on me that what I'd kept for myself was a fake.

The clerk looked confused. "All of the details were in the paperwork we provided you."

I nodded. I hadn't even looked at the bill of sale. Gabriel had glanced over it for me. And pocketed the money. I hadn't noticed. I'd been too caught up in the excitement and the story he'd woven for me—that I'd woven for myself. I'd wanted so badly to believe the fairy tale that I'd been played for a fool.

Again.

As I left the shop, the words of the Widow rattled around in my head. *Simply do the next right thing.* The problem was that I didn't *know* what that might be. I stood on the Pont des Arts, my feet and back aching from all the walking. Padlocks covered the bridge railings, thousands of them. Couples inscribed their initials on the side of a padlock with Sharpie or nail polish, locked it to the railing, and then tossed the key into the Seine, their love locked in place forever. It seemed to me that the bridge must be ready to sink under so many locks. The weight of all that love was hefty.

Was the next right thing to go to the police and tell them about the pendant? It might help convince them I was a victim in all of this too. Or it might just cement their theory that I was as dumb as a stale baguette. I could just imagine the female officer's face as I explained how, yes, I let someone I just met broker the sale of possibly the most expensive item I owned without even glancing at any paperwork.

The next right thing could be to call Molly and tell her every-thing and beg forgiveness for what I'd said in our last call. She'd likely forgive me. We'd been friends a long time. She might even be able to avoid telling me she told me so. And yet I still didn't want to reach out. Just as it had been for the Widow, having to make that apology seemed a step too far. And yet, Molly worked in a law office. She would know how to handle the police, maybe even call someone here to ensure I wasn't in any real trouble. For all I knew, I should go to the American embassy and ask for asylum.

There was the option of taking Sophie's advice and simply chalk-ing the whole experience up to a learning opportunity. Jesus, I was tired of the universe teaching me things. I could continue my vaca-tion, take a food tour or a river cruise, and try to act like everything was fine.

Or I could go home a week early, cut my losses. If I called the airline, they would change my flight. This entire trip had been a mistake. I thought I was living out some made-for-TV movie where, after a makeover montage, I would find true love in the shadow of the Eiffel Tower.

Was Gabriel out there somewhere, laughing at me? I pictured him with his feet up, counting his money, a glass of fine wine on the table next to him. Thinking about how he spun things until I volunteered to be his reference. Asking him to sell my ring. Begging him to sleep with me. Or maybe he wasn't laughing; maybe he felt pity. And somehow that seemed even worse.

My hands gripped the railing, my fingers nearly white with the strain. The worst part was—and this was impressive because there were a lot of worst bits to choose from—that the person I most wanted to talk to, the person I wanted to help me, was Will. I wanted him to pull me in, rest my face on his chest while he rubbed my back in circles, and whisper that it would all be okay, that he would fix things. The sound of his heart and the smell of his starched shirt acting like Valium. He had been my person for so long. My friend and my partner. Unlike Barbe-Nicole, I wasn't sure I was strong enough to handle everything on my own, and I wasn't even dealing with invading armies. I was used to knowing that I always had someone in my corner, someone to back me up.

And now he was there for someone else.

I'd almost forgotten the news of him and Gwen. Will was getting married. He'd stepped out of our marriage and into another relationship without even a pause while I was stumbling around on my own. I'd been replaced.

I should be able to think of the next right thing to do without having to run it past anyone, and yet the first person I thought of to help me when I'd been conned was the person who had pulled the ultimate con on me. How could I trust someone like Will to help, but not trust myself?

I took a deep breath. Will's betrayal had been the worst thing I could have ever imagined. But the one advantage of bad things happening is that you learn, just like the annoying Hallmark cards tell you, that you're stronger than you think.

I'd been smitten with Gabriel, but I hadn't loved him. The police would realize I wasn't involved. I had no record of past criminal deeds. For crying out loud, I worked in insurance and was so risk averse I didn't even buy heels over three inches. I was the person you could count on to have Tylenol and Band-Aids and spare Kleenex in my purse. I wasn't exactly an international woman of mystery.

The financial loss of the ring stung, but it wouldn't bankrupt me. If I was honest, if this whole thing hadn't happened, the ring would have likely sat in my jewelry box at home on the dresser gathering dust.

The biggest damage from all of this was a sense of embarrassment. I felt humiliated.

Again.

What is the price of your own worth?

The Widow's words echoed in my head. Did I really value myself so little that I was simply going to accept what had happened, to just walk away with my tail tucked between my legs?

Hell no.

The Widow faced down people who didn't believe in her. She didn't rely on others to solve her problems. She got spiders to do her wishes, for crying out loud. Sophie hadn't lain down and fallen apart when she'd been fired; she'd picked herself up and moved toward her dream, knowing it might be harder but that she could still do it. Women all over the world dealt with all manner of horrible things and still managed to fight their way back.

Why did I assume they had something that I didn't?

What if the way to be a stronger person who didn't take bullshit was simply to choose the next thing that led me in that direction, instead of waiting for someone else to help, or worrying about how to cross the finish line?

I knew what the Widow wouldn't do: stand around a bridge feeling sorry for herself. She would use the darkness to find her new North Star. As she said, strength wasn't a state; it was a series of choices. Which meant I needed to start making them. I tore the pendant from my neck, feeling the sting of the metal chain breaking, and hurled it into the river below.

The Delphine hotel's business center held a few computers and a printer. After ordering a pot of coffee and an egg salad croissant sandwich, I got to work. I pulled out my journal where I had carefully made the list of what I wanted to accomplish. I was tempted to cross out the item *Have Great Sex* but realized that while things had gone horribly wrong with Gabriel, it was still on my to-do list, although no longer with him. In the meantime, however, I added two bigger priorities.

1. **Stop being a doormat.**
2. **Make Gabriel pay.**

Then I settled in for a crash course in wine fraud. Turned out Gabriel hadn't been a particularly inventive con artist. The techniques he used were on the first few hits of my Google search "How do con artists fool you?" He was vague on details, letting me fill in the rest. There was a sense of urgency, that only he could help me navigate the jewelry stores, and that this big dinner event was a one-time shot. He took the things he knew about me and then spun a tale I wanted to hear. Instead of creating my own story, I lapped up the one he gave me.

Even the con he pulled was small potatoes compared with what was possible. There was a guy named Rudy from LA who had auctioned off millions of dollars of fake wine, $24 million at one auction alone. There was another guy, a European, who had allegedly discovered a rare stash of wine owned by Thomas Jefferson. He sold a single bottle alone for over $100K back in the 1980s. I couldn't decide if I was relieved that I hadn't gotten mixed up with a criminal mastermind or disappointed that Gabriel was so mediocre.

Gabriel had done the bare minimum: buying old bottles, filling them with cheaper wine, and creating fake labels. The bottle he sold me had likely been legit. A good con sprinkled some real bottles in as bait and then, when the customer was ready to buy a case, substituted the fakes.

If he hadn't screwed up the label, he likely would have gotten away with it.

Wine made for a perfect con. Some people bought bottles only to stick them in cellars, not intending to drink them for years, or ever. And if they did drink them, who wanted to admit after paying top dollar that they didn't think it tasted that great?

We believe what we want to believe. Hell, I knew that better than most.

I flopped back in the seat and stretched my hands and wrists while looking over my notes. Sophie was right. The local police would make some inquiries, but assuming Gabriel was smart enough to lie low, they wouldn't launch a countrywide manhunt. Interpol likely hadn't been contacted; he wouldn't be considered worth the effort.

If the police couldn't find him, how did I think I was going to? I'd snapped a photo of him that first night in the park. I supposed I could take it to various hotels around Paris and see if Gabriel had checked into any of them, but a quick search showed that there were over 1,500 hotels in the city, not counting Airbnb and other less official options. Not to mention he might have his own apartment in the city.

Kate MacIntosh

There were hundreds of antique stores and flea markets. I could circulate his picture, see if anyone had seen him buying up old bottles, then hope he'd used a credit card with his real name. All I would need was fluency in French, weeks more time to go to all the shops, and the luck of a thousand lottery winners.

I turned over our conversations to see if there was anything I'd overlooked. Working in insurance had taught me it was all about the details, filtering line by line to find out what was important.

I made a list of the things he had told me or that I knew objectively. His name was fake, so there was no point in searching that. He was knowledgeable about wine, at least enough to fool people who knew it better than I did. He knew the basics of classical music. He knew the artist Caillebotte had done the painting he liked even before he saw the museum label. He hadn't seemed to know most of the other impressionists that well, but I was certain he'd seen and liked that painting before.

He had said that painting was his favorite because he'd worked in construction when he was younger. I added that detail to the list. So, I needed to find someone with a construction background who liked to drink and could recognize a Mozart tune. How many of those could there be in the world?

Shit.

"Madame? Would you like more coffee?"

I was already jittery from the caffeine. "No, thank you."

"Anything else?" The waitress gathered up the debris of my afternoon spent in the business center onto her tray. Two empty cups and the plates holding only flakey remains of the egg salad croissant and a couple of salted caramel macarons.

I shook my head, then changed my mind. I wasn't going to figure anything else out today. "Actually, I'd love a glass of wine."

"Of course." She passed a thick creamy card-stock menu over to me. My eyes traveled down the list of what they offered by the glass. There was a Sancerre.

"I'll have this," I said, tapping the name on the menu.

"Of course. I will bring it right back."

"I'm going to move to the lobby." I stood stretching. I was still in Paris, after all. I should at least enjoy the view out the hotel window. Learning about cons had been interesting, but it hadn't given me any ideas of what to do next. I only had a week left in France and no idea how to best spend it.

After moving into the front room, I dropped into one of the velvet chairs, the Widow's book tucked under my arm. The waitress carefully placed my glass down on the white marble side table. If nothing else, I suppose I'd at least learned about wine on this trip. I could imagine dropping random facts at a dinner party when I was back in Chicago. As long as no one asked any follow-up questions, I'd sound very worldly.

I sat straight up. Gabriel had said something else that first day we met. Something about one of the wines. My mind strained to go back in time and pick out the conversation. It was a wine that went well with a picnic. Oat something. No. Haughty. No. Hot Palmer? Nothing was right.

I jumped up and went to the bar. "Excuse me, have you ever heard of a wine called Hot Palmer, Oat Palmer, something like that? It's a small vineyard."

The bartender's face crunched up in thought and then his expression cleared. "There is a Château Palmer, but it is not small. Or, ah, do you mean Haut-Palmer?"

"Yes! That's it!"

"I regret we do not have any here," he said. "Is the Sancerre unpleasing?"

"No, the Sancerre is great. Do you know where that wine, the Haut-Palmer, is made?"

"Oui. It is from Reims. The Champagne region, madame."

I could have reached across the bar and kissed him. Gabriel had said that wine was made near where he lived. What were the odds the bastard had headed home? It was all coming together. Sophie was there, and that was where the Widow was from—my only friends in France there to help me. It was destiny.

I knew what my next right thing to do was. I was going to Champagne.

Barbe-Nicole

■ REIMS ■

REGARDING THE EVENTS OF DECEMBER 1813

My sweet petite fille,

Far be it from me to chastise you, but I must also be honest. You allow yourself to become bothered too easily. While I recognize that you did not wish to see your former friend after all that had passed between you, to skip the event altogether was not the behavior I expect of you. There are people in this life with whom we do not wish to spend time. Words that we do not want to hear. Things we do not wish to do. However, to hide from them will not make them disappear and only makes us look the weaker for the avoidance. If you think I am being too harsh, know that I have learned this lesson through my own failures.

■ ■

"There is someone here to see you." Madame Martin stood at the door of my office.

I glanced up, annoyed. "I am not expecting anyone." There were not enough hours in the day as it was without people showing up un-invited. The stack of correspondence I hadn't dealt with threatened to topple. My head throbbed daily with worry, and the sight of our led-gers was enough to make me grind my teeth. The business for which I had given everything teetered on the brink. No one had thought the war could go on for so long. And with war came constant problems. The money I had set aside that I was sure would see me through was depleting at an alarming rate.

Since the debacle of Napoleon's defeat in Russia, more and more trade restrictions had been imposed. Other countries hoped to choke us off, to bring France to her knees. Our foreign orders had dried up. In theory, we could still sell here in France, but most of our country lacked the funds for champagne, let alone any cause for celebration. With the war growing closer, I had told Louis to not risk his safety with travel. It was best he should stay with his family. I wanted to ask him his opinion on what to do, but our long-ago fight had altered our relationship, and the distance between us now felt too vast.

Everyone in town was on edge. My wise cellar master, Pharaoh, had been right last year when he came to me with his concerns. The Russians were at last coming to France. The newsheets broadcast that troops were near the border. There were rumors the Cossacks were more monsters than human. Those in town talked of flight, but there was nowhere to go where the Russians wouldn't follow, and our homes were here. No, we would stay.

"It is Mademoiselle Margot," my housekeeper said, jolting me from my thoughts.

The Mouse? After all this time. Unease crept into my chest like the tide. "What does the girl want?"

"She would not say."

I drummed my fingers on the desktop as I considered my options. It was tempting to send her away. I did not wish to see her again; Margot was a sign of what I'd done.

"She asked me to give you this." My housekeeper passed over a handkerchief. The embroidery around the edges was novice yet tidy, but it was the initials in the corner, CC, done in faded pink silk, that caught my eye. Clémentine's.

"Send the girl in."

I fidgeted at the desk, trying to decide if I should stand or remain sitting, then was annoyed that I was at odds with myself. There was no reason for me to be nervous. I decided against standing. It was not as if she were an honored guest. I adjusted my sleeve, folding the fabric just so to hide an ink stain.

When she entered, I was glad I was seated. The sight of her may have buckled my knees. The years had been harsh to Margot. She was thin, far too thin, and her sunken cheeks made it clear she was missing teeth. She had the fishy stench of unwashed body about her. The Mouse scratched at her ill-fitting dress.

"Margot," I croaked. I had not thought about how far she may have fallen after leaving. I hadn't wanted to think about it. The guilt of my actions, which I'd managed to pack into a tiny part of my heart, bloomed and swelled now that she was in front of me.

"I come to ask you something," she said. Her reduced circumstances had not changed her attitude. She literally crawled with vermin, and yet it did little to alter her sense of pride.

"How did you get this?" I held up the handkerchief.

"Clémy gave it to me."

I twitched. "The nuns allow you to see my daughter?" I could not fathom how the good sisters, even if they encouraged charitable works, would allow young women of stature to consort with someone such as Margot.

The Mouse shrugged. "The nuns provide occasional food to those of us that need it. Clémy saw me and convinced Mother Superior to let me work in the laundry. She's a good and godly person, your girl. Kindhearted."

Is she implying I am not? "I see. I'm glad you found work as a laundress."

"The work is better than being a whore, but it pays worse." Her eyes didn't leave mine.

I flushed. Women did not speak of such matters.

"There was little else I could do. Not if I wanted to feed Bara," she said, although I had not asked her for any accounting of her choices.

She'd named her child after a revolutionary. Interesting. "You had a son," I said.

Mouse nodded, and her face softened. "He's a good boy. He's two years old now. You can tell he'll be a smart one."

I would have to speak to the nuns. Clémentine should not have contact with this woman or her son. She was entirely too tenderhearted. And the Mouse entirely too manipulative.

Margot straightened, as if deciding to focus on business. "I came to tell you that you need to fetch Clémy. She's not safe in Paris. I would have brung her, but I hadn't the funds to travel with another."

I shuddered to imagine Clémentine traveling with this woman. The roads to Paris were dangerous enough in a coach. "The weather and roads this time of year are too poor. I don't—"

"The Russians will be there soon."

"Bonaparte will hold Paris," I said with a conviction I suddenly didn't feel.

Margot shook her head. "He won't. Any who say thus are just wishing."

I fidgeted with the things on my desk. Foreboding clouds of memories of when I had to escape from my own school as a child crowded at the corner of my mind as my mouth grew dry.

Shaking my head to clear the dark thoughts, I forced the past back into its locked cage. That was then; this was now. I had known things were dire, but certainly not so bad that Paris itself would fall.

Margot scratched again at her sticklike arms. "There will be the sound of cannons in days. I know you don't want your daughter here, but you need to get her."

My head snapped up. "I love my daughter."

"I don't doubt that. But I suspect you find it easier to focus on business with her far away."

My mouth pinched. "You know nothing of my child or my relationship to her." My breath was shallow, as if my corset were too tight. Had I been too busy with thoughts of work to realize the dangers in Paris? I would have to find a way to get Clémentine. My brain spun with options and challenges, juggling them the way a player might. "I thank you for this message. I know you risked yourself to bring it." I reached to the desk to get some coins to pay her.

"It's not your money I've come to ask for."

I stiffened. "I see. And what have you come for?"

"I want my son to stay here. The coachman's family could take him in. Bara's a quiet boy, no trouble. Then when he's old enough, he could train to work with the horses, or in the kitchen. He is smart. I can tell."

"You want to leave me your son?" I'd rid myself of the Mouse, but just like real vermin, she would leave the place infested with more. It was one thing to pay her for warning me of the danger to Clémentine; it was another to expect me to support her child until majority.

Her chin thrust in the air with insolence, but I suspected it was to keep from crying. "I want him safe."

"I cannot impose on any of my staff to take in—"

"You impose your will whenever you want. All I ask is that you do it to save my child. You owe me."

I pulled back, ready to argue.

"I know you paid Henri to leave me."

I blinked. "I do not know what—"

"Do not lie," she snapped. "His brother told me. Henri left some of the money you paid him for the care of our child. He at least felt bad about what he'd done."

Standing, I placed my hands on the desk and leaned forward. I would not be lectured like a child. "Any action you took was your decision alone. I did not force you to bed the man." I pushed away the truth that I had known the man was trouble.

"If you wanted me gone so bad, you could have given me the money direct. You didn't need to give it to him."

Ha. Had I given the girl money, she would have returned every few months with her hand out for more and more. No, once I knew she was capable of telling the priest François's secret, she had to go. *And* she had to be discredited, so that the door back would be shut forever. I would not be shamed for saving my own reputation. And I hadn't known she would fall pregnant. I hadn't wanted this outcome for her. I could not be blamed for it all. "You wonder why I wanted you gone? After you used what you knew to get what you wanted?"

"I would never have shamed this family," Margot said.

The girl was a liar. She had done that very thing. I sniffed dismissively. "You would have done whatever it took to get what you wanted. Please do not pretend any loyalty to this house."

She stepped forward quickly, and I nearly put my foot through my own skirt as I moved back out of her reach.

"Yes, I did use what I knew. I wanted more for myself," she said. "Is that so bad? I wanted to be a lady's maid to raise my station." The Mouse was close enough that I could smell the sourness of her unwashed body. "I could have been a good lady's maid. The Revolution was supposed to change things. To make us all citizens, and yet those of you who have so much still find ways to make sure the rest of us have none. I love Clémy. I would have done right by the girl."

"You didn't know the last thing about being a lady's maid."

"I could have learned!" she cried.

I shook my head. This conversation was ridiculous.

"You learned, did you not, to run a champagne house?" Margot waved out the window to the fields outside. "You learned to blend the grapes, to do the books, to sell your wine. In town, they say your champagne is some of the best."

"Not some of the best, it *is* the best," I snapped back.

She smiled, as if satisfied. "You used what you had," Margot said. "The money from your family, your father-in-law's investment. You used the death of your husband, and the goodwill that gave you, to make your opportunity. You act as if what I did was so wrong, when you and your kind have used your advantages for centuries. Why did you begrudge me the chance to use what very little leverage I had?"

I pinched my mouth tight, and we stared silently across the desk at each other. How dare she say I used the death of my beloved? How dare she tell me what I did not want to hear? I forced my breathing to calm. "You confessed to the priest about François. You risked every-thing, and I did not, I will not, stand for that."

She shook her head. "I told no one what I knew."

Her lie cooled the fury in my chest and lifted any guilt. No one else had seen François with the bottle. It had been her. She lied now because she had nothing left, as no one would believe her.

"Someone on the estate will take in your son," I said calmly. "I do this for the past service you have done for the family, and for you coming here today for Clémentine. I do it because despite what you think, and despite how you have treated me, I am a good person."

"I did not betray you."

"You used what you knew to make your load lighter. To escape work. You would use me."

She nodded. "I would. And I admit it. Which is more honesty than you've shown. You dislike me because we are alike, and you dislike your daughter because she is so different from you. Perhaps the issue is not with either of us, but with yourself."

I wiped my sweaty palms on my linen skirt, glad the dark color would hide any mark. "I think it is best if you leave now. Madame Martin will give you food for the road and some coin. You can leave the child with her. I'll see that he's found a home with one of the staff."

"And given a position when he's older."

I paused; I didn't like how she had backed me into a corner. "I will not promise a position here." I raised a hand when she opened her mouth to argue. "But I will ensure the boy is trained in a skill. We shall see what he has an aptitude for when the time comes. Perhaps the horses or somewhere in the cellars."

"And you'll see that he's fed and kept safe."

"As much as I can in these times," I agreed.

With that, the fire went out of the girl. Her shoulders dropped and even the spark in her eyes dimmed. She suddenly seemed smaller. "Very well. I'll be gone. You'll tell Clémentine I wish her well?"

"I will."

Margot shuffled to the door and paused, then turned around. "We're a lot alike, you and I." She smiled and glanced about the furnishings of the room, taking in the silk-covered chairs and the oil paintings on the wall. "What I could have done if I had been born you, and not me."

"You shouldn't return here," I said. "It will be too hard on the boy if you are coming and going."

The Mouse nodded and then slipped out of the room.

I crossed the office and shut the door, my hands shaking. Her rudeness was almost more than could be borne. I reached for the decanter that I kept on the side table for guests, poured a glass of brandy, and downed it in one go.

Natalie

APRIL 23

I stepped off the train in Reims early in the morning, hauling my suitcase behind me. The sun beat down on the platform, and I instantly peeled off the sweater I'd worn for the trip. It had only taken an hour to get here from Paris on the express, not even long enough for a nap.

My roller bag thumped over the cobblestones as I walked toward the center of town. I'd considered calling Sophie to tell her I was coming, but I was afraid if I did, she'd try to talk me out of the plan. It was the same reason I hadn't called Molly. If Molly thought sleeping with a guy I barely knew was a bad idea, I was 100 percent convinced she'd think chasing down the same guy, who I now knew was a con artist wanted by the police, was a *really* bad idea.

Molly would also point out that "find Gabriel and make him pay me back" was a million miles away from being an actual plan. However, I did know the first step, which was to go to Sophie. Molly might observe that Sophie and I weren't friends; in fact, our entire relationship was built on a lie. It was also possible Sophie had been nice only because it was her job, and because she thought I was a widow, too, but I believed it was more than that. I liked her and she liked me. We might not be *friends*, but it didn't mean we weren't becoming so. I would tell her the truth about Will when the time was right.

Sophie might be putting a brave face on things, but Gabriel had screwed her over too. I was certain she'd be willing to help me. Or at least almost certain. I didn't have her home address, but I had found the address of her shop.

I stood outside. Taped to the door was a sign: CHAMPAGNE WIDOWS: ÉDUCATION ET BOUTIQUE DE VIN. As I peered through the grimy windows, it looked to me like there was a hell of a lot to do before opening would be even a remote possibility. In Paris Sophie had said her future wine bar was still in the renovations stage, but I hadn't realized that meant stage one. The building looked like it had last been inhabited around the early 1700s. A patina of dust covered every flat surface.

But I could see why she'd chosen the location. Large windows looking out on the narrow street would flood the space with natural light. The walls had built-in wooden shelves for display. The ceiling was high and crisscrossed with ancient wooden beams. Sophie emerged from a back room, and when she saw me peeking in the window, she dropped the box she was holding, her mouth falling open.

"Natalie?!" she yelled.

I waved and held up the bakery bag of treats I'd stopped to buy on my way.

Sophie stood there in shock, then shook her head and unlocked the door. Her hair was tied up Rosie the Riveter–style with a floral silk scarf. "Natalie from Paris! I cannot believe you are here. In my shop!" Her voice was loud and echoed around the space.

"Surprise!"

Sophie laughed. "It is very much a surprise. Natalie! From Paris!"

"Yep, it's me." I rustled the bag in the air. "Can I come in?"

"Of course." Sophie opened the door wider and waved me in. "I am afraid I am not ready to host you." She looked around at the mess. There were piles of construction supplies stacked in the corners, and a spider the size of a gerbil hustled for one of the corners of the beams in the ceiling. There was a musty, dusty smell that made me think the place had mice.

"Come, sit." Sophie motioned toward a small bistro table, a couple of coffee mugs still half-full sitting on it. She swooped them up by the handles and used her sleeve to wipe the table clear. "Let me get us some fresh coffee."

"Don't go to any bother," I said.

"If I can make coffee for the tradespeople who rarely show up and leave early with excuses when they do, I can certainly make coffee for a friend." She disappeared in the back and came out a moment later with two fresh mugs. "Now, tell me what brings you here?"

I wrapped my hands around the mug and inhaled the rich smell. "I wanted to see your shop."

Sophie laughed. "I am afraid there is not much to see yet."

"That's pretty." I motioned to a large wooden bar that dominated one end of the room. I opened the bakery bag, pulled a croissant out, and passed it over to her before grabbing one for myself.

"Merci." She took a tiny bite and smiled. "The bar needs to be sanded and cleaned, but it is walnut. I was lucky to find such a piece. But it will have to wait. First, I need to do some tile on the floor, paint the walls . . ." Sophie rolled her eyes. "Let us just say there are many things on the list before the bar."

"I can help," I offered. "I tiled both the bathroom and the kitchen in my old house. I can help you get it done. And I don't want to brag, but I'm a pretty damn good painter too."

"I cannot ask you to do that," Sophie said, shaking her head. "You should not spend your vacation time working."

"I don't mind. I'm happy to help." The truth was, I enjoyed this kind of project. Unlike so many things in life, there was tangible proof of progress when you did renovations. Something was a mess and then you made it into something better.

I could easily see Sophie's vision. When she was done, the shop would be quaint and cozy. She could use baskets to display extra items to go with the wine: bar towels, aprons, corkscrews. I brushed dirt from my jeans and glanced around. "You know, if we get the walls clean, we could start painting today. You'll want to do that before putting down any flooring, and trust me, a new coat of paint can make everything look a million times better."

Sophie appeared small as she looked around the space, surrounded by the building supplies, ladders, and the stack of tables she'd tucked in the corner. She'd guided me through Paris, but now it was clear how young she really was. I could tell she was overwhelmed. It was one thing to say you didn't care you were fired and that you were going to embrace your dream. It was another to stand in the middle of your dream's construction zone.

"This is supposed to be your grand French adventure. I would not be able to live with myself if you spent it here painting walls." Sophie smiled. "I tell you what: I will take today off and drive you around for a tour of the Champagne region. We will visit all the great houses. Including that of our friend, the Widow Clicquot."

"I don't want to mess with your work."

Sophie rolled her eyes. "You Americans, always with the working. One always has time for champagne and friends. But I cannot ask you to help me with the shop. We cannot have you painting walls when you haven't even gazed upon the Matisse they have in the Reims museum. You will see; it is beautiful."

Sophie reached over and squeezed my hand. "It touches me you would come here to see my dream and then offer to help. I know your trip has not gone as it should, but for you to extend this kindness says so much about you. Especially after so much loss in your life. We shall have a good time and then I will send you back to Paris to see real art, not this paint." She lightly kicked a can of paint on the floor.

A flicker of guilt fluttered in my stomach. Maybe I could wait to tell her about Will. "I have to be honest. I didn't come just to see you." I took a deep breath. "I'm going to find Gabriel."

Her expression clouded. "I do not think this is possible. It is like seeking one grape in an entire field. France is much too large."

I put my croissant down and leaned forward, excited to tell her. "But I don't need to search all of France. I'm almost certain he lives in one of the villages around here."

She pulled back, clearly confused. "How? Have the police said something?"

I shook my head. It was unlikely the police would share any details of their progress with me even if they had any. "I haven't told the police I'm in Reims. Technically, I wasn't supposed to leave Paris. I promised the detectives I would stay in town."

Her eyes widened. "Then you should return."

"If they can't bother to hunt down Gabriel, then I'm certain they won't come looking for the middle-aged American lady." I said this with a confidence that was more bluster than fact. Coming to Champagne was turning me into Bonnie minus a Clyde.

"I do not know, Natalie. To come so far on a guess . . ."

"It's not a guess—or, I suppose it is, but it's a good guess. The first time I met Gabriel he was talking about wine, and he mentioned a winery, Haut-Palmer. It's from here."

Sophie nodded. "Yes, I know this wine. It is one of the few houses in this region that make still wine instead of sparkling."

"Gabriel mentioned how much he liked that wine and that he knew it because it was made near where he grew up."

"So you have come to find him," she said, looking impressed. "How can you be sure he told you the truth? He is, after all, a professional liar."

I slumped back in the chair. "I don't know for sure, but I think he said it without thinking." When Will spun his lies about the affair, he had sprinkled them with things that were true. No one, not even an experienced liar, is able to remember everything. It made sense that minor details, things they didn't think were important, were left in their stories. "It isn't just the wine con. Remember my wedding ring? He took the money from the sale. The pendant he told me was in exchange was a fake."

Sophie nodded, her mouth set in a grim line.

"You don't seem surprised," I said.

"I feared when we met in the café that it was the case, but I thought perhaps if you didn't know for sure, there would be no extra pain."

"I can't keep hiding from things that are unpleasant," I said firmly. "I need to at least try to find him."

Sophie wiped the crumbs from her shirt. "Do you have a plan?"

A ripple of excitement ran through my body. "I do. But I could really use your help."

"Of course, I will help you in any way that I can."

"I have basically six days left before I fly home. I'll help you with the projects for your shop, but I'm also hoping to go to a bunch of the small towns and villages around here and ask about him." I fumbled for my phone in my back jeans pocket. "Look, I have a picture." I flashed the shot I'd sent to Molly from that first date.

Sophie leaned in and used her fingers to zoom in on his face. She looked up, shocked. "That is him! How lucky you were able to get your repaired phone back."

"I could drive around by myself, but I don't speak any French. And if French small towns are anything like American small towns, the locals are going to be reluctant to say anything to a total stranger."

Not to mention I was terrified by the idea of driving by myself. Even with GPS, I had zero sense of direction. Will had always been the one to do the driving on any of our road trips.

Postdivorce, I'd realized how many everyday-life tasks I had outsourced to my husband. Hooking up the printer, fixing the garbage disposal, spider killing, and auto navigation. My life was like a company that had massive layoffs and now everyone was wandering around trying to find someone who knew how to operate the coffee machine. I was determined to master everything I needed to know, but I wouldn't mind leaving the long-distance driving until I was back in my own country.

"People may be reluctant to talk," Sophie agreed. "But if they know he has been involved in wine fraud, they will want to help. Reputation is everything to these growers. Some of their families have been growing grapes on the same land for centuries."

I nodded. "That's another thing that makes me think Gabriel is from here. None of his fake wines were from this region. And he was careful with who he conned. He didn't pick average people; he picked people he figured could lose the money. I don't think he's completely thoughtless, but it still doesn't make it okay."

"I believe you have considered everything," Sophie said.

"He assumed I was an easy target," I replied. "Heck, I *was* an easy target, but not anymore. I'm going to find him and I'm going to make him pay me back every single dime."

"I can see he has pushed the wrong woman."

I couldn't tell if Sophie was impressed or worried that I was some type of revenge heat-seeking missile. Gabriel thought I was some rich widow who wouldn't even miss the money, but I was over letting people decide what I could afford to give. How could I explain that I'd spent my entire life making sure things were easy for other people? I was so busy every second of the day figuring out how to manage everyone else's emotions and desires that I forgot I had my own. I was sick of being disappointed in myself for this and ready to start doing something. I wasn't going to hide from unpleasant people and facts anymore. I was done wandering around trying to figure out how to pick up the pieces.

I knew what I wanted now. I wanted my money back. I wanted to prove to myself that I was through being that pliable doormat. And while I knew it didn't make any sense, I couldn't escape feeling that if I stopped Gabriel, it would get my entire life on the right track. And that if I didn't find him, then I was doomed to keep repeating the same mistakes over and over.

Sophie cocked her head. "And if I tell you that while I think it is noble you want justice, it would be better that you spend your time enjoying your vacation?"

"I would tell you no way," I said.

She smiled. "So be it."

I nodded and glanced at my watch. "Okay, what do you say we

clean this place until lunchtime? It will go faster with two people. If we get the walls washed, they can dry while we drive around looking for Gabriel. Then we can paint tonight and plan the next day."

"You've thought of everything," Sophie said.

"Plans are what I do," I said.

Sophie raised her coffee mug in a toast. "To your plan being a success."

I clinked my mug against hers. "To success!"

Barbe-Nicole

■ PARIS ■

REGARDING THE EVENTS OF JANUARY 1814

Anne, mon ange,

I adore that you think of me so fondly, but be aware it is much easier to appreciate one's great-grandmother than their mother. It is easier to hide one's flaws with time and distance. While too often women are taught to be modest, also do not allow too much pride in what you accomplish to keep you from reflection of your failures. There's much to be learned in both experiences. I am proud of all I have done, but I have often learned more in times when I have failed. There were times that I was so certain of my view (some may dare to call it a pigheaded perspective) that I missed the truth until it was too late.

■ ■

I was desperate to get Clémentine. The Mouse's words had burrowed into my mind and eroded my confidence. Had I kept my daughter away as punishment for being the type of girl I knew I could never be, innocent and pliable? If I had allowed my focus on work to take away from my duties as a mother, I would never forgive myself. It had taken nearly a week to ensure we would have fresh horses along the route, and I dared not even think of the cost. The money I had squirreled away to support myself and the champagne business was dwindling faster than water through cupped fingers. It had seemed like so much initially, but with the war dragging on, soon I would run out. I bit my lip, angry that I was once again thinking of business.

I had known the road to Paris would be difficult, but I had underestimated the deplorability of the conditions. The roads were little more than frozen mud, a chilling rain flew sideways in the wind, and all of Paris seemed to be trying to leave as we tried to enter. The entire journey I spent perched at the edge of the seat as if I could coax the horses to go faster, frightened that we may already be too late.

My father-in-law, Phillipe, insisted on accompanying me. I'd told him it wasn't necessary, but now I was ever so grateful. He was outside the convent guarding the coach with the driver, both of them armed. A coach with two horses was more valuable than gold when all of Paris wanted to flee.

As I stood in Clémentine's room, the distant sound of cannon fire like thunder, I shook in my boots, my bowels watery. The only thing that comforted me was the sight of my girl.

"Clémentine, leave your trunk," I demanded as my girl dawdled and fussed.

Her eyes were wide as saucers. "But, Maman, my things—"

"Are just things," I snapped. I regretted my tone immediately when her eyes filled. How quickly love can turn to impatience.

"Ma fille, your things will be here when you return," I said, forcing my voice to remain calm. There was no need to tell her that we needed to keep the coach as light as possible to put the least amount of strain on the horses. Speed would be our ally. "For now, just bring your most important items. Perhaps your doll."

Clémentine rolled her eyes. "I am too old for dolls, Maman. I am nearly fifteen." She surveyed her corner of the room. "I will need my poetry text. And my friend Renée made this for me." She scooped some knitted item to her chest as if it were a babe.

I nodded, a thin, tight smile on my face. "That sounds perfect. Be sure to take an extra shawl. It is chilly." The truth was it was freezing. My hands burned with the cold.

"I will have one of the sisters place a hot brick from the kitchen in the coach," Mother Superior said from the doorway. "It will help to keep your feet warm."

I nodded my thanks. The two of us exchanged a glance as the cannons roared again in the distance. Was humanity doomed to always be at war?

"Come, darling, it is time we made our departure." I put my hand firmly on Clémentine's back and guided her toward the stairs.

"Is there anything I can do to assist you, Reverend Mother?" I asked as Clémentine descended, still muttering about her classwork.

She shook her head. "Most of the girls have gone home, or to stay with relations here in the city. The nuns and I will ensure those that remain are safe. We can retreat to the church crypt if needed."

I nodded, knowing there would be little the sisters could do if the Russians beat down the doors to the abbey. They would need to pray that the Russian reputation for destruction did not extend to children or those with holy orders.

We paused at the door, the wind outside howling. Clémentine

waved a greeting to her grandfather, but he didn't take his eyes off the street beyond. The coachman faced the other direction, both of them on edge, with their guns resting in the crook of their arms. My mouth was dry with anxiety. The relief I had felt when we pulled into the school dissipated as I realized we still had to return to Reims. At least this time we wouldn't be going against the flood of people.

Mother Superior pressed a rosary into my hands and made the sign of the cross in the air between us.

"Wait!" Clémentine cried. "What about Monsieur Souris?"

I looked at Mother Superior in confusion. Mister Mouser?

"He's a cat. He belongs to no one, but Clémentine has affection for him."

"Darling, the cat will be fine. We must go."

Clémentine stamped her foot. "Monsieur Souris relies on me. I cannot simply abandon him!" She called his name and made a clucking sound as she clapped her hands together, wandering the small courtyard.

Dear God, the Russians would storm the city and we would still be here seeking some flea-bitten bag of fur.

"We do not have time," I insisted.

"One does not leave someone they love because times are difficult," Clémentine stated, her face set with determination.

Her tone stopped me short, and without further discussion both Mother Superior and I began to call for Mister Mouser, our voices tinged with desperation.

After a moment, a thin gray cat, like a liquid shadow, appeared and ran toward Clémentine and pressed against her skirt. I couldn't imagine it would ever allow her to touch it, let alone permit itself to be bundled up into a coach. However, perhaps the cat understood the dangers ahead better than my daughter, for he submitted willingly to her grasp.

"We can go now," Clémentine said, standing with the bearing of a queen, the creature tucked under one arm. The two of them clambered inside the coach, and I watched her with a sense of pride.

"Que Dieu vous protège," Mother Reverend said, making one more quick sign of the cross.

"May God keep you safe as well," I replied as I climbed up into the carriage, and with a jolt, we were off.

■ ■

Hours later my bones ached as we bounced over the ruts in the frozen mud along the road. For an exorbitant amount we had hired fresh horses not too far out of the city and were making decent time. I pushed away the worry that it was an expense we could ill afford. My eyes were gritty with exhaustion, but I was too afraid, and too cold, to give in to sleep.

Clémentine lay on the seat next to me, buried under the blankets we had brought. Her rosebud lips parted as she slept. The cat, despite my efforts to discourage him, had curled up in my lap and promptly fallen asleep as well. Now I found myself grateful for the extra warmth even as his claws kneaded the fabric of my dress, pulling threads free as he dozed. I wondered if Monsieur Souris knew how his life circumstances had improved so much for the better. And if he was aware he was destined for a bath, should he wish to live inside my home.

Philippe sat across from me, occasionally pulling the leather curtain in the window aside and staring out into the dimming light. He still held the gun on his lap. He was in his seventies. By all rights he should be home in front of his fireplace on a winter's evening enjoying a glass of brandy, not here on the road.

"I'm glad to have her with me," I said softly, so as to not wake my daughter. "My cousin would have taken her in, but I feel better with her in my sight."

Philippe nodded, his face softening at the sight of his grand-daughter. "Moi aussi." He chuckled. "And the way she would not leave the cat, cannons booming and her still searching."

I shook my head in annoyance. "She can be willful."

"Yes, but like her mother, I suspect it will serve her well," he said with a smile. "And she is loyal to those she loves."

"Like her father," I said. Clémentine had so many of his tender traits. Perhaps they bothered me because I fretted that they would leave her vulnerable, as it had my husband. We rarely brought up François's name. The years had dulled the pain of his loss, but it was still there, like a bruise you press on occasionally to remind yourself of the hurt.

"When he was a boy, François found this turtle and wanted to make it a pet. Did he ever tell you that?"

"A turtle? No."

"He insisted on having it in his room. It crawled away, no doubt seeking its way back to the pond. It died, but we could not find where it was hiding. His mother was so angry about the smell." Philippe chuckled. "I had forgotten about that until now. You think you will remember everything, that there is no way you will forget, but memories slip into the cracks and out of sight before you know it."

"Like the turtle."

He winked at me. "Yes, like the turtle."

"Do you think we're safe now that we're so far from the city?" I asked after a moment, aware that he had no way of knowing more than I what lay ahead, but still wanting his assurances.

"If the driver can keep the coach from overturning, and we can avoid any ruffians, then yes, I think we will be fine. The Russians will still need a few days, maybe a week, to take the city."

"How long until they reach Reims?"

Philippe shrugged. "Not long. It may go better than we fear. Rumor has it that the Russian generals are keeping their men in check. They haven't destroyed the towns they've already taken. But they are eating and drinking their fill, so the cupboards are likely to be bare when this is done."

"I've hidden most of the 1811 wine," I admit. "Pierre walled it up in the cellar. I know the troops will take what they want, but with luck, they won't find the best of it."

"The officers will search for soft mortar. They'll know what to look for," Philippe said, his voice tense.

"The mortar is long dry. I started over a year ago."

An enormous smile spread across Philippe's face. "You are a genius. If our government was run by you, we would not be in this position."

I warmed at his words. "I think Napoleon will fall," I admitted.

His expression darkened. "As do I." He checked out the window again. "He's not a man to bet against in a fight, but he is still a man. There are limitations even to the mighty Bonaparte."

"We are fighting the Russians now, but when peace comes, they will be the ones to buy our wine."

Philippe nodded. "They say the czar cannot get enough champagne."

"The first to get their wines into the hands of the Russians will take the market," I said.

Philippe appraised me. "True. But the trade blockades will keep everyone out until there is peace. To circumvent the blockades could be considered treasonous."

"Wine doesn't know politics," I replied, gritting my teeth as the wheels bounced through a particularly deep rut. I prayed we didn't break an axle.

Philippe grimaced. If I found the ride uncomfortable, I could only imagine how he felt.

"If someone were caught trying to sneak champagne through the blockade, it would all be confiscated," Philippe replied. "Wine may be neutral, but men are not."

"This is why they should allow women to run all things," I said.

He chuckled. "Perhaps, my belle-fille." His face grew serious. "I am proud of you. What you have accomplished is impressive for a woman or a man. Few I can think of could have done better in these difficult times. You have been a good steward of the land and the name Clicquot."

My throat grew tight. We were not a family to speak of emotions. "Merci." I stroked the cat in my lap, enjoying the thrum of its purr through the fabric of my dress. "It has not always been easy, but I take great pleasure in the business." There was again that distant twinge that I took too much pleasure in business. That it pushed out all other things and people.

Philippe sighed. "It is not easy for me to admit, but you have done better than François would have."

"No," I hastened to say. "That is not true."

He reached over and patted my knee. "It is all right, dear girl. As I have grown older, my vision for the world and objects around me has grown weaker, but my vision for myself and those close to me has become stronger. That is one of the few benefits of aging. One may not be able to read the small print in a book, but one knows themselves much better. The energy to keep falsehoods up and dancing as distractions becomes too wearying." He sighed. "François had many talents, but you are better at running a business."

"François was a wonderful man," I said.

Philippe nodded. "He was indeed." He motioned toward Clé-mentine. "You discover as a parent that it is hard to let go of your own hopes and wishes for a child to let them be who they are. I always felt that perhaps I should have done more for François."

"You were a good father," I protested.

"At times. Other times I failed him." He waved off the argument I was about to make. "I struggled with his moods. It frustrated me when he could not see the reasons for joy. You would see the clouds come over him and then there would be nothing one could do."

I lowered my eyes. When François fell into a period of darkness, it was a very deep pit.

"Before he died, we had cross words." Philippe looked out into the countryside. "It is one of my deepest regrets. He was back from Germany and still abed days later complaining of illness. I suspected it was not a fever, more likely one of his states. I came by the house, and you were in the office working. It angered me that he was not the one conducting business. He claimed sickness, but I accused him of coming up with excuses. I told him he had a wife, a daughter, and a business, that there was no time for weakness and lying about."

His confession stole the breath from my lungs.

"I didn't say that he wasn't a man, but—" Philippe's voice cracked with emotion, and he stared down at his lap. "I was unkind."

My hand grasped his and squeezed. "François knew you loved him."

"I hope so, but I fear he also knew I was embarrassed by him. Frustrated that he couldn't be the man I thought he should be. I held expectations that were unfair." He shrugged. "We so often dislike in others what we do not have the strength to recognize in ourselves."

His words cut my heart.

"And then when he died just a day later . . ." Philippe shook his head, unable to continue.

I sent up a prayer of thanksgiving that I had never unburdened myself of the details of François's death with his family. I patted Philippe's hand, making a comforting sound.

He sighed and leaned back, his eye releasing a single tear. "There was an apothecary bottle mislaid from our home. Poison for the rats. When François passed, I feared for a long time that he . . . that he might have . . . that I had pushed him to . . ."

"No," I said. This was not a lie. Any decision François had made had always been his own.

"At one point, I confessed my fears to the priest."

My heart seized. "*You* spoke to Father Joseph?"

"Yes, but it was a mistake. I forgot that God is forgiving, but a priest is no God." Philippe looked at me. "Don't appear so concerned, Barbe-Nicole. I realized I had given in to despair by speaking to him, wanting him to cleanse me of my worries. A mislaid bottle meant nothing. I had to let go of these thoughts."

I tried to respond but was only able to mumble an incoherent word.

"Now look what I have done. I have upset you needlessly, my dear. I shouldn't have spoken of such things."

"No, it's all right," I managed. "I didn't know."

"There's no need to drag up old worries. There are plenty of new ones to contend with. What happened with François is most likely exactly what it appeared to be, a fever." He smiled softly. "And if it was not, then that is between François and God, not you and I, or any other."

"I don't believe a loving God harbors anger," I said.

He shook his head. "Nor I, my sweet girl. I believe that when the good Lord takes us from this earth, he will ask us two questions. It is our answer to those questions that determines the outcome of our everlasting souls."

"What are the two questions?" I asked, now nervous.

"What did you do with the talents that were given to you by God, and what did you do with the time you had on this earth? Nothing more. Nothing less."

I nodded and absently patted the cat on my lap. I had done some good, but I had also cast out a young woman for a wrong she had not committed. I punished those around me for holding a mirror to the traits in myself that I either lacked or disliked. My throat was tight with shame. I vowed more patience with my daughter and to reach out to Louis. I vowed to do better so I could face those questions when the time came.

Natalie

APRIL 27

I hung on to the steering wheel with a death grip, hating every second of the drive. I had no one else to blame. I'd volunteered to take the car on my own. Honestly, how this thing was allowed on the road without first needing to be wound up with a rubber band was beyond me.

Operation Find Gabriel had started off great, with Sophie and me bombing around small towns in her clownishly tiny Citroën. But despite our best efforts, there had been no progress in days. There were entirely too many small towns in this region, and exactly zero indications anyone had seen or known Gabriel.

Last night as we split a bottle of wine, our feet up on an empty box of glassware, Sophie had declared it a lost cause. I couldn't blame her for wanting to give up. Even if Gabriel had told the truth about being from this area, there was no guarantee that he'd returned.

Sophie hedged until I pressed her, and she admitted that she didn't have the time to drive me from one end of Champagne to the other. She needed to focus on the shop. In a few days she had a meeting with a city official for the final step of her business license approval. I'd felt a wave of shame at taking advantage of her willingness to help. This was my project, not hers.

Which was how I ended up white-knuckling a drive in Sophie's clown car down a path that seemed more sheep trail than road. I'd offered to pick up some used stools she'd purchased for the bar, leaving her free to work at the shop. I ground the gears as I tried to shift into a higher speed. The car behind me was so close we were practically riding piggyback. Barbe-Nicole had to deal with Cossacks hot on her tail as she escaped Paris; I had this guy in a Renault.

French road signs bore little resemblance to those back home. There would be a number that could be anything from the speed limit to the road name, or another alarming incomprehensible sign that was simply an exclamation point circled in red. I'd passed another that had the outline of a horn with a line through it and wondered if wandering jazz bands were that much of a problem in rural France.

Finally, I spotted a tiny patch of dirt on the side of the road that was just big enough to fit a chunky cocker spaniel. Or this car. I slowed down and pulled off. The other driver careered past with a blare of his horn.

I sat letting my heart rate return to normal. It would have been better if I had stuck to the larger road, but this was where I had broken my word to Sophie. I told her I would pick up the stools and then drive straight back to Reims to finish the grout, but I'd decided to take a small side trip.

While I understood she didn't have any time, it didn't seem like it would hurt for me to ask around in the village where I was picking up the stools. No one in the bakery had admitted to speaking

English. The gas station attendant had simply shrugged his shoulders as he smoked, apparently unconcerned with the risk of explosion as he pumped gas.

However, the woman who loaded the barstools into Sophie's car—in a game that appeared to defy the laws of physics—gave me a lead. She didn't recognize the photo of Gabriel but told me that two towns over there was a union hall for people working in construction. If he had worked in that profession, there was a chance someone there would know his real name.

I knew Sophie would think it was a waste of time, but if I didn't check, I'd never forgive myself.

I poured water from my water bottle onto the hem of my shirt and lightly dabbed my face and neck. I missed Molly. She was the kind of friend I would have normally counted on to stay on the phone with me while I made a stressful drive. The past several days were the longest we'd gone without talking in years. I couldn't be mad at her for not calling. I'd told her to give me space. But now I found the space lonely.

My finger hovered over my phone, then I shoved it back in the console. I was five minutes out from the town with the union hall. I gripped the steering wheel and focused. If the Widow could make it all the way to Paris and back in a coach in January during a war, I could make this drive.

■　■

The phrase "union hall in France" might lead a person to picture a medieval guild, with soaring timber-braced ceilings and heraldic shields mounted along the wall. Alas, it looked more like a Department of Motor Vehicles office somewhere in rural Indiana. Lots of cheap Formica counters, metal filing cabinets, plastic chairs, and staff with the eyes of people resigned to their own slow death by bureaucracy.

The good news was that I had found a clerk who watched a lot of crime documentaries as a hobby and was thrilled to be a part of my investigation. The bad news was that she'd found nothing.

The clerk heaved a thick binder onto the counter. "This is the final place I can think to look."

I plucked at the dusty binder.

"Sorry it is so old-fashioned. I have tried to take our office digital, but half of the management here still believe mobile phones are too new." She flipped pages and then turned the book to face me. "These are pictures from a conference last year. Perhaps he is in the crowd?"

I scanned the faces, hoping to see Gabriel's sly smirk looking back, but there was nothing. I checked the following pages. Groups of people clustered around tables in a banquet room. Speakers at a lectern, faces serious. Other photos of people standing next to booths in the trade hall advertising power tools and cement. Not a single shot of Gabriel.

"He's not there." I deflated like a slowly leaking balloon. I'd been so certain that if I kept looking, I'd find him. I'd risked my life driving here and for nothing. "Are you sure you can't think of anything else?"

The clerk sighed. "If we had his correct name, and if he were a member of the union, then I could find his address in our system. Or if not an address, one of the past contractors might know how to locate him. But, without his name . . ." Her voice trailed off.

I couldn't fault her for trying. She'd studied his picture with the focus of a neurosurgeon about to cut into someone's brain.

"I am certain he is not a contractor," she said. "They come the most often here to the office. But the laborers?" She shrugged. "They are not here so very much. Some of the old-timers are more active with organizing labor marches and protests, so they are well known, but otherwise it is hard to say. Do you know the last time he would have worked as a laborer?"

I shook my head. I couldn't even be certain that he did. One throwaway comment about liking a painting because it showed people redoing a floor wasn't exactly like getting a sneak peek at his résumé. It was possible he'd helped a family friend with a home project. Hell, after all I'd done to help Sophie over the past few days, I could consider myself a construction worker, but it didn't make me eligible to join the union.

"You may try asking at the Mastiff. It is a bar. I know it is quite popular with our members." She shrugged. "Maybe someone there would know him?"

My ears pricked up. "Like a wine bar?" That would be a place I could imagine Gabriel.

She wrinkled her nose. "No, more like a bar where the tables are sticky. Many people go there to watch the footie games on TV."

I couldn't picture Gabriel in his custom suits tossing back beer, but I would still check it out. It wasn't like I was flush with any other great ideas. "Can I walk to the bar from here?"

"Oh no, it is a village over, Épirinal, maybe ten or twelve kilometers to the east."

Great. More driving.

"I really appreciate your help."

"I will hope for you that you find the bad guy. Maybe your story will be a podcast!" She said this with the same level of excitement as if I had a chance to win a Pulitzer Prize.

"If it becomes a podcast, I'll be sure they interview you," I said.

Her eyes lit up. "That would be fantastique!"

I trudged back down the stairs, my stomach rumbling. I was going to have to stop for lunch soon. Checking the time on my phone, I wondered how long it would take me to stop at the bar. Of course, the village was in the opposite direction from Reims. Sophie was going to wonder what happened to me. I'd have to tell her about this side trip.

When I stepped onto the street, it took me a second to identify what was wrong.

The car was gone.

I looked up and down the road. It was a small car, but still large enough that it shouldn't have been able to hide. I pinched the bridge of my nose, closed my eyes, and then opened them again in case the car was playing some type of elaborate peekaboo.

Had someone stolen the car?

I patted my pocket. I still had the keys.

An old man leaning against the entrance to the union hall smiled at me as he picked a loose piece of tobacco that had come from his hand-rolled cigarette from the tip of his tongue. "American woman, you are missing your automobile, yes?"

"Yes! Did you see who took it?" I dashed to his side, ready to call the cops, then I paused. Could I call the police, or was my name flagged as a fugitive on the run?

The man gave a chuckle, which slid into a liquid cough that made him sound one step from a raging case of TB. I went to pat him on the back, half-afraid chunks of his lungs were going to splatter down on the sidewalk, but he waved me off.

Gaining control of himself, he took a deep drag of his cigarette as if it were the pesky oxygen that had caused the problem. He took a few inhales as he gathered himself.

"Oui, I did see who took your car." His eyes twinkled with mischief.

Was this where he told me it was him before dragging me into a panel van, making it a dual car-woman-napping situation?

"It was the tow truck!" he crowed finally. He seemed disappointed I didn't find this as amusing as he did.

"My car was towed?" My stomach went into a free fall. Sophie was going to be pissed.

He nodded. "You park where you should not."

"How was I supposed to know—"

The man pointed to an incomprehensible sign. Merde.

Barbe-Nicole

■ REIMS ■

REGARDING THE EVENTS OF FEBRUARY 1814

My darling girl,

I am surprised you wish to hear tales of those darker times. At first no one who lived in those days wanted to speak of it at all, as if we could deny things that happened. Then we wanted to talk, but our children had no interest in the past. Perhaps this is the benefit of living a long life. The generations that follow find us intriguing. Very well, I will tell you of when the Russians came to Reims. It was a time when my life held so many clouds that I wondered if the storms would ever break and there would be sun. When you face these times, you must remember to not borrow tomorrow's fears today, as they will keep you from action. And when all seems darkest, reach toward those who are reaching out to you. You are a brave and independent girl, which you know I admire, but do not be so independent as you miss the value of good friends.

■ ■

I fixed a smile upon my face like armor as I strode out to meet the Russians. It was easier now that they were here. The waiting had been harder. The night before, I had heard them in the streets. Thousands of men streaming into the city, dreaming of their homes back east. And this morning there were four soldiers on horseback invading my courtyard, dressed in their dark-green jackets, brass buttons polished but white trousers streaked with dust. A man in a plumed hat with a braided aiguillette nudged his horse forward.

"Welcome," I said, as if this were a planned visit and not an invasion. My stomach churned and my ribs felt too tight to hold my beating heart. My mind strained to race about searching for all the ways things might go horribly wrong, but I held it at bay. Panic could be deadly.

"Madame Clicquot?"

I bowed my head and risked a glance back at the house. I'd ordered Clémentine to remain hidden with my lady's maid, but I half expected to catch her peeking out from a window. The entire staff was agog to see the foreign troops. Rumors had swirled about them, from sharpened teeth to their being the size of bears, but of course the truth was duller. They were simply men.

The rumors my father-in-law heard had proved to be correct. The Russian generals had held an iron grip on their troops thus far. There had been none of the destruction or rampant violence that had been feared, but I knew that in these situations, things could tip to the other direction at any moment. I had no intent of risking my most precious resource, my daughter. The maid was under strict instructions that if there was any hint of trouble, she was to take Clémentine and disappear into the cellars beneath the house. With miles of stone tunnels beneath the city, they could hide or seek refuge with another family in the village until it was safe.

"We've heard of your champagne and have come to try it for ourselves," the ranking officer called out in French.

"I'm grateful to know my wine's reputation for excellence has spread," I replied. I motioned to Pharaoh, who came forward with bottles in hand. The officer grabbed one, the horse dancing back and forth as if it, too, were excited for a taste. Between controlling the horse and keeping his grip on the bottle, the man was unable to open it. I could see his growing frustration.

Mon Dieu, was I expected to be hostess as well? Was it not enough that they were going to take the wine without payment? Did I have to open it for them? Put out some cheese and bread, perhaps?

"Use your blade," I suggested. "It seems appropriate for conquering heroes, after all."

The officer stared at me, trying to decipher if I was being sly or fawning. He quickly pulled his saber from its sheath with a metallic whisper as one of his men held the horse's reins. The other officers cried out what I assumed to be encouragement in Russian. Holding the bottle by the base, he ran the blade up the side of the glass. With a quick blow he decapitated the bottle, the froth of the champagne burbling over the side and dripping into the dirt.

The officer laughed, tipped the bottle up to drink, and guzzled down a vast quantity.

"Perhaps not the wisest plan to remind them to use their weapons," Pharaoh said, quietly enough that his voice didn't carry to the Russians.

"It is all right. They are but boys playing games," I said, hoping I spoke the truth. We both watched the other officers slice the tops from their bottles, one of them nearly taking off his thumb in the process. They were unlikely to hurt any of us, provided we gave them what they wanted. While this idea comforted me, I still watched them closely, like a bird watches a cat.

Pharaoh was unable to control his expression. He looked at the officers with distaste as they drank, spilling almost as much wine on their uniforms as down their throats.

"Today they will try for free," I told him in a whisper. "But they will develop a taste, and someday they will pay handsomely for my wines."

"Madame, your champagne is excellent," the officer declared.

I lifted my chin in pride. "I already know this, sir. Perhaps you could be so kind as to give that review to the czar when you return home."

He threw his head back and laughed. "Indeed, madame, I shall." He lifted the bottle in the air. "To the Widow!"

"To the Widow!" the officers repeated, already beginning to look fuzzed from the wine. Or perhaps it was the ease of their victory. I allowed myself a small amount of relaxation. They were less an army at this point and more men on a holiday trip through the French countryside. Drinking our wines, eating our food, with no regard or concern. Napoleon was not yet to be counted out, but there were few now who remained confident in his eventual victory.

The officer motioned over his shoulder, and two infantrymen hustled forward through my gate, leading a mule-driven cart that groaned and creaked.

"The men will load your wines, madame."

"My cellar master will show them the way." I bent slightly at the waist, gesturing them forward.

Pharaoh and I exchanged a glance. This was the moment of greatest risk. Moët's cellars in Épernay had been looted of nearly every bottle. With luck the Russians would be satisfied with the crates easily located and not go searching further. The vintages we had walled up would hopefully stay hidden. Even I could barely spot the difference in mortar and brick, and I knew where to look.

But if they were to discover our subterfuge, there would be a heavy price to pay. If they knew we'd lied . . . My mouth went dry, and my barely held facade of control threatened to crack.

Watching the crates being carried out and loaded onto the cart, I nearly allowed myself to give over to weeping. Each of those bottles represented hours upon hours of labor. It was time caught and suspended in liquid form. One could never get the past back, but for a moment, a person could taste it.

My gaze strayed to the cellar workers, who watched the Russians with a mix of disdain and fear. I knew they trusted me to see them through these difficult times. I was afraid to let any of them know that I didn't know how much longer I could do it. I shoved the fear down, walling it away like my wine. I could do nothing today about those worries, so there was no reason to entertain them.

My coachman stood at the gate, his mouth in a snarl holding back what he likely wished to say to the troops. At least the Mouse's son, Bara, was thriving. The coachman's family had taken him in. With eight children of their own, one additional small boy hardly seemed to make a ripple. The coachman's wife had taken one look at the lad and pulled him toward her skirts like she was a roosting hen and he a chick trying to escape. She'd fattened him up and now the boy looked at full health when I saw him about the estate. It was almost enough to dampen my guilt.

"We will take our leave of you now, Madame Clicquot."

My attention back on the men in my courtyard, my eyes instantly tallied up the wine on their cart. One of my field workers hoisted the last basket filled with straw and bottles into place. The lost inventory would be painful, but not too deep a blow. We had fared better than Moët.

Two of my field workers went to the gates so we could close them behind the officers. It would do nothing if the soldiers wanted to return, but it made me feel better to pretend to have the rights to my own space. I should count myself lucky they had not commandeered the house for their troops, but it is hard to count your blessings while you are still cursing misfortune.

As the gates shut with a clang, I noticed the bearing of one of my laborers, straight-backed and walking with almost a swagger. Could it be?

My hand shot to my chest when he turned to face me. Louis!

I lifted my skirts and ran down the drive to greet him, not caring that I was behaving in a way that did not suit my station.

"Louis!" I embraced him and felt him go rigid at the unusual affection. I pulled back, looking him up and down, his clothing dusty and worn. "What in the heavens?"

"You wrote that I should come."

"But you look like you were dragged behind your horse on the trip."

"I arrived in town just before the troops and thought it best to not draw attention to myself. A traveling man coming to your home could be seen as someone from Napoleon's army. I've risked being called a spy enough, thank you very much."

"Come inside, I want to hear of your journey." My eyes filled with tears at the sight of him. Striding back inside, I barked for Madame Martin to have drinks and refreshment sent to the parlor.

Louis stood near the door. He stank of horse and sweat, and I had rarely been so glad to see another. When I had written to him I wasn't sure he would come. His face was lined and creased. It struck me how much older he was, how long we had worked together—and then it occurred to me that I, too, must look older. The years were sliding past. My throat grew tight.

"Please sit." I motioned for him to join me. He hesitated for a moment and then dropped into a chair.

The maid bustled in with a tray, the china clattering atop it. Everyone was still on edge from the army arriving. Louis was lucky she didn't spill the entire thing down his jacket.

"I didn't recognize you in that outfit," I said. I poured coffee for the both of us and placed his in front of him.

Louis had become a bit of a dandy in the past few years. His German wife had a love for fine fabrics and prints, and her appreciation of color had rubbed off on him. He said the fancy dress made him memorable, which, for a salesman, was a trait to be admired, but I suspected he liked it. His favorite was a bright-yellow waistcoat that shone like a hen's egg yolk in the light. He called it lucky and wore it whenever he could.

He brushed his hands against his coarse woolen trousers, his mouth curled in distaste. "Yes, I apologize for my state. I intended to wash up before seeing you, but when I heard there was a detachment of officers coming here, I wanted to come as quickly as possible."

There would have been little he could do had the meeting with the Russians not gone well, but I appreciated his loyalty. He quickly devoured the small slice of cake on the plate, and I made a mental note to make sure the cook fed him. Who knew how long he had been without a proper meal.

"It seemed they did not take too much," Louis said, brushing the crumbs from his face.

I lifted my shoulders in weary agreement. "I did what I could to hide the best for sale later."

"As long as the blockades exist, there will be no sales," Louis sighed. "I never believed I would say it, but I almost wish Bonaparte would fall so that we can declare the war finished."

The end of the war was all anyone wanted to discuss, but for once, my mind wasn't on politics or the impact of it on business. "I asked you to come because I need to speak to you." I fidgeted in my seat. Now that that time had arrived, I felt as awkward as a child. Embarrassment and humility were not emotions that fit me well. He cocked his head, appearing leery.

I took a sip of my coffee before putting it down. I felt as anxious as I had with the Russians. "I owe you an apology."

Louis blinked but made no other response.

"You have been a loyal employee," I continued. I had practiced this speech in my head dozens of times, but now that the man was in front of me, the words had slipped away. "You have offered me good counsel and I was wrong to have spurned your assistance in the past."

"I was wrong to overstep my position."

"Your position as a salesperson perhaps, but not your role as my friend." Now that the words had flown from my mouth, I felt naked. I fussed with my skirts, unable to meet his eyes. "There are few that I trust in this world, few who have supported me in this plan to run this house, and you have been one. I was angry because you told me what I did not want to hear. I realize now that the truth is one of the most valued things a person can offer."

"The truth is that I hold you in the highest estimation," Louis said. "It would be one of the great honors of my life should you consider me a friend in addition to your employee."

A tear spilled down my cheek and I wiped it away quickly. I didn't trust myself to speak. We sat in silence for a moment and then I cleared my throat. "I have need of your advice. In a matter not related to the business." I motioned for him to eat the slice of cake that had been brought for me.

"You were right. It was a mistake to let the girl, Margot, go. I behaved poorly. I have been trying to find her to fix the situation but have not had any luck. I tried the school, as she worked there briefly, but Mother Superior said Margot has not returned to them. She was doing some work . . . entertaining, but I don't know how to find her at that type of establishment." My cheeks flamed red.

"Would she find work in a finer bawdy house that served gentlemen?"

I thought of Margot's sunken cheeks and shook my head. "No. She's not likely associated with any formal establishment. I would pay for any information."

He broke the cake in half and swallowed a large piece whole. "To pay would be the beginning of giving away money endlessly. There are many struggling in the city. There would be sightings of her on the hour, all from people with their hands out. Are you even certain she is in Paris?"

I shook my head.

"The best plan may be to wait. Surely, she will come back to see her son."

I plucked at my top skirt, unable to meet his eyes. "I told her not to return."

"I see."

My thoughts swirled with what may have become of the maid. I tried to not consider how she might fare on her own with foreign troops in the city. Not a sou to her name. At night, my brain played over our last conversation. How I hadn't believed her. How she'd accused us of being cut from the same cloth and I rejected the truth. How I had left things up to Henri so that I could play the innocent. I flushed with the shame of it all.

"I wronged the girl," I said, my voice cracking.

Louis nodded.

I appreciated that he did not argue with me. I hadn't told him all of what I'd done; I would take that secret to my grave. If I was unable to find Margot, there would be no way to repair the situation. We cast ourselves as the hero of our own stories, and it is humbling to realize you have acted as a villain. My entire life, I had taken pride in my ability to think ahead, to cope with challenges. But this was a situation that could not be righted through sheer will.

"You know what they say when there is a heavy burden?" Louis asked.

I shook my head.

"That it is lighter once shared." He reached his hand across the table, and I grasped it as if it alone would keep me from falling.

Natalie

APRIL 27

Sophie had arranged for a friend to drive her to the village so that she could get the car from the tow lot. I'd tried to pay, but she'd ignored my offer, slapping her card onto the counter with a sharp snap. Her face was as dark as the storm clouds the Widow was worried about.

On the drive back to Reims, I apologized several times. I explained I'd only meant to pop into the union hall for a moment, but she didn't even glance over. Her hands held the steering wheel firmly, as if she thought I might try to wrest it from her control. You would think I'd stolen the car instead of taking it on one small unsanctioned side trip.

We sped down the narrow road, the hedges alongside my passenger window zipping past. If I stuck a finger out, it would be torn off. I considered asking her to slow down, but the set of her jaw made me keep my mouth shut.

I understood Sophie was concerned about her business. I felt bad that I'd dragged her out of the shop after I told her I wouldn't eat up any more of her time. "It won't take long to set the grout," I mentioned to smooth things over. "We can get you caught up on your to-do list in no time."

No response.

"I can pay you cash for the tow fees," I offered again. "And pay your friend for their gas and time to drive you."

There was a twitch in her right eye, but otherwise, nothing.

"I got a good lead on finding Gabriel," I offered.

Her hands clenched the wheel. "I do not care about Gabriel," she spat.

"He screwed you over, too, you know," I pointed out. "If it hadn't been for him, you wouldn't have lost your position at the Delphine."

Sophie stomped the brakes, and we screeched to a stop in the middle of the road. The seat belt snapped into a locked position, and I nearly hit the dash. The smell of burnt rubber hung in the air.

"Do not dare to imply that any of what you are doing is for me," she snarled. "This"—she waved her hand around—"is all for you."

Sophie wrangled the stick shift back to first with a metallic groan, and we shot off with a plume of dust. I winced but stayed quiet.

Once in Reims, we spun through one of the city's roundabouts, and she pulled to a stop in front of my hotel. We sat there in silence for a moment with the engine ticking.

"There is a train tomorrow morning back to Paris," she said eventually. "I got you a ticket." She fished it from her pocket, then pressed it into my hand.

I stared at her and then down at the ticket, my mouth agape. "You can't be serious."

"I am very serious. It is time for you to go." She got out of the vehicle, walked around, and opened my door. Sophie looked prepared to drag me out.

"Look, I understand you're upset." I stepped slowly from the car. I hadn't realized she was *this* angry.

Sophie's nostrils flared. "I am not upset. I am *done*. You need to leave Champagne. Go back to Paris, finish your vacation, and go home."

My lungs felt too small, unable to hold the oxygen I needed. "I know I messed up and I get you're stressed for the meeting with the city officials. I can help."

"I do not require your help."

"Of course you don't require it, but I *want* to help." I had no idea that Sophie had been this close to the edge. I should have realized how anxious she would be with everything she'd invested in the wine shop. I would be that hand reaching out to her, just as Louis had been there for the Widow. "There's still a lot I can do. And this business is important. I love the idea of teaching more women about wine and getting them involved in the industry."

"Stop!" Sophie commanded. "This is my dream." She pounded her chest. "*My dream*. The one I created with my husband and is now mine alone. You knew nothing of champagne before you came here. Do not pretend that you care about this industry, or how hard it is to be a woman in it."

I swallowed hard, feeling like a child caught being naughty. "I care."

Sophie rolled her eyes. "Get your own dream. Is your life so lacking in its own purpose that you must latch on to what others want? Are you truly too frightened to be your own person?"

I sucked in a breath. People on the sidewalk paused to watch.

"Who are you, Natalie Taylor? Do you exist as your own person, or must you find life only in others, first your husband and now me?"

Her words pummeled me like a fighter going for the knockout punch.

"That isn't fair," I managed.

Sophie pulled back, her hands clenched in front of her, her face a mask of exaggerated concern. "Oh, is my speaking of your dead husband too painful?"

I blinked, shocked at her rage and spite. Then a hint of dread began to creep in. I had a bad feeling that tomorrow's worry had caught up to today.

"I reached out to your friend Molly," she said. "I wanted to tell her I was worried about you and your focus on Gabriel. Do you know what she told me?"

I shook my head, feeling myself shrinking, getting smaller and smaller.

"She said that you were likely upset, lashing out at Gabriel, because you couldn't lash out at your husband for getting engaged to his mistress."

"I can explain," I said, not certain that I could.

"You can explain a dead husband coming back to life to marry another? Impressive. It is a miracle. Your husband lives!" She threw her hands up in the air.

"I didn't know how to tell you," I said, desperate to make her understand. "Things were complicated. Will had this midlife crisis, and I ran away here to find some way to get over the divorce, and then there was the mix-up at the hotel, and it seemed easier to just let it stand—"

"It is not so complicated. You could have told me, but perhaps you were too ashamed. It is not that he didn't want to be married, or that he wanted to be free and young again. He simply did not want to be with *you*." She shook her head and slammed the passenger door shut. "And I do not blame him. I do not want to be with you either. What you are running from, Natalie Taylor, is that you have no life of your own."

The last bit of my heart crumbled.

Sophie lowered her voice, suddenly looking exhausted. "Go home, Natalie."

"Please," I managed. "Let me fix this. You're my friend." I reached for her arm.

She stepped back and walked around to the driver's side. "We are not friends. Friends do not lie to one another." Sophie wrenched her car door open and then paused. "We were people who met when we needed each other, but that need has passed. Go home."

Sophie dropped into her car and sped off, leaving me standing on the sidewalk in front of the hotel with a crumpled train ticket in my hand.

I went to my room and lay down on the hard hotel bed with its scratchy sheets. The room smelled faintly of lemon cleaner and mildew. CNN International was on in the background. You know life isn't good when you'd rather listen to economic disasters, floods, and the occasional violent crime than the thoughts in your own head.

Gabriel had been an escape. The illusion that he'd been attracted to me was a distraction from the fact that Will and I were truly over. Yes, I knew we were divorced, and yes, I also knew there would be no way we would ever somehow magically get back together, but a tiny part of me had hoped.

When Gabriel had turned out to be a lie, it had seemed like something I could fix. That I could teach him a lesson in a way that hadn't been possible with Will. You can go to jail for being a con artist. The only sentence for being a shitty husband is losing half your dishes in the split.

I began to cry. I hadn't allowed myself to give in to tears for so long it was like my eyes had forgotten how to do it. My breath caught in my throat as I sobbed into the pillow. The feelings rushing out like a tsunami.

The night dragged on. I would turn off the TV and try to sleep, but then find myself tossing and turning. I'd get up, turn it back on, and mindlessly watch the news or old *Friends* episodes dubbed in French. I would feel numb and then suddenly discover that I was crying again. It felt like the first few days after I'd discovered the affair.

I rolled over onto my side and curled up. Sophie was right. I didn't have a dream of my own. My dreams had been entwined with Will's since we were young. I was the type of person the Widow disdained, someone who saw my worth only in how others regarded me. Since the divorce, I realized there were all these things I didn't know about myself. I slept on the same side of the bed because that was the side I always had. Every meal I'd cooked for over twenty years had been with him in mind. I never made brussels sprouts because he hated them, and I wasn't that crazy about salmon but still prepared it on regular rotation. In being the ultimate we, I had lost me.

I lay there watching the news circle around again to the same stories. Nothing had changed. There was still a flood in Poland. The EU was still worried about the economy. The stories blended into each other like my own thoughts.

My gaze caught on my suitcase, my new slingback shoes on the floor next to it. I loved my new clothes, how they fit, how they made me feel. The Widow's book sat on the desk. She made mistakes. What she'd done to the Mouse was horrid and yet she kept going. She apologized to Louis. She kept fighting. She didn't stay in bed with the covers over her head. If I was going to find my worth, I would have to do it myself. I sat up, swinging my legs out of bed. I marched to the bathroom and ran the water until it was ice-cold and then used the rough washcloth to wipe my face.

I was not stuck in a loop. I had picked up and traveled to France on my own. If I didn't like where I was, then I would have to be the person to change it. Not wait for my ex to turn into the person I'd wanted him to be, or a friend to fix things, or some man to sweep me off my feet.

I dug out the discarded journal in the bottom of my suitcase. It was time for another list.

Barbe-Nicole

■ REIMS ■

REGARDING THE EVENTS OF MARCH 1814

Dearest Anne,

Bravo to you on your recent accomplishment! Do not dismiss it as luck. There may have been an aspect of fortune, but it is also your efforts that brought the results. Business and life both require a balance sheet. You must know your assets and your losses. It is not to fill you with pride, or despair, but so that with a full accounting you can plan. I look forward to hearing what you will accomplish next. And to think you considered giving in. Did I not tell you to press on? I have known those bleak moments, and I assure you, most do surrender. It takes fortitude and planning to move ever onward. It was the same during the darkest portions of the war. You will enjoy this tale, in part because it involves your grandmother meeting Napoleon when she was not much younger than you.

■ ■

My father's staff looked at me with wide eyes, scared and uncertain, hoping I would take the lead. One could hardly blame them. The emperor was dismounting from his white horse and moments away from discovering that my father had abandoned him. Napoleon's allies were like leaves in late autumn, falling away at an alarming rate.

Clémentine at least was thrilled with the opportunity to meet the great man. She took a step forward and made a deep curtsy. She'd been practicing in the mirror.

"Welcome, Emperor," she said, her voice clear and loud. It likely carried to the crowds outside Father's gates. It seemed all of Reims had come out to see him return to the City of Kings and to determine for themselves how much fight was left in him.

Bonaparte looked worn, the years etched into his face. He still managed a smile for my daughter, although I could tell he was surprised she was the one welcoming him when he had reason to expect it would be my father, the man he'd made mayor.

While Napoleon's men had retaken Reims from the Russians, there were few in town who thought he could hold it for long. My father admired Napoleon and did not want to risk offending Bonaparte, but he also did not wish to be seen too aligned with the man, should the emperor's enemies vanquish him in the end. And so he had simply run, leaving me and my siblings to handle the situation in his absence and allowing him to appear neutral.

I dropped to a curtsy. "All of Reims is grateful for your return, Your Imperial Majesty," I said. I didn't mention that we would also be grateful if he could find a way to peace so the rest of us could focus on commerce.

Napoleon's face was sharp, like that of a hawk. His curved nose and small eyes that missed nothing. "And where is the mayor on this auspicious day?"

I ducked my head. "Unfortunately, my father was called away on unavoidable business. But my brother, Jean-Baptiste, and his wife greatly look forward to hosting you and your men."

There was a slight twitch at his mouth. "I see." His words were pregnant with disapproval. I wondered if he felt the sting of being cast aside after being so adored.

"My brother's home is on Rue de Vesle, but I would be most pleased if you would allow me to offer you refreshments here before you depart." I motioned to my father's house behind me. "Our family is honored that you would grace us again with your presence."

Bonaparte stared at the front of the house as if he could see through the windows and doors to when he had been here with Joséphine. How the entire world had seemed alight with possibility.

"Merci, Madame Clicquot. I appreciate your offer. However, if your father is not . . . available, then I will ride on to your brother's home. While I wish I had the time to enjoy your company, there's work to be done."

"Of course, Your Imperial Majesty." I bowed my head. From the corner of my eye, I saw Clémentine pout. She'd looked forward to writing to her friends at school and telling them the tale of entertaining the emperor. No doubt in the story she would be the center of the action. While she was still quite young at fifteen, she was not so young as to not notice the handsome men that served the emperor in their military uniforms.

My father's groom moved forward to place a mounting block, but Napoleon shook his head, then leaped astride his horse with little trouble.

"Your Majesty, may I offer the company of my daughter, Clémentine Clicquot? She would be honored to escort you to her uncle's house," I said.

Clémentine vibrated with excitement, her eyes lighting up as if it were Christmas morning. I could see that Napoleon had been inclined to turn me down until he saw her expression. It was well known that despite his penchant for being irritable, he loved children. He nodded his approval. "It would be most kind of her."

Clémentine curtsied so low this time that she nearly stumbled. The groom assisted her into the saddle. She sat prettily on the horse, her hands dainty and soft on the reins, but with a sense of control. Clémentine was a strong rider with no fear. She'd always had an affinity for animals, just like her father.

With a pang, it struck me how proud François would be of our daughter and the woman she was becoming. If I closed my eyes, I could imagine him standing beside me, his face in a wide smile. He would be grateful that she had not inherited his tendency to melancholy. Clémentine could be stubborn, but she was almost always in good spirits. She had no interest in business or studies, but she was gentle and most often in pleasant spirits. A good person.

"Assist your aunt Thérèse," I instructed my daughter. She looked at me, irritated at being treated as a child in front of others. I curtsied low until Bonaparte rode out.

Walking back into the house, I found the staff lined up in the hall ready to greet the emperor. "Bonaparte has ridden on to Jean-Baptiste's."

The butler's shoulders drooped; he'd been looking forward to seeing the man despite the work that would be involved.

"Just as well," Madame Pieter said. Her son had been one of the lost in Russia. She shooed the cluster of maids. "Back to work then."

"I'll take refreshment in the parlor," I said. "Have Louis join me."

Moments later, Louis strode in. "The great man has moved on, has he?" He clapped his hands when he saw the tray Madame Pieter had one of the maids bring in. "A meal fit for an emperor!"

I motioned him forward. "Eat as much as you like. The cook made enough for the entire army."

Louis piled food onto a plate, pausing only long enough to pop a small morsel of sausage into his mouth. He murmured his approval and then stacked more food atop what he already had. It was a wonder he wasn't as wide as he was tall. I watched him eat with pleasure, glad to have him in my confidence again.

"How are the others faring?" I asked.

He pushed the rest of a piece of cake into his mouth and wiped his hands on his trousers. "It varies from house to house. Most have lost at least fifty percent of their stock."

"All to the Russians?"

"Our troops have taken their share as well. You were wise to wall up what you did."

"I owe Pharaoh for that wisdom."

Louis smiled. "He's a good man. Worth his weight in grapes."

I chuckled. "Indeed. I would pay him more if there were a single sou to spare." The thought of finances made my stomach tighten. Over the past years I had held things together by supplementing weak sales with selling off my belongings, but there was little left. I put down the slice of cake that had been in my hand, appetite gone. "And the fields, how have they fared through all this?"

Louis rubbed his chin, the rasp of whiskers filling the quiet room. "Several more have been trampled. We should be able to buy root-stock from other houses to replant in the spring," Louis said, sensing the pain the loss of the vines caused me.

"Assuming we have confidence anything new won't also be destroyed." Every time I moved forward with the business, the war pushed me back further. All those years ago the fortune teller had neglected to mention just how many mountains there would be to climb.

"And our sales, any change?" I asked. Perhaps he would have good news that would raise my spirits.

Louis sighed. "Who can we sell to in these times? The blockades and trade agreements have nearly every foreign market closed to us."

I unclenched my hands. "I see." I had suspected as much, but I had hoped Louis would see a solution I had not spotted.

Louis wiped a smear of cream from his lip. "The wine will keep behind the wall, safe and sound until peace comes."

The wine would be safe, but the business would not. I opened my mouth to tell him to share the burden, but then stilled my tongue. I did not want anyone to know the truth of the situation. While I had done everything I could, I still felt shame. I had risked so much for this business. If it were to not survive, then what had been the point?

"And when peace finally arrives?" I asked.

He nodded, pausing to think. "Our own market will stay small for some time, years maybe. Too many people have lost too much."

I agreed.

Louis drained his coffee, turning positive. "The British will buy, but for sheer volume, the Russians will be our best market. Give it another year."

I bit my lip. I did not have a year. There would be nothing to pay the workers in the spring. The list of expenses ran through my mind like a river. New vines, the field workers, bottles, workers for the cellar—on and on they came, as relentless as the Russian army.

"And how is your family?" I asked. For once I did not want to talk business any longer.

Louis's face broke into a wide grin. "You should see your busy godchild! His mother spends her day chasing him from one end of the home to the other." Louis tugged on his vest, his chest swelling with pride. "He's only two, but you can tell he's clever. Gets his intelligence from my wife, I'd guess. And he smiles too, has the charm of a salesman."

"He must get that from his father."

Louis blushed. "Perhaps if he is very lucky, he'll be able to work for you when I am too old and gray to travel."

"Perhaps." My throat tightened. Would I even have work for my dearest friend in a few more months, or would I have to shutter the entire house? Retreat to living on the kindness of relatives? Or, God forbid, have to seek out a new husband? It was not just my business that hung in the balance, but my hard-won independence. Having tasted freedom, I did not know how I could live with the lack of it.

Louis looked out the window. "In times of war, when things seem difficult, I enjoy imagining my son's son, and then his son, and his son, a long line of my family, all working in this business. Selling the best champagne all over the world in times of peace and prosperity." He leaned back satisfied, the tray of food meant for a large group now nearly bare.

"What about your daughters, won't they be in this business—or are you foolish enough to imply women shouldn't be?" I asked with mock offense.

He laughed and stood, giving me a bow. "Madame Clicquot, I have no doubt with models such as you, women will run the world in the future."

"If they did, it would run a far sight better, I would think."

"Well, we men certainly haven't done the best job these past few years."

I stood as well. "Don't be ridiculous, Louis," I said. "Men have been mucking up the world for far longer than that."

■   ■

After Louis left, I wandered my parents' house. I should have returned to my own, but I felt an overwhelming sense of exhaustion. I'd always been up before the sun, spilling over with energy, but lately my vigor had disappeared.

Tears trickled from the corner of my eye. Without a miracle, I would lose the business. Some would say that it was a foregone conclusion, that a woman was not meant to run a vineyard. But I could not shake the conviction that it was not wrong for me to want something for myself. Something that was not about filling a role for another.

But I had regrets. I had covered up any questions of François's death. Hidden what I knew and feared, even from his father. And the time spent on the business did not come without a cost. I was often not the best daughter, mother, or friend. And then there was what I'd done to the Mouse. The weight of my worries seemed to drag me down further. I caught sight of myself in the window reflection.

Who was this slumped creature? I immediately stiffened my spine, straightening. Enough of this circling of my losses. I had made the best champagne in the world. In Louis, I had a good friend. Clémentine was safe and thriving. Moreover, I had my brain and wits. I would find a way.

Natalie

APRIL 28

My eyes snapped open as the train squealed to a stop. I'd barely slept the night before. I'd finally drifted off for what felt like mere minutes before my alarm blared in the morning. A cup of overly strong coffee at the train station had done little to make me feel more alert. My eyes felt gritty, and not long after we'd pulled out of the station at Reims, they had drifted shut.

The train wasn't direct, it was scheduled to stop in every small town between Reims and Paris. Relieved that I hadn't missed my stop and woken up somewhere in Poland, I was about to close my eyes again when I noticed the sign on the platform.

Épirinal.

The name rang a bell. As soon as it clicked into place, I was up and out of my seat. The whistle was blowing as I yanked my suitcase from the overhead rack and bolted for the door. The train jolted, ready to move, and I jumped. My suitcase thumped down loudly on the platform next to me. My heart hammered overtime as the train I'd been on a second ago pulled out of the station.

Okay, I was awake now.

I was going to find that construction bar. I didn't have anything left to lose by trying this last thing. I patted my tote bag and the book inside. Catching my own reflection in the station windows, I stiffened my spine and raised my chin. After I ditched my suitcase in a locker at the station, a quick Google search gave me an address and a map. Then it was as easy as following the narrow streets to the location.

Hands on my hips, I considered the Mastiff. It wasn't going to be featured in any tourism magazines as a "hidden gem." The street outside smelled like stale urine and fried food. There were posters in the window for various sporting events, some faded and long out of date.

Cupping my hands around my face, I peered in the window. The place wasn't large. Chairs were stacked on top of tables so that, in theory, someone could clean the floors. However, I was willing to bet these floors hadn't been mopped since "Like a Virgin" was topping the charts.

A voice behind me made me jump.

A wiry woman stood a few steps back, a cigarette pinched between her fingers. She repeated whatever she'd said in French.

"Do you speak English?" I asked.

She took a drag and blew the smoke up through her bangs. "I say, 'You want something?'"

"Do you work here?"

"No, I am just a concerned citizen." She rolled her eyes when I was silent. "Of course I work here. You think anyone else is worried about this shithole?"

"I need to ask you about a customer," I said. "I'm trying to find someone."

She tossed her cigarette into the street, where it sizzled out in a puddle of questionable origin. "You might as well come in. I am Cerise." Moving past me, she opened the door and turned off the alarm. She dropped her bag on the bar and pulled her hair up, using a rubber band that had been around her wrist.

"I'm Natalie," I said.

"This person you wish to find, is he your boyfriend?" She picked a wet cloth out of the sink and gave it a quick sniff before wincing and tossing it into an empty bucket on the floor.

I sat on one of the tall barstools. "It's complicated."

She gave a raspy laugh. "My friend, it is always complicated. You have until the supplier comes for delivery to ask me anything you want. I must restock everything. We had a full house last night and tonight is Les Bleus." She caught my expression. "It is rugby. Very popular here."

"I'm not really into sports," I admit.

She waggled her eyebrows. "Who cares about the sport? Have you seen the men who play? Rugby boys. Give 'em to me any day, even over a footie player." She kissed her fingertips. "Natalie, they have such cuisses—you know this word?"

I shook my head.

Cerise slapped her thigh. "And le cul." She cupped her ass cheeks and then fanned her face. "Footie boys all think they're so pretty, but a rugby player, he's a man first. You won't see one of them stealing your fancy face cream. The bar sponsors a team, local boys who play for fun. They do not play well, but no one is watching them for the game."

"I'm looking for this guy." I slid my phone over the counter with the photo of Gabriel.

Cerise wiped her hands on her jeans and picked it up, scrutinizing the picture. "I do not recognize him. You say he's a customer here?"

279

The tiny spark of hope went out like her cigarette had on the street outside. "I know he works, or worked at least, in construction. I heard a lot of construction guys come here."

She looked at the photo again. "I do not recognize him. I cannot say that he never comes in, but he's not a regular."

I slumped in the seat. "I knew it was a long shot."

She nodded, passing the phone back to me. "Life is all about chances. He is handsome."

"He's also an asshole," I said.

"Funny how those often go together, no?" She reached into the low bar and pulled out a bottle of hard cider. "On the house."

"It's not even lunchtime," I pointed out.

Cerise shrugged, pulling one out for herself and twisting the top off. "It is basically apple juice. What do they say, for health."

She had a point. And I had nowhere to be until hours from now when I could catch the next train to Paris. I took the top off my bottle and clinked hers. "To health." I sipped the cider while she wiped down the bar and began stacking glasses, holding two or three in one hand. "Have you worked here long?"

"My whole life I am growing up in places such as this. My mother's parents owned one. To me, they are like a home. But here, I have only been about three or four years."

I watched her move with practiced ease around the tight space. She hefted a keg of beer into place under the counter with barely a flex of her biceps. She restocked the fridge with drinks, making quick notes of what they needed to order with a stubby pencil she kept behind her ear. Each step seemed almost choreographed, in sync. More than that, she seemed happy, living in the moment.

"Is this what you always wanted to do?" I asked.

She arched an overplucked eyebrow.

"Sorry. Things are messed up lately. I'm trying to figure out what to do with my life."

Cerise tipped up her bottle, draining it. "If you are trying to figure out your own life, my advice is to stop following what other people are doing." She rinsed her bottle out with a swish and dropped it neatly into a carton of empties. "And as for life being messed up? That is what it is. A series of up and down, messy and not. C'est la vie." There was a loud honk from the back and the sound of a truck backing up.

"Ah, that will be the supplier." She tossed her bar towel over one shoulder.

"I'll get out of your way." I reached for my phone and started to stand.

Cerise waved for me to sit. "Finish your drink."

"Do you have a bathroom I can use before I go?"

Cerise pointed toward a hallway. "It will be all right, Natalie. Have a little faith that you'll find your way and that things that are meant to be will be."

"You should be a philosopher," I said.

She winked and then moved to meet the truck. "In France, bartender and philosopher are the same thing." The fire door scraped on the cement as it opened, and she called out a greeting to the delivery person in the alley.

I turned my phone over and over in my hand. As the Widow pointed out, it was time for me to do some accounting. I had a debt owing. Just like she hadn't wanted to hear what Louis had to say, I'd also lashed out at my friend. It was up to me to make it right. I opened the messaging app and typed a text to Molly.

I'm sorry. There's no excuse for what I said. Things got complicated, but everything's fine. Will explain when home. Drinks on me.

I hit Send and felt a small weight lift. Molly had acted like my mother, but I'd encouraged it. I wanted someone to take charge so badly I'd put her into that role when it was my job all along.

I slid my empty bottle over the bar and put a few euros down for Cerise.

In the hallway that led to the bathroom, there were a bunch of framed photos. I paused to look them over. While a few were of events held at the bar (including one that appeared to be the saddest New Year's Eve party on record), most were team photos. Groups of mud-covered guys, some sporting various injuries, with their arms around each other and holding the team sign ÉPIRINAL MASTIFFS.

Cerise was right. These men were built. Their thighs looked like they'd been carved from solid marble. One shirtless fellow looked like a late 1990s Abercrombie & Fitch model.

The photos had no logical order; a group shot from 1978, complete with short shorts and porn-star mustaches, hung right next to another from 2015. In some shots, the girlfriends or wives hung on the players, seemingly unfazed by the mud or blood. There were a few years documented when someone must have had an actual mastiff dog as a pet, as the pony-sized, drool-covered creature was front and center in every picture.

The women's hairstyles and outfits were more fun to track by year. For someone who had lived through the 1980s, I'd apparently blocked out just how bad fashion had been. Is there anyone who can wear neon orange without looking like a walking traffic cone?

I was just about to turn away when I saw him. I blinked and then zeroed in, wondering if it was wishful thinking combined with drinking before noon. My mouth went dry, and I quickly licked my lips. It *was* him.

Gabriel.

He was in the second row of players, from a team twelve years back. He was younger, but I'd recognize that half smile anywhere, even with the slightly longer hair flopped over one eye. The frame covered the list of player names. I tried to take it off the wall so I could pull the photo out, but it was attached with screws. Making a note of the year, I quickly scanned the rest of the photos.

There was another! From the year before. And there was Gabriel again. This time, he had his arm around a woman kissing him on the cheek. Black dots peppered the sides of my vision.

I backed up until I hit the wall opposite. I stood staring at the picture while the faint sounds of glass bottles clinking together and the thud of kegs being unloaded came from the bar. There was a rushing sound in my ears, and it occurred to me I might faint. I slid down the wall and dropped my head between my knees, forcing myself to take slow, deep breaths.

Once I started thinking about what disgusting things might be on the floor near the men's room, I knew I was no longer at risk of passing out. Standing, I took a quick photo of the picture in the frame and then another with a close-up of the names.

My shaking finger traced the list at the bottom of the photograph. *Gerard Rancourt and wife Sophie Rancourt.*

They were married.

Barbe-Nicole

■ ROUEN ■

REGARDING THE EVENTS OF APRIL 1814

Dear Anne,

You stated in your letter that you would have been frightened to face Napoleon. While he is a figure in your history books, I can assure you he was still just a man. But I was frightened by many things during those dark years. Fear makes some cower, and others respond with action. You may intuit which type I am. I have long believed that if it appears all is lost, one must keep trying, for you never know how the winds of chance will blow.

■ ■

I hadn't expected the captain's home would be so cozy. Although, in truth, I had no idea what to expect of pirates other than what I had read as a child from the *Robinson Crusoe* book in my father's library.

Louis maintained that Monsieur Rondeaux was not a pirate, simply a shipping merchant with loose morals who would not mind taking a risk.

"I want the wines taken to Königsberg," I repeated, my mouth dry with anxiety. "It would not be acceptable if they were off-loaded anywhere else." My Russian distributor, Monsieur Boissonet, had assured me that if I could deliver the wine to the Prussian port city, he would get it to Russia.

Rondeaux nodded, stroking his beard in a way that struck me as lewd, although I couldn't say why. The man had a way of looking at me as if he was imagining me without my chemise. "So you have said, madame." He turned to Louis. "How much wine is to be transported?"

My mouth pinched shut. I loathed men who wouldn't discuss matters of business with me. It was my name alone on the house, Veuve Clicquot Ponsardin, and yet I might as well have been invisible. I had half a mind to tell him I would take my business elsewhere, but I had no other options.

The man risked his ship by flaunting the law. Most shipowners were staying put, anchored securely in the harbor until it was declared safe, but I knew I could not wait until then. Opportunity was in the risk.

Napoleon had abdicated; his reign was over. In the end, it had come quicker than expected. Nary a week after returning to Reims, he'd been driven out again. It still didn't seem possible, but it was fact. Crates and crates of champagne had been opened to celebrate the peace treaty. The Bourbon kings would rule again. C'est fini.

International trade had not yet resumed, but it would soon, and with it would come a flood of product onto the market. I heard that Rémy Moët had tripled the workers in his employ. Unlike me, he had the funds to do so. The Russian czar, Alexander, had ordered wines from the house Moët. Rémy strode about the region, bragging of the connection to Russian nobility. No doubt he suspected with the czar's favor he would corner the market, but first he would have to get his wines to Russia.

I aimed to beat him there, and I was prepared to risk everything I had left on this one spin at the wheel of fate. I would not wait for trade to open; instead, I would smuggle my wines out.

"Over ten thousand bottles," I said. The number made me light-headed to say aloud. Louis had argued that we should not send so much. If our plan failed, we would be ruined. But we needed to make our mark, and that is never done meekly.

Ten thousand represented all our reserves, every last bottle of the 1811 comet wine that we had tucked away safely during the war. If the shipment were to be lost or seized, it would be the end of Veuve Clicquot. The end of my freedom as its head. I would return to the quiet world of women, where action was taken only through others. I could not bear the idea.

The risk was enormous. We would be sending the wine without permission or any security. Not only was I flaunting the law but breaking every common-sense rule. If any of my competitors were to learn what I was plotting, Rémy Moët in particular, they could beat me at my own game.

Ah . . . but if I won.

Rondeaux had returned to rubbing his beard. "You will have to get the wines here quickly. I won't hold the ship for you."

I nodded, but the man still looked to Louis.

"We will have the wines here," Louis replied, his gaze steady and serious.

"Pack them well. I will not be held responsible."

"I will travel with the wines all the way to Russia," Louis said. "I'll take responsibility for them. And ensure that others take due care."

I spun toward him. This was not something we had discussed.

The shipping merchant slapped his thighs. "So be it. Have them here as soon as possible."

"And you will tell no one of this arrangement," Louis said, stressing again our need for privacy in this matter.

Rondeaux gave a clipped nod.

"And it will not be whispered about in kitchens or markets either," I said pointedly in the direction of his wife, who had stood in the corner of the room while we met.

Rondeaux laughed. "No, I shall also see that it is not whispered among the skirted set."

He could laugh all he liked, but the truth was that more secrets than he knew passed from lip to ear among women. If more men employed women as spies, they would find that news could travel in half the time. I waited until I saw her nod as well. Only then did I rise.

"We thank you for your time, monsieur." I thrust my hand forward to finalize the deal.

Rondeaux's hands were calloused and rough; it was like shaking hands with rock and rope. The salt of the sea seemed to be trying to preserve him even as he lived and breathed.

"Don't thank me, Madame Clicquot. All I ask is that you pay on time."

I had borrowed the funds to pay for the project. I would rather not, but I had nary a spare coin that hadn't already been squeezed. Either this gamble would pay off or I would have to shutter my doors and retreat to the country, relying on the charity of my family. My stomach rebelled at the thought.

■   ■

I pulled my shawl tight when we were back in the street. The wind blowing in from the river that led to the sea carried the cold of the deep. Even the spring sun couldn't chase it away. I moved quickly to warm my blood.

"Did you plan to tell me you were going to travel with the wine?" I asked.

"What choice do we have? You know as well as I there isn't anyone else you can trust." Louis held out a hand to hold back any argument I was about to make. "You have good men in your employ, but none who can do this."

The wind chilled the tip of my nose and made my eyes water. "It won't be a pleasant journey." I felt bad that he would have to take the trip and yet also envious that he could.

"Life in your employ has been many things, but it has never been dull."

I was flooded with a sense of affection for my old friend. He had stood by me throughout our entire journey even when I had pushed him away. I wish I could tell François what an excellent choice he had made when he hired this man.

Louis loved this business as much as I. He did not question every decision I made as if I were empty-headed, but he also did not agree with each choice if he thought it unwise. It is a rare person who finds the balance between support and mindless approval. If one finds such a friend, they should keep them close.

"We shall pack your bags with as much comfort as possible," I said. "I will expect you to update me at every opportunity."

Louis chuckled. "Madame, I expect you to try to stow away in my bags."

Oh, if only I could. We paused at the top of the street to watch the port. The tide was in, and ships moved up and down the water-way, their sails out and rounded. My nose twitched, and I told myself I could smell the salt of the open sea.

"One day women will go wherever they please," I said, half to Louis and half as a promise to myself. It wouldn't be Clémentine; it would take more time than that. Perhaps her daughter, or the generation after that, would take to the sea and overland to travel wherever they wished.

Louise crooked his arm, and I took it as we walked toward the river. "It has been my experience, madame, that most people, when given a choice, be they man or woman, rarely choose adventure. It's far too easy to stick to known paths."

"True. But it is nice to have the option."

"It seems to me, madame, that some like yourself seize the choice regardless of whether it is offered."

"You make me sound pigheaded," I protested, while secretly pleased with his assessment.

Louis bowed his head slightly. "I apologize for any offence. Shall we seek out a pair of breeches and a pirate hat so that when you stow away, you have the right clothing?" He smirked. "Dare I say that Rondeaux would be quite pleased if you were to make the journey instead of me? I sensed he would prefer your company."

I scowled at him and whacked him lightly on the shoulder. "Never you mind. I will trust you to get the wines there. And to get the best price for them too."

Louis nodded and began to talk of how best to pack the wines to avoid breakage. We'd need more straw, and we'd have to pull some of the field workers from the vineyard to make the crates if we were going to be ready to leave soon.

As he spoke, I allowed my mind to wander. I knew I would try to think of any possible things that could go wrong to avoid disaster, but I also would allow myself to think of how it could all go right. There was a warmth in my chest as I pictured it. I may never leave France, but I would have my own grand adventure right here at home. The comet never left its place in the sky, and yet it still impacted the world. I would be the same. I simply needed to shine brightly enough.

Natalie

APRIL 28

I sat in the restaurant determined to take my time before making any decisions on what to do next. I hadn't given myself time to think since I'd landed in France. Hell, I hadn't been thinking much since Will walked out the door over a year ago. Instead, I'd pinballed from one decision to another, most of them made, or suggested, by someone else.

No. It was time to slow down. Figure out what I wanted. I wasn't so foolish as to think that fixing things here in France would somehow magically make the rest of my life fall into place, but I was damned if I was going to let other people get away with treating me badly anymore. I'd believed all was lost, but I should have listened to the Widow, because the winds of chance blew in my favor for once. I caught myself—it wasn't simply chance; I hadn't given up. It had been my decision to stop at the Mastiff.

The waiter paused at my table and refilled my wine, a Beaujolais.

I sipped it while I watched the door, keeping track of who came in and out. I'd asked to be seated in a corner, someplace where I'd be unlikely to be seen, even if someone was looking for me.

But no one was looking. Sophie and Gabriel—excuse me, *Gerard*—would have assumed I'd returned to Paris. They would have no reason to suspect I'd snuck back into town. But I still didn't intend to take any chances.

There was a limited menu on the chalkboard hung near the bar. So far, I had taken the waiter's advice on what to order. There had been an appetizer of cubed ham, le jambon de Reims, cooked in stock with nutmeg and shallots. The main had been a mix of rabbit and pork with garlic and onions cooked in a puff pastry, which was also a regional specialty. Now I was waiting on a course of cheeses: a Chaource that was supposed to taste like mushroom, a salty firm Langres, and one called Barberey, a soft cheese that he promised was delightfully smelly. The food had been delicious, and letting the meal unwind over two hours had worked its magic on calming me down.

The shock of realizing Sophie and Gabriel were married had shaken me to the core. That she had been in on the scam the entire time had shut down my system for a moment. Everything I thought I knew had turned upside down, and like the Widow had taught me, it had a way of making things clear. The knowledge of Sophie and Gabriel's relationship slotted into my brain like a missing puzzle piece, making sense of everything.

Sophie must have spotted me as a mark the moment I'd checked into the hotel. Emotional. A widow, at least in theory. Rich enough to stay at the Delphine for two weeks and able to go shopping with abandon. I'd practically offered myself up on a platter.

Sophie had given me the idea of wandering the bookstalls, and told me the perfect little café to have a glass of wine at when I was done. I went exactly where she told me, just in time for my "chance" meeting with Gabriel. It had all been very well planned between the two of them.

Sophie used the shopping trip to learn more about me, feeding Gabriel information that allowed him to transform into my perfect mate. And I had to hand it to him—he knew how to be charming.

No one had stolen my phone. Unless you count Sophie seizing the chance to nab it from my bag on the Metro and then finding an opportunity to smash it, making it harder for me to communicate with friends back home. The police had tried to tell me. They'd said they didn't see any criminal; they'd suspected her of something, but she'd explained it away so easily.

Without Molly or anyone else to urge me to take things carefully, Gabriel set me up for the final stages. And I'd done all the rest myself.

I called the Delphine hotel. The front desk manager laughed when I asked about Sophie being fired. No, she'd quit without notice. I could have told him the reason she left was that she didn't need to work there anymore. Between the wine scam and the money from my ring she and Gabriel were set up to do what they really wanted.

I squirmed in my seat, and then took a large sip of wine. I wondered if any part of Gabriel had been attracted to me or if it was just part of the con. Sophie had interrupted us with news of Molly's messages just in time to keep anything from happening. After Will's betrayal, all it had taken for me to fall for Gabriel was his attention. I should have spent the time falling in love with myself instead.

The waiter glided up to the table and placed the cheese plate down. Each piece was arranged with a sprig of grapes and a seedy whole-grain cracker, like a Picasso painting. I admired it for a moment before cutting into the Langres.

I smiled, picturing Sophie's face when I'd shown up at the shop in Reims. They hadn't expected that. I wondered, when she had called out my name so loudly that first day, if it was to alert Gabriel so he could run out the back door. They must have imagined I would slink through the rest of the vacation dejected and embarrassed or run back home after the con was exposed. I bet they never expected me to come looking for Gabriel. Sophie was going to wish she'd never introduced me to the Widow Clicquot and the idea of having a spine, because it was getting stronger every second. I lightly touched the Widow's book where it lay on the table.

Sophie and Gabriel must have decided it was better to keep me close rather than let me run around playing Sherlock Holmes in the Champagne region on my own. Sophie drove me from village to village in the search for Gabriel. She knew where to take me, where there would be no chance of finding him. Not to mention I had no idea what she'd even asked people. For all I knew, she inquired if they wanted a crazed perimenopausal American to move in. A quick shake of the head no, and we were off to the next place, and I was no wiser to the real discussion.

They assumed I was stupid. Or that my broken heart had made me naive. Or that I was easily manipulated. And I couldn't say I hadn't been all those things. But I was much more complicated than they'd counted on. That was something I had learned from Clicquot, that women were a complex mix of things. I may have been foolish, but I was also clever. And persistent. And willing to think outside the box. And my broken heart meant I wasn't afraid of much anymore. The worst had happened when Will walked out the door. But once you get up from being knocked down, you're less scared than you used to be. If I could survive it once, I could survive it again, and this time, I was going to take my own shot.

■ ■

I had the cab driver drop me off a block from the shop. The rain had petered off to a faint drizzle by now. As I came around the corner, it was impossible to miss Champagne Widows. The lights were on inside and I could just make out two figures moving about from where I stood. The meeting with the city inspectors was the day after tomorrow, and they were likely trying to get as much done as possible.

Part of me wanted to go up and lean my face and hands on the glass, horror movie–style, just to watch their expressions when they realized I was back. But while that would give me instant gratification, it wouldn't solve my problems.

When I first spotted the texts between Will and Gwen, I'd confronted him right away. There had been tears and accusations, pleading on my part and lies on his. He convinced me it wasn't what I thought, and I'd wanted to believe him. It had dragged the entire split out for months, not to mention increased my own heartbreak.

Reading about the Widow had taught me some things. She'd been rash when she blamed the Mouse, and she'd regretted it. She learned her lesson and I needed to learn patience from her.

And that was the problem. I still wasn't entirely sure what I wanted. If I called the police, they'd arrest Gabriel. There might be some hassle about my leaving Paris against police orders, but I doubted it would be much. I wasn't certain what the authorities would do about Sophie. While I liked the idea that Gabriel would spend the rest of his life rotting away in jail for what he'd done, for all I knew he'd be let out with a slap on the wrist. Even if a court required him to pay restitution for the wine theft, I wasn't sure I could prove that he'd conned me out of the money from my ring as much as I'd been foolish enough to give it to him.

And I wanted that money back. I'd earned the value of that ring in twenty years of marriage. If anyone was going to use the money from its sale to make their life better, it should be me. My hands clenched tightly.

I leaned against a building and watched the two of them. The stone still held a faint bit of heat from earlier in the day, and I found it comforting. In one of the letters in Clicquot's book, she talked about focusing on what you do well. For her, that was making champagne. But for me? That was evaluating risk. Paying attention to details.

My travel journal had morphed from my initial lists into a plan of action. I had things to check out in the morning. I wanted to know as much about the two of them as possible and everything I could learn on French law for fraud cases. And when I had all that information together, then I would act. I planned to shine as bright as Clicquot's comet.

Barbe-Nicole

■ REIMS ■

REGARDING THE EVENTS OF JUNE 1814

My darling great-granddaughter,

Waiting is hard. The in-betweenness of things. I've long believed that I could handle any situation, but the space where a situation is unknown is difficult for me. I recall the endless time after Louis took the wines. Either all was well, or all was lost, and I could only wait to discover which way the fates had decided. When situations arrive where you must bide your time, then your task is to do it as patiently as possible and put into place what you will do next. Remember: when in doubt, do the next right thing, and allow it to lead you to your destiny.

■ ■

I stretched at my desk, considering the papers in front of me. My father was busy convincing everyone that he had always been a friend of the nobility and the Bourbons. He was planning endless soirees and inviting all his connections, doing his best to wriggle closer to Louis XVIII or his diplomat Talleyrand. Personally, I thought it was a fool's quest. I doubted the new king would take anyone to his bosom who had stood for any revolutionary cause. Although what did I know: men can change allegiance in the blink of an eye.

I would rather thrust a pen in my eye than attend, but I would go if for no other reason than my attendance meant I could secure an invitation or two for my social-climbing creditors. Anything to buy their forbearance and patience. I pushed away the ledgers. There was no point in adding the numbers again. I knew them backward and forward. Everything hinged on the outcome with Russia. Until then my task was to distract my creditors with music, dancing, and vapid conversation.

Clémentine looked up from a settee where she'd perched with a book. She'd taken to spending the afternoons in my office, along with the damned cat. My daughter longed to return to school. I hadn't the heart to tell her that unless my plan was successful, I didn't have the fees for her tuition. Instead, I told her she'd fallen behind and she needed to catch up on her schoolwork before Mother Superior would allow her to return. As a result, she now daily made a show of reading or practicing her needlework.

"Is everything all right, Maman?"

I smiled with the fake heartiness of a consummate salesman. "Yes, darling, of course all is well. Just a bit of a headache." It wouldn't do to worry her. Her happiness was one of the few pleasures I had of late.

She perked up. "Would you like me to get you some water? Perhaps some headache powder?" The girl would do almost anything to be free of a book. It had already been discarded, flopped open on the floor next to where she had been sitting.

"That would be kind."

Clémentine stood quickly, much to the displeasure of Monsieur Souris, who had been enjoying a nap, and scurried from the room to fetch me a drink.

My finger traced the map I kept on the desk. Louis had departed on June 10. Unless the ship had grown wings and taken flight, they wouldn't have arrived yet. The earliest would be the end of the month, more likely early July, or if the winds were disagreeable, even as late as the middle of the month. And it would take even longer for word to reach me.

Although I longed to be with Louis on the trip, I was also glad that I was not. It was late in the season for such travel, and the captain, Cornelius, would be doing all he could to run at speed to avoid detection. Rondeaux assured Louis and me that this was the best man for the job. We would see.

The cat stalked over, regarding me as a feeble second choice for his couch.

"Come on then. There won't be a formal invitation." I patted my lap. Monsieur Souris leaped up and spun in circles before lying down. I petted him carefully. The cat and I had something in common. We liked touch, but only on our own terms. You could stroke him behind the ears peacefully one moment, and the next he'd bite down as if you were his mortal enemy. He purred. We both seemed to need some comfort this afternoon. My finger traced the route again on the map. If sheer will could blow the sails forward, the boat would make good time.

"Here you are, Maman." Clémentine bustled in, the maid a step behind her with a tray. "I had Madame Martin include a couple of sweet biscuits. I find when I have a headache it's often hunger," she said, playing at being my mother.

A glance at the plate as the maid placed it on the desk made me smile. "Oh, it seems Madame Martin has included too many biscuits. I could never eat them all."

"Shall I return them to the kitchen?" the maid offered.

Clémentine fidgeted; her mouth skewed up into a scowl.

I held my smile. "Would you like some, Clémentine, to save the girl from taking them back?"

My daughter scooped up the biscuits so quickly it could have been a magician's trick. "If it is helpful, then I suppose I could."

"Thank you, that will be all," I instructed the maid.

The maid handed over a letter sealed with wax. "Madame Martin asked me to bring you the post as well."

Clémentine had already clearly inspected the handwriting.

"It's from Mother Superior! Do you think she's saying I can return to school?" She bounced up on her tiptoes, crumbs escaping from her mouth.

"It could be any number of things," I said, motioning her to take a seat as I opened the letter. A small child's bonnet fell from the center of the pages once I had the letter open. It was dark with grime, but the stitches upon it were well made.

The letter itself was short.

Madame Clicquot—

I trust this letter finds you and your family well. We have sent up many prayers in gratitude for peace and a return to more simple times. We look forward to Clémentine returning in the fall. She's well liked here at the school and her friends speak of her often.

However, I regret I am not writing merely to send good wishes, but to share some troubling news.

The Champagne Letters

Mademoiselle Margot has left this life and gone to the next. I wish I could say it was an easy passing, but alas, it was not. Her relationships with various members of our military appear to have led to the development of the French disease. This weakened her constitution, and then when exposed to consumption, she went quickly.

One of the laundresses who was friends with her alerted me to her illness. I went to Margot's side. There was little I could do but summon a priest, as her health was too far gone. Margot did not speak or waken in the brief time that I was with her.

The only thing Margot had in her possession was this cap. It belonged to her son when he was a babe. Margot had requested scraps from the laundry to make it when she first came and had shown the finished work to me in the hope that I would allow her to take on more needlework projects. I have enclosed it here with this letter so that you can let her son know her thoughts were of him until the last.

Margot was buried in a pauper's grave in the city.

It was kind of you to look after your former maid even after her troubles while in your employ. She was a headstrong and ambitious woman, which contributed to her downfall, but with God's grace she will find peace in the next life.

Sister Maria
Mother Superior

"What is this? It smells unpleasant." Clémentine's nose wrinkled as she held the child's hat between two fingers.

"Don't touch that," I said, snatching it from her and holding it to my chest. At Clémentine's wide eyes, I forced myself to moderate my tone, wincing at my sharpness with her. "Sorry, ma chérie. I am simply out of sorts today. This belonged to someone I knew, and Mother Superior thought I may want it."

The questions in Clémentine's mind could be seen in her expression, not the least being why anyone would want the stained and foul item. She chose to focus on what was most important to her.

"Did she speak about me returning?"

I nodded. "Yes. She was pleased to hear that you have been working on your studies. She states that your friends miss you."

"Do you think I shall have the same room when I go back? I do hope so. I like everyone, but Juliet and Marie are my most bosom friends. Have I told you of Juliet's brother? He is nineteen and quite handsome, although she says he was horrid to her when she was little. But he seems very kind to me. He likes dogs." Clémentine chattered away about her friends and the school, her words a soft background to my thoughts.

I fingered the thin fabric of the cap, the stitches at the edge making the faintest bumps. The work was fine, better than I would have imagined. Perhaps Margot would have made a good lady's maid. My heart pinched. Mother Superior had called her ambitious. And clearly not as a compliment. But that had not been her downfall. Nor the pox. Her downfall had been my own stubbornness. I had overlooked anything that did not fit with the story I'd chosen to believe.

How could the Mouse be dead?

I pictured her gaunt face when she had been here. Her arms were like twigs. She would have had no reserve if a fever came over her. And I'd sent her away.

The Mouse was dead, and it was my fault.

"Clémentine," I said, cutting off her prattle. "Do you know what would make my headache better?"

She stilled, eager to be of service.

"Would you go out and collect some flowers? Something to make a nice bouquet for my bedroom."

Her eyes lit up. Clémentine loved the outdoors. She would spend hours deciding between one bloom and the next.

"Of course, Maman." She straightened as if she were a soldier being given orders.

"Take a few more biscuits. It will be hard work."

As quick as an imp, she palmed two more of the biscuits and was out the door in a flash. I waited until I heard her steps on the stairs before I gave over to tears.

I cried for Mouse in a way I had not let myself cry for François. I cried for two lives much shorter than they should ever have been. I cried for time and experiences lost to my business and because I knew I would not change that. I cried for the fact that at thirty-six years old, I was finally having to let go of the image of who I wanted to be in this life and accept the truth of my character, both good and bad.

There was a protest from the cat, who stirred in my lap. I was disturbing his rest. His stern face made me blot my tears. I could not change the past, but today and tomorrow still stretched in front of me. All I could do now was make sure those mistakes did not define me. I picked up my pen to begin. I would pay for masses to be said for Margot's soul; that I could do now. And when the ship arrived and we sold our wines, then I would make plans for how else I could alter the course of future events.

Natalie

■ REIMS ■

APRIL 30

"It is good you asked me to call. You had made a mistake," the librarian said, putting down the phone.

"I knew it." I shook my head ruefully. "My French isn't great, and I just started to get that bad feeling that I'd screwed it up."

She smiled. "Your appointment today with the inspector, Monsieur Reynold, and the city tourism director, Madame Boyle, is at *two* in the afternoon, not at four."

I placed my hand on my heart as if overcome with relief. "Thank goodness I had you confirm. Can you imagine if I had missed it?" Granted, before she called, I didn't have a clue as to the time of the meeting. I'd made several mistakes since arriving in France, but this hadn't been one of them. No, now I was busy altering the course of future events.

"Your new business sounds very interesting," the librarian said. "A good addition to our city."

"Thank you so much. You'll have to come once we're open. In fact—" I rummaged through my tote bag. "Be my guest." I wrote in my notebook *Champagne Widows: Good for one free tasting or class.* I tore the sheet out and scribbled Sophie's name at the bottom. "What is the point of owning a business if one can't treat people who deserve it?"

The librarian's eyes lit up. "Merci, but are you sure? I do not mind assisting you."

"It's completely my pleasure. You've been a huge help."

I'd spent most of yesterday here in the Carnegie Library across from the Reims Cathedral. With its chevron-patterned wooden floors and huge stained-glass windows, it looked more like a fancy estate home than a library. But it had what I needed most of all, which was free Wi-Fi and access to a computer.

Hours of research meant I knew more about Gabriel, Sophie, and French fraud laws. I spent hours last night tossing and turning, trying to determine where I'd gone wrong. Then I realized that much like the Widow Clicquot, I had to stop focusing on the mistakes I'd made and instead on how I was going to learn from them and go forward. It was going to take a leap of faith, perhaps not as much as hiring a pirate ship to cart my wines to Russia, but not without risk.

I'd decided not to call the police. Getting justice for me wasn't going to be their priority. And if I was honest, I didn't want Sophie to risk going to jail. Gabriel yes, but Sophie no.

But I did want my money back. Which meant the fact that both she and Gabriel had underestimated me would end up being their mistake.

I made notes, putting the plan together, trying to figure out where it could fail. I needed to know what time Sophie's meeting was with the city officials. I considered calling the office myself but knew my French wouldn't be good enough. Instead, I had the librarian call on "Sophie's" behalf.

I thanked the librarian one more time, then checked my watch. There was still time to kill. I wandered across the square to the Reims Cathedral. At the top of the steps, I found the smiling angel, a stone sculpture near the entrance.

There was a moment of disconnect when I remembered a passage from the book. Barbe-Nicole had looked up at the same figure. She'd written about it. I paged through the book, looking for the section. I stared up at the angel's face, then back down at the words on the page. There was something eerie about knowing we were standing in the same place. On the same stone. All those years, over two centuries of time, compressed and lay flat between us. It seemed as if I could almost see the Widow out of the corner of my eye walking up the steps. I wished I could thank her, to let her know what an impact she'd made.

I slipped inside the building. A guide spoke to a tour group in a low whisper as they moved toward the door. "Next, we'll go outside to see the statue of Joan of Arc, who insisted on having King Charles VII crowned here in 1429. While she was a French hero, she would not be recognized as a saint until 1920."

Barbe-Nicole would be glad to know the woman finally got her due. All it took was being burned alive and five centuries. A reminder that some things take time.

The ceilings soared upward, and my nose twitched at the faint smell of oiled wood and incense. I slipped through the nave, my footsteps like soft whispers on the stone floor, and went to one of the side chapels.

If candle lighting was good enough for the Champagne Widow, it was good enough for me. I wasn't particularly religious. My family had been a much bigger fan of sleeping in on Sundays than it was of the Almighty. But while I might not be a big believer, prayer seemed the right thing to do now. If I was going to take a leap of faith, it seemed I should have some.

I dropped coins into the holder with a clank and used a taper to light a small votive in one of the red glass holders. Slipping into one of the empty pews, I watched the flame flicker and stared back into the eyes of the Virgin Mary statue. I thought I might have second thoughts now that I was about to take the first steps, or that a part of me would try to talk myself out of taking action, but there was nothing but stillness inside me.

It might mean I was doing the right thing, approved of by God, the Virgin Mary, and the wandering spirit of Barbe-Nicole Clicquot.

Or maybe I was simply done questioning everything I did.

■　■

An hour later, I got into position and texted Sophie.

I'm sorry about everything. I need to fix things between us.

I imagined her rolling her eyes at Gabriel, at my persistence. Then three dots appeared as she composed her reply.

It is okay. We both have a lot of emotion. I wish you well.

My fingers flew over the phone. I need to meet with you. I'm coming to Reims.

Her response was quicker this time. You should stay in Paris. There is no need to come here to fix anything.

I typed back quickly. I figured out how to find Gabriel's real name. I'm going to go to the police. You can come with me.

I enjoyed the pause. The two of them would be on edge with that nugget. Not scared yet, but nervous. They would assume they could still manage the situation.

 The Champagne Letters

After what felt like forever, Sophie finally responded. Wow. Great that you found something. But I want to focus on my future now, not the past.

I fired back an answer. I understand. It's okay I can go to the police on my own.

Hre response came quickly this time. What did you find?

I tilted my face up to the sun and allowed them both to wait for my answer.

I kept the wine bottle he sold me. It will have his fingerprints. If he has a criminal record, he'll be in a database.

There was no question of Gabriel having a record. A search of the newspaper archives at the library turned up that he'd been convicted of petty theft about eight years ago. Since then, he'd either kept his nose clean or, more likely, hadn't been caught, but his fingerprints would still be in the system. And while he might have only one conviction, I was betting there had been other run-ins with the police.

The criminal record was real, even if the bottle wasn't. I hadn't saved it. I barely had room in my luggage for my own things—I didn't need to hang on to old recycling—but they didn't know that.

How lucky you kept this item. Since you are leaving, mail it to me and I will take it. That way there is no chance officials will delay your return. She sent the eye roll emoji. Police can be a hassle.

I'm sure they were worried about a hassle.

I could NEVER trust the bottle to mail system. It's the only proof I have. I don't let it out of my sight.

I let that fact sit with them for a beat. Let them start thinking how they could get the bottle. Then I texted the real bomb.

Besides, I'm already on the train. I'll be in Reims in 20 mins.

They didn't answer right away. I chewed on my lip, watching the front of the store and then glancing down at the phone. A minute went by.

What would I do if they didn't respond?

Another minute.

C'mon, all that prayer and candle lighting had to count for something, right?

One minute more ticked by and then finally the three blinking dots, meaning they were writing. Tension dropped out of my shoulders when I saw the response.

Sophie's message was short. Wow. This is great. I'll pick you up. Will send directions where we can meet outside the station.

See you soon! I dropped my phone back in my bag, not bothering to wait for whatever location she sent since I had zero intentions of going. I checked my phone. 1:20.

As the registered owner of the business, according to the law, Sophie had to be at the store for her meeting with the city officials. It wasn't the kind of thing where you called and rescheduled. With French bureaucracy it could be months before they would schedule another. That meant she couldn't take off to the train station to meet me.

But the two of them also couldn't let me run off to the police. They needed that bottle. They couldn't take the chance that it might still have any fingerprints and that the police might take it seriously. Not when they were this close to reaching their own dreams. That meant Gabriel would have to intercept me. If I went to the train station, either he'd try to charm me out of the bottle, or I'd be the victim of a mugging in whatever corner out of the view of the CCTV cameras they'd arranged for us to meet. My purse and the bottle would be conveniently stolen.

Lucky for me, I was staying right here. I wanted to speak to Sophie alone.

A couple of minutes later, the door to the shop opened and Gabriel slipped out. I was too far away to hear what they were saying, and wouldn't have understood it anyway, but they seemed to be in an argument. Eventually, he threw up his hands and jumped into Sophie's car parked just a few doors down.

I waited until I was sure Gabriel wasn't about to turn around and come back for anything. Then I closed my eyes to gather my strength and pictured the Widow. If she could kick ass in a corset, I could do it in expensive French underwear. I strode down the sidewalk and swung the door to the store open.

There have been many moments in my life when I realized I would always remember them. The first time I saw the ocean as a kid. The moment the priest declared Will and me husband and wife. Finding the texts between Will and Gwen.

And now this. The expression on Sophie's face when she saw me in the door was exquisite, and it burned itself instantly into my long-term memory.

She stared at me and then at the door and then back at me. "Did your train arrive early?"

I could tell even as she asked, she knew that wasn't possible. My message had come through only minutes ago.

"I thought it would be best if we talked, just the two of us." I paused. "Without your husband around."

The only reaction was a twitch in her jaw. She looked out the front window.

"Gabriel's already left for the train station. Have a seat." I motioned toward one of the bistro tables. Strolling around the back of the bar, I selected a bottle of champagne from the fridge. Taittinger.

I pulled a couple of glasses from the back counter and then put them down so I could fiddle with the wire cage on the bottle. "You know, the Widow Clicquot started initially with a partner her family made her take on, Alexandre Fourneaux. He had a son, and every-one thought Barbe-Nicole should marry him, but she didn't. The son went on to start a different Champagne house, and that eventually became Taittinger." I waved the bottle in her direction. "Funny how things are all interrelated, once you know the details."

Using a crisp white bar towel, I twisted the cork, and it popped with a satisfying sigh. I poured us each a glass and sat across from her. There were a few drops of sweat on her forehead.

"Put your phone on the table," I instructed her. "Don't worry, you can talk to him later."

She paused and then slid it over toward me.

"I'll give it back to you when we're done. I just don't want you distracted. Unlike some people, I won't break your phone to keep you from having an inconvenient conversation."

She flinched. "How did you figure it out?"

"Which part? That you were the one who took my phone, or the whole con? This helped answer some questions." I opened my phone and held it up to show her the picture from the bar. Gabriel with his arm draped around her. The close-up of their names.

"So, there is no bottle with fingerprints."

I shook my head. "Your husband wasn't memorable enough to keep mementos." I sipped the champagne. It was Taittinger's Nocturne Rosé. The wine was a bright bubbling pink, the color of watered-down cranberry juice. I motioned for her to drink. "It's nice, a bit dry, but I like it."

Sophie didn't touch her glass. There was another twitch in her jaw. "What do you want?"

I leaned back in my chair and glanced around the shop. There were still things that needed to be done. The shelves weren't full, just a few bottles placed around for show. Behind the bar hadn't been tiled yet, and the iPad cash register was still in a box on the counter. But you could see that it would be a beautiful space. "It looks nice in here."

"You want something, or you would have come with the police."

I nodded. "If we never met, I wouldn't have heard about the Widow Clicquot. I've learned a lot from her."

"She was a great woman."

"She was."

Sophie shifted in her seat. Her eyes darted to the clock on the far wall. 1:35. "You came to talk about the Widow?"

"Last time I saw you, you said that I needed to get my own dream."

"You have come for an apology?"

I refilled my glass. The first had gone down easily. "No. You were right. I spent my whole life supporting other people's dreams. I thought my husband's dreams were our dreams. Well, you already know how that turned out. I think that's partly why I let you believe he was dead. I was ashamed that he left me. That he didn't find me good enough." I sighed. "I've spent all this time trying to figure out where I went wrong when instead I should have been focused on where I wanted to go from here. The thing is, it was never about me. Not his dreams, and not his failure to be a decent husband. If there's any shame, it's on him."

Sophie nodded.

"Just like Gabriel's decision to come back to my room should make him ashamed. He already had the money from the ring and wine by then."

Sophie bit her lip. "He wouldn't have slept with you. He was going to come up with an excuse to leave, but I arrived first."

I shot her a look. "Tell me you don't believe that."

Sophie looked away, glancing at the clock again.

I followed her gaze. "Ah, am I taking too long to rehash my marriage and the importance of fidelity? Sorry. I'll move my story along. Here's the thing. You and Gabriel took my money to help with this place. To build *your* dream."

She swallowed and then nodded, unable to meet my eyes.

"So, I guess that makes your dream partly my dream now." I leaned forward so our faces were inches apart. "I'm done investing in other people's dreams without being paid back."

"We don't have your money."

I arched an eyebrow. "You haven't spent it all. You're too smart a businesswoman. You need capital in the bank to carry you for a few months until this place gets off the ground. You may not have told Gabriel, but I'm betting you've tucked some aside."

Sophie fidgeted in her seat. "If I empty our bank accounts, the business won't survive. We need a cushion until we get busy."

I shrugged. "That's not my problem. Besides, do you really think you can thrive in this business knowing that you stole from another woman to make it happen? The Widow sold her own jewelry, not someone else's."

There was a tiny tremor in her lip.

"Did you know I'm angrier with the woman my husband had the affair with than I am with him?" I chuckled. "I used to think it was because I had so much history with him, it was easier to blame her." I sighed. "And that's part of it, but I also think women should stick together. Enough men in this world are careless with women and our feelings. Don't we owe each other better than that?" I swallowed, feeling a fresh wave of sadness, and then I released it.

I leaned back in my chair. "The letters from the Widow got me thinking. We're harder on other women. We let men get away with things that we'd never accept from a female friend."

"Do you want an apology? I am sorry." Sophie spit out the words, her voice cracking. "The original plan was only to use you as a reference for the wines. It was Gabriel who thought of the ring. It gave us the extra money we needed. It meant not having to risk a second wine sale. As I got to know you, I had regret for what we were doing."

"Not so much regret that you didn't take my money," I pointed out. Hell, for all I knew, Gwen felt regret over her part in my marriage falling apart. But that regret didn't stop her from participating in the betrayal. "Making mistakes isn't the problem. Doing something about them is."

"You said yourself that you didn't even wear the ring. You didn't need it. This place is all we've ever wanted." She waved her hand all around the space.

"You don't get to decide how I spend my money. Or what is important to me." I sat up straighter. "No one gets to decide for me anymore."

Sophie's shoulders slumped. "So now what? What do you want?"

"I got rid of Gabriel because I want you to know that what happens next is your decision."

"Do I have a choice? You have taken my phone."

I pushed it across the table. "You can call him if you don't think you can make this decision on your own, but for what it's worth, I know you'll choose better than he will. After all, you said taking my ring was his idea, and I think we can agree that was a mistake."

Her mouth was pursed in a pout, but she didn't touch the phone. "So, what is the decision?"

"I want the money from my ring, and if I get it, I'll leave you alone," I said.

"How do I know you will? That you will let us go?"

"You don't. You have to trust me. One woman to another. But

what I can tell you is that if you don't give me my money, I'll be sitting right here in fifteen minutes when the city officials arrive. A new joint business partner in your dream. I'll tell them to add my name to the license, and if you object, I'll call the police. So, I walk out of here with either half this business or my money, or you and Gabriel go to jail. Those are the only three options."

"The money from your ring did not pay for *half* of this place. You cannot ask to be an equal partner."

I shrugged. "What can I say? Interest. Look, that's the deal: pay me back the money you stole from me, not a penny more, or I will be an equal partner in the business."

"That is not fair."

"It's fairer than how you treated me."

Sophie locked eyes as if she expected me to break, but I didn't look away. I knew she wouldn't want to give me half ownership. If nothing else, she was a smart businesswoman and that was a bad financial decision. Better to be short on operating capital now than to have me around forever. "Fine. I will get your money."

I smiled and pushed away from the table. "Okay, let's go."

"There isn't time," she insisted. "The meeting is in a few minutes."

"Your bank is just a few doors down." I jerked my head in the right direction. "They can wire the money direct to my account. C'mon, I'll go with you." I stood. "If you don't want to share your dream with me, then you don't get to take anything. I'm not doing one-way relationships anymore."

Sophie sat there. I suspected she was trying to figure a way out of the situation. "If you ask to be on the business license, it makes you tied to the wine fraud in Paris. The police could connect you with us."

I nodded. "Yep. It's a risk."

"And you are willing to take such a risk? Maybe you go to jail. Or you ruin your reputation." She leaned forward, her words sharp.

I nearly laughed. How little she knew me if she thought I cared anymore about what others thought. I lifted my glass and finished it all in one gulp. "I've learned taking risks isn't nearly as scary as living your life without taking chances. C'mon, let's go. We need to hurry if you're going to make your meeting."

Sophie stood. "As if you care."

"I do. I wouldn't be here otherwise giving you any options. You should think about that later. Would Gabriel give you any options? If you want some free advice, you should consider carefully how someone who is so comfortable lying and cheating might treat you someday. If you want this business to succeed—hell, if you want a life without certain heartache—you should dump him."

"You don't know Gabriel," she said, her face pale.

"Oh, I think I do. And I think you do too."

Barbe-Nicole

■ REIMS ■

REGARDING THE EVENTS OF AUGUST 1814

My dearest Anne,

You asked if I wished I had traveled. My wines have reached the farthest edges of the world, and yet I have not left my own small corner of France. The world and its circumstances kept me here in Champagne, but I have never allowed restrictions to hold me back. I seek adventure in books, in tales from others, in new foods, and by challenging myself with new ideas and thoughts. No, my dear sweet girl, the purpose of travel is to expand our mind, and that does not require the traversing of distance, only the willingness to embrace something new. Do not allow yourself to feel hemmed in by any border.

■ ■

I took the letter from Louis to my office when it arrived. I thought I would tear into it immediately, but as I sat there looking at the wax seal, I couldn't bring myself to open it. As long as it remained unread, it had possibility. I could spin tales of what I would do and how I would respond.

My hands ran over the items on my desk as if I were blind. Inkpots, a leather ledger, two empty bottles for me to consider in case I wished to change makers. There were letters that needed a response. Bills from creditors. Notes to myself about things that needed to be done. All the debris that accumulates with a business. The things that fill hours of a day and expand to fill the corners of one's mind when one can't sleep.

If my gamble did not pay off, all of this would disappear. I was luckier than many others. There were still enough funds to avoid ruin, although there would need to be economies. Clémentine wouldn't return to school. I would need to sell the house in Bouzy. I could move in with my brother and his wife. A spare room. A need to stay out of their way, always ensuring that I was no substantial burden.

Or I could marry. I stroked the edge of my face. I was not old, but my flesh was not as it had been in my youth; like overripe fruit, it was a touch too soft. I was passing into the stage of being overlooked by men. It surprised me how little I cared. Yes, if I could find a true partner, that would be nice. But I required a man who added to my life, not drove it.

It seemed foolish to me that men were so easily led by looks. True, young women were beautiful, but those of us who were older had other advantages. Wine improves with age: it becomes richer; the flavors blend and soften. It is no longer attempting to figure out what it will become. It is less changed by the hands around it and more of its own unique thing, and women are no different.

At thirty-six, I felt I was finally becoming the woman I was always meant to be. A good vintner uses the grapes they have, balancing their advantages and disadvantages to create something remarkable, and so I was learning to do with aspects of myself. Like a vine, I had trained myself to grow where the soil suited me best and was no longer quick to bend at every wind. I was deeply rooted in myself.

I knew there were marriages that were true love matches, and I missed the touch of François, the way he could look at me in a way that made me feel seen. But I no longer needed a man to be visible, and if I did not find true love with another, I preferred to have it with myself, uncontested and uncompromising.

What I wanted was this business. Not merely to grow a few grapes to earn the funds to make my child's life better, but to build something that would last. I wished to stride on this earth and make a mark. To be untamed and to proclaim my accomplishments loudly and without shame. I wanted to be the very best at what I did.

I lifted the letter and allowed myself to trace the seal before putting it back down. So much hinged on the contents.

Does it?

From the corner of my eye, for just a moment, I saw François. Sprawling across the settee as he used to enjoy. He'd watch me work. He said he liked that I had such purpose. I would glance up from fretting about a column of figures and he would be there, a half smile on his face.

I still felt his loss, but I had endured. Just as I had every other time life had presented me with failure and loss. That was what I did. I moved on. I moved forward. It is what strong women have done since the start of time, and it is what they will need to continue to do, as life itself is a challenge. Failure should be as expected as ease and joy. Had not the fields taught me that over all these years? One poor harvest does not mean one removes all the vines. You consider your losses, you prune, you feed the soil, and you bide your time until the sun shines again. You hold your breath for the next season. And if need be, the one following. But one does not simply give up.

Whatever this letter contained would not change who I had become. It might mean that my current path had ended, but it did not mean the end of my journey.

I opened the letter.

July 15, 1814
Königsberg
My esteemed Madame Clicquot,

I will not force you to read to the end of this letter to know that our outcome has been good and that you have cause to celebrate. However, I hope you will indulge me in sharing the details.

The crossing was difficult as we had expected so late in the season. To avoid difficulties with blockades, the captain ran us at full sail and far from shore. Traversing the water felt like traveling over a rock-strewn road in a carriage with no springs. The nights were so cold I could barely feel the tips of my fingers and my teeth rattled in my head. And then the days were too warm. I fretted over our bottles like a mother does a babe in the crib.

The ship itself was infested with rats. Some were so large I thought them at first to be dogs. Alas, the ginger cake you packed for me was a victim of their onslaught. In fact, they ate a hole right through the hamper while I slept. I count myself lucky that my person itself was not assaulted, although I know some members of the crew were not so lucky. Although perhaps I should be offended that the rats preferred to nibble upon these men who smelled of onion and cheap sausage.

Our ship, the Zes Gebroeders, *made the harbor of Königsberg on July 3. The following morning, it was already alarmingly hot at dawn. I supervised the unloading of our wine, opening the first case with a heavy heart. I could not see how the wine could have survived such foul treatment.*

As my eyes flew over the letter, I found myself falling between the lines of ink until I could imagine myself standing next to Louis on the deck of the ship.

I would pull that first bottle free from the packing basket and see it was crystalline, nary a single broken bottle in the case. The same for the second and third cases I opened. The condition of the wine would be perfect, and my heart would take flight from my chest. I would open a bottle to taste the quality, and perhaps for a touch of celebration. It would be like heaven, as strong as the wines of Hungary, as yellow as gold, and as sweet as nectar.

Ours was the first ship to arrive in the area with wines from our region.

And, oh, how these people have hungered for champagne! In my imagination I am on the dock next to Louis, overseeing the unloading, when we are besieged by those who have heard we have wine aboard. Grown men begging for a chance to buy even just a single bottle if that is all we will spare. People wait for us at the hotel; they find us on the street; they leave pleading notes at the dock. All of Prussia is mad for my wine.

The wine merchants come en masse, all clamoring for the chance to purchase. A few even come to blows with one another! Some are calling it the Comet Wine, based on the emblem in the cork. Others scream out, "Give me the Widow!" The fever for consumption shows no sign of breaking.

We had set a price for the bottles, but we take advantage of the unprecedented desire. We raise the prices higher and higher, and yet they still leap for the chance to give us their money. We sell some bottles for five and half francs apiece! A single bottle selling for what I paid in wages for a week of labor. It is madness, and it is glorious.

I pictured myself striding about, preparing to take the next leg of the journey into Russia, eager to be on the road. The czar demands his men bring the champagne to him immediately; they are en route to meet us and hasten our arrival. Louis teases me that my vanquishment of Russia shall be far more swift and far more successful than Napoleon's efforts.

I placed the paper down, almost surprised to still find myself in my office, and began to cry. We had succeeded. Not success beyond my dreams, because I had always reached high.

"Maman?" Clémentine hovered in the doorway, her face pinched in concern. "Was the news bad?"

I leaped from my desk and rushed across the room to gather her in an embrace. "Oh, my darling girl, the news is wonderful!"

"So, business is good?"

I laughed. "The business. Life. All is good. Vive la vie!"

Natalie

MAY 1

Paris was waking, the sun stretching between buildings and warming the sandstone. I needed to leave soon for the airport, but there was time for one last walk around the city. I wove through the crowds on the sidewalk, my suitcase trailing, trying to imprint as many memories as possible in my final moments here.

A text from Molly popped up.

Travel safe.

The message made me smile. I considered calling her back. I had so much to tell Molly. Not just about everything that happened but also how sorry I was about our fight. About how I realized I'd lost myself for the past year. How much her friendship meant to me. I glanced at my watch. There wouldn't be time for an in-depth heart-to-heart, and the streets of Paris likely weren't the place. It was a story that was going to require wine and hours to tell completely.

Across the street the bookstalls were starting to open for the day, the sellers calling out what I suspected were well-trodden insults to each other. They lit up Gauloises and talked of possible rain.

I walked over and perused the offerings. I pulled a thick travel guide from the stack, *1,000 Must-See Destinations*, and paged through it. The glossy photos begged for more time and consideration. There were so many places to see, so many adventures to be had. As I put the travel guide back, I impulsively pulled my Widow Clicquot book from my bag and placed it on the stack. When the seller turned around, he picked it up, clucking as if chiding it for almost getting away. Then he jammed it into a shelf, lost in the middle of cookbooks and old issues of *Vogue*, copies of Dickens and Voltaire. My throat tightened, and I almost called out for him to stop, offered to pay for it all over again.

I didn't know why I'd done it. I'd planned to bring the Widow's book home with me. I assumed I'd reread it over and over, but in that instant, it struck me that the book should remain in France, waiting for the next person who needed it. The Widow would want it that way.

I turned my back and flagged down a cab. It was time to go. As I dropped into the back seat, the cabbie began speaking in rapid-fire French and I had to stop him.

"My apologies, madame, I assumed you were French."

I took that as the compliment it was meant to be and instructed him to take me to the airport. I leaned back, watching the city pass by as he darted through traffic. Then I suddenly sat straight up, gripping the seat.

"Wait! Stop! Can you pull over here?"

With a muffled curse, the taxi driver wedged the cab into a small spot on the street. I had recognized the antique jewelry store instantly. I suddenly knew what I had to do.

"If you wait, it will just take me a few minutes." I jumped out of the cab and dashed inside as the closed sign flipped over to open. I walked to the cabinet where I had seen it when I was with Gabriel and pointed it out to the clerk. "That one right there," I said, tapping on the glass. There was a sense of relief when he dropped the ring into my hand.

I turned my hand to the left and the right, letting the sun light up the dark stone.

"It fits as if it were made for you," the clerk said.

I nodded. I'd liked it better than the pendant, but I'd let Gabriel talk me out of it. That was never happening again. This was what my wedding ring money was meant to buy.

"I'll take it," I said. "Do you know anything about the history of the ring?" I asked as I handed over my credit card. The counter smelled of lemon furniture polish, and the floor creaked companionably under my feet. It was as if they were personally greeting every person who walked in.

The clerk shook his head, likely pleased to have made a sale so early in the day. "We don't know very much, I'm afraid. Some things come in with provenance of past owners, but unfortunately not this one. The seller purchased it in an estate sale some time ago but couldn't recall the name of the owner. The setting is early 1800s. The jeweler who made it wasn't very well known, but their specialty was making new pieces from older ones."

I held the ring in the palm of my hand, seeing the dents and scratches in the band. Without a polished shine, the gold looked almost soft, like fur. I liked the idea that it had been worn on other fingers, passed down woman to woman until it found its way to me.

"At the time, many of the wealthy and nobility had to sell their jewels to survive," the clerk explained, writing up the sale with a fountain pen, his handwriting like calligraphy.

"The Napoleonic Wars."

He nodded his head. "Madame knows her history."

"Those that don't learn from the past are doomed to repeat it," I quipped as I passed the ring back to him.

Pushing his too-long jet-black hair from his eyes, he chuckled. "Indeed. The jeweler of this piece specialized in taking some of the larger, more elaborate pieces that people used at court. Then they made them something that could be worn more easily. Ofttimes we think something must be showy, but true value and elegance is often in the simple." Noticing a blot of ink on his index finger, he licked it quickly and then rubbed it off with his thumb. He fished through a large wooden cabinet behind him. "We have the original ring box in here somewhere."

The cab outside tooted its horn. The cabbie was awful impatient for someone who had left the meter running.

"I should go," I said. "I'm going back to the States today." And I realized in that moment that I was glad. I pictured my condo, still full of boxes waiting for me to turn it into a home. I made a mental note to stop in duty-free at the airport and buy a bottle of champagne. I'd invite Molly over.

"It shouldn't take but a moment; let me just match up the item number. Aha!" The clerk pulled his head from the cabinet with a cry of victory while holding a small faded red leather round box. He flipped the metal clasp with his thumbnail and tucked the ring into the worn velvet interior. "Here you are, madame. May you wear it in good health."

Taking the ring from the box, I slid it onto my finger and noticed the jeweler's name embossed into the leather, the letters faint and almost unreadable.

Poette.

I blinked in shock and then ran my fingers over it. *Poette.* It was the same name as the jeweler Barbe-Nicole had used when she had to sell her emerald brooch. I glanced down at the ring.

Could it be?

Madame Poette must have remade hundreds if not thousands of items. Emeralds and rubies, diamonds, and every other stone possible, torn from one setting and redrafted into another. There would be no way to know if this emerald had once been a part of a brooch. And even if it had, the odds that this stone in this ring had ever belonged to the Widow Clicquot's brooch were thousands, if not millions, to one. It wasn't probable.

But it was *possible.* And I was coming to believe in possibilities.

Perhaps it was as simple as deciding that it would be the story I told myself. How I came to France when it seemed like my entire life had fallen apart and how a woman from the past had come into my life to teach me what I needed to know.

It didn't matter what others thought of the story, or if they believed it to be true. I wasn't telling it for them.

Epilogue

Barbe-Nicole

■ REIMS ■

JUNE 1866

There are still so many stories I could tell you, my darling great-granddaughter, but I find myself growing weary. What is a life but a series of stories we tell, and retell, until we edit out those we don't like and burnish the ones we do? I have tried to be honest in these pages, but I suspect I've been too kind to myself at some points, but I prefer that to the tendency to be overly harsh, which most women do. If one can't give grace and kindness to ourselves, what is the point?

Make a note of that as well, sweet girl: while it is good to strive for betterment of oneself, it is equally noble to mark what makes you unique just as you are.

You know the rest of the story of our champagne house. I made my fortune in that risky run to Russia. Louis sold our entire stock, for prices I could not even imagine. And more than the money, or at least as nice as the money if I am attempting honesty, was the reaction of the public. They loved the wine. Czar Alexander declared that he would drink nothing else. Say what you will about the Russians—at least they know good champagne.

When Louis Bohne passed in 1821, I lost perhaps my dearest friend. Some thought us too close for employee and employer, but never again did I meet someone so aligned with my mind. There was never an affair of our hearts, only our minds. I assumed we would work together until the end. For such a good man to be taken from this life by a slip from an icy bridge seemed too absurd to be real. Life often laughs at our effort to have it make sense.

He had worked for me for decades, but he was much more than an employee. He believed in me and my dreams. If one dares bold things, you will need people like Louis by your side. Someone who can hold your belief for you when you waver. Now that he is gone, I hold on to my memories of him, keeping that tiny spark of him alive to pay him back for all this work and kindness. This is what love and friendship can do—make one immortal.

After Louis was gone, I found others to help me. There was a touch of scandal, some saying I dallied with younger men. Holding out the possibility that I might take them on as business partners or even as a spouse, but instead merely playing with their affection. As if men haven't dangled opportunity in front of women for years!

No, I have no regrets there, nor any desire to share my private life with you or anyone else. Be it enough to say that I did not find myself lonely over the years, nor does anyone who spent time in my company have reason for complaint. If they wanted more, it was never because it was promised to them, only that they desired it.

While there are things in my life I would change if I could, my largest regret is how I treated the Mouse. That sin weighs on my soul, but I have done my best to balance the scales. I ensured her son, Bara, went away to the best schools and was for want of nothing in pursuing his own dreams. His mother, I suspect, would have been proud of him. He had her ambition, although I do like to think some of his willingness to work hard was influenced from years in my household.

I continued to repent by establishing a home for poor children in Reims. Perhaps by that point it had stopped being a form of repentance and instead was an acknowledgment by me that while life offers opportunity to all, it is not equal in the meting out of good fortune to seize those opportunities.

There were other charities I gave to as well. And all of that giving came with its own form of joy. The fountain in Épernay that I donated resulted in the locals joking that I was willing to give even my rival Monsieur Moët a drink. That alone made the donation worthwhile.

And while I believe those who say money does not buy happiness are typically those who have never been without, I agree that it cannot replace the most valuable things: good friends, a clever mind, and a willingness to pursue one's dreams. The Mouse taught me to recognize my own flaws, but it was my responsibility to address them.

It is my hope that by sharing my story with you, my darling great-granddaughter, I've been able to impart what I've learned, including that challenge is to be expected. While some may wish for hardship to pass them by, it is in hardship that we push ourselves. If a seed remained a seed, it would produce nothing. It is only by rupturing itself from the inside, through pushing itself through rock and soil toward the light, weathering storms and drought, that it finds its true purpose. And so, the same shall be with you.

I shall tell you a secret, my chère Anne—you are the most like me. You have audacity and I predict you shall live a grand life. To dare things before others contains risk, but it achieves so much. I look now at the portraits painted of me and I wonder, Who is this old woman? In my mind's eye I am still young, still smooth skinned and brimming with energy.

As a woman of faith, I do not fear death. What is it except for the next grand adventure? But I will tell you, I hate the idea of missing what will happen in this world. I long to see you grow, and your children, and your children's children. I wonder what new and amazing things the world shall bring to pass. They are driving ships now with steam and making machines that sew! I tremble in anticipation of the things you will see, ma chérie. The world is in perpetual motion, and we must invent the things of tomorrow. I tell you to act with audacity. To live your life without apology and not in service of any other. I hope for you, my sweet, darling girl, that you live.

Le vin, c'est moi.
Barbe-Nicole Clicquot
The Queen of Reims

Historical Notes

The first time I heard of the Widow Clicquot was more than twenty years ago. I was living in Belgium and traveled to the Champagne region for a vacation. Despite the copious free samples that were imbibed at various vineyards, the story of Barbe-Nicole Clicquot stuck in my mind. I scribbled in my journal that she would make an amazing character for a book. At the time I'd never completed a novel, although I'd dreamed of being a writer since I was a child—but the Widow was an undeniable force. Thanks go to the tour guide who ignited that spark, although I regret I never wrote down her name.

Roughly ten years ago, I came across the biography *The Widow Clicquot: The Story of a Champagne Empire and the Woman Who Ruled It* by Tilar Mazzeo. Remembering that long-ago tour, I bought it immediately and found myself immersed in Barbe-Nicole's story. I cannot recommend the book enough for those of you who would like to know more about her life and the champagne business.

I reached out to the Veuve Clicquot champagne house when I decided to write this novel, and their heritage manager, Isabelle Pierre, was kind enough to answer many of my questions. In terms of historical dress, A. G. Angevine was generous with her time and knowledge, and I'm very grateful.

As this is a novel, I have imagined scenes and conversations that may not have existed; I've also bent some historical truths so they would fit my story. Any errors I've made are my own and occasionally even on purpose. And while I request a novelist's indulgence for my changes, the following details may offer clarification for those curious about Clicquot's history.

The death of François Clicquot was publicly listed at the time as a "malignant fever," what was most likely typhoid. He had been sick for several weeks before he passed with increasingly harsh symptoms, and there were rumors that François had died by suicide. Barbe-Nicole likely was aware of this gossip. François had suffered previous bouts of depression, but there is no direct evidence that his death was self-induced. The truth of his cause of death remains unknown.

The Mouse, Margot, is a completely fictional character. The Mouse is my stand-in for the challenges that Barbe-Nicole faced, including people who tried to undermine her, as well as her own possible doubts about her ambition. While Barbe-Nicole Clicquot supported various charities, including establishing a home for disadvantaged children, there was no boy named Bara whom she directly fostered.

Barbe-Nicole was an innovator in the world of champagne. She created the process known as remuage, or riddling (storing bottles on their necks, or "sur pointe," versus on their backs, and rotating to allow the sediment to collect near the cork). However, she created the process in approximately 1816. I moved the event up in the timeline so it could occur during the span of the novel.

The act of opening a bottle of champagne with a sword, sabering, dates to the Napoleonic Wars. According to legend, soldiers who couldn't be bothered to dismount their horses to uncork the wine lopped off the top with their blade. I had this happen at Barbe-Nicole's direction in the book. While there is no evidence she was ever involved, I like to believe that as a woman who was always looking for efficiencies, she would have approved of this method.

The scene where Barbe-Nicole sees a fortune teller exists only in my imagination. However, the fortune teller Lenormand was a real person. She did give readings to Empress Joséphine, and according to historical accounts, she did have a bat nailed to the wall of her home. This was a decorating choice that was too juicy to leave out of the story.

Barbe-Nicole's home was in the city center of Reims. For this novel, I moved it out so that the vineyards and cellars were located directly on the estate grounds. Her actual home was destroyed during the First World War. However, her childhood home, the Hôtel Ponsardin, is still standing and is now the headquarters of the Reims and Épernay Chamber of Commerce.

While some of the Widow's actual correspondence does exist, I created the book of letters to Barbe-Nicole's great-granddaughter. For those interested in learning more about champagne, the Napoleonic era, or wine fraud from less imaginary sources, these are some books I found most helpful.

The Widow Clicquot: The Story of a Champagne Empire and the Woman Who Ruled It by Tilar Mazzeo (HarperCollins, 2008)

Champagne: How the World's Most Glamorous Wine Triumphed Over War and Hard Times by Don Kladstrup and Petie Kladstrup (William Morrow, 2005)

9000 Years of Wine: A World History by Rod Phillips (Whitecap Books, 2017)

Napoleon: A Concise Biography by David A. Bell (Oxford University Press, 2015)

Napoleon: A Life by Andrew Roberts (Penguin Books, 2015)

In Vino Duplicitas: The Rise and Fall of a Wine Forger Extraordinaire by Peter Hellman (The Experiment, 2017)

The Billionaire's Vinegar: The Mystery of the World's Most Expensive Bottle of Wine by Benjamin Wallace (Crown Publishers, 2008)

Thank you for your time with the book and indulging me as I created my view of history. I kept a copy of the painting of the Widow Clicquot posted above my desk as I wrote. When I found myself faced with challenges, I would ask myself, What would the Widow do? I am indebted to her memory and hope that my effort to bring her alive on the page will interest others in her story. And in her champagne! If you haven't had it, try a bottle—you won't be sorry. I keep a bottle in the fridge; you never know when you might want to celebrate. Cheers! Or as they say in France—à votre santé!

Acknowledgments

always read the acknowledgments when I finish a book. It's a mix of being fascinated with just how many people are involved in the creative process and a secret desire to see my name in the back. Feel free to write your name in here _____. Every step of writing this book had me thinking about future readers, so I couldn't have done it without you. And, as one who has a looming stack of to-be-read books, I truly appreciate you giving this book your time and attention.

Writing a novel is a long journey. And, like any good road trip, it requires high-quality snacks, a willingness to get lost in pursuit of the right direction, and the best company possible. The people along for the ride make reaching the destination possible, and even keep you from driving off the road.

There is a special breed of people who will read early drafts of a book and provide feedback. These people are both kind and not afraid to tell you when you've left a giant plot hole in the middle of your novel. Thank-yous go to: Jamie Hillegonds, Crystal Hunt, Kelly Charron, Robyn Harding, Liza Palmer, Elizabeth Boyle, and Bonnie Jacoby.

Acknowledgments

I will admit to being a lover of wine and champagne long before I wrote this book. And while I am an enthusiastic amateur, both the Veuve Clicquot Champagne House and the amazing team of sommeliers at North Vancouver Everything Wine did their best to help me learn so much more. Any mistakes or errors are completely my own.

It is not going too far to say that this book would not exist without the guidance, wisdom, and occasionally inappropriate humor of my literary agent, Barbara Poelle, and the crew at Word One Literary. I feel so fortunate to work with you, and even more fortunate to consider you a friend.

The entire team at Gallery Books deserves a shout-out for taking a stack of pages and turning it into the book you're holding. Book people truly are the best people. My editor, Abby Zidle, deserves a crate (or two or three) of champagne for her creativity and insight. This book is so much better because of her involvement and, if I were dreaming of an editor (and I was), she was the perfect fit. Ali Chesnick ensured I didn't drop any balls (or deadlines) all while staying patient and cheerful. Nicole Brugger-Dethmers provided copyedits and, as my high school English teacher will vouch, I never learned to use a comma correctly, so thank you for your eagle eye. Sophie Normil and Jessica Roth provided marketing and publicity. Writing a book is fun but sharing it with others is even better. I owe them gratitude for helping the book find its way into the hands of readers. Thanks also go to Associate Director of Copyediting John Paul Jones, and the book designer Kathryn Kenney-Peterson.

Thanks to the authors who took the time and generously offered blurbs. As huge fans of their novels, I could not have been more excited, and I appreciate their support as a writer.

I am so fortunate to have so many strong and amazing women in my life who have acted as guides on my journey, celebrating the

Acknowledgments

wins and carrying me through the times when things were bleak. My grandmothers, both long gone but very much not forgotten. My mom, my aunts (Joan, Barb, Carol, Bonnie, Pat, Noreen, and Kira) and so many friends including Laura Sullivan, Molly Sullivan, Stephanie Marie Candiago, Serena Robar, Jeanette Caul, Kaiti Caul, Joelle Anthony, Maribeth Ruckman, Roz Nay, Renata Verhagen, Sheri Radford, Alisa Luke, and everyone at the Creative Academy for Writers and so many others. Cassandra Evans deserves my endless gratitude for taping me back together after my divorce and I'll take her voice in my head anytime. And while he's not a strong woman, my dad did his part to raise one, so thanks to him as well.

Last, I want to thank booksellers, librarians, and book influencers. Thank you for all you do to get books into the hands of people. I truly believe it's through stories that we learn and grow by seeing different worlds and perspectives. You're changing the world one book at a time.

Please join me in raising a glass. Every day is a champagne occasion if you want it to be.